Phantasia presents...

Exile

by Martin Owton

This book is a work of fiction. The characters, incidents, and dialog are products of the author's imagination, and any resemblance to actual events or persons, living or dead, is coincidental.

Copyright © 2015 Martin Owton

Published by Tickety Boo Press
www.ticketyboopress.co.uk

Edited by Andrew Angel
www.andrewangel.co.uk

Copy-edited by Emma Compton

Cover Art by Gary Compton
Book Design by Big River Press Ltd

ACKNOWLEDGEMENTS

'Exile' took a long time to write and a long time to get right so there are a lot of people who had a hand in it, some of whom I haven't seen for ages, so if I miss anyone I apologise and thanks for your help. Firstly I would like to thank my long-time trusty critique partner Patrice Sarath, the T-Party Writing Group and Rushmoor Writers. Many people read early drafts of 'Exile' and offered comments; I would like to particularly recognise Gaynor and Sue, Mad Kate, Mike Brunavs, Dr Alex Chatterley and Helen Anderton. My agent Ian Drury took a chance on me, I thank him for his support and hard work. I thank my wife for her patience and support, my webmaster Robin and finally, Gary Compton for sharing the vision.

Martin Owton

Exile

The Nandor Tales

Book One

THE EXILE OF DARIEN

PROLOGUE - THE BETRAYAL OF DARIEN

Lord Tirellan looked out across the valley from the doorway of the farmhouse he had taken as his command post. The campfires of the army of Caldon, his army, speckled the darkened land like the stars of the night sky. Beyond them a few lights showed where the town of Darien sat behind its walls in a curve of the river.

Too late, thought Lord Tirellan, his jaw clenched tight. He picked a lump of dried mud from the fur collar of his cloak. *We should have been here ten days ago. The town was wide open then.* But the quick thrust with his cavalry had been hindered by the unseasonable weather and the Earl of Darien's small, but well-trained army. Now he lacked the heavy forces necessary for a successful siege. He crumbled the mud between his manicured fingers. *And we are not allowed to fail.*

He dug in a pocket of his waistcoat and found the leather wristband his emissary had returned with. *It is time.* He closed the door to the rain and the night, unfastened the heavy cloak and turned to the interior of the farmhouse.

He settled himself in his chair in the bedroom; he had given orders that he was not to be disturbed for anything less than the end of the world. No doubt his secretary was fuming at his exclusion, and at this very minute scribbling a letter to his true master, the Duke.

He put his hand to the steaming mug on the small table beside him; too hot to drink. He had brewed the contents himself from dried mushrooms and herbs bought the last time he was in the Holy City. It might well be some time before he could purchase more; the least he could expect was banishment by the High King for the attack on Darien. *I shall miss the pleasures of the Holy City, but it will be worth it in the longer run.* He shifted in his seat. *Only if we take Darien swiftly though. How much will this clansman want?* He had considerable latitude, but there were limits to Caldon's resources. *I can go to ten thousand crowns, perhaps twelve at most. I hope he's not too greedy.* He sat rehearsing his arguments and strategy as he waited for the infusion to cool.

He put his hand to the mug again; cool enough. *Time to resolve the matter.* He took a deep breath and, readying himself for the foul taste of the brew, drank deeply. It took a physical effort to keep from vomiting the bitter fluid straight back up. He snatched up a jug of clean water and rinsed his mouth three times before sitting back in his chair. Eyes fixed on the plain whitewashed wall; he sat very still and tried to concentrate on the slow rhythm of his breathing.

Gradually the noise of the camp faded and, it seemed to Tirellan's eyes, a mist began to form in the corners of the room. He picked up the wristband and rubbed it slowly between his hands, trying to think only of the man who had worn it. The mist grew thicker until it filled the room. Lord Tirellan felt a brief moment of vertigo as the potion took him and his spirit broke free. He stood up and strode into the mist still grasping the wristband.

For a moment the swirling mist was all he could see. Then darker areas loomed up before him which became walls, the mist thinned and he stepped out into a candlelit room. Two men sat on a dark red carpet waiting for him. Lord Tirellan was momentarily taken aback at the second man, but quickly calmed himself.

"Good evening gentlemen," he said evenly. "I am Lord Tirellan, the Duke of Caldon's field commander."

"We wait for you," said one of the men, a squat muscular figure with fierce moustaches, his dark hair in a braid that reached the floor. "I am Tentra, clan chief. He is shaman. He will know if you lie. Sit with us." His guttural accent so mangling the words that Lord Tirellan could barely understand him.

Lord Tirellan lowered himself to sit cross-legged on the carpet. He flicked a glance at the shaman. The tattoos on his shaven head seemed to swirl briefly in the candlelight. Lord Tirellan felt a cold shiver of fear as he looked into the unfathomable dark eyes that stared back. *A reminder of the stakes.*

"There will be no lies. A simple price for a service is all that I seek," said Lord Tirellan.

"Not so simple that I break my word," said Tentra.

"But once the choice is made the rest is simple," said Lord Tirellan. This was one of the possibilities he had considered. "And I presume that the choice has been made since I was invited here. Do you wish to discuss the price? That's what I came here for." He folded his arms across his chest and waited for their reply.

"You presume big, Lord Tirellan," said Tentra with a scowl.

"I presume that you are realists. You must know that we outnumber you, and that you have little prospect of relief."

"We are not afraid to fight you."

"The courage of the clans is well known, but ultimately you will lose and you will die, and for what? This is not your fight. Has Darien become a clan territory? Did you bring your warriors so far to have them buried in an unmarked pit?"

Lord Tirellan watched Tentra's face intently. The last thing he wanted to do was push the clansman into a show of defiance. Tentra spoke a few words to the shaman in a harsh tongue that Lord Tirellan could not understand. The shaman replied with a longer speech. Tentra was silent for a moment then looked at Lord Tirellan. "What is the price?" he said.

"Five thousand crowns," said Lord Tirellan.

"Not enough."

"Seven thousand."

"Eight."

Lord Tirellan took a deep breath and set his face to stifle the smile. "Very well, eight thousand."

"In gold."

"In gold."

"Five thousand now."

"Five thousand as soon as my representative can get it to you." His emissary had been optimistic of being able to re-enter Darien. Lord Tirellan silently hoped that optimism was not misplaced.

"One thing more." Tentra's eyes glittered in the candlelight. "All Darien soldiers die."

Lord Tirellan was silent for a moment as he thought about the codes of war and the implications of Tentra's demand.

"All die," said Tentra.

"A small price to pay," said Lord Tirellan permitting himself a smile this time. "When can you move?"

"When you pay us. We have gold, we open gates."

"Excellent," said Lord Tirellan. "Then I think our business is concluded. I'll bid you goodnight, gentlemen." He stood up and turned towards the wall of mist that hung just beyond the carpet. As the clouds closed around him he allowed himself a sigh of relief. *A deal my Lord of Caldon will be happy with I think.*

***

Ivo, Earl of Darien, knelt before the altar of Martis, his sword laid at his side. Unable to sleep for another night, he had decided to spend the hours until dawn in the temple that adjoined his apartments in the hope that the Soldiers' God would show him some way to save his people and town.

A sound that rose above the steady drip of rainwater interrupted his prayers. He held his breath and gave all his attention to listening for a repeat. Again. This time he had no doubt. The main gate of the castle was being opened. He seized his sword, grabbed a candle lantern from its niche and ran for the courtyard.

He hauled open the door and stared out at the dark courtyard. The light of the lantern showed him little beyond the wet cobbles and falling rain. All was quiet; too quiet. Where was the gate sentry? He should have reacted to the lantern.

I'll flog him if he's sleeping in some dry corner. He advanced a few steps, lantern held high, searching for anything that would give a clue to the sentry's whereabouts. A dog barked followed by another. From beyond the gate came the clatter of horses on the cobbles of the market square. Torchlight flickered through the dark tunnel of the gateway. The blood froze in Ivo's veins. Three shapes detached themselves from the dark bulk of the gatehouse and ran towards him. The lantern showed him enough to identify them as clansmen. He turned and fled for the guards' barrack room barely closing the door before his pursuers.

"To arms! We are betrayed," he cried as heavy blows crashed against the stout door at his back.

Within a few heartbeats the Earl's guard were roused. Men pulled on boots, groped under pallets for weapons and armour and lit torches from the night lanterns.

"What's happening, my Lord?" Eamon, blademaster of Darien, appeared at Ivo's side.

He must sleep in his mail to be ready so quickly, thought Ivo.

"Gate's open. The clansmen have turned. Horsemen in the marketplace."

"We must shift them, my Lord. We can't defend the castle otherwise."

"I agree," said Ivo. There was another crashing impact on the door.

"We have to get to them before they get in here," said Ivo. "Sergeant!"

The guard sergeant stepped forward at Ivo's call. "My Lord."

"Form the men up."

The sergeant turned to the soldiers behind him. "Form two

columns and spread when you're through the door." The men lined up smartly, swords drawn. "Ready, my Lord."

The pounding on the door ceased.

Ivo looked at Eamon and nodded. The blademaster's face was expressionless. *He knows our chances as well as I do*, thought Ivo as he took his place in the second rank of the column beside him.

"Open the door, Sergeant."

The guard sergeant lifted the locking bar from its cradle and another man hauled the door wide open. The two columns of soldiers charged through into the courtyard and spread out in an arc with Earl Ivo at the focus.

The courtyard was filled with Caldon's soldiers. The torches they carried showed their ranks to be at least three deep with cavalry behind them. The front rank of infantry dropped to kneel; their spears levelled at the Darien men. Behind them a rank of archers, arrows nocked, waited. Ivo, his stomach ice, took in the scene and then threw down his sword.

Oh my son. I have failed you.

Beside him Eamon stared at the enemy, his face blank as if he saw nothing. Very slowly he drew his sword and let it slip from his fingers. All along the Darien line weapons clattered to the cobbles. All was still for a moment. Then a harsh voice cried an order from behind the ranks of soldiers and the archers loosed their arrows.

CHAPTER 1

The tavernkeeper pushed the potboy out of the backdoor of the Black Lamb. "Run and fetch the guard, right now." He reached for the blackthorn cudgel that hung on the back of the kitchen door and returned to the common room where he carefully took down his treasured mirror from behind the counter. There were three people left in the common room and two of them were trouble. The tables were littered with mugs, some still half-full, that his customers had abandoned in their hurry to be out of harm's way.

At a table in the middle of the room sat Marek, the Earl's Blademaster, and Davo. Marek drained his mug and thumped a massive fist on the table. "More ale," he roared, throwing the mug across the room. The tavernkeeper filled a mug from the barrel and cautiously brought it to the table. The last time he had seen Marek in this mood it had taken six guardsmen to subdue him and the common room had been wrecked. He glanced at the third person in the room, the young stranger who had walked in an hour ago, and thought about warning him of the danger; but the tavernkeeper had no doubt if he did so he would become the object of Marek's attention instead. He collected the empty mugs and retreated behind the relative safety of the counter, counting the minutes until the guard could arrive.

The young stranger looked no more than twenty. His mud-splashed legs showed he had arrived on foot rather than horseback, though his clothes were of good quality, and a sword hung at his left side in an old black leather scabbard. He had spread his travel-stained cloak across a chair beside the fire to dry and then sat alone at a small table in a corner with a bowl of mutton stew and a mug of ale. Sitting back in his chair, eyes half-closed, he appeared to be nodding off to sleep.

Davo was staring at him too. The tavernkeeper thought Davo was almost more dangerous for all that he was two heads shorter than Marek. Davo had quick hands and a quicker tongue, and liked to play tricks on people. Davo started fights, and Marek finished them.

Davo scooped a lump of mud from his boot and tossed it at the stranger's cloak. It landed squarely in the centre. The young man did not stir. A second blob landed beside the first. Still he did not move. Annoyed by the lack of response, Davo looked around for something more offensive to toss at the still figure. His eyes lighted upon a large beetle crawling across the floor. Smiling mischievously he picked up the insect and gently lobbed it towards the bowl of stew. The somnolent figure flicked out his right hand and caught the beetle just above the bowl then looked over at the grinning Davo and Marek.

"What're you looking at, sonny?" Davo sneered.

"A man who eats insects." His voice was light with a slightly foreign accent.

He flicked his wrist and the beetle flew across the room again to land in Davo's half-full beer mug. Davo swore and, leaping to his feet, threw the mug at the youngster, who tumbled off his chair avoiding it and rolled in the rushes and sawdust on the floor. Davo stepped forward reaching beneath his jacket to the knife at his belt. The young man put his right hand on the hilt of his sword, and stared up at him.

Davo stopped and looked back at Marek with a grin. "The lad's got a blade, Marek."

"So he has, Davo. Looks a bit large for him, don't it. Reckon we ought to take it off him before he hurts hisself."

The young man rose to his feet, giving Marek and Davo the opportunity to size him up. He was two hand-widths shorter than Marek and lacked the big man's bulk in the shoulder, though he moved with an easy grace. He wore a loose flowing long-sleeved shirt of dark blue and black trousers cut snugly. He was clean-shaven and his dark hair was long enough to be caught by a thong in a short ponytail at the nape of his neck. Hand on his sword hilt; he looked calmly at the two grinning soldiers.

Marek stared back for a long moment then stood up, pushing aside the tables; he stretched himself to demonstrate his considerable size, and drew his own blade, tossing aside the scabbard. The young man flicked his blade clear of the gated scabbard and waited for the big man to make his move, the weapon resting lightly in his hand. Something about his stance and calm made the tavernkeeper think *this fellow knows what he's at. A gated scabbard too, a crown to a penny he's no mug.*

Marek eyed the sword scornfully and raised his own heavy blade. He was big and strong and that was the way he fought; it had been enough to keep him cock of the walk in the Earl's guard for years, and he was well used to being the best swordsman for leagues around. He stepped forward swinging his sword right-handed at the young man's neck. The young man ducked lithely under the blow, and his blade flicked out to stab Marek's right foot. Marek yelped with pain and drew back a moment cursing before swinging a chest-high slash. The young man danced backwards and Marek struck air. Marek stepped back half a pace and rebalanced.

Marek's favourite move was a heavy single-handed swing to the neck followed by a left hook to his opponent's stomach. The tavern keeper could see him trying to work into position for it; circling to his left, feinting a thrust and then stepping in with the right-handed swing. To his surprise the young man lunged forward and then, using the strength Marek put into the blow, flicked Marek's blade with his own over his head as he ducked. The momentum of the stroke threw Marek off balance and he stumbled with his back half-turned to his opponent. Marek caught himself, turned and took the young man's blade full in the throat.

Marek would have screamed if he still had a larynx. Instead he gurgled as the blood sprayed from the severed arteries. He clutched at his neck in a vain attempt to hold his life in, stumbled over a stool and fell on his face in a widening pool of blood.

The stranger watched calmly and then turned to look at Davo. Davo, eyes wide with terror, looked first at him, then down at the dying Marek, and ran for the door. The tavernkeeper still stood behind his counter clutching his blackthorn, staring in disbelief at his blood-splashed common room. The young man reached down and wiped his blade on Marek's jerkin before sheathing it.

The door crashed open.

"No-one move," a harsh voice commanded. Half a dozen guardsmen in scruffy red livery over chainmail rushed in, swords drawn, and surrounded the stranger. The young man stared disdainfully at the soldiers, his right hand resting on the hilt of his sheathed sword until he saw the crossbowman who had followed them, then his hand fell away. The guard captain, a stocky middle-aged man with greying hair and a bristling moustache, strode into the room.

"You! I'll take your sword. Now!" he barked, pointing at the stranger. The young man stared back at him for a long moment, as if weighing the odds, then slowly unbuckled the belt that held his blade and let it fall to the ground. The captain gestured to one of the remaining guardsmen who stepped up and searched him for weapons. The guard's eyes widened slightly as he retrieved slim throwing knives from both sleeves and a dagger from one boot. He stepped back and showed the captain what he had found.

"Right, you will come with me," the captain commanded the stranger. "You too," his eyes turned to the tavernkeeper. The guardsmen herded the stranger towards the door. Outside another four guardsmen stood with Davo. Beyond them a crowd of townsfolk was gathering to gawp at the scene

"You and you." The captain gestured to two of the guards. "Get a cart and bring the body."

The tavernkeeper locked up his tavern under the captain's gaze, and then they set off for the castle accompanied by Davo. Behind them, the soldiers formed up around the young man and marched him away with two spears at his back. The crowd of townsfolk followed them shouting insults; a couple of urchins threw clods of earth at the young man until the guardsmen chased them off. The troop made their way up the wide strip of mud between the buildings of Nandor town; most were, like the tavern, wooden with overhanging shingled roofs, but as they came closer to town centre there were a few stone buildings.

A squall of rain blew up the valley sending the townsfolk scuttling for cover, lashing at the soldiers and their prisoner whose heavy travel cloak had been left spread across a chair in the tavern. The tavernkeeper looked back at the young man; muck from the soldiers' boots had splashed him up to his waist, the rain had soaked through his shirt and plastered his dark hair to his scalp. By the time they reached the castle at the far end of the town, the prisoner looked thoroughly bedraggled and disreputable.

Welcome to Nandor, thought the tavernkeeper.

CHAPTER 2

Nandor castle was neither large nor impressive. Though the main gatehouse was stone-built, there was no great curtain wall of stone, just a high fence of wooden stakes. Aron looked up and noted that no body hung from the gibbet that stood atop the gatehouse. *Yet,* he thought bleakly.

The guard party surrounding him entered the compound through a postern beside the main gate and stood in the rain, facing the keep on its raised mound in the middle of the cobbled courtyard, the grey stone stained by lichens and the runoff from the gutters. Next to the gatehouse was a two-storey stone-built barrack block where a few men in the same livery as the guards lounged around the door staring at the prisoners. Beyond that was a set of stables roofed with wooden shingles, and a collection of flimsy-looking sheds. A gust of wind carried smoke spiralling upwards from one shed; the forge, Aron guessed.

The captain brought the prisoners into the gatehouse and left them guarded by liveried men armed with spears and crossbows. The tavern-keeper, the little man called Davo and Aron were allowed to find seats, the guardsmen stood and kept hold of their weapons. Aron settled calmly onto a rough wooden bench, barely looking around; he did not look at the other two though he felt their eyes on him continually. The captain returned in a few minutes and took the tavern-keeper away with him. Davo's agitation increased. Time passed; the guards watched Davo, Davo watched Aron. Aron leaned back and closed his eyes.

Contrary to appearances Aron was awake; through half-closed eyes he was studying the guards. Their worn livery, the dull and notched edges of the spear heads, and with the poor state of the castle's stonework drew him to the conclusion that if he had to fight his way out then he had a respectable chance. He hoped it would not be necessary; bloodshed always caused complications. *But I cannot allow myself to be detained here too long.* This trip escorting a wool merchant into the back of beyond was supposed to have kept him out of harm's way for a week or two while the Duke of Caldon's Saxish mercenaries took Oxport apart looking for him. Now it looked as if he could be diverted for months. *How much harm can Caldon and Lord Tirellan do to the exiles in that time?*

He reviewed the actions of the past hour. *Could I have avoided getting myself into this mess? Perhaps I shouldn't have put the beetle in Davo's beer.* No, he decided. Once he had entered the tavern the fight was inevitable. The big swordsman - Marek, Davo had called him - was drunk and looking for trouble and had settled on him as victim; nothing he could have done would have prevented the confrontation. Once Marek had drawn his sword then there could only have been one outcome. If fate was involved, it had determined that he kill Marek and take the consequences. There was nothing more he could do.

The captain returned. "You're for the Earl," he said gruffly, nodding to Davo. Davo stood up reluctantly and crept out past Aron, who opened one eye and watched him go. *I won't make any move before I hear what the Earl says,* Aron thought. *Who knows? He may turn out to be a just and honest man.*

***

Alice, Countess of Nandor, strode into the gloomy little room that was her husband's study, noting with disapproval the clutter of riding tack and empty bottles on the floor.

"What is this I hear about Marek?" she said.

"He's dead," said Baldwin, Earl of Nandor, mournfully. He gazed up at his wife from the chair where he sat, clad in mud-splattered britches and a wine-stained shirt, his favourite hound sprawled over his feet.

"How? Where?" She caught the half-formed braid of her hair, still unmarked by grey ribs, and tossed it over her shoulder.

"Murdered by some vagabond sell-sword in the Black Lamb." Earl Baldwin drained his goblet and refilled it with wine from the earthenware jug on the table. "He's in the guardroom. I'm going to hang him at sunset," he said with heavy satisfaction.

"You will do no such thing." Lady Alice glared down at her husband, hands on hips. "If there was a fight in the Black Lamb, then Marek started it. You know very well what he was like."

"It's what father would have done. I won't have people killing our guardsmen." He ran bony fingers through his thinning hair.

"Don't be ridiculous. This is all your father's making. Without his pig-headed obstinacy we wouldn't be in this mess. If he'd given you some part in the running of Nandor years before he died, then we might have mended our relations with Sarazan. Now you want to make it worse."

"How could it be worse?" Earl Baldwin took another mouthful of wine.

"A swordsman capable killing Marek and you want to hang him? Madness! Don't hang him, use him. Use him to get Maldwyn back."

"How?"

"Send him in place of Marek. He could hardly be less reliable."

"Why should we trust him? He might betray us to Sarazan. Lead us into a trap. I want men bound to us by blood in this."

"And we have few enough of those that we can ill afford to toss away a skilled warrior. Madness twice over. Even your father would recognise that."

"What if he refuses?"

"Leave that to me," said Lady Alice firmly. "You have Thalon find out what he is capable of, and I will persuade him to join us. And for your honour's sake put on a clean shirt before you speak with him." She turned and swept out.

***

Time passed slowly in the guardroom, rainwater dripped steadily from the broken gutter of the gatehouse, the room grew dim as night drew on. A servant came to light the oil lamp that burned smoky yellow on its shelf, providing little light and filling the room with its stink. Eventually the Captain returned. He beckoned to Aron, who stood up; the guardsmen's spears again a handswidth from his chest as he stretched. Two of the guardsmen fell in behind him, spears still tracking him as he followed the captain. They crossed the small courtyard and, by the light of the Captain's lantern, climbed a flight of stairs cut into the keep mound to the door which stood ajar. They passed into the keep, directly into the main hall. The Captain led the party towards a chair and table that sat before a fireplace set into the far wall. Light from a line of oil lamps splashed onto the straw-strewn floor. Threadbare tapestries and ragged banners, that emphasised the dark stone between them, hung above the benches that ran the length of the room against either wall. Aron could smell the smoke from the fire that smouldered in the hearth. The far end of the hall was lit by a single crown of candles that hung by a chain above the table.

As Aron's eyes adjusted to the light he noticed that his confiscated weapons lay on the table. He measured the distance to the table then relaxed and shifted his gaze to the man who sat in the chair. Earl Baldwin of Nandor was like his castle in that he was neither impressive nor in good repair. A thin balding beak-nosed figure in his mid-forties peered at Aron with bloodshot watery blue eyes. It was difficult to imagine that he had ever been magnificent even on his wedding day. *One might indeed wonder what his wife had ever seen in him,* Aron thought *except, of course, he is an Earl.* At a nod from the captain, one of the guardsmen reversed his spear and struck Aron a blow in the back of his right thigh that drove him to his knees.

"I will have your name, young man." Earl Baldwin's voice was a high pitched, nasal whine.

"My name is Aron, son of Eamon, of the county of Darien." Aron answered. *At least the straw is clean,* he thought. *Someone keeps up standards.*

"So Aron, son of Eamon, you have robbed me of the service of my finest swordsman," the Earl said, almost petulantly to Aron's ears.

"It was nothing of my making, Lord." If Marek was the finest swordsman in Baldwin's retinue it did not say much for the rest. Aron, though, thought better of saying so.

"I well know that, otherwise your head would already be adorning my gate," said Baldwin. "Be that as it may, you are greatly in debt to my house. However, there is a way at hand for you to repay that debt. Stand up."

Aron relaxed; at least he wasn't going to have to try to cut his way out, though it sounded very much as if Earl Baldwin had a nasty job for him. He stood up, rubbing his hands together to remove the fragments of straw.

"My only son, Maldwyn, was captured by soldiers of House Sarazan twenty days ago. They hold him to a ransom of five thousand crowns," said the Earl, almost choking over the words. Aron could smell wine on the Earl's breath.

Aron's heart sank further. The Duke of Sarazan sat on a rich estate with a well-equipped and drilled army of considerable size and renown; he was also a confidant of the High King and no friend of Darien. Looking about the hall; at the Earl's tunic, which showed signs of darning, and his chipped and scratched chair, Aron could see how finding a five thousand crowns could be a problem. "House Sarazan, my Lord?"

"The House of Sarazan has laid false claim to certain border territories. Maldwyn was leading a troop of my guard to assert our rights. He was seized in ambush by a superior force."

An equal number of Sarazan troopers is likely to be an overwhelmingly superior force, Aron thought. He did not say so. Instead he asked. "What does the High King say?"

"His opinion has not been sought," said Baldwin dismissively. "He is unlikely to go against one of the men who put him on the throne."

True, thought Aron. *Though he claims he deals justice fairly to all.*

"I was," Baldwin gestured to the guard captain, who had taken up station behind Baldwin's chair, "with Captain Thalon here, even today preparing an expedition to rescue Maldwyn."

Aron hoped his face betrayed none of the feelings of a man who has just had his worst suspicions confirmed. "Where is he being held, Lord?"

"Sarazan. Where else? They sent two of the men who were taken with Maldwyn as couriers of the ransom demand."

"The main fortress, my Lord?" Aron had seen the Duke's castle there. It had withstood a four month siege in the civil war half a generation ago, and had been reinforced since.

"You know it?" Baldwin asked. Aron nodded. "Good. Then you know its weaknesses."

Aron tried hard to think of one and failed. "You could pay the ransom, my Lord." Aron knew the words were a mistake as he was saying them.

"What? Never!" Baldwin leapt from his chair and drew himself up to his full height, namely Aron's chin. "The honour of Nandor would never permit it."

Aron had not heard of the honour of Nandor before he had arrived in the little town this morning. All he knew were a few vague tales of an Earl of Nandor who was renowned as a fierce warrior, hunter and drinker and it was difficult to believe that his blood flowed in the veins of the man before him.

"Our plans must go forward and a swordsman without Nandor in his voice will be an asset. You will take the place of the man you killed, on your sworn oath of loyalty to Nandor, and make ready to free my son." The Earl sat down triumphantly. "I will have your belongings collected from the town. You will live in the barracks until you leave for Sarazan. See to it, Thalon."

"Is that wise, my Lord?" Thalon spoke cautiously from behind Baldwin's chair. "He has just killed one of them."

"Ah yes, quite so. I see your point. You had better put him in one of the guest chambers." With that the Earl rose from his seat and ambled towards one of the staircases that led off the hall.

The words, "I shall speak to you later, young man," floated down the stairs.

***

Aron sat on his straw mattress cleaning the mud off his boots, thinking on the day and reflecting that Earl Baldwin of Nandor must be the greatest fool in the high kingdom if he thought that any oath Aron swore under these circumstances would bind him anywhere outside Nandor. Aron took obligations of honour very seriously; indeed such things were what elevated him in his mind above the level of other sell-swords and kept his conscience clear, but there were limits and this was well beyond them. *Just do what you have to to get away from here as soon as possible*, he thought. *Even if it means swearing an oath you know you've no intention of keeping.*

There was a knock at the door, and a grubby kitchen girl pushed it open without waiting for Aron's response. She carried a tray with a large bowl of stew, half a loaf of fresh bread and a flagon of ale. Staring at him with fierce red-rimmed eyes, she laid the tray on the floor beside his bed, next to his pack which had been fetched from the tavern. Then she left and Aron clearly heard her exchange words with the guardsman outside the door. No matter that the stew was rich with mutton and the ale was dark and strong, he was still a prisoner.

CHAPTER 3

The ringing of a bell woke Aron. He took a moment to remember where he was, then rolled out of the low bed. He went to the narrow window, lifted the waxed linen blind and looked out. Yesterday's rain had blown over and the sky was speckled with white clouds. In the courtyard below the servants and guardsmen were beginning the day's duties. Maids carried baskets of fresh bread from the bakery, and two ragged children chased a pair of dogs around a wagon by the forge. Aron watched for a while, counting the number of shingles missing from the roof of the stables, wondering what the day held for him.

He did not have long to wait. Heavy boots clattered on the wooden floor and the door to his cell was thrown open. Captain Thalon marched in.

"Get dressed, lad," he said gruffly.

Aron put on his still damp shirt and pulled on his boots as Thalon watched.

"Right, follow me." Thalon turned and marched out. Aron followed him, hoping he would mention breakfast. He didn't. Instead they walked across the courtyard, out of the postern gate and along beside the wall to a bare field of beaten earth. About two dozen men in scruffy livery were waiting in the chill morning air, standing around in little knots gossiping. They fell silent as Thalon and Aron approached.

"What is to happen here?" Aron asked.

"You killed their instructor. I want to know if you are fit to take his place," Thalon replied, his eyes cold. "Take a practice sword." He pointed to a box of wooden practice blades. Aron took a sword and tried it for weight, he paused a moment, tried another and another, then went back to the first.

"This one will do," Aron said, gently hefting it. Thalon pointed at the nearest soldier, who already held a wooden blade.

"Begin."

The soldier lifted the wood in salute then approached Aron sideways. His unbalanced stance instantly told of his poor level of training. Aron executed standard blocks, waiting for the mistake. He did not have to wait long. The man over-extended in a lunge and was unable to recover quickly enough to prevent Aron's wood striking him firmly under the ribs. He doubled over with a grunt, and two of the watching group stepped forward to assist him to one side as Thalon called the next opponent forward.

So it continued. One by one, Thalon called them forward, and Aron despatched them, each one no more skilled than the first. After the first few, Aron had thought he would have proved the point, but to his annoyance, Thalon seemed determined that they continue until Aron failed. He resigned himself to taking on each one to satisfy Thalon, reining back his anger to ensure that none of them took more hurt than a bruise. *Good practice for my basic bladework*, he thought, almost hoping for a man with a bit more skill so he could be truly exercised. No such man appeared, so he repeated the exercise of block and counter while the soldiers grew more restless and frustrated. One or two attacked with real anger, aiming wild slashes at him, but fared no better. *These fellows are disgraceful. It would take months to turn them into a worthwhile fighting force. I hope the Earl doesn't intend any serious fighting.*

Aron counted twenty-six men fall before Thalon gave way and called a halt. Aron had not noticed the passage of time, but now saw that the sun stood high overhead and he became conscious of his empty belly.

"Right. We'll break now. You, you and you." Thalon pointed to three soldiers. "Take him along with you and get him fed." He turned to Aron. "Go with 'em, if you want to eat." Then he turned and strode off towards the castle.

Aron walked silently with his escort back to the barracks where, in the mess hall, stew and coarse bread was ladled out by a taciturn cook. Aron found a place at the end of a rough table; the other soldiers kept as far away from him as possible even though that meant several ate standing up. No-one spoke to him, though a few glanced his way and then looked away. He ate in silence, avoiding catching anyone's eye, but his ears caught snatches of the soldiers' talk.

"Don't like the bastard coming in here showing us up."

"You want Marek back?"

"Alright so Marek was a bastard, but he was our bastard."

"Know what you mean. I don't like him either. Cocky little pisser. Reckon a few of us should give him one of his own lessons."

"You can try if you want, but Cap'n'll have the skin off your back for it. I'm just gonna keep my head down. He'll be gone soon enough, soon as he sees there's no money be made here." There was a murmur of assent around the group.

Fine by me, thought Aron. *I want to be gone from Nandor just as soon as I can be.*

The soldiers talk died away into silence as Captain Thalon came into the mess hall. "Right lads, break's over," he said. "Finish up and get back to the practice ground."

A grumble of discontent ran around the room as Thalon turned away, but the soldiers finished their meals and within two minutes were all heading back outside.

"That was piss poor this morning," said Thalon once everyone had arrived. "So we're going to do it again."

He nodded to Aron to pick up a practice blade. Aron did so, wondering just what this was going to prove. Out of the corner of his eye he noticed someone standing on the castle battlement. He turned to see Earl Baldwin watching them as the first Nandor soldier stepped reluctantly forward. Aron felt a moment's sympathy for the fellow; he was overmatched and he knew it. Aron saluted him and swept in the attack, aiming a forehand cut at his neck, then backhand to his groin and forehand again. The soldier blocked the first two blows competently enough, and made the same block to the third. Aron softened the blow, twisted his wrist and ran his blade down the length of the soldier's sword to catch his wrist. The soldier dropped the sword with an oath and looked up to see Aron's swordpoint a handswidth from his face. He retreated back to his fellows rubbing his hand and Aron took guard again. No-one came forward to meet him so Thalon picked a man out. Aron could see the fear on the soldier's pimply face as stepped forward. *He's already beaten*, thought Aron. He waited a moment as the soldier hesitantly took guard then swung a strong forehanded cut at waist height. The soldier blocked it with his wood but failed to turn with the blow. The momentum knocked the blade away from his body leaving him wide open to Aron's backhand. Aron's wood thumped into his stomach, knocking the air out of him, and he doubled over.

"Next," called Thalon.

As before lunch, each of the twenty-six men faced Aron and fell before him. Captain Thalon looked on stone-faced until the exercise was finished.

The soldiers gathered up the practice blades and started to drift back towards the castle. One or two directed hostile looks Aron's way. Aron wondered what he was meant to do next. At the Blademaster's academy a vigorous exercise session like that would have been followed by a good long warm soak in the bathhouse, but he very much doubted that they even had a bathhouse in Nandor. He looked to the Captain for a clue. Thalon said nothing, but gestured that Aron should follow him. Aron fell in behind him, conscious of the sharp wind that chilled him through his damp shirt. They walked in silence back to the castle.

Thalon escorted him back to his guest room and just before he closed the door said, "Get yourself cleaned up. You'll dine with the Earl tonight."

Aron was astonished. He sat down on the bed and took off his boots. His first thought was to hope that he wouldn't be dining alone with Earl Baldwin, otherwise he foresaw a very dull evening ahead. His second thought was whether or not his other shirt was wearable. He stripped off the shirt he was wearing and dug in his pack for his other one; it was cleaner than the one he had taken off. He went to the washstand that stood in the corner of the room and poured water from the jug into the cracked bowl. He tested it with a finger; it was icy cold. With a grimace he took the washcloth and washed as best he could.

Aron didn't remember going to sleep. He had laid out on the bed to relax for a moment, but now the room was dark and someone was knocking at the door. This time whoever it was waited for him to call out "enter" before coming in.

"Dinner is served, good sir." The speaker carried a small candle lantern; by its dim light Aron could see a young footman.

Aron blinked the sleep from his eyes and pulled on his boots. Even though Captain Thalon had said he would be dining with the Earl, he was still surprised at the summons. He followed the footman down to the main hall, drawn by the enticing smell of roasted meat. He was shown to a place setting at the wooden table which took up fully half the width of the room. Captain Thalon was already at the table with another man who had the look of a clerk. A bell was rung and the two men stood up, so Aron did too. The Earl entered followed by his family. The unimpressive figure of Earl Baldwin occupied Aron for less than a second. His wife was a different matter, very different.

The Countess of Nandor was in her mid thirties. Her dark hair curled to her shoulders, her blue eyes sparkled and her firm but well-rounded figure betrayed no hint of the children she had borne. A dozen or more years ago she could have paralysed an entire army with a smile. In any other company the girls - Aron presumed them to be her daughters - who accompanied her would have stolen breath and turned many heads with their lustrous dark curls, blue eyes and slim figures; in their mother's company they were merely a promise of good things to come.

Aron was seated at the end of the table next to the Countess with one of her daughters directly across from him. Aron guessed the girl to be a few years younger than himself, perhaps sixteen. Servants brought in the first course; the fierce-eyed kitchen girl put a pewter bowl of soup before Aron, and a pale wine was poured. Aron wondered about starting conversation, but the rich dark soup, thick with vegetables, seemed good enough to occupy his full attention. The girl opposite finished her soup and looked hard at Aron.

"So you're the man who killed Marek," she said.

Aron paused for a moment to think about his reply, unsure whether he was the hero or villain of this story.

"Yes, I'm sorry to say I am, my Lady."

"This is my younger daughter, Lady Edith," the Countess broke in. "And you need not be sorry on our account, Aron son of Eamon. You have done us a service ridding us of that loathsome lout."

Edith grimaced. "I won't miss the way he used to look at Celaine and me. He was horrible."

Aron felt able to relax a little at this; clearly Marek was not going to be missed in this part of House Nandor.

"And now you're going to rescue Maldwyn for us," said Edith, fixing Aron with an intense wide-eyed stare.

Someone should warn her about staring at young men like that, thought Aron. *An impressionable young fellow could do himself serious damage looking into those eyes.* Aron became aware that several seconds had passed and he had not answered Edith's question. "I believe Earl Baldwin intends that I should take the place of the late Marek," he said cautiously.

"And I'm sure you'll be a big improvement," said the Countess with a smile. "I have never been to Sarazan. What do you know of it?"

"The fortress of Sarazan is large and very solid," said Aron, certain that he spoke no secrets. "It is built on a low promontory into the lake so that there is only one approach. Much of the old city near the fortress was destroyed in the siege and the new building is farther away so there is no cover during the approach. The Duke's army is large, disciplined and has a good reputation. The Duke has a firm hand. There is some crime, but the town watch are efficient and thieves are publicly hanged; most of the officials are obstructive but honest. It would be easier to pay the ransom."

I hope she doesn't share the Earl's views on the honour of Nandor, he thought.

"Yes. I'm sure it would be, but the Earl will not hear of it. Such monies as we have must go for these ladies' dowries." She gestured with an elegant hand to indicate her daughters.

Edith was still focused on Aron like a kestrel on a mouse. Of course, it would be essential to House Nandor that the daughters made good marriages. They were pretty enough, certainly, and of an age, but the dowries were what mattered to suitors. Ransoming Maldwyn would strip the estate and leave the girls unmarriageable.

"Could you not resolve this by offering a marriage to Sarazan?" asked Aron. "The Duke of Sarazan has two unmarried sons."

"We proposed such a marriage several years ago," said the Countess with a touch of bitterness. "The Duke has greater alliances in mind."

"What manner of man is the lord Maldwyn, if I may ask?" asked Aron.

"Maldwyn is a boy filled with energy and enthusiasm for life," said the Countess. "It breaks my heart to think of him confined."

"He's tall, dark and handsome and always at some sport or other," chimed in Edith. "He's a wonderful swordsman, almost as good as Marek." Her flow of words stopped abruptly as she realised what she had said. "I suppose he is not as good as you." The words came out awkwardly and she blushed. Aron felt slightly pleased. The Countess came to Edith's rescue.

"My Lord tells me you are from Darien. You are a long way from home; what brings you to this far corner?"

An assassin's crossbow bolt and a Saxish wizard, thought Aron, gripping his fork tightly.

"I'll wager you're the son of some great noble unjustly wronged and seeking your fortune, so that you can return and set all to rights," Edith said enthusiastically, her eyes shining dangerously.

Aron paused over his reply, not wishing to tell an outright lie.

"Darien is now submerged in the dukedom of Caldon, is it not?" asked the Countess.

"Since the war, that sadly is true. It will not always be so."

The Countess raised her eyebrows at the tone of his reply. "And Caldon now calls himself king and stands against the High King."

"Caldon grows strong on the wealth of Darien, but the High King makes him look stronger by refusing to confront him," said Aron grimly.

"Perhaps he fears such a move risks a wider war," she said, her eyes, the same blue as her daughter's, fixed on his face. "Is that weakness?" Her gaze turned aside. "We all fear a return to the bloodletting," she added softly.

"Caldon's ambitions will bring war if they are not opposed. He will use the army he is building."

"So the High King can ill afford to snub an ally as important as Sarazan. Any rescue of prisoners must be done subtly lest it give Sarazan a pretext to march on us. The High King would not stay their hand."

Aron was impressed. The Countess had very clear grasp of the realities of their situation and he found himself drawn to sympathise with her plight.

"And what is your position within this game of great powers? My daughter thinks you a vengeful son of a noble house."

The question was slipped in so effortlessly that Aron was drawn into answering before he had a chance to think.

"The Earl of Darien sent me, with his son Cordra, from the fortress before it was encircled. We fled to the Holy City to the care of the Duke of Kyria, Cordra's uncle on his mother's side. When the news of Darien's fall reached us, the exiles proclaimed Cordra Earl. We still hope the High King will confirm him in the title and back us against Caldon."

"So you are a companion of the Earl in exile," said Edith with a sigh, blue eyes brighter than ever. "How romantic."

There's one who has listened to too many bard's tales, thought Aron, once he had remembered to breathe.

"Earl Cordra has been a good friend to me," said Aron. "But these days his time is mostly consumed by the game of great powers, as you put it."

"But you have been to the court of the High King?" said Edith.

"My ladies have not been to the court," said the Countess. "Indeed, my Lord and I have only visited once, before the war."

Further conversation was curtailed by the arrival of the main course, a roasted haunch of mutton; unsurprising as the wealth of Nandor, such as it was, was in the wool trade. At the far end of the table Aron heard the Earl complain that the meat was undercooked and call for more wine. He glanced that way and caught Edith's sister looking at him, though she quickly turned away.

Aron tried to concentrate on his meal, but as he ate he could feel the Lady Edith's gaze on him. He knew that if he looked up from his plate he was sure to meet her eyes. His first thought when he had considered the situation had been that he would go along with whatever scheme Earl Baldwin cooked up until he was out of Nandor, and then he would disappear. Pretty as Lady Edith undoubtedly was, there was no reason change that view. *Don't get caught up in this. Just be polite and think about how you're going to get back to the Holy City.*

Aron tried to hide behind a second helping of mutton, but Edith would not be denied. Once she had extracted from him the information that he had been to the Holy City and spent time at the court of the High King, the questions were endless. Aron had only been on the fringes of the court, but had been close enough to see beneath the initial glamour, and he found her excitement about the possibility of being presented at court naive and a little tiresome. The Countess again rescued him with questions about the political manoeuvring and alliances. Aron felt out of his depth before her probing and was glad when the meal was over and the Countess withdrew with her daughters. *No doubt her father thought it a good match to marry her to Baldwin,* he thought *but he should have been more ambitious for her. She is wasted in this backwater.*

After the ladies left Captain Thalon took Aron to one side and curtly told him to present himself at the practice ground in the morning. As Thalon strode out Aron thought to take his leave, but the Earl was already deep in conversation with the clerkly fellow and a bottle, so he sought the stairs and climbed up to his chamber, his head swimming.

***

"Well, she made a fine spectacle of herself, didn't she?" Lady Alice, Countess of Nandor turned from the door of her chamber to look at her elder daughter Celaine.

"If you mean Edith, then she was doing as I asked," replied

Lady Alice through pursed lips. "And I can't fault her enthusiasm."

"Embarrassing, wasn't it?" said Celaine. "I've no wish to flirt with a common soldier."

"A soldier yes, but far from common," said Lady Alice. *You foolish girl, just because he's not a Duke's brat. You haven't seen how he moves, you haven't looked into those dark eyes. You'll change your mind when you do.* "And the one man who could rescue your dowry, or have you forgotten?"

"I don't see why we can't just borrow the money."

"That's because you haven't seen the ruinous terms the moneylenders offered."

"This is all my idiot brother's fault."

"Be quiet, Celaine," said Lady Alice sharply. "I will not have you talking like that. Now you will do as I ask and spend some time with Aron. Take him for a walk tomorrow. I'm sure you will find it a pleasure. Show him your herb garden."

Lady Alice watched her daughter's face. For a moment she thought she was going to argue the point, but then Celaine said "Yes Mama," and with a suggestion of a curtsey flounced out.

CHAPTER 4

It was still deep in the night when Aron awoke convulsed by a stomach cramp. He managed three steps away from the bed towards the washstand before the contents of his stomach were violently expelled. He collapsed to the floor as another spasm took him and his arse let go a stinking flood. He tried to cry out, but all that came out of his mouth was more bitter vomit. He tried to stand, to reach the waterjug, but bright lights flashed in his eyes and his head span; he took a step sideways and toppled against the wall. He clutched at the wall, trying again to stand, but his legs would not support him and he crumpled in a miserable retching heap. He could not feel the floor beneath, for his body seemed suspended in swirling dark water that tossed him over and around. He heard a voice calling his name, a voice that he had not heard since he was in his cradle. *I'm here Mother. I'm coming,* his mind replied. The turbulence of the water subsided; stars appeared in the darkness, dancing before him. One star grew, its light reaching out to him, warming him, until it resolved into his mother's face. She loomed larger and larger, dark eyes filled with love, taking over his whole field of vision. Her mouth opened and the world went dark again as he was swallowed.

The next thing Aron was aware of was women's voices, singing in harmony words that he could not make out. He opened his eyes and, to his surprise, found himself looking down on a group of four women who stood at each corner of a bed. He recognised one of them as Lady Alice; the others he did not know. The song ended; Lady Alice took up a small bowl and held it to the lips of the figure on the bed. The figure did not move. Aron looked more closely at the dark hair and pale face and, with a jolt, recognised himself.

What's happening here? he thought. A cold surge of fear ran through him. *Am I dying?* He remembered being ill, sicker than he had ever been before. *Is this what it feels like?* He watched in fascination as candles were lit, bunches of herbs were burned and Lady Alice anointed his brow with oil. Then they began another song, but again he was unable to discern the words or even the language. As the song swelled and the candlelight grew brighter Aron felt a glow of warmth flow through him. The vision of the room slipped out of focus and faded.

The next time he opened his eyes his view of the room was more conventional. He tried to sit up but found he did not have the strength.

"Thank the Lady. You're awake at last." Aron turned his head to the voice, the speaker was a motherly woman with a care-lined face. "How are you feeling?" She brought a plain earthenware bowl to his lips. "Drink."

Aron drank and was surprised to find himself thirsty. He drained the bowl which she refilled from a jug and he drained it again.

"How long was I asleep?" he asked as she took the bowl from him.

"Four days. We thought we'd lost you. Now you lie quiet while I fetch milady."

She smiled and bustled out of the room leaving Aron cringing with embarrassment as he realised that she might very well have had to wash him all over. He tried again to sit up and this time succeeded, though the effort left him feeling light-headed. The weakness in his muscles confirmed that he had been very ill.

He looked around; there was glass in the window and a faded tapestry on the wall; a small charcoal-filled brazier warmed the room. The sheets he lay on were linen, with soft woollen blankets piled on top. This was a much finer room than he had been put in first.

Feet clattered on the landing and the door opened. Lady Alice walked briskly in followed by the motherly woman.

"Thank the Lady, Glynis," said Lady Alice. She came to Aron's bedside and laid a cool hand on his brow. "No fever." She smiled and Aron could see the relief on her face. "You must be hungry. I'll have something sent up." She turned for the door.

"Eat, then sleep. Tomorrow you'll be stronger," said Glynis briskly. "And make sure you drink plenty of water."

The women left the room leaving Aron to his thoughts.

Eat! The last meal I ate put me in this state. If it was bad meat surely others would have been affected. And I've never heard of bad meat giving such strange dreams or making you sleep for four days. This was something else, something that seems very like poison. But who? Not the Countess surely. If the bizarre vision was true, then she had worked mightily for my recovery, and her relief seems real enough. No, there are other enemies here. Is Caldon's arm truly so long that it can reach me even in Nandor?

A short time later two maids appeared with the promised

supper tray and a small short-legged table that sat comfortably on the bed. There was a large bowl of soup, fresh crusty bread, a slab of pale cheese and a large mug of buttermilk. Aron lifted the lid of the soup bowl and realised that he was very hungry. He put all thoughts of poison to the back of his mind and tucked in.

***

"Will he live then?" asked Earl Baldwin as Lady Alice stepped into his study.

"He will, I think. He's past the worst of it." Her brow creased as she looked for somewhere to sit but found all the chairs piled with clutter.

"The Gods nod our way at last." He reached for the bottle that stood on the table beside him.

"Perhaps," said Lady Alice gravely, "But no thanks to Peg."

"Peg? What has she to do with this?"

"It's the talk of the kitchens that she was carrying Marek's child, and now she can't be found. And Glynis found brown bonnets hidden in her bedroll."

"Brown bonnets! Then he is indeed fortunate to be alive." He paused a moment, bottle in hand. "He must never learn of this."

"Why do you think that?"

"How would he ever trust us enough to join our cause?"

"And how much more would he distrust us if he found that we hid the truth from him? No, we must tell him and he will trust us all the more."

Earl Baldwin stared at his wife and shook his head.

"Are you sure? We must have him. He's the finest swordsman I've ever seen."

"I will take care of it. You see to it that you have a plan worthy of him."

"Oh I will. With him at my side how can we fail?"

"At your side? Baldwin, you will not be going to Sarazan."

"It's what father would have done."

"I have no doubt it is," Lady Alice said tartly. "But you are not your father. Besides the risk to Nandor is too great. What would become of us if we lost you and Maldwyn? No, it must be someone else. Thalon. He is a proven man and a seasoned warrior."

"And there is no-one I would trust more, but he is too old for this. It needs a younger man. Tancred."

Lady Alice pursed her lips in displeasure. "Certainly he's young, but he's completely unproven."

"Then let him prove himself. I don't doubt his valour, and with this Darien lad to advise him he should do well enough."

Lady Alice frowned but said nothing.

***

Aron woke to the ringing of the morning bell. Cautiously he eased himself out of the bed and stood on the floor. To his great relief, he was able to stand and, though he was unsteady, he managed to walk to the window. Outside the castle was waking up to a damp grey morning. Hearing footsteps on the landing outside his door, he hurried back to his bed before Glynis came into the room.

"Awake? Good. You've got a much better colour," she said. "No headache?"

Aron shook his head. "No."

"And hungry I've no doubt. I'll send up a tonic with your breakfast, make sure you drink it all." With that she was gone.

A short time later a shy maidservant brought up a tray of breakfast. There was fresh bread, cold meat and more of the pale cheese and a tall mug of something warm, dark and bitter-tasting. After a deep breath, Aron took a mouthful of the tonic and, to his relief, found it wasn't as bad as he had feared. *I've passed evenings drinking worse ale than this*, he thought and finished the mug in three draughts before turning his attention to the food.

Outside the rain fell steadily. Aron put aside the tray and lay back on the pillows. *I really don't mind staying in bed today.* The beat of the raindrops on the stones of the keep lulled him to doze. He wasn't sure how long he'd slept when more footsteps sounded on the landing. He sat up with a start and had just about blinked the sleep out of his eyes when Lady Alice came into the room, a troubled look on her face.

"Good morning," she said, her tone much more formal than yesterday. "How are you this morning? I hope you slept well." She paused and looked distractedly out of the window. "I fear we cannot expect much of the day. My maid tells me it will rain until nightfall."

"I slept well, thank you my Lady," said Aron. "I feel much stronger today."

She turned to face Aron and he knew that she was about to say something of great importance. "I must tell you of the shame of Nandor. Your illness was nothing natural. I believe you were poisoned, and by one of our household. This morning a fisherman found the body of one of the kitchenmaids in the river. Her name was Peg. She was Marek's lover. The kitchen gossip says she was carrying his child." Aron thought about the wild-eyed maid; was she Peg?

"We searched through her things and found some mushrooms. They're called brown bonnets. They grow in the woods and everyone knows them to be poisonous. She was seen to be cooking something the evening you dined with us. Those that eat them suffer as you did; they usually die."

Lady Alice, her face grave, stood by the window waiting for his reaction. Only her hands, clasped in front of her, betrayed her tension.

Aron felt a momentary stab of sympathy for wild-eyed Peg, too young to know any better, another victim of Big Marek's fondness for a fight.

"It was not of your doing, my Lady, and you have shown me nothing but kindness," he said and watched her face relax into a relieved smile. "And now thanks to your kindness, I think I am well enough to get up today."

"It will be a quiet day around the castle with the weather as it is. I'll send a maid to get your clothes. We must have you decently covered."

Aron looked around the room and realised that his clothes were nowhere to be seen. He started to put the sheet up to cover himself, but then stopped as he realised the stupidity of his action. Lady Alice smiled at him in amusement and, after a moment, Aron smiled too.

"I shall send my ladies to entertain you. Be careful that you do not overtire yourself." She said and still smiling left the room.

A few moments later a maid appeared at the door with Aron's clothes and deposited them with a giggle on the end of the bed. Aron dressed and made an attempt at tidying his hair. When he opened the door the maid was standing on the landing. Her mischievous smile made him wonder if she'd been watching through a crack.

"My Lady said I should look after you sir, and take you to the parlour."

Aron walked a few paces and then accepted her offer of an arm to support him as they made their way down the dimly-lit stairs. At the foot of the stairs he was caught by a sudden feeling of shyness. The women he'd grown up around had been cooks, serving maids and the like, not the daughters of the nobility. He thought about asking the maid to take him back to his room but by then they had reached the door. Feeling awkward, he followed the maid into the parlour.

The room was small and snug, hung with tapestries and a cheerful fire burned in the grate. The Ladies Celaine and Edith sat on stools before the fire with sewing baskets at their feet. Both stood up with welcoming smiles as Aron came in. Glynis came forward to take his arm.

"It's good to see you up on your feet," she said. "Come and sit down here by the fire."

"Everyone's been so worried about you," said Celaine. "We were all praying for you."

"All of us," said Edith, her blue eyes shining. She was slightly shorter than her sister, Aron noticed, and her blue woollen gown showed signs of having been darned in several places.

Glynis guided Aron into a comfortable chair. "Now ladies, what shall we do? It would be very dull to watch Lady Edith unpicking her embroidery. Do you play cards, young man?"

"I do know some card games," Aron said, thinking that the games he had learned from the soldiers of Darien would be most unsuitable for playing with nobly-born girls.

"That's settled then. Bring the cards, Edith."

Edith produced an ornate wooden box from a shelf behind the hangings and they settled down beside the fire around a low table. Edith dealt out the cards and the game began.

Glynis, Aron learned, was very good at cards, and he was glad that no coin was involved. Her lined homely face betrayed nothing of her thoughts and she won consistently. Lady Edith was quite the opposite; she was reckless and flighty, taking great delight in the few hands she won and teasing Aron when he lost. Lady Celaine was quieter than Edith and a cautious player, but as the afternoon passed her reserve melted, she smiled sweetly at Aron and sometimes glanced at him with the same dangerous blue eyes as her sister.

As the afternoon stretched into evening and the candles were lit Aron began to grow weary.

Glynis caught his eye and frowned. "Bedtime for you, young man."

"Oh no. Not yet," cried Edith. "Can't he stay for dinner?"

Aron yawned widely and the argument was settled. The cards were put away and, after bidding the girls goodnight, Aron made his way back up to his room. He undressed and climbed into bed; his mind filled with mischievous smiles and sparkling blue eyes, and was asleep before the maid arrived with his supper tray.

CHAPTER 5

The ringing of the morning bell again woke Aron. He walked to the window and was relieved to find he was much steadier on his feet than yesterday. Outside the sky was grey with cloud but it was not actually raining. He dressed slowly, wondering what the day would bring. His stomach reminded him that he'd missed supper last night. He pulled on his boots and cautiously made his way down the stairs to the main hall, where a handful of people sat at breakfast. Aron did not recognise any of them. He helped himself to fresh bread and white cheese and sat down to eat on his own, conscious of being looked at.

He had just finished and was on his way out when Lady Celaine walked in. She smiled sweetly at him. "Good morning, Aron. I trust you slept well," she said.

"I slept very well, thank you," Aron replied politely, trying not to grin like an idiot.

"My sister and I did so enjoy our games yesterday," Celaine said and stepped closer.

Aron caught the tantalising scent of sweet roses. *And which games did you enjoy most? The cards or the flirting?* he thought.

"It would please me if you would walk with me this afternoon." She looked up to give him maximum benefit of her blue eyes.

Indeed it would, thought Aron. *It would also annoy Edith, I'll wager.* He was not best pleased with the prospect of being a toy for sisters to fight over, but a refusal would definitely seem churlish.

"If my duties permit, I would be honoured," he said, half-hoping that duty would not permit.

Duty approached in the person of Captain Thalon. He nodded briefly to Celaine. "Milady." Then he turned to Aron. "I heard you're well again," he said, with no trace of sympathy. "Are you fit enough to be useful?"

"If nothing too vigorous is involved then I believe so, Captain."

Thalon frowned at him as if he suspected Aron of malingering.

"Training," growled Thalon. "I know you can beat them, now I want to see if you can teach them. Not too testing for you, is it?"

"I should be able to manage," said Aron. He nodded to Celaine and was rewarded with another mischievous smile and blaze of blue eyes before she turned to walk away. Thalon grunted impatiently and Aron fell in beside him as they set off for the practice ground.

None of the soldiers looked pleased to see them, and they took their time when the Captain formed them up in two ragged ranks.

"Right. Pay attention," he bellowed. "The last practice session showed you up as a sorry bunch of clowns, so we're going to work on your basic bladework. You will listen to Aron and you will do what he says." There was a mutter of dissent from the ranks. "Silence. Does anyone want to argue? There's a month's guard duty waiting." The muttering died. "Now." He turned to Aron. "What do you want?"

"Take two men to give me an example," said Aron. "I'll work from there."

"Right." Thalon turned back to the soldiers. "Jako and you, Vini. You were particularly poor last time. Step forward."

The two men reluctantly came forward, picked up practice swords and stood facing each other.

"Begin," ordered Thalon.

It took only a few exchanges before Aron intervened.

"Stop." He stepped forward. "Your feet are in the wrong place. That means that your weight isn't behind the block."

He took the practice wood from one of them and demonstrated the stance just as his father had taught it to him, ten or more years ago in Darien. The soldiers looked towards Thalon as if seeking reassurance that what they'd been doing was not wrong.

"He's in charge," said Thalon. "Now, try it again."

Aron handed back the practice wood and stepped out of their way. The two men resumed their practice, showing some signs of having listened.

"Better," said Thalon. "Now, all of you. Break into pairs and practice this."

The men did as ordered, and Aron went from one pair to another observing and correcting, the Captain's eyes on him all the time.

Other drills followed and Aron spent the morning taking the Nandor soldiers through the basic exercises of bladework as he had been taught them, but as Marek clearly had not. Eventually Thalon called a halt.

"Enough," he ordered. "Adequate, I suppose, 'til Tancred gets here. You're dismissed."

Aron caught the name, but decided that now was not the time to ask who Tancred was.

With no duty to go to after his meal, Aron was hoping that Celaine had forgotten about their walk but, as he left the barracks hall, a maid stepped towards him.

"The Lady Celaine would speak with you, young master, if you would follow me," she said. Aron followed half reluctantly, aware that his clothes were splashed with mud from the morning's coaching.

The Lady Celaine did not appear to notice the mud and, in fact, seemed very pleased to see him. She had changed her gown from the morning and, Aron suspected, had put on her best and had artfully twisted a dozen pale flowers into her dark hair. She dismissed the maid who returned to the castle. Aron looked around for a chaperone, but there was no-one in sight. *They do things differently in Nandor*, he thought. *I would certainly not be strolling alone with an Earl's daughter in the Holy City. Not if she, or anyone in her family, cared about her reputation.*

"Would you like to see my herb garden?" Celaine asked demurely.

"I would be delighted," said Aron. Celaine led the way out through the postern and a short distance away from the walls to where a stream ran through a small valley. Ahead of them was a cultivated area enclosed by a low fence.

"This was my mother's garden, and when I was little I used to help her with it," said Celaine. "She gave it over to me five years ago, and I've planted it with as many herbs as I could find would grow here. I've always loved growing things." She opened the gate. "We must have a fence to keep the sheep out. They would eat everything." Inside the fence healthy green plants flourished in neat rows, on one side in beds raised up from the surface on piles of broken rock. "The raised beds give better drainage to those plants that prefer a dry soil."

"I don't know much about herbs," said Aron, walking down beside one of the beds. "What is this one?" He stopped beside a clump of knee-high plants with feathery leaves.

"That's tansy," said Celaine. "It's really useful. You can cook with it in stews, make a draught for treating worms and stomach aches, and if you mix it with elder leaves, it's really good for keeping flies away."

"Really. I never knew," said Aron. "What's this next to it? It looks like a daisy to me."

Celaine smiled at him. "That's feverfew. It treats pain and

nervousness, and next to it is costmary." She knelt and plucked a broad leaf from the spindly plant before her. She rolled it between her fingers and held it out to him. "Smell it."

Aron knelt beside her and took the leaf, lifting it to his nose. "It reminds me of the ale they brew in Darien."

"I wouldn't know about the ale, but we eat it in salads and leave bundles on our pillows."

She took the leaf from him and as their fingers touched there was a moment when Aron thought she might kiss him. Celaine smiled sweetly at him and the moment passed. She stood up with a toss of her curls, turning her shoulder to him.

"Would you care to sit with me awhile?" she said. "There's a bower down by the stream."

Without waiting for his reply she walked back down the path to the gate.

The bower stood beside a willow tree on the bank of the stream where the water chattered most agreeably over a set of stepping stones.

"This is my favourite place," said Celaine as she made herself comfortable on the wooden seat.

Aron sat at the other end of the seat so that their knees almost touched.

There they sat as the afternoon passed and throughout Celaine kept up a barrage of questions about life at court. A lot of the questions concerned nobly born young (and not so young) men. Aron knew a few of those she mentioned and answered where he could; it occurred to him that these were possible husbands that the Earl and Countess might have tried to interest in Celaine of Nandor. Several were already married, and probably represented early disappointments for the pretty girl by his side. Others had dreadful reputations as seducers and wastrels, and certainly represented escapes. She carried her setbacks well as she chatted about one thing and another, and her eyes had a very definite sparkle when she looked at Aron, though there were no more moments when he thought a kiss was promised. Her hair held shades of chestnut where it caught the sun, Aron noticed, and her nose turned up ever so slightly at the end.

"Who is Tancred?" Aron asked, remembering the name Thalon had dropped after the practice session. The sparkles vanished from the blue eyes.

"He is a snake and I won't marry him." The words were spat out.

That's a little uninformative, my Lady. "I merely wished to know who he is. Captain Thalon implied he would be here soon."

"He is my cousin, and sees himself as Earl of Nandor if Maldwyn does not return. He thinks marriage to me would strengthen his hand." Celaine said scornfully. "He tried to kiss me last midwinter. Actually put his tongue in my mouth. I was sick. Marry him? I'd sooner go to the priestesses."

That was what happened to daughters who refused the marriage their fathers chose for them, Aron thought. *Celaine would be wasted in a temple.* He struggled to think of something to say that would not sound either insensitive or stupid, but came up with nothing.

Celaine slipped off the seat. "I must return. I feel a headache coming on." Aron walked beside her, but she did not speak until she reached the gate.

"Thank you for your company; no doubt I shall see you at dinner." Then she was gone.

Did I do what was expected of me? Aron thought as he climbed the stairs. When she'd talked about Tancred, he'd wanted to take her in his arms and tell her it wouldn't happen, but he couldn't do that. Not now, his life was already complicated enough. Though the way she'd looked at him suggested he would have been welcome.

***

There was a new diner at the table that evening though Aron was not introduced to him. A few years older than Aron, he was tall and dressed in a dark tunic of fine cloth with a discreet embroidery of gold; his thick dark hair flowed over his broad shoulders and he seemed naturally at ease in his surroundings. He was placed at the far end of the table beside Baldwin and Thalon whilst Aron was surrounded by the ladies. It may have been the wine, which was a great improvement on the previous night's, or the sparkling eyes that watched his every move, but Aron began to relax and felt moved to tell one or two humorous stories. Lady Alice laughed gently and smiled a great deal. Celaine collapsed in a fit of giggles that had Edith laughing so much that she gave herself hiccups and had to leave the table. At the far end of the table the effect was different. The new diner glared down at Aron, his eyes sending a message that was precisely the opposite of the one that Edith and Celaine were sending. Aron suspected he knew who the newcomer was, but asked Lady Alice anyway.

"That is Lord Tancred, my husband's nephew. Baldwin has been persuaded that someone else should command the expedition to liberate Maldwyn, and he has chosen Tancred." Aron felt an icy inevitability descend upon him at these words. It must have shown on his face as Lady Alice said quietly. "We will not speak of it here. I will send for you later."

For the rest of the meal, Aron sat in the focus of the opposing sets of body language. Edith and Celaine were fully aware of the icy looks from Tancred and played up to them as much as possible. Aron had never before been the centre of so much female attention, and while he basked in it, he was certain it was not likely to help in his dealings with Tancred.

After the meal, when Aron had retired to his room there came a knock at the door. He opened it to Glynis, who looked him up and down and sniffed loudly.

"My Lady wishes to see you. Follow me."

She turned abruptly and set off up the corridor, not waiting to see if Aron followed. *Who's put grit in your slippers?* thought Aron as he trailed after her.

Glynis halted before a door, knocked once, then held it open for Aron to enter. He stepped into a small room hung with tapestries. Before a cheerful fire Lady Alice, clad in a long robe of rich blue wool, sat in an easy chair, her hair falling loose in a dark torrent down her back. Aron tried not to stare but failed miserably.

"Thank you, Glynis. You may serve the wine now."

Glynis poured the wine from a silver jug and handed Aron a fine glass goblet.

"So, Aron son of Eamon. I believe you are what you say you are," said Lady Alice. "Master Robert, the wool buyer you travelled here with, gives a good account of you and tells me you performed a fine service for a merchant of Oxport, who is also known to me. It pleases me greatly that you are not a creature of Sarazan."

She took a sip of her wine and leaned forward a little, the loose neck of her robe offering a tantalising glimpse of the treasures within.

"As I said at dinner," she continued, "the Earl has been persuaded that the risk to his person is too great, and he has given command of our expedition to Tancred. No further plans have been laid, but I do not trust Tancred."

"What manner of man is Lord Tancred? Is he competent to command?" Aron asked, hoping without much cause that the unfavourable opinion he had formed of Tancred was inaccurate.

"Tancred was a most objectionable child, spiteful and selfish, and has not improved with age." The Countess wrinkled her pretty nose in displeasure. "He is a man entirely consumed by ambition."

"He is heir to the Earldom after Maldwyn."

"That is so," she said slowly, her tone neutral and controlled.

"He has much to gain if Maldwyn doesn't survive the rescue attempt he is to command."

"My husband refuses to see any danger in this. Because Tancred is the most fearless horseman in the chase, he thinks he is to be trusted, and doesn't believe that one of the blood of Nandor would harm another."

"So the fox is in charge of the hen coop."

"A cunning and determined fox. We are quite in your hands." The blue eyes turned sharply on Aron and the warm, red lips opened slightly. "I would value any advice you could offer. You will find Nandor grateful. It is a quiet place, and we are not rich, I fear, but I'm sure we could find something for you that you would think a worthwhile reward." Aron caught the hint of an amused smile as she looked at him, assessing his reaction.

"As we said before, the main difficulty is to keep Sarazan from the throat of Nandor." Aron said thoughtfully. "If we cannot go openly as an army we must go covertly as thieves. A few men only, better if they are not Nandoran. I know Sarazan a little, but there must be men in the garrison who know it better. It would also be useful to talk to the men captured with Maldwyn that Sarazan returned."

"There are a few outlanders among the guard. I will speak to Thalon. He is a good man; I trust him and I hope you will also. He holds the good of Nandor close to his heart."

Aron thought Thalon had already made up his mind about him, and did not think him a man who changed an opinion easily.

"I can arrange passage of a small group into Sarazan. There will be wool merchants looking for guards for their pack trains. I'm sure Tancred will enjoy being a muleteer for a few days."

Lady Alice laughed warmly at her own joke and opened those blue eyes wide. Aron forgot to breathe for a while. He was aware of what she was trying to do. Being aware of it didn't stop it working. The blue robe had worked looser exposing an enticing amount of white bosom. Aron became aware of another pair of eyes watching him very closely. Glynis sat on a stool in the corner of the chamber glaring at him in a thoroughly disapproving manner.

"My husband will be here soon. Best you leave now. I shall send for you tomorrow evening that we may further discuss this." The Countess's eyes held the promise of far more than mere discussions.

"As it pleases you, my Lady."

Aron stood up and headed for the door, his head swimming.

In his bed that night Aron thought about the enterprise laid before him. It was undoubtedly a most risky undertaking, but he owed his life to the nursing skill of the Countess and her ladies; of that he felt sure. The debt had to be paid, so it had to be chanced. Tancred could well be an obstacle; but surely Aron had endured worse, and if he became too awkward, well then there were ways of dealing with that too. His honour demanded that he give the undertaking every effort. But what then? Return to the quest to see Darien free, to seek revenge against all who had brought it down?

Looked at realistically, the recovery of Darien was further away than ever, and the land was already much changed from the home he knew. From the tales the steady stream of refugees had carried, Caldon had spared little effort in tightening his grip over the last five years; driving out the native folk with fire and sword, bringing in settlers to displace them, building new fortresses and filling them which his soldiers. Among the great houses, with the honourable exception of the Duke of Kyria, there was no appetite for a confrontation with Caldon. Even Kyria's support for the exiles was uncertain; the Duke was an old man, in poor health, and his heir much less disposed to the cause of Darien. When the Duke died they would be friendless and his own future that of a sell-sword or worse. He remembered the crossbow bolt that had snuffed out the life of his friend as he walked beside him in the Holy City. *I lived because the assassin made a mistake. I may not be so lucky the next time.* And if he carried on living the way he had been then there certainly would be a next time. *Am I wasting my life on an impossible dream?*

He wondered about his reward, if he lived to collect it. The gratitude of Nandor? Not in gold, that was evident. What then? A wife from the house of Nandor and a position in the household? That had its attractions and better prospects than the life he'd been leading for the last four years. Looked at that way, the position of Blademaster of Nandor, married to the pretty daughter of the Earl, had a lot to recommend it. *If the House of Nandor is true to its word.* He'd heard too many tales of daring rescues where the rescuers became inconvenient when they came to collect their promised lavish rewards. Some he'd heard first-hand from survivors. Though it was possible that Baldwin, obsessed as he was with the honour of Nandor, would keep the promise. *And even if he wouldn't Lady Alice would. That I should live long enough to collect. The most likely outcome is failure in Sarazan that leaves me free of any obligation to Nandor, so worry about the reward when it's been earned.*

Sleep eluded him for a long time, and when it finally came he dreamed of blue eyes.

CHAPTER 6

Captain Thalon found Aron immediately after breakfast. "You come with me, lad. Her Ladyship favours you, it seems, and has given me a list of duties that all revolve around you." The old soldier looked hard at Aron, but with less hostility than before. "Lord Tancred was asking about you too."

I'll bet he was, thought Aron.

"You'd better watch yourself around that one," Thalon continued. "He has a nasty temper. I'll take you now to see the fellows who were with young Maldwyn that Sarazan sent back, and then get together the men that'll be going with you. Few years ago an I'd a bin first in line, but I'm getting too old for those sort of high jinks."

"And you are too obviously Nandoran," said Aron, not unkindly.

"Forty years, man and boy, in the service of Nandor. Thirty years I served the old Earl. Now there was a man you could follow to the end of the world."

The old man puffed out his chest. The two of them marched towards the soldiers' barrack. When they reached it Thalon went into the mess hall and called out two names. Two men, both short and dark-haired, appeared quickly and Thalon handed them over to Aron. They both eyed him cautiously, no doubt remembering the sessions in the practice yard, but relaxed when he sat them down at a table in the mess hall and asked them to tell him everything they knew about Maldwyn and the circumstances of his captivity. Maldwyn seemed popular with his men-at-arms, and the two men were genuinely eager to produce any titbit that might be of use. Aron spent over an hour with them trying to extract the last drop of information, and he had dragged the bottom of the well several times when Thalon returned.

"I have the crew that'll be going with you, if you've finished here."

The old soldier's attitude was almost respectful, and Aron wondered what the Countess had said to him. Thalon led them into another room where Davo and four other soldiers waited.

"Right, you men," said Thalon. "You are here because you

have been selected for a signal honour. You are to rescue the Lord Maldwyn. Aron here will be going with you and the Lord Tancred is in command. Are there any questions?"

The four soldiers said nothing, but shuffled their feet and looked away to hide their frowns. Davo, though, was distraught. The little man backed up against the wall, fell to his knees wailing.

"No, you can't send me back there. You don't understand, they'll hang me. I can't go back."

Thalon was unmoved

"You can and you will. You know why? First, because you're the only man we've got who is from Sarazan and secondly, because it's the one place in the world that I can be sure you won't get yourself into trouble. Now stop snivelling and listen."

Surprisingly enough Davo did shut up. Thalon continued with his briefing

"You've been chosen, not because you're the finest soldiers in the garrison, but because you're not Nandoran. If this goes wrong, you're nothing to do with Nandor or Earl Baldwin. If you make it back with young Maldwyn, you'll each receive a farm of land to hold for yourselves and your heirs."

There were more frowns and shuffling of feet in response to this promise. One of the soldiers turned his head and spat on the floor. Thalon ignored him.

"You'll be going out as caravan guards just as soon as we can find you a caravan, so have your gear ready to go on one hour's notice. That's all."

Thalon dismissed the men and then turned to Aron.

"Lord Tancred wishes to see you."

Aron felt he almost added sir, but changed his mind at the last moment. Thalon led the way out of the barracks into the main keep with Aron a stride behind. *Got to get it over with sometime*, Aron thought as they climbed the narrow spiral stair to Tancred's quarters. *Just keep your mouth shut and hold your temper.* Thalon rapped on the door, a voice called "enter" and they went in.

Lord Tancred was sitting back in a chair with his feet on the table and a goblet in his hand. His gaze took in Thalon briefly then settled on Aron. Close to, Aron could see there was a softness around his jawline and he looked slightly overweight.

"So you're the murderous upstart I've been saddled with thanks to Baldwin's weakness." Tancred's voice had a similar whining edge to Earl Baldwin's. "Well, let me tell you. I'd have had your skin for killing one of my men. There's a story going round that you're some kind of gentleman, but that cuts no ice with me. You'll do exactly what you're told, when you're told, and if you cross me, I'll flog you myself." His tone left Aron in no doubt that he expected nothing more than a; "Very good, my Lord". Aron supplied one, concentrating hard on not letting his anger show.

"Good," said Tancred, taking a drink from his goblet. "My uncle directs me that I should lean on your advice in the matter of this expedition. Do not imagine that this gives you any status in my eyes. I shall ask for your advice when I want it and not before. Have you anything to say?"

"No, my Lord," said Aron, keeping his eyes on the table.

"And one more thing." Tancred got up and walked around the table to stand face to face with Aron. "You'll stay away from my cousins, is that clear? Now get out."

Aron needed no encouragement to leave. Thalon clattered down the stairs behind him. They stepped out into the courtyard in silence. Not completely sure of Thalon's view of Tancred, Aron said nothing of their interview.

"I would like to take an hour or two in the practice yard with the men going with me. Would that be possible?"

"Excellent idea. I'll chase them out," Thalon said and walked off in the direction of the barrack block.

Aron headed for the practice yard, needing to work off the anger that boiled in him. It had been a long time since someone had spoken to him like that, and he'd killed that man. *React to him and the whole scheme is ruined*, he thought. *Think of Maldwyn and the reward. Time enough to deal with Tancred afterwards.*

He worked for the best part of three hours trying to kick the soldiers out of the sloppy techniques they had picked up. The main problem was that, as the previous day had shown, they had never been taught from the beginning, and under pressure they always reverted to their old ways and mistakes. Thalon watched silently, shaking his grizzled head when one of the outlanders looked to him for support.

Aron worked the anger out and replaced it with a deep sense of foreboding. If it came to serious sword work, these were dead men unless their opponents were equally inept. Aron thought that unlikely; Sarazan employed at least four blademasters that he knew of, and maybe more. *The swordsmen of Sarazan will be well drilled.*

Eventually Thalon reminded him that, even if he was not hungry, the others were. Reluctantly Aron put down the practice sword and they headed for the barracks where the same taciturn cook ladled out the same stew. Aron went to sit with two of the outlanders who grudgingly made space for him at the table, but said nothing.

Aron finished his stew and looked at his companions, one dark and the other blond; both were big men and at least ten years older than himself, the blond fellow's hair was thinning. *If I'm going to be on the road with them,* thought Aron. *I should at least find out their names.*

"Where are you fellows from?" he asked. Both stopped eating and stared at him.

"What's it to you?" The dark one grunted.

"Just curious, I'm from Darien."

"Wheresat then?" said the blond one.

"Long way from here. East and North."

"Thought you was from the 'Oly City?" said the dark one accusingly. "I 'eard you bin to that fancy 'cademy."

"Been there, but I'm not from there."

"Reckon you think we're just stupid country boys," said the blond one. Aron was acutely aware of the hostility of their gaze. *Marek was probably a good friend of theirs.*

"No I don't. I'm a country boy myself." Aron wished he hadn't started this conversation.

"But you're a gen'lman."

"It's a good story, but it's not true." Aron lifted his head to look directly at them. "I'm the son of a soldier, like you. My father was blademaster of the guard at Darien." He saw the doubt on their wind-burned faces and decided to press his advantage. "What are your names? You know mine."

The two men looked uncertainly at each other then the blond one spoke. "I'm Thomi, he's Kriss."

"Glad to know you, Thomi and Kriss," said Aron.

The two men grunted in reply and then stood up from the table leaving the remains of their meals.

"See you 'round," said Kriss as they made for the door.

Aron sat until they were out of sight, his sense of foreboding deeper than ever, and then headed for the well to rinse away the sweat that was now drying on him.

***

ron had sluiced himself off with a bucket of startlingly cold water and had his head buried in his towel when Edith spoke. "I rather expected heroes to have more hair on their chests."

Aron started, he hadn't heard her approach and became very conscious of the goose flesh on his chest and belly.

"You shouldn't be here like this, my Lady," was all he could think of to say. She was dressed in a loose shirt of undyed wool and what looked like a pair of her brother's cast-off leggings, pale skin showing through one knee. Her dark hair flowing over her shoulders did not appear to have seen a brush that day and she smelled slightly of stables.

"Nonsense. I've seen my brother without his shirt many times. He hardly keeps it on in summer. Anyway, I don't like men with too much muscle." She looked up at Aron with that high intensity stare again; the one that stopped Aron talking. "Would you like to see my horse?"

Nothing would annoy Tancred more, he thought silently as he said "I would be delighted, my Lady."

Aron followed her across the courtyard towards the stables, expecting Tancred to appear at any moment. Edith, oblivious to any watchers, said nothing but kept turning those dangerous eyes on him as they walked. She led him into the dim dusty interior, past empty stalls, to the far end where a plump pony munched contentedly on a bundle of hay.

"Isn't he lovely?" she said, patting the pony's nose. "He's called Kestrel."

"Hello, Kestrel." Aron reached at stroked Kestrel's neck. The pony turned and nuzzled his hand.

"He likes you," said Edith. "Help me get him some more hay."

She pushed open a rickety wooden door in the wall next to Kestrel's stall. Aron followed her through the door, the sweet smell of hay in his nose. *This is unbelievable.* He thought. *No nobleman's daughter I've ever met would behave like this.*

As soon as he was through the door, Edith spun around, threw her arms around his neck and kissed him with a great deal of enthusiasm and very little expertise. Aron was so startled he nearly lost his balance and fell over, but after a moment the surprise wore off and his instincts took over. He pulled Edith close and her body moulded to his shape, her firm young breasts pressing against his chest. They kissed for a long time and then, as they gasped for breath, Edith turned the eyes up to full intensity. Aron felt his reason begin to melt.

"You've got to get Maldwyn back, then you can rescue me and we'll have wonderful adventures together," said Edith breathlessly. "You can teach me sword-fighting. I can already use a bow."

What did I do to start this? thought Aron his mind reeling at the sudden explosion of Edith's passion. *She's an Earl's daughter.* He thought of explaining how adventures entailed a lot of going hungry and sleeping under hedges in the rain, but it did not seem likely to deter Edith at that moment, so he settled for reaching out for her hands. She took this as an invitation to kiss him again.

"I can't just stay here," she said still holding him. "There's so much to see in the world and I want to see it with you."

A part of Aron wanted to pick her up and carry her off then and there, but he suppressed it for a more sensible approach.

"Where I'm going is going to be very dangerous. I can't make promises about the future beyond it, because I may not come back, and I don't like to make promises I can't keep."

No lies there, he thought.

Edith responded by throwing her arms around him and kissing him again. Aron stopped thinking about consequences and surrendered to the moment. Edith seemed to have discovered a technique of kissing without breathing which Aron had missed out on, and his lungs were starting to burn when Kestrel whinnied. Edith reacted instantly, jumping backwards away from Aron as Glynis appeared in the doorway.

"So there you are, miss. You're late for your singing lesson, and you've made me come and find you in this filthy stable." Glynis's voice would have curdled new milk. Edith stepped through the door and walked out of the stable without a backward glance. Glynis however, gave Aron a long hard sour-faced look before she followed Edith.

Aron sat on a hay bale trying to reassemble his thoughts as the blood surged through his veins. Edith might think that he was a dispossessed noble, but he was under no illusions about his real status; he was a swordsman for hire. Expensive and with scruples, but for hire none the less. One thing was clear; this was going to cause trouble. Tancred had already warned him off, and half the castle must have seen him come in here with Edith. Aron had no doubt how he would react to being crossed. The whole venture was risky enough without Tancred adding to it. Of course, once they were out of Nandor there was nothing to stop him sticking a knife in Tancred and going his own way - nothing save his honour and the debt he owed Lady Alice.

Aron arrived back at his guestroom still deep in thought. He took out his gear and did what he always did when he needed to create peace in which to think; he pulled out his whetstone and set to sharpening his blades, losing himself in the work.

When it grew too dark to see he put aside his gear and stood at the window watching night creep over Nandor, caught between cursing the circumstance that had brought him to here and wondering just how difficult a rescue would prove. Too frequently the memory of Edith's lips against his intruded. *How old is Edith? Older than poor stupid Peg. Old enough to be wed certainly.* At court he'd seen plenty of girls who looked her age, or younger, married off, with a fine dowry, of course; and back in Darien many of the young village girls would have one child with maybe another on the way. Then there was Celaine as well. She had looked at him with the same eyes as Edith and, he was sure, the same thoughts in her heart. Edith, maybe, had suffered fewer disappointments than her sister and possibly that made her bolder, but the possibility for the worst sort of trouble was very strong. *It would have definitely been better if I had never come to Nandor and better again if I never returned.*

***

"Dinner is served in the main hall, good sir."

A footman in the usual tattered Nandor livery stood at the door holding a candle lantern.

"Very well, I'll be down directly."

Aron left the door open for the light as he searched for his comb. He made a largely vain attempt to bring order to his hair then hurried downstairs.

When Aron arrived in the hall, he was left with no choice of seat and had to sit at the foot of the table with the pasty-faced clerk on one hand and Glynis on the other. The clerk slurped his soup and snuffled his way through the main course, but did not actually speak to Aron, and Glynis glared at him as if she was eating unripe lemons. The only warmth in the scene came from Celaine, seated further up the table next to Tancred, who favoured him with an amused little smile and sparkling eyes whenever Tancred's attention wasn't on her, which wasn't often. Edith was not at the table. Aron considered asking Glynis where she was, but thought better of it almost immediately; Glynis's narrowed eyes and the white-knuckled grip on her knife gave him ample warning. Celaine continued smiling at him and Aron suspected that she knew very well why her little sister wasn't at dinner.

At the end of the meal, bottle in hand, Baldwin and Captain Thalon settled beside the fire to refight old battles. The ladies withdrew and Aron headed for the stairs rather than seek Tancred's company. He had barely closed the door to his chamber when the knock came. He was not expecting his caller to be Glynis.

"My Lady wishes to see you. Follow me." The command was delivered in as haughty and contemptuous manner as Aron had ever heard. The Countess might wish to see Aron, but Glynis did not approve and made no effort to hide it. Aron followed her brisk footsteps to the Countess's chamber. Glynis rapped firmly at the door, even her knock was disapproving, and held it open for Aron. He stepped inside and felt a cold wave ripple down his body as he passed her.

"Thank you Glynis. You may leave us," Lady Alice said from her chair by the fire. She wore the same blue robe as the night before, and again her dark hair was loose about her shoulders.

"Very good, my Lady."

One final blast of arctic disapproval washed over Aron before the door closed.

"My Lady," Aron said, unsure of what was expected of him.

"A caravan leaves tomorrow for Sarazan. The merchant has been bought, and you will leave at first light carrying all our hopes. There is much to talk of."

As Lady Alice stood up her robe fell away leaving her quite naked.

CHAPTER 7

In the shadow cast by the overhanging upper storey, two figures stood in a doorway looking down Coopers Lane at a three-storied house built of dressed grey stone. There were no ground floor windows, and those higher up had thick metal bars across them.

"Are you sure this is the house, Cristoff?" asked the first.

"My informant was sure, and he has proved reliable in the past, Petter," said the second. "There should be at least a dozen of them in there."

"Very well then. It would be inconvenient if he proved to be wrong." He raised his arms, took a deep breath and spoke a word of command. The night was split by a pulse of blue-white light. The house across the lane was starkly outlined against its surroundings for a moment and then unnaturally bright flame roared through the interior, engulfing the shingles of the roof, lighting up the sky above the Holy City.

Cristoff turned his face away from the heat of the inferno. "Impressive, Petter."

"Thank you. It was intended to be."

"Most impressive, but also noticeable."

"That too was my intention. A wildcat flung into the middle of the complacent pigeons of the Wizard's Circle. They will not recognise the signature, but my power will leave them quivering." He smiled, his teeth flashing almost red in the firelight.

"Where did you learn to do that? Galgulla?"

"Yes, amongst other things. I foresee this as being a most fruitful association."

The door of the blazing house crashed open and a screaming figure, alight from head to toe, staggered out. Further up the lane another door opened and two men ran towards the burning man.

"Time to be gone from here, Petter."

"Yes, indeed." They pulled their dark cloaks around them and slipped quietly into the dark alley behind them as the whole street came to frantic life.

"That's one nest of Darien rats we won't have any more trouble from," said Petter as they walked briskly down the alley; the blaze behind them casting leaping shadows on the dank walls. "Now that that is taken care of, I must be on my way to Caldon to report back to his Grace. I'll take the usual escort."

"As you wish, Petter. Will you have time before you leave to entertain Bazarkis's latest offering?"

"Of course. I've been particularly looking forward to it. I have something to show you."

"Another gift from Galgulla?"

"Not a gift, an exchange. I provided him with what he asked for, and he gave me a pack of the finest hounds you've ever set eyes on. As I said, this promises to be a most profitable alliance."

"You trust him?"

"Come now Cristoff, he's an immortal. Of course I don't trust him. But for as long as I supply him with what he wants, he'll give me what I want; and what he wants most is a temple filled with worshippers."

"And you intend to give him this."

"High Priest of Galgulla. It has a certain ring to it don't you think, Cristoff?"

"You don't think Caldon will object?"

"I do not intend that he will even notice us, and by the time he does I will be too strong for him, even if he does gain the throne."

They reached a small square where an unliveried servant stood holding two horses. They took the reins from him, mounted up and rode away into the night.

CHAPTER 8

The rescue expedition did not leave at dawn. Instead Aron, Davo and the other soldiers stood about in the cold drizzle as they waited for, first the merchant's train, then Tancred, and finally Earl Baldwin. It was fully two hours after dawn before Baldwin appeared on the steps of the keep with Thalon. He did not look a well man; his eyes were glazed and bloodshot and his nose was running. He clapped Tancred on the shoulder and shook his hand, and then waved in dismissal to the rest of the expedition. He did not look at Aron. Thalon, however, made a point of coming down the steps and speaking quietly to each man. When he reached Aron he took him by the hand.

"I misjudged you, young man," said Thalon. "I thought you were some good for nothing sell-sword who'd taken advantage of a man well gone in drink. It took my Lady to show me, but there's more to you than that. I believe you can pull this off. Bring him back for the future of Nandor."

There were tears in the old man's eyes. He gave Aron's hand a last firm squeeze and then turned away to remount the stairs. Aron turned to follow the caravan which had started to move out of the gate, as he did so a figure slipped past Thalon in the keep doorway and ran down the steps. Aron turned at the sound and stood still in the middle of the courtyard as Edith ran towards him. She halted two paces from him and held out her hand with a piece of cloth in it.

"Take this with you. Wear it for me, it will bring you luck," she said breathlessly.

Aron took the cloth and looked at it, frozen with embarrassment. It was a handkerchief embroidered with the crest of Nandor and an ornate E.

"I would be honoured to," he said softly.

Then she stepped forward and kissed him chastely on the cheek.

"Come back to us," she whispered, and then ran for the steps. Aron was sure he'd seen tears in her eyes as she turned. Aron moved to follow the caravan and saw, looking at him from the gatehouse, Tancred.

***

Lady Alice watched the caravan until it was out of sight then, with a sigh turned from the window to face Glynis's disapproval. "Did you find any?" she asked.

"Only these, my Lady, and they are mould eaten." Glynis held out a small woven basket. "And it is far too early in the year to be looking for any new leaves."

"I know that well." Lady Alice took the basket and inspected the contents. A handful of blackened leaves sat in one corner. "These will just have to serve." She passed the basket back to Glynis.

"They'll not work, my Lady," said Glynis. "And there would be some who would call it the Lady's judgement."

"Indeed?" said Lady Alice. "And what would those people have me do? Push gold at him?"

Glynis said nothing but glared at Lady Alice.

"He is our only hope, and I don't believe him to be a man whose loyalty is bought with coin. So I must buy it with something else."

"Clearly," said Glynis sourly. "And did you? Or have you dragged your good name in the mud for nothing?"

"Gods! I don't know, but what else could I do? I had to play every card I could to bind him to us."

"I hope he proves to be worth it and that my Lord never learns of it."

"Why would he? Only three people know and he's not going to learn of it from me. I spent years enough trying to give him another son so why would it happen now?"

"The Lady's judgement."

"If the Lady has a price for this, then I will pay it to get my son back." She turned towards the door. "And if that price is a child, then a way will be found. Now there's an end to it. We will not speak of this again."

***

The caravan moved slowly through the soft rain away from Nandor town. The rough muddy road wound between dry stone walls bordering the pastures where the sheep that had provided the load grazed. Only the merchant rode. Everyone else, the merchant's servants and the Nandorans, in keeping with their disguise as guards, walked beside the laden mules, including Tancred. The displeasure was evident upon his face as the mules splashed through the ruts left by the local farm carts. Aron walked at the rear of the caravan as far away from Tancred as possible, and smiled to himself at what he took to be Lady Alice's manoeuvre of making Tancred play the caravan guard. No-one spoke, and as the rain dripped off the edge of his hood and ran down his face, Aron had plenty of time to think: the road ahead, what was happening in the Holy City, how to avoid clashing with Tancred. All these passed through his mind, but mostly he thought about the women of Nandor.

The caravan made about a dozen miles before they stopped at dusk at a dismal inn in a grim little village. The inn was clearly much used by trade caravans as there was a dormitory for guards and muleteers built over the stable. Tancred, spurning the fiction of being a caravan guard, bought a room in the main part of the inn. The rest of the men grumbled to each other and played a little dice over mugs of ale in the taproom. Aron retired to the dormitory conscious of his exclusion but uncaring. He checked over his gear and cleaned his boots, giving them an extra layer of waterproofing grease. Then, damning the rest of the group to sore heads in the morning, Aron took to his bed, his stomach growling in protest at the undercooked vegetable stew he'd been served for supper.

He spent an uncomfortable night on the verminous straw mattress, disturbed at least twice in the night by someone retching into the bucket that had been left by the door. The next day dawned similar to the previous, with rain clouds smeared across the sky. After a meal of watery porridge and stale bread the party set out again. Tancred, looking fresh and well-rested, rejoined them having breakfasted in his room.

The mules plodded onward through the mud in a generally south-easterly direction and Aron plodded after them. The clouds hid the tops of the hills and the wind whipped a stinging drizzle into Aron's face. There was little need to keep a look-out for bandits as the trade on the Nandor road was too thin to sustain even a modest band of thieves.

The rain ceased as the day drew onward, and the caravan reached a major junction where two other roads joined the route to Sarazan. A large inn and market stood nearby bustling with activity. The merchant took his party into the compound and Aron found that they were to share their lodgings with two other sizeable caravans. At least their party had their own dormitory; it was not unknown for parties of guards to take a savage dislike to each other, and it was poor business for the innkeeper to have to rebuild his inn because he had only one sleeping area.

Tancred again bought a private room and retreated to the dining room without a word to the rest of the party. The other men took themselves down to the taproom to discover if the other guards knew dice. Aron had no interest in watching them lose their money and lay down on his bed with the aim of catching some extra sleep.

The sound of a heavy impact, angry voices and splintering wood woke him. He sat bolt upright in his bed. The fight was in the next room. There was no sign in the dormitory of any of the others in the Nandor party. The row transferred to the landing outside. There was a hefty thump on the door, more shouting and then the sound of many boots on the stairs. Aron's curiosity was aroused; he sat up, pulled on his boots and then made for the stairs.

There was no-one about, but there were drips of fresh blood on the steps. Aron followed the trail out into the courtyard where the scuffs in the dirt showed something or somebody had been dragged towards the paddock. Raised voices floated through the cool evening air from the far side of the field. The rain clouds had dispersed leaving the sky clear, the first stars of evening were beginning to show, but there was still enough light in the sky for Aron to see by. In the far corner of the field five men were beating a sixth. Two men held him by the arms, two others took turns to swing blows at him and the fifth roared encouragement. Aron ran lightly across the grass with a sickening certainty growing in his mind. The five men carried no weapons he could see, but they were large and hard-faced with an air of muscular solidity; caravan guards. They were so intent upon their victim that they did not notice Aron until he spoke.

"What's going on here?" The five turned as one and their victim slumped to the ground. It was Davo.

"Caught him going through our packs, so we're teaching him a lesson."

The man who had been encouraging the others to beat Davo spoke. Aron weighed him up; he was at least ten years older and a handswidth taller with a deep chest, thick shoulders and the face of an unshaven pig.

"That's enough. He's had his lesson." Aron spoke firmly and evenly.

"We're goin to hang 'im." One of the others said, sticking his unshaven chin forward in challenge.

"No, you're not."

"You gonna stop us?"

The five spread out as if to surround Aron. It had to be quick and it was. The short-bladed knife came from Aron's left sleeve. His left hand caught Pigface's right arm in an armlock and Aron had the knife pressed against his throat before he had time to react.

"Step back," He said to the four men that faced him. "Tell them to step back." He pressed harder with the knife, a spot of blood appeared at the tip.

"Alright, alright. Do what he says, lads."

Sweat broke out on Pigface's brow. His cohorts moved back leaving Davo sprawled in the dust.

"Run. Get away from here. I want to see you head over that hill."

Aron waved at the road that climbed a hill away from the inn. The four roughnecks paused. Aron twisted the knife slightly.

"Run, run you dogs," Pigface choked.

The four turned and loped off towards the road. Davo moaned and stirred in the dirt.

"Pick him up."

Aron released the armlock, but kept his knife pressed against his prisoner's throat. The man bent slowly and lifted Davo across his broad shoulders. Aron removed Pigface's belt knife with his left hand and then stepped back satisfied that he could handle anything the man might try.

"Carry him back to the inn," Aron commanded.

Pigface moved off slowly with his burden bouncing awkwardly. Davo groaned again. Aron kept three steps back all the way back to the inn. The caravan guard may have considered all manner of schemes, but they reached the dormitory without incident.

"Put him down." Aron gestured to the nearest pallet. Pigface deposited Davo in the bed. "Out," Aron commanded and followed the man out into the yard. Aron threw Pigface's knife at his feet. "It finishes here if you want."

Pigface bent down to pick up his knife keeping his eyes on Aron as his fingers searched for the blade. He found it and straightened slowly still looking at Aron. Aron held his gaze coolly, knife in hand. Pigface did not speak but slowly sheathed his blade, turned and walked stiffly away. Aron watched him out of sight and then headed back to the dormitory.

Davo was sitting on the edge of his bed dabbing gingerly at his nose, one eye closed by a bruise that covered one side of his face. Aron did not remark on his recovery, suspecting that Davo had had much practice at playing dead.

"Guess I owe you my life," the little man said, his speech slurred by his swollen lips.

"Guess you do."

"None of them other bastards would've bothered. They'd have hanged me there but for you. I may not be much, but I pays me debts."

Aron did not feel overwhelmed with gratitude. Indeed he wanted to kick Davo for creating the situation, but he knew it was pointless. If beatings were going to cure Davo of thieving then it would have worked a long time ago.

"Let's get one thing straight. You were going through their gear." Aron did not make it a question.

The little man nodded and opened his still-bleeding mouth to justify himself. Aron held up his hand to halt the flow before it began.

"I don't want to hear it. You can start paying back your debt by staying out of trouble. No more thieving and no more tricks."

Davo was right about the attitude of the rest of the party as word of the confrontation spread quickly. Aron headed for the taproom to get a drink, but the story was there before him. No sooner had he got a stoup of ale than Thomi and Kriss left their dice game and came over.

"S'true then?" Thomi's tone was certainly not approving. "You saved the little bastard's neck."

"True enough," replied Aron, looking into his ale.

"Don't know why ye bothered. I wouldn't have."

Aron looked up at Thomi for a long moment.

"Do you know your way around Sarazan? We're going to need him."

He took a long pull on his ale. Thomi and Kriss looked at each other for a moment then turned to return to the dice game. Aron finished his drink and returned to the dormitory. He lay down on his bed and tried to sleep, but his mind was too alert as he relived the evening's events. *That was a desperately dangerous thing to do. All it would have taken would have been one caravan guard who was drunk enough to move and I could not have withstood them all. I'll leave him next time.* But there was still a thrill of pleasure at the danger survived, that he'd bested the lot of them.

***

Next morning Tancred was beside himself with anger when he found Davo too damaged to walk, and Aron had to take charge of him to prevent him being left behind. Rearranging the burdens of the pack mules, Aron made space for Davo to ride for the day's journey. The two of them travelled at the back of the caravan, studiously ignored by the rest of the party. Davo was not a great conversationalist when intact; injured he said nothing for hours on end. Aron, plodding uphill through the mud behind Davo's mule and trying to avoid the mule dung and larger puddles in the track, found his mind wandering to a pair of blue eyes.

I wonder if Lady Edith would find this adventure enough? He thought as the mule slid into a puddle splashing him with dirty water.

So the day passed until the caravan reached the next stopping place. The inn was the largest they had yet stopped at, reflecting the growing number of trade-routes that had joined the road. The rest of the party continued to ignore Aron and Davo through the evening meal; no-one invited Aron down to the taproom so when Davo headed for the dormitory, Aron went after him.

Sitting on his pallet Aron reached into his pack for his mail shirt. Tomorrow they would cross the border into Sarazan where, despite the Duke's fearsome reputation, serious banditry was not unknown as the trade routes grew richer. Aron drew out the steel chain shirt and, as he did so, a piece of cloth fluttered to the floor. He bent to retrieve it and held it up to the dim lantern. It was a lady's fine linen handkerchief embroidered with the crest of Nandor and an ornate E.

"Beautiful girl, Lady Edith, but then so's her sister." The words were barely distinguishable so swollen were Davo's lips.

"So?" Aron did not conceal the edge of annoyance in his voice.

"Can't keep nothing secret in a castle." Even through bruised lips Davo's satisfaction was evident.

A thrill of alarm ran through Aron. *How long would his visit to the Countess stay a secret?* "What are you getting at?" he said, trying to keep his voice level.

"Just wondered why you're going along with this. Now I know. Which one d'yer want?" Aron relaxed. *If Davo doesn't know about the Countess, then no-one else does.*

"What makes you think I'm doing this for them ?"

"Yer gorra better reason for doing it? Yer crazier 'an I thought."

"Thanks very much. What makes me crazy? Saving your skin?"

"That too. Crazy for thinking we can ger 'im out."

"You don't think it can be done ?"

"Gerring in maybe, gerring out even. Stayin' alive afterwards is the trick."

"How come?"

"Yer don't know Sarazan like I do. Place's rotten with spies and snitches. I ain't bin there for ten years, but everything I've 'eard says it's worse than I remember it were, and it were bad enough then. Soon as e's missed, the whole place'll go up like a dry haystack. Be impossible to hide."

Aron pondered this information for a minute before speaking again. "So we'll have to get away from the city as soon as we have Maldwyn."

"Yeah, if we can ger him at all. So which one d'yer want?" Davo's bloodshot eyes glittered with interest. "Celaine's got bigger tits."

CHAPTER 9

The road was busier as they drew near the border, with several merchant caravans as well as smaller groups of travellers and lone horsemen. They reached the border around midday, Aron sweating uncomfortably under his mail shirt in the thin sunlight. The post on the Nandor side of the border was deserted. On the Sarazan side, however, a large squad of hard-eyed men examined trading permits and meticulously searched the packs of everyone who sought entry. Davo cringed back under their scrutiny, pulling his hood down as far as it would go over his face and trying to hide behind Aron, but the guards paid him little notice and concentrated on the contents of the packs. Tancred's temper frayed by the minute as everyone in the merchant's train had their goods probed thoroughly. Aron watched with mounting concern, expecting an eruption to blow their cover at any minute. The wool merchant also looked nervously at Tancred. *He'll sell us out the moment Tancred causes a scene,* thought Aron.

At last the guards waved them on their way before Tancred reached boiling point, but his temper smouldered dangerously for the rest of the day. The caravan marched into Sarazan making much better time along the well-paved road. The rocky hill country of Nandor gradually gave way to gentler slopes, scrawny sheep replaced by plump cattle grazing lush fields between neat hedges as the milestones marked their progress towards the city.

As evening approached they reached a large inn; its yard crowded with wagons and mule trains. Horses and livestock churned about as men unloaded wagons and unhitched horses and led them off to the stables. Stallholders shouted their wares; chickens, children and dogs ran underfoot; and beggars and whores accosted anyone who stood still. Beside the inn stood a small stone-built barrack compound large enough to house fifty or so soldiers, although there were only a dozen men visible.

The merchant went into the inn to arrange lodgings leaving the rest of the party standing outside. Davo became very interested in the girth of one of the pack mules; ducking down behind the coarse-haired beast to conceal himself from the gaze of two men who sat, not drinking from their mugs, under the tree in the inn courtyard.

Aron stood silently taking in the scene, watching a small squad of soldiers go through their weapons drill in the barrack square. The merchant returned with two servants from the inn; one collected the merchant's bag, the other called on the rest of the party to follow him.

The servant directed them to a flight of stairs and handed Tancred a key. Tancred headed for the stairs followed by the others, Aron and Davo last. The dormitory was clean but spartan, with enough bunk beds for twenty. At the end of the room a canvas screen concealed, Aron presumed, a bucket; that he could not smell it spoke a great deal for the cleanliness of the inn.

Tancred looked around the room. "Good enough for you lot, but I'll need my own room."

He turned and began to make his way back to the stairs until Aron blocked his path.

"What do you think you're doing?" said Tancred. "Get out of my way."

"Do you think this will go unremarked? Have you not considered the fact that we are in disguise and our safety depends on us staying unnoticed?" Aron kept his voice low and level.

"I'll take your advice when I ask for it." Tancred tried to push past Aron, but Aron stood his ground until their faces were only a handswidth apart.

"Caravan guards do not have their own rooms," said Aron struggling for control. "And Sarazan has eyes everywhere."

Tancred's face flushed red and his eyes bulged, his right hand strayed towards the knife at his belt and Aron caught his wrist.

"No, my Lord. We'll all finish up in Sarazan's dungeons," said Thomi.

Tancred twisted around at his words and stared wildly at the half circle of Nandor soldiers.

"Seize him, you men," he gasped. "Don't just stand there."

Aron watched their faces to see if anyone looked likely to stand with Tancred, his right hand gripping the hilt of the knife in his left sleeve.

No-one moved.

"No, my Lord," said Kriss. "Thomi's right. We'll finish up in Sarazan's dungeons. That merchant will sell us out at the first sign of trouble."

Tancred stood for a moment glaring at them, then he turned to Aron. He tugged his arm free of Aron's grip.
"You forget yourself, sellsword. We will speak of this when we return to Nandor." With that he stalked down to the end of the room.
Thomi stood in front of Aron and favoured him with a broad wink and a slow nod of his head.
"You done right, my lad. We'll see the Earl knows it."
Aron let out the breath he'd been holding and released the knife hilt. He felt the sweat trickling down his body underneath his shirt. He chose a bed and sat down, using the breathing exercises he'd been taught to calm his racing pulse. Everyone in the room was silent, their heads down to avoid meeting another's eyes.
Aron was undisturbed overnight, but did not sleep much. Tancred had always bid fair to be a difficulty, but now a major confrontation seemed inevitable. He was not worried for his own survival, but any return to Nandor was going to be next to impossible if Tancred died at his hand.
This just keeps getting worse. Why on earth am I worrying about it? This really isn't any business of mine. Why not just slip away from the party in Sarazan and then goodbye Tancred, goodbye Maldwyn, goodbye problem? I need never concern myself with Nandor again. This appealing thought was answered with the memory of the women chanting around his bed as he lay in the grip of Peg's poison. *I owe the debt.*

***

Aron kept a nervous eye on Tancred for the rest of the passage to Sarazan, but Tancred kept well out of the way and did nothing reprehensible other than glare sourly at everyone, especially Aron. The attitude of the other members of the party changed though; Thomi and Kriss invited him to join their nightly dice games, which he declined. The wool merchant, who had not previously spoken to Aron, bought him a mug of ale the next evening, and expressed his hope that Tancred could be kept out of trouble until they reached Sarazan.
The caravan made good time along the busy, well-maintained road and stayed overnight in large inns each a close replica of the one before. Aron slept every night with a knife under his pillow, but was undisturbed.

***

Their first view of the city of Sarazan came when they crested a line of hills above Sarazan lake. The city stood at the far end of the lake where the Sarazan river flowed out on its way to meet the sea at Oxport.

"Zat Sarazan then?" said Thomi as he and Aron rested from the climb up the ridge. "Big, in't it?"

"It is," said Aron. "Biggest inland port in the land. The lake is as far as you can get upriver with a cargo boat of any size."

"Rich place then."

"Markets for anything you can think of. Wool and cloth, timber, pottery, glassware, spices. Some of the finest metalworkers in the country if you want armour or swords. The Duke takes a good cut of all of it, of course."

"That's how he can afford that then." Thomi pointed to the great fortress that squatted on a spit of land running out into the lake beside the river, the neck of the peninsula defended by a stout high wall with one massively reinforced gate. "Don't fancy 'aving to lay siege to that."

"They tried that in the civil war. See all that open ground." Aron pointed to a wide area of grassland before the fortress wall. "That used to be the best area of the city. It was all destroyed in the siege and the Duke wouldn't allow their rebuilding, so there's clear lines of sight all around the castle."

"Zat where Maldwyn is?"

"Probably," said Aron. "That's one of the things we've got to find out."

"Don't fancy it much," Thomi said gloomily and spat into the ditch.

CHAPTER 10

The caravan wound its way down from the highlands and approached the city on the highway, which was still busy in the late afternoon.

"Them's all new," said Davo staring at the fine stone houses and gardens that stood on either side of the road. "What happened?"

"When did you leave Sarazan?" asked Aron.

"Year before the siege. All this was just fields."

"All the nobles' and merchants' houses round the castle were flattened in the siege, I believe," said Aron. "The Duke wouldn't let them rebuild so they all moved out here."

"Makes sense," said Davo. "Yer get a load of stink and flies down by the lake in the summer."

As they drew nearer the city the quality of the houses declined until they were passing artisans' workshops and open areas where markets for all kinds of beasts and goods thrived. The city had long ago outgrown its wall, so there was not the usual inspection at a gate; they simply followed the main road into the city, crossed the ancient stone bridge over the river and then turned to track the river towards the docks area where the wool merchant's warehouse lay. Once there the merchant bade them farewell and they were on their own.

Here Davo was useful for the first time; though he was still terrified on every occasion someone looked at them for more than one glance, he was growing bolder as he hadn't been recognised and arrested as soon as they entered the city. His memory of the poorer areas proved adequate to finding them a sleeping loft in a filthy and disreputable tavern that was in keeping with their cover.

"We will make a tour of the city and establish which taverns the Duke's guards drink in," said Tancred, looking at Aron as if he expected him to interrupt. Aron avoided meeting his gaze and said nothing. "Keep your ears open, and we shall learn how to get into the fortress. You and you will stay here and keep our room secure." Tancred gestured at Aron and Davo.

Aron had doubts about the orders, but kept these to himself.

On the face of it they seemed sound enough, but it made little sense to confine him to guarding their room. If there was loose talk about the security of the castle it would be in a soldiers' tavern and he reckoned himself better able to look after himself in such places than anyone else in the party. What bothered him most was that he felt he was the only person with real motivation to find solid information about Maldwyn; the only thing he could trust the Nandor soldiers to do was to get drunk and attract the attention of the watch. Of Tancred's motives he had darker suspicions. Davo was delighted at being able to keep hidden and settled in the taproom with a large flagon of ale and looked prepared for a long evening's drinking.

Aron took a few minutes to find his way into every corner of the Tavern and then settled down to do his laundry. Lady Alice had given him two new shirts so he now possessed four, and he'd put on his last clean one three days ago. He bent to the task glad of the respite from the tension induced by Tancred's presence. Tomorrow would be time enough to think of how to rescue Maldwyn.

It took only a few minutes with warm water and washboard before the shirts were hanging on a line strung between the rafters of the loft. Once that was accomplished he wasn't tired enough to sleep and had little choice other than to join Davo in the taproom. Davo was sitting on a stool in front of the broad fireplace with a mug in his hand and a girl on his knee. Aron blinked hard to confirm his eyes did not deceive him; the girl was strikingly ugly with a heavy jaw, protuberant nose and eyebrows that met in the middle. Surely even Davo couldn't get drunk enough to change that.

"Hullo there, mate. Come and ger warm, I'll ger yer a drink. Off yer go darlin', and I'll see yer later."

The girl slid off Davo's knee and flounced past Aron with a wink and a saucy roll of her ample hips. Aron's nose was filled with a sickening mixture of unwashed body and cheap scent.

"I think she might be my cousin," Davo said with a smile as he passed Aron a mug full of dark bitter ale. "She's a little sweetie, isn't she? An' she told me a thing or two. They're wasting their time out there, she told me."

"She told you what?" said Aron, whose head was reeling from the smell of the hideous girl and the thought of her being a sweetie.

"The Duke's guards. They got their own tavern in the castle. She bin up there. Duke likes to keep an eye on 'em, see. Tancred an the rest o'them's wasting their time." Davo chuckled into his mug.

"Did she say anything else?"

"Ooh, she said a few things she did." Davo leered at Aron. "She said some real interestin' things."

"Anything useful to us for rescuing Maldwyn?"

"Nah, but I'll talk to her again soon." The leer continued. "You want me to see if she gorra friend to bring along?"

"No." Aron shuddered at the prospect. "I think I'll get some sleep." He finished his ale and headed for the stairs.

"Suit yerself then." Davo's cackle floated after him.

***

Aron was asleep when the others returned, but their drunken noise, living up to the pretence of being caravan guards, must have wakened most of the inn. Aron decided to leave it until the next morning to see if they had learned anything.

In the morning, Aron was awake with the sun; he rose immediately, leaving his snoring companions to their hangovers. There was no sign of Davo. Aron scrounged a small loaf of bread from the kitchen and set out to explore the city, reckoning that he had plenty of time before Tancred or any of the others would be up and about.

The streets around the tavern were busy with commerce of all kinds. Porters pushing laden barrows disputed the narrows vociferously with muleteers. Horse-drawn carts rattled over the cobbles, ragged messenger boys weaved their way in and out of the throng and hawkers cried their wares. Aron slipped through the crowd with lithe ease, keeping one hand on a knife hilt; the pickpockets of Sarazan were famed for their skill. He headed back towards the ancient bridge from where his memory of his previous visit to the city could take over. Two people tried to rob him on the way; one caught the point of Aron's knife across his hand for his trouble. Aron saw neither of them, so crowded were the narrow streets.

When Aron reached the bridge he turned away from the river and into an area with wider, cleaner streets paved with pale stone. The air smelt fresher and the shops were busy with prosperous, well-dressed womenfolk. The street led to the marketplace with its fine inns where Aron had lodged on his previous visit, and then beyond to the courthouse and the watch barracks. Past the barracks, he took a street that paralleled the lakeshore. Fine houses hid behind high walls on either side, fountains tinkled in shady courtyards and gatekeepers eyed him suspiciously as he strolled past.

At last Aron came to a lane that led down to the lakeshore and followed it to a small beach where the waters of the lake lapped against the dark rocks. He sat on a rock tossing pebbles into the water, looking out at the grim bulk of Castle Sarazan; to anyone passing he was an idler wasting a fine morning. He gazed at the rear wall of the fortress which rose vertically from the water. It was clearly smaller than the landwall wall, after all the lake guarded that approach. He tried to estimate its height, a plan forming pebble by pebble in his mind.

Looking away from the castle, he saw that where he stood was in fact in a bay; away to his right the lakeshore curved back towards the castle. Close to the beach there were still some lakeside houses, but these grew sparse further around the shore. The point closest to the castle seemed to be unoccupied open woodland. *So much the better,* Aron thought as he measured in his mind the distance across the mouth of the bay.

In the distance the courthouse bell tolled the hour, nothing moved on the surface of the lake save a few ducks. Aron threw his last pebble and then turned towards the lane that led back into the city.

***

The sun was high in the sky when Aron returned to the tavern, yet the carousers were still abed. Davo, however, had returned and was sitting in the taproom looking very pleased with himself.

"Where yer bin then?" said the little man through a mouthful of bread, spreading crumbs before him.

'Having a look around and doing a bit of thinking."

"Nor as much fun as what I bin doin'," Davo grinned displaying yellow teeth and half-chewed bread.

Aron did not think this deserved a reply, so it was a few moments before he spoke. "Would your new friend have any contacts down in the docks?"

"Maybe. What're yer thinking of?"

"We'll need to get out of Sarazan sometime soon, whether we get Maldwyn or not. A riverboat looks like a good bet."

"Reckon she knows a lot of sailors." Davo laughed.

"I need captains, not deckhands. Can you get her to find us a few candidates and find how much money they'd need?"

"I guess she might be able to find the time, if I let her."

"You'll be needing to get out when the time comes, or have

you forgotten you're a wanted man here?" Aron was not in the humour to appreciate Davo's lightheartedness.

"Well, 'spose so," was the grudging reply.

"I need to know a few more things too. The farside of the lake beyond the bay, it looks like open country, what's up there?"

"Duke's deer park. He hunts up there, no-one goes in there if they want to keep their hands." Davo took another mouthful of bread.

"The lake itself. I saw no fishermen, does anyone fish the lake?"

"No. Duke don't allow it," said Davo scattering more crumbs. "Anyway, there's a monster in the deep."

"Really? And you've seen it, have you?"

"No, but my da's brother he seen it, years ago mind."

"So no-one goes on the lake. Can you swim?"

"Swim? No." Davo started with alarm. "Don't go near water me, nor do anyone in Sarazan. The monster, see."

Aron's nose told him Davo's avoidance of water extended to the domestic situation.

"Are all the Duke's guards local men?" Aron changed the subject abruptly.

"Far as I know. Always used to be. Whassat got to do with the lake?"

"So they wouldn't be able to swim and would be afraid of the lake?"

"Probly, if they're local lads. What's you getting at?"

Any further discussion was curtailed by the noisy arrival of a dishevelled and sweating Tancred. Aron forbore to mention the futility of the previous night's expedition, Davo felt no such inhibition.

"You 'ave a good night then?" Davo leered disgustingly at Tancred. "You find anything, other than a bottle?"

Tancred stared for a moment at Davo as the little man grinned at him then abruptly lashed out, catching Davo across the side of the head and tumbling him to the floor. Aron forced himself to stay still. *Now is not the time*, he thought.

"Get out! Get out of my sight." Tancred turned his ill temper on Aron as Davo fled the room. "You too!" Aron stood up and walked slowly to the door feeling Tancred's eyes on his back.

"He had no call to do that," said Davo, wiping the blood from his face where one of Tancred's rings had caught him, when Aron joined him outside.

"You asked for it," replied Aron, glad to have got Davo out of the tavern. "At least he's off our backs for a while and we can get on with searching out some way of undertaking our mission."

"Whas we gonna do then? You know some better way 'n drinking with soldiers?"

"Yes. I can think of several. Drinking with the Duke's guards and asking too many questions won't get you many answers and only attracts attention," Aron said, though he suspected it would work well in Nandor. "What I need now is a wise woman. Can you find me one?"

"You feeling ill?" said Davo uncomprehendingly.

"No," said Aron. "I need one who knows how to walk the mist."

"Wassat?"

"It's a way of finding out things through using the spirit world."

"I don't want nothing to do with it then, 'at's witchcraft," said Davo making a sign against the evil eye.

"Never mind then," said Aron shrugging. "Just find me a wise woman."

CHAPTER 11

Aron and Davo had made their way around the poor quarter of the city at least four times in often fruitless searches for Mother this or Granny that, only to find that the wise women they sought were out, not wise at all, or, in one case, dead.

"At least she knows what I'm talking about," said Aron.

"That's more'n I can say. I never 'eard of walking the mist. I'm hungry, let's find a tavern," pleaded Davo. The cut Tancred had inflicted had stopped bleeding and faded into the rest of his injuries.

"You're a wanted man in this city, or have you forgotten?" said Aron, though in fact the reason he wanted to keep out of a tavern was an acute shortage of money.

"Umm," Davo grunted in assent." Why'd yer have to be right all the time? I only wanna drink." He shrugged and the two of them carried on walking.

The route back to their lodging seemed to take them past every baker's shop and pie stall in the city. At every one, the enticing odours reminded Aron of how hungry he was and how little money they had. He added it up in his mind: the wise woman would need paying, not a great sum, but more than he had. Supplies would be needed and, finally, a clandestine passage downriver would not come cheaply. Tancred held the expedition's funds and, as they walked, Aron thought of the various ways of persuading him to part with some of it. None seemed likely to result in anything other than a sneering dismissal.

"Davo. Do you know where Tancred keeps the money Earl Baldwin gave him for the expedition?"

"So what if I do?" Davo said suspiciously.

"So we need money to make this work. He's got it, and he's not likely to give it to us. Does that put ideas into your head?"

"I thought yer didn't approve of my thieving."

"That was then. You were putting all our necks in the noose by doing something stupid and unnecessary. Now we are the only ones pursuing the purpose for which that money was intended. Do you see the difference?"

"No." Davo said in genuine puzzlement.

Aron was silent for a minute as he pondered on Davo's mental processes; finally he spoke. "I'll worry about the difference then. You just see if you can lay your hands on some of the money."

As they drew closer to the inn, Aron wondered whether Tancred's ill-temper would have subsided. He knew a confrontation, probably fatal, was inevitable and knew also it would bring the fragmentation of the group and the unwelcome attention of the city authorities. This was sufficient reason to try to delay it.

Tancred's temper had not improved. He rounded on Aron and Davo the instant they entered the common room of the inn.

"Where have you been?" he demanded harshly.

"You told us to get out, so we've been through the city searching for information," said Aron meeting Tancred's gaze with a sinking heart. "I've found someone who claims to know the fortress, but information costs money in this city."

"And you expect me to give you the money?" sneered Tancred

"How else do you propose to come by information?" Aron kept his tone calm and reasonable to avoid antagonising Tancred further.

"That is for me to decide. If this source you've found has worthwhile information you bring them to me, understand?"

"I doubt they'll talk to you. They don't have much time for the aristocracy. You'll just have to trust me on this."

"Trust you? You must think I'm simple."

Aron did not have time to answer this as Davo laughed in a tone precisely calculated to tell Tancred that's exactly what he thought. Tancred's temper boiled over. He leapt up from his chair and grabbed Davo in a stranglehold, lifting him off his feet and choking him.

"You little weasel, I've had enough of you." Tancred roared as he shook Davo and pressed him up against the wall.

Everyone in the room stood stock still for a moment as Tancred strangled Davo. Aron stepped forward, knife in hand. *I can't avoid this*, he thought as he put the knifepoint to Tancred's throat.

"Enough, put him down."

Aron's tone was cool and measured. Tancred froze for a long moment then relaxed his grip on Davo, lowering him to the floor, as he glared at Aron, his bloodshot eyes almost glowing red.

"Let. Him. Go," said Aron firmly, still holding the blade to his throat.

They stood locked in that posture for several breaths before Tancred released Davo who immediately scuttled towards the door. Tancred stood breathing like a man who had just run a mile race; the sweat streamed down his face as his mouth worked, but no words came forth. Aron watched him, poised to respond to the attack he expected. *If he attacks, I have to kill him,* he thought. Abruptly Tancred turned and strode from the room, almost walking over Davo who still stood, hands behind his body, with his back against the door.

Davo scrambled up from the floor where he had retreated from Tancred's exit and triumphantly produced his hands from behind his back. In them was a canvas pouch.

"Won't have to ask 'im again, will we?" The little man grinned.

Aron grinned back at him.

"That was well done," he said slipping the knife back into its sheath. "You were hungry a while back, shall we get something to eat? Call the potboy, Davo."

One of the other Nandor soldier passed him a mug of ale with a nod of approval and went back to his seat.

CHAPTER 12

Aron moved cautiously through the narrow streets between overhanging buildings, letting his ears become attuned to the little sounds of the night, listening for anything that might betray an attacker. He plucked at the chainmail under his shirt and loosened his knives in their scabbards. This part of the town had a bad reputation for thieves and footpads. Only a few householders obeyed the Duke's edict to hang lanterns for streetlighting, leaving a multitude of deep-shadowed corners and doorways where an ambusher might lurk. He started at a scuffle from an alleyway, and then relaxed as it became the familiar howl of tomcats disputing territory.

He lost his bearings several times in the maze of alleyways and little courtyards, and had to backtrack, squelching through the mud and worse, all the time wary for a stalker tracking him. The few people about at this hour hurried along avoiding eye contact. A thin rain was falling, blurring vision so that Aron could see only a few paces in the darkness. Usually he would trust his sense of direction to get him anywhere he had visited before, but this time he was defeated; the streets all looked the same and the only landmarks were the taverns that had been closed when he had walked through in daylight. Eventually he found a street urchin begging at a tavern door and paid him a penny to bring him to the wise woman.

The child led him swiftly down a lightless alley, across a courtyard, down a second alley, in all a distance of less than fifty paces before knocking at a door that Aron could barely see in the gloom.

"Come in, young warrior," called a voice from within.

Aron pushed the door open and warm yellow light flowed out to greet him. He stepped into a cluttered little room; bunches of dried herbs hung from the roofbeams, pots and jars were stacked in every corner. A pair of oil lamps provided the comforting glow, and in the middle of it all the wise woman sat in a rocking chair before a small fire. She shooed a cat from her lap and gathered her shawl about her shoulders.

"You took your time getting here," she said, her voice

sounding surprisingly young to Aron. "So you want to walk the mist. You can pay? It's not cheap trickery I'm selling, mind." Aron pulled out the pouch of coins he'd brought and spilled them into her gnarled hand. She counted them and then smiled again. "Think you're strong enough?"

"I was last time," said Aron confidently.

The wise woman smiled at him displaying the gaps in her yellow teeth. "So you know the rules then."

"I believe so."

"Tell me them, warrior."

"I can walk in the spirit world as I am or was, but nothing more. I cannot bring anything with me, but any wound that I take there I will suffer here."

"Quite so, warrior. If you die in the spirit world then you die here also. But you neglect the most fundamental thing."

Aron looked at her, puzzled.

"So you don't know it all." She smiled at him again. "The will. It is all under the control of your will. If you stay focused it will take you where you want to go, but if you allow your mind to wander so will your spirit, and believe me, there are places there you do not want to go. Still sure you want to do this?"

"Yes," said Aron firmly.

"Good. Then how well do you know the man you're looking for?"

"Not at all, I've never met him."

"Then how do you expect to find him out there in the mist?" The woman sat back in her rocking chair, steepling her fingers. "Do you know his location well? Have you been there? Have anything that belonged to him?"

"I've a rough idea of where he is but no, I've never been there and I've nothing of his." Aron replied, feeling somewhat awkward.

"Then you're a right fool, boy. I should give you your money back now and send you on your way." She rocked forward towards Aron. "But I like your face, so lets me think about it and see if there isn't some other way of doing this."

She rocked back, stretching her arms behind her to hold the chair in that position as she thought. For a while the only sound was the hiss of a kettle on the grate.

"Is there someone you know well, who also knows him well?" she said. "If you can find them, then they can lead you to him."

The image of a pair of sparkling blue eyes rose in Aron's mind.

But whose eyes? Edith would probably be better, she had craved adventure.
"Yes. I think I know someone who meets that description." Aron smiled to himself.

"Will they be asleep at this hour?"

"I would expect so," said Aron.

"Do you trust them and, more important, do they trust you? If you lose them in the mist there's no telling where they may end up."

Aron stopped to think. He hadn't considered that there might be a risk to Edith walking the mist with him. Could he trust her to be sensible and do what she was told? If not, he had no business taking her there. But equally this was the only way to gain the information he needed. He remembered the look on her face as she had handed him her handkerchief when they left Nandor and made his decision.

"I trust her and she trusts me," he said.

"Then it is worth the attempt."

The wise woman got up from her chair and fetched a pottery jar down from a shelf. She drew out a handful of the contents, sniffed them and then tossed them into the kettle.

"This will help you to walk the mists with me and see if we can find the one you seek." She lifted the kettle from the grate and poured dark, steaming fluid into a mug which she passed to Aron. "Don't let it get cold now."

Aron's stomach turned at the memory of the taste. He lifted the mug to his mouth and the foetid, bitter smell of the brew rose to meet him. He screwed up his face in disgust and turned away.

"You must drink it." Her dark eyes glittered with wry amusement. "Come on, warrior. How many have you slain then? And a cup of broth is beyond you, shame on you."

Aron drew a deep breath and then filled his mouth with the contents of the mug; with a determined effort he swallowed and forced his throat to stay closed. The woman passed him a second mug filled with liquid.

"Drink this. It'll take away the taste," she said sympathetically.

Aron took a swig and his mouth was filled with gentle lemon flavour. He swallowed and took another mouthful; the awful taste of the first draught receded.

"Sit down now and wait." She lifted a pile of clothes from a wooden chair beside the fire. "When the draught begins to work you must clear your mind of everything but the one you seek.

Concentrate on them alone, start with your strongest memory of them and build them in your mind's eye. Put your whole being into creating their image. Take this picture and reach out across the darkness to them. Mayhap they'll dream of you and that'll aid you. Now sit back and relax, the better to focus."

Aron sat back his chair as the woman instructed, his churning stomach the main focus of his mental processes. He belched a couple of times, and gradually the urge to vomit eased. Eyes closed, he sought calm and focus as the blademasters had taught him - be the eye of the storm - then his mind lifted with a surge of vertigo. He gasped.

"Good. It begins. Concentrate, warrior. Build the picture in your mind."

The words echoed as if spoken down a long corridor. Aron smiled as he remembered looking deeply into a pair of blue eyes, soft lips warm against his and firm young breasts pressing into his chest. Opening his eyes Aron found the room filled with swirling mist, the woman was nowhere to be seen, but she spoke as if she could see him.

"Step into the mist. Find the one you seek."

Aron stood up and stepped cautiously forward into the billowing white clouds, expecting to walk into the wall that he knew was three paces from where he had been sitting. His arms stretched out in front of him, Aron kept moving encountering nothing but chill mist.

"Focus your mind. Think only of your quest," called the disembodied voice from a vast distance.

Aron pictured dark curls framing a smiling face with sparkling blue eyes and kept walking. The mist thinned and the outlines of disordered shadows firmed to become solid objects: stepping around a chair Aron found he stood at the foot of a bed in a room whose walls were white cloud. One of the occupants of the bed sat up, opened her eyes with a squeak of delight and then leapt up, throwing her arms wide in welcome. Aron stepped into Edith's embrace, savouring her warmth after the coldness of the mist. Behind him the mist solidified into tapestry-hung walls.

After Edith had kissed him a mere half dozen times she finally spoke. "Oh my darling, how I've missed you. How is it you come to me now?" Then she kissed him again.

Aron indulged himself for another minute before pulling free from Edith's embrace. "I need your help, my Lady. Come dress yourself; I need you to help me find Maldwyn."

"Do you not like me dressed as I am?"

Edith skipped a few dance steps so that her shift swirled about her thighs. Aron felt his cheeks warm as Edith turned her high intensity blue gaze upon him.

"I like you very well, my Lady, but you sought adventure and you cannot go dressed like that."

Edith kissed him again, then released him and turned to her clothes piled carelessly on a chair. "If it's an adventure then I'd best wear something that I can move easily in."

She rummaged through the pile and pulled out the pair of leggings she had worn in the stable. "These were Maldwyn's until he grew out of them."

A further rummage produced a woollen shirt and pair of light boots. Aron turned his back as she dressed,

"Am I suitably dressed or will I need a hat?" She smiled a mischievous smile at Aron.

"You're fine as you are, my Lady. Take my hand and we'll be on our way."

Edith did more than take Aron's hand; she came and put an arm around his waist and looked up at him, her blue eyes seeming large enough for him to fall into.

Aron closed his eyes and tried to remember what he was there for.

"You must find Maldwyn for me. Build a picture of him in your mind so strong that you can touch him, then send it out into the night. Clear your mind of everything except Maldwyn." Mist began to rise from the floor. "Hold the picture in your mind," Aron said as the mist swirled around them.

They stepped forward in the direction of the door but never reached it. Edith's arm gripped him very tightly as they walked through the featureless cloud, unable even to see their feet to tell what surface they trod. As before, insubstantial shadows thickened to firm lines, and then they stepped out of the mist into a small stone-walled room furnished with the bare minimum of rough furniture. Edith pulled Aron closer and shivered against the chill. On a pile of straw in a corner a figure huddled under a single blanket.

"Maldwyn!" Edith cried and pushed forward towards the sleeper.

Aron pulled her back as Maldwyn stirred.

"No. Do not wake him. We haven't time to talk with him. We're here to find a way out."

"But...."

Aron silenced her by turning her back to him and kissing her. When she released him he pulled her towards the door of the chamber. They stood for a moment while Aron thought about how to open it.

"If this is a dream then we can walk through it," said Edith, pulling Aron forward.

There was a moment of darkness, and they found themselves on a landing with a spiral stone stairway leading both up and down. Aron led them cautiously down. At the bottom an archway led out into a cobbled courtyard lit by flaring torches. Keeping tight to the wall they edged out passing within an armslength of a crossbow-carrying sentry. Aron was holding his breath and trying to keep as still as possible when he looked down and saw that though the sentry cast a shadow, he and Edith did not. Cursing his foolishness, he stepped away from the wall, around the corner and set out across the courtyard. The sentry did not deviate from his path. Aron walked quickly across the yard drawing Edith after him. Several carts were parked in front of a series of wooden huts which were built up against a solid stone wall. Aron made for the gap between the last cart and the hut with the lowest roof. Edith squeezed in beside him and looked up, blue eyes shining with excitement.

'What do we do now?" she whispered as her arms slipped around his chest. Aron pulled her close for a moment and then whispered. "We climb."

Wriggling free of Edith's grasp, he put one foot on the hub of the cart wheel and pushed himself up, catching the roof timbers of the hut he swung onto the roof via the top of the cartwheel. Then he stretched down, caught Edith's hand and pulled her up as she scrambled onto the roof beside him. Walking along the hut wall they came to the stone wall. Aron reached up and pulled himself up to look over.

"What can you see?" Edith asked.

Aron lowered himself carefully back down. "Water, the lake."

"What place is this then? Castle Sarazan?"

"The very same."

"Where are you then?"

"In Sarazan city, seeking a way into this fortress."

"Then this is a truedream." Edith's face drew close to Aron's, her voice a husky whisper. "You'll remember this, remember you were here with me."

"I'll remember every bit." Aron pulled her closer still and she rested her head in the hollow of his shoulder. Aron held her there and looked back across the courtyard trying to spot any further sentries in the moonlight. The farther corners of the yard started to blur as a mist began to rise from the cobbles.

"We haven't got long, the spell won't last much longer. Tell your mother I'm in Sarazan."

"Promise me you'll come back to Nandor."

Aron felt the desperation of her plea in the strength of her arms encircling him. He said nothing, but bowed his head to kiss her one more time as the mist grew thick around them.

CHAPTER 13

Aron trudged wearily back towards the group's lodging house. It was late even for the most desperate of thieves, so he was less watchful as he traversed the dark streets, the memories of his walk in the mist turning over in his mind. On one level the trip had been fruitful; he knew where Maldwyn was, how he was guarded and of a possible way in. On another level he was confused; if he accepted the dream of Castle Sarazan as real then he had to accept Edith's reaction to him as equally true. His blood raced as he remembered the passion of her embrace. *But she's an Earl's daughter. How have I managed to set the girl on fire like that? All I did was be polite, listen to her talk and kiss her when, with no prior encouragement, she kissed me.* He tried to concentrate on his plan to free Maldwyn and failed utterly.

The tavern was locked and shuttered when, after many a wrong turning, he reached it some time in the small hours. It took a lot of sustained and forceful hammering before he roused a dull-eyed kitchenboy and convinced him to unbar the door. Tired to his bones, Aron climbed the stair to the loft dormitory and crept in hoping to avoid waking Tancred. The room was as quiet as a mausoleum. In the pitch darkness Aron was unable to even hear breathing. Weariness overcame curiosity and sleep claimed him before he could investigate further.

Morning answered the mystery. Aron awoke to find himself alone in the loft, the other beds not slept in. Davo's absence he could explain, but the others? He made his way to the kitchen where he scrounged a loaf and a pot of small beer and learned that his companions had gone out late in the evening as they had done every night previously.

"Probably been taken up by the Watch," laughed the cook. "You'll find them locked up in the watch house nursing sore heads."

Aron decided to leave them there, glad of anything that kept him away from Tancred and the inevitable confrontation. He and Davo had more urgent business in finding a quick way out of Sarazan for themselves after the rescue attempt; successful or otherwise. There was little to do until Davo returned.

***

"The wards were breached last night, my Lord," said Ezrin. He stood before the table in a small wood-panelled study at the heart of Castle Sarazan. Facing him across the table, Lord Hercival, younger son of the Duke of Sarazan, sat back in a fine carved chair. His dark hair and finely chiselled features with a prominent hooked nose marking him as one in whom the blood of the Sarazan dynasty ran strong.

"Again, Master Ezrin?" said Lord Hercival. "This is the third time in as many weeks. What is it this time?"

"Someone or something was within the castle last night, My Lord."

"Are you so sure? What was it last time, Nicoras?"

"One of the lads had a wench in the hayloft, my Lord," said Nicoras, his battered face impassive. With the Duke away at the court of the High King, having taken his eldest son Lord Reginal, the guard commander and a select company of bodyguards, Nicoras was in command of Castle Sarazan's forces, under Lord Hercival.

"Can you be sure that it is nothing so ordinary, Master?" asked Lord Hercival sharply, his dark eyes fixed accusingly on Ezrin.

"It was a response quite different to the last one, my Lord."

Ezrin almost succeeded in keeping the annoyance out of his voice. He wished that he was speaking to Lord Hercival's father or even his elder brother Lord Reginal. His Grace, the Duke, would not have spoken to him like that; he knew the value of Ezrin's arts.

"The sentries saw and heard nothing, my Lord," said Nicoras.

"I did say someone or something, my Lord," said Ezrin. "If the sentries saw no-one then I stand by my statement. Something was within the castle last night. I would speculate that someone using the arts of sorcery was exploring our position."

"Which part of the castle?" The hook nose pointed at Ezrin.

"I cannot tell that, my Lord. The wards merely warn of breach of the perimeter."

Lord Hercival pursed his lips and frowned in thought. "I'm at a loss to know how to respond to such a vague warning. What think you, Nicoras?"

Nicoras folded his powerful arms across his barrel chest. "Difficult to assess a threat that no-one else sees, my Lord. I can double the guard detail for the next few nights if you wish it."

"I don't believe that will be necessary, Nicoras. Who would be so bold as to assault us here?

"There's a squad of Nandorans holed up in a cheap tavern down in the city," said Nicoras. "Their leader is Baldwin's nephew, Tancred."

"What on earth do they think to do?" Lord Hercival laughed. "Rescue that flea-bitten wretch we've got in the south tower? Nicoras, you surely jest with me."

"They could be a threat, my Lord."

"A bunch of sorry sheepherders. Very well, Nicoras, go down and collect them if you think they're a threat. We'll send Earl Baldwin a reminder of the stakes in this game. And as for you Master Ezrin, may I suggest you go back to your tower and work at refining your guard spells rather than casting horoscopes for the maidservants, popular as they are."

Ezrin pulled his long silver cloak about him and stalked out with as much dignity as he could muster.

***

It was a very sorry bunch of Nandorans that sat in a cell in the watch house. Despite a fine selection of battered heads and bruised limbs they bore their discomfort in silence, except Tancred. He complained if someone coughed, complained if a flea bit and complained loudly if any feet sounded in the corridor beyond the door. If he had nothing to complain about, he told his long-suffering comrades and the world in general, that he had done nothing to deserve this state. This was untrue. He hadn't intended to start a fight, but it had directly resulted from his actions. A serving girl, admittedly clumsy and more than a little plump, had spilled a mug of ale over Tancred in a crowded taproom. Tancred had cursed her, then slapped her, and the whole tavern rose against them. The entire room exploded into a maelstrom of brawling men, the Nandorans at the centre. Then the Watch arrived and, in all probability, the Watchmen Tancred was now abusing had saved their lives.

***

"I don't want to know about what you did with that girl last night." Aron was losing patience with Davo. "Just tell me that you've found a boat that'll get us out of here."

The little man had finally arrived back at the tavern around midday, reeking of cheap scent.

"You're just jealous, that's what." Davo grinned. "But I got us a boat. Her ma's got a boyfriend that's a boatman. He'll take us downriver. Won't be cheap, mind."

"How much?" Aron said resignedly.

"Twenty silver for each man."

Aron drew breath through clenched teeth like a man pulling a splinter from a finger. Sixty silvers. Most farmers in Darien didn't earn that much in a year. "Is he reliable?"

Stupid question, Aron thought as soon as he said it. First, he wouldn't trust Davo's judgement and second, anyone asking that much to perform a minor illegal act was certainly criminal.

"Doubt it, but we got no choice 'ave we? You know anyone else?"

"No. You're right, we need passage out and we'll need it soon. Maybe within a day. How soon can he leave?"

"Soon as he sees the silver."

"Good, then we go tonight. We'll make a try for Maldwyn and go direct to the boat. When can you take me to this sailor?"

Davo went quiet for a long moment before answering. "Not till after dark. I know where to find him then."

"Fine, we'll wait here. But get your gear together and bring it down here. Just your gear, mind." Davo gave him a dark look which he ignored. "There's no knowing where Tancred and the others are, or when they'll show up. I just hope they've kept their mouths shut if they have been taken up by the Watch. Although, if they hadn't, we'd have had a platoon of guardsmen on the doorstep with the dawn. So you keep quiet if they do show up. I don't want to have to explain to Tancred why we're getting our kit ready for the road."

***

"It seems you have an excess of energy and aggression." The magistrate fixed his cold gaze on Tancred. "Fortunately here in Sarazan we know of a cure for that." The frosty stare took in the other four men of the Nandor expedition. "Five days labour in the quarry will cool your tempers, I think. Take them away please, watchman."

The party were hustled out of the courtroom by half a dozen black-clad men and led to a waiting room. Chained one to another and the wall they sat in silence watched by a selection of the criminal class of Sarazan and four Watchmen. Tancred looked around the room, his fists clenched very tight. It was not the physical prospect of the quarry work that annoyed him; it was dishonour that he, a nobleman of an ancient house, should be lowered to this, and in the company of common soldiers. Yet to have declared his station would have landed him in far deeper trouble, joining Maldwyn as a hostage.

The other Nandorans avoided catching his eye; they knew that the witnesses of his discomfort would suffer for it later.

As the day progressed the room filled up with the lowlife of Sarazan until, when it seemed no more could be contained within the walls, the watchmen unbolted the chains from the wall and led the convicts out in chained-up groups of four or five.

The prisoners were herded onto large open wagons, the chains were shackled to a ring on the wagon body and then the horses were whipped up. As the wagon clattered through the streets the people they passed jeered and threw whatever came to hand. Urchins ran alongside and lobbed handfuls of filth, some with remarkable accuracy. Tancred crouching in the bottom of the wagon received a double handful of stinking ordure across the back of his neck. None of the Nandorans dared to laugh.

***

Aron stretched out on the bench in the common room beside the cold remains of last night's fire; his head resting on his pack, and closed his eyes. The lack of sleep was catching up with him, and he foresaw still less in prospect for the next few nights. Davo settled similarly on another bench beside the door to the tavern's interior: it appeared that he too had had little sleep. Breathing slowly and evenly, Aron sought the dark pool of sleep; sinking into its warm depths he let his mind wander where it would.

Maybe some residue of the wise woman's potion remained within him, or maybe it was his spirit that now knew the way of itself, but Aron dreamed of stepping once more into the mist. As before, insubstantial shadows thickened into solid objects, and he emerged from the cloud into a meadow. Looking around, he recognised the herb garden at Castle Nandor and then seeing the bower beside the willow tree, smiled to himself. Who waited within dreaming of him? He walked up the path, his boots silent on the soft turf, and stepped into the bower. Celaine sat alone on the double seat, her head bowed. She looked up at Aron, the red in her lovely eyes showing that she had been weeping. A smile spread across her face like the sun breaking through rain clouds and she reached out to take him in her arms. She buried her head in his chest and held him very tightly. Aron ran his fingers through her dark hair and whispered soft words of comfort, waiting for her to speak. After a long while Celaine's grip loosened and she turned her face up to look at him, eyes moist with unshed tears. Aron pressed his lips to hers and they held each other close for further long minutes. Finally she released him.

"I've missed you night and day since you left, but today I need you more than ever." She looked into his eyes and tears threatened to flow again.

"Tell me," Aron stroked her cheek with his fingers.

"Just another rejection. I should be used to it by now, but...."

Her shoulders heaved and the threatened tears flowed. Aron held her close and wondered what he could say. Then the dream disintegrated as the door of the common room crashed open. Armed men, the crest of Sarazan on their breasts, burst into the room by the street door.

Aron was suddenly back in the inn. His reaction was immediate; the first man through the door fell with a thrown knife in his throat. The second stumbled over his fallen comrade and the third died with Aron's second throwing knife in his left eye. Aron snatched up his sword and attacked while he still held the initiative. The man who had stumbled died on his knees, unable to avoid Aron's thrust. The fourth man tangled with the fellow behind him as he tried to avoid the assault. He died quickly too, and the fifth man backed out into the street. Aron slammed the door, dropped the locking bar and then wedged a bench against it to keep the assailants at bay.

"The other door. Get it closed. Put your bench against it. Now!" Aron yelled at Davo who sat wide-eyed. The little man did as he was told, and then stood in the middle of the room shaking his head in confusion. "What the hell is going on?" Looking at the dead guardsmen he said unnecessarily, "We're in the shit."

There was a loud noise from the street door as if something heavy had struck it.

"That won't hold them for long." Aron looked around at the plain room. There was one window high up in the wall, too small for even a child to wriggle through. He stooped to retrieve his knives, wiping them on a dead guardsman's tunic.

Davo looked at Aron with an odd measuring gaze as if trying to decide something, then he looked at the wall, finally he spoke.

"The chimney. We can climb the chimney."

Aron looked at him open-mouthed.

"It's wide all the way up. I know 'cos I was a chimney boy. I've climbed thissun before, there's lots of room."

"That was a long time ago, you've grown since," said Aron.

Another crash at the door reverberated around the room, this one accompanied by an ominous cracking of timbers.

"Yer got a better idea?"

"No, let's climb. You first."

Davo picked up his pack and stepped into the wide fireplace. He fastened the pack to an ankle and then began to climb. Aron snatched up his pack and, in similar fashion to Davo, tied it to his ankle. There was another thump, this time from the other door leading to the interior of the inn. Aron stepped into the fireplace, looked up and received a small avalanche of soot in his face. He spat the filth out of his mouth and decided to wait until Davo was clear before starting the climb. He didn't want to be half way up with Davo blocking the way above, an enemy below and no way to turn. There was another charge on the street door, but the tortured wood withstood the blow. Soot continued to fall in the fireplace; the door was assaulted again but held. The soot fall ceased. Aron looked up the chimney and saw nothing but a ragged patch of sky. He listened intently for a moment... nothing, then Davo's urgent whisper. "C'mon, get moving."

Aron began to climb, feeling for handholds in the dark. In the room below he heard a splintering crash. Voices echoed up the flue. The street door had yielded to the enemy. His shoulders and hips scraped on rough, warm brickwork, but handholds presented themselves; this was a way that had been climbed regularly, though by climbers smaller than he. His head emerged into clean air. Davo caught hold of his shoulders to pull him clear.

"C'mon, we've gotta get away from here."

Aron needed no such urging, pulling his pack clear of the chimney they set off across the rooftops of Sarazan.

Up on the roof, Davo was transformed; certain in his movements he directed Aron away from the besieged inn. Taking command effortlessly, he stepped with assurance from roof to roof as they left the Duke's troops behind. Two hundred paces they travelled, leaping from house to house, until Davo thought it safe to descend to the street. Then he led Aron through the alleys of the poor quarter to a dilapidated wooden shanty that seemed held together with pitch. Davo rapped on the door with enough force that Aron expected it to fall into the hovel. It didn't, instead it swung open revealing the face of the serving girl from the tavern.

"Oh sweetheart, come in." Then spotting Aron, she added.

"Maybe I'd better find Annie or Babs for your friend. I thought you said he weren't interested."

Aron stepped into the gloom of the interior. "I'm just looking for somewhere to keep out of the way for a few hours. I don't think you need trouble your friends on my behalf, but thanks for the offer."

Aron thought about asking if there was somewhere he could wash off the filth he had acquired in his ascent of the tavern chimney, but a brief look at his hostess and surroundings convinced him that no such facility existed. Davo had already made himself comfortable with the girl on a straw-filled sack. Aron shrugged, put his pack down on the beaten earth floor and sat on it.

"Before you get too comfortable, Davo, remember that we have a few things to acquire before dark," he said, but got only giggles in reply.

***

"How many?"

The young lieutenant stood before Nicoras in the guardroom of Castle Sarazan, his career prospects in ashes. "Four dead, Captain."

"And how many Nandoran sheepkissers were responsible for this slaughter?" Nicoras's gaze turned to the guardsman standing stiffly at the lieutenant's side.

"Two, sir. Two that I saw anyways. Fought like demons, Captain."

"No doubt they did. Then vanished away into thin air." Neither man dared to look Nicoras in the eyes as he paced before them. "Well, did they?" he bellowed.

"We searched the whole tavern, Captain. I swear it. There was no trace." The lieutenant answered.

"We did sir. Top to bottom," the guardsman added.

"Who asked you?" Nicoras roared. "Keep quiet until I ask you. So where did they go?" Nicoras put his face close up to the young officer. "Did they turn into birds and just fly away?'

"I don't know, sir. We found no trace. The men are saying its magic, Captain."

"Are they indeed? I might expect that from the common soldiery, but I expect more intelligent reasoning from the officers of this guard. There is no evidence of a wizard in Sarazan. Master Ezrin has not told me of any unexplained use of magic. Can you think of no other explanation?" The young officer said nothing. "Then let me do the thinking for you. Was there a chimney in the common room of this tavern? Did you examine it? Was there a great deal of soot in the hearth?" Nicoras noted the young man stiffen with surprise and realisation. "Is it possible they escaped up the chimney and across the roof? Did you consider that?"

During this tirade Nicoras had resumed pacing the room; now he put his face very close to the lieutenant again. "No. You did not. That is how your assassins escaped. Not magic, they climbed up the chimney. Now get some men on the roof, follow the tracks they left and find them, you moron!"

CHAPTER 14

Midnight found Aron and Davo in the Duke's deerpark on the opposite shore from Castle Sarazan. Crouching in the bushes by the water's edge Aron readied his gear.

"If I'm not back by the first lightening of the sky, I'm not coming back. You're on your own then. But do me the courtesy of waiting till then before you go back to sweetie. And look after my boots; they're the only pair I've got."

Aron pulled them off and passed them to Davo. He wound the rope around his body and tied one end to his left wrist. The grappling hook they'd bought earlier in the day was attached to the other end and secured at his side.

"How do I look, have I missed any bits?" Aron asked.

Wearing a dark shirt and breeches and with the soot from the chimney smeared across his face, Aron should have been almost invisible to Davo as a cloud front covered the sky.

"Real good, can't 'ardly see yer," said Davo. "Hope e's fit enough to get out."

"He's a nobleman being held for ransom, that's very different to languishing in a dungeon. The Duke will respect the conventions; Maldwyn'll have enough to eat and he'll get exercise daily. He's probably in better shape than we are." Aron looked up at the advancing cloud. "Now is as good a time as we'll get," he said and stood up. "Good luck then," Davo said. "Bring him out. Master Maldwyn's a good lad, it's a shame what's 'appened to 'im."

Aron stepped into the water and stifled a curse as the cold bit into his legs. Gritting his teeth he pushed forwards until his shoulders were underwater then struck out with a purposeful breaststroke. He was a strong swimmer; long summer evenings beside the Darien river had seen to that. The back wall of the castle looked to be less than a long bowshot distant, but he had reckoned without the cold. This was not Darien at midsummer and the chill drank his strength like a thirsty horse. "*This settles the debt,*" he thought as he pushed through the dark water. "*After this no-one can say I didn't try.*"

He concentrated on breathing regularly; trying to focus all his awareness on the rhythm of the stroke and ignore the distant bulk of the fortress.

The wall loomed over him, seeming much higher than he knew it was. It was too deep for him to touch the lakebed so he trod water and unwound the rope from around his body. He took hold of the shank of the hook right-handed, testing its weight with a couple of trial swings, then he took a deep breath and relaxed to let his body sink down into the water. Then, with a great kick of his legs, he surged out of the water and tossed the hook and its trailing rope high into the air towards the wall. There was a clatter as the hook landed beyond the wall, and Aron carefully began to pull the rope in. It tautened as the hook caught on something, came loose and tautened again. Aron pulled harder to test the solidity of the grip and then began to pull himself clear of the water and up the wall.

He cautiously lifted his head over the wall and looked down into the rear of Castle Sarazan. He was very close to where he had intended to be. The sheds he'd climbed in the dream world were a few paces off to his right. The night breeze, gentle as it was, thrust cold knives into his wet body. Trying to keep as low as possible, Aron swung his body over the parapet and wormed his way along to where the solid shed wall joined the perimeter wall. He lowered himself seeking a solid footing, doubting that the roof would take his weight. His bare feet sought and found the stone, he stepped down and, dropping to a crouch, looked around. Nothing moved, no-one called the alarm; not a single light shone out from the dark bulk of the keep. He crept forward until he could see over the edge of the roof; below him was a line of wagons parked beside the sheds just as in the dream. Water dripped from him down onto the nearest wagon. Still in a crouch, he jumped and rolled as he hit the ground to finish up under one of the wagons. He crawled up the line to the farside of the first wagon and looked across the yard to where the sentry should be. The man was concealed in the deep shadow under the keep and Aron wasn't sure he was there until he stamped his feet to ward off cramp. There was no approach to his position that was not in plain view.

Concealed in the shadow under the wagon, Aron reached into his belt pouch and drew out a smooth round pebble and a soft leather sling. He fitted the pebble into the sling's pouch and crept out from under the wagon. He stood concealed against its dark body and stared intently into the darkness towards the sentry, awaiting his moment, shivering with cold, right hand cocked at his shoulder. Time passed and he began to suspect the man had fallen asleep at his post when, boots crunching on the cobbles, the sentry stepped out of the shadows towards him. Aron took a slow deep breath and sought the focus and inner balance that he had been taught. He held the stillness for a moment then, in a single flowing movement, launched the slingshot at the oncoming man.

The stone struck the sentry just below the rim of his helmet, he grunted in pain and collapsed, his crossbow clattering on the cobbles. Aron paused for a long moment, not daring to even breathe, to see if there was a reaction from anywhere, any further sentries he'd not seen. Nothing happened, so he scuttled to where his victim lay and dragged him back to the cover of the wagons as quietly as he could manage. From his pouch he drew out leather thongs to truss the unconscious man and a gag to keep him quiet.

Aron left him beneath a wagon and scurried, as quickly as his bare feet would allow, to the shadow of the keep and the stairway that the sentry had guarded. The stairwell was very dark and Aron felt his way up, listening intently all the time for any sound that might warn of an enemy above. The only thing he could hear was the rasping of his own breathing echoing back from the stone walls. The first level was utterly dark and silent as Aron crept on upwards past its entrance to the second level where the dream had placed Maldwyn.

It was as quiet as the first. Aron stepped slowly out into the passageway, his hands held out before him like a child's game of blind man's bluff. His fingers found the wall and he followed it until he reached a door. He raised the locking bar, gently laid it to one side and lifted the latch. The door creaked open and Aron slipped inside. A window provided sufficient illumination for him to make out the mound huddled on a narrow bed. He walked over to it and pulled the thin blanket off the sleeping man. He put a hand over the sleeper's mouth to stifle any cry and whispered in his ear.

"Keep quiet and do what you're told. We're getting out of here."

There was no response. Aron muttered a curse and shook the sleeper roughly by the shoulder. There was a grunt but he didn't awaken. Aron searched with his free hand, found an ear and dug his fingernails into the lobe. The sleeper started violently and tried to sit up. Aron hauled him downwards cursing him the while.

"Maldwyn of Nandor?" The man grunted in acknowledgement and tried to bite Aron's hand. "Be still, the Gods rot you. I'm here to get you out. Now keep quiet and I'll release you."

Maldwyn relaxed under Aron's grip and Aron removed his hand. Maldwyn began to speak and Aron replaced his hand quickly to silence him.

"Questions later. Now you do what I tell you and keep quiet." Aron removed his hand again. Maldwyn kept gratifyingly silent. "We're leaving - now! You come as you are, carry nothing. I hope you can swim."

Maldwyn stood up slowly, his hands pawing at Aron. Aron caught his arm and pulled him towards the door. Maldwyn stumbled after him, feet scuffling on the floor.

"I need my boots," he said.

"Sssh," Aron hissed at him. "Our lives depend on keeping quiet. Get your damned boots then."

Maldwyn groped in the darkness and collided noisily with the chair. Aron ground his teeth in frustration. Maldwyn tugged his boots on and then kicked the chair again as he tried to step round it.

"Where are you?" he whispered.

"Here." Aron reached out and caught hold of Maldwyn's arm. "Keep as quiet as you can and just listen." They stood for a long moment. The passageway was as quiet as before. Aron kept hold of Maldwyn with one hand as he felt his way along the wall with the other. He found the edge of the stairwell, stopped and Maldwyn blundered into him. Aron grunted in pain as Maldwyn stood on his cold bare right foot. Maldwyn began to apologise, but Aron silenced him abruptly with a hiss.

"Stairs next. Keep two steps behind me to the bottom." Then he stepped into the stairwell feeling for the edges of the steps with his mistreated toes. Behind him Maldwyn scuffed and stumbled on the uneven stone, leading Aron to fear that he would fall and sweep both of them downwards in a tumble that would surely end the adventure.

Aron breathed a silent sigh of relief as he reached the bottom of the stair where the open doorway was outlined against the night sky. The dim light gave him his first chance to take a look at Maldwyn of Nandor. Edith had described him as a great tall dark hunk of a man, so Aron was not surprised to find Maldwyn topped him by a handslength; however, he doubted that many girls would consider him handsome. His nose, which clearly proclaimed him his father's son, dominated his face beneath a thatch of straight dark hair, and his limbs seemed to be just too long for his body. Aron supposed that in a few years he might fill out, so that his proportions would seem more natural; then a girl might look twice. Of course, he'd be an earl someday - if he didn't tread on Aron's toes too often.

Maldwyn was also staring at Aron, probably sizing him up in the same way, so Aron turned to look across the courtyard at the wagons where he had left the immobilised sentry. All was quiet as he whispered his instructions to Maldwyn, pointing out which wagon to head for, and then sent him on his way. There was no reaction to Maldwyn's passage across the yard, so Aron followed him, silently cursing as the cobbles bit his cold bare feet.

Halfway to the wagons Aron heard the tread of nailed boots coming from the direction of the main castle buildings. He sprinted the remaining distance to the nearest wagon and ducked into the shadows beneath it as two men, one carrying a torch, appeared in the archway that lead to the front of the fortress. They crossed the courtyard heading for the stairwell from where Aron and Maldwyn had just come. Aron thanked whatever gods protected the bold and foolish, grateful that he hadn't met the guards on the stairs.

They had only a few moments before the sentry's absence was discovered. Aron crawled to the far side of the wagon and stood up in the space between it and the line of huts. Maldwyn was easily located in the darkness; Aron could hear him moving around beneath another wagon. Aron called to him softly and then cursed as Maldwyn struck his head on some protruding piece of the wagon's body, the noise echoing across the yard. The sound of boots on cobbles ceased suddenly. Aron pulled himself up on the wheel of the wagon and risked a look back; the torch was stationary. He was silently thankful for the guards' stupidity in carrying a torch; they'd be able to see nothing beyond the pool of illumination it provided. Maldwyn reached his side and Aron hissed him to stillness, waiting for the torch-carriers to turn back to the stairwell. The guards stood for several breaths and then started walking towards the wagons.

"You climb first," whispered Aron. "I'll deal with these two if they get too close."

Maldwyn paused for a moment, but Aron gave him a shove to get him moving. Maldwyn scrambled up onto the wall with ease and, to Aron's surprise, did not put a foot through the roof. The guardsmen paused halfway down the line of wagons. Aron took the opportunity to climb up onto the perimeter wall. He did so as quietly as he could in his haste, but evidently not quietly enough because a shout went up from the two men in the yard and they broke into a run towards him.

"What now?" asked Maldwyn as he looked back to the commotion.

"Jump. And I hope you can swim," replied Aron as he scrambled onto the top of the wall and launched himself feet first into the darkness.

The chill of the water bit into his body as he kicked out to bring himself to the surface. There was a large splash a few armslengths away as Maldwyn joined him. Aron struck out for the opposite shore with silent powerful strokes but Maldwyn, though he kept up a reasonable progress, thrashed around like a drowning man. Behind them in the castle bells begin to ring.

A light showed at the foot of the castle wall and was joined by more. There were curses and a large splash followed by smaller more regular splashes. Two of the lights began to move, bobbing, away from the wall. A boat had been launched, and was headed towards them guided by Maldwyn's noisy strokes. Aron looked for the shore and then looked back at the boat, measuring the distance, and concluded that the boat would catch them before they reached the shallows. He called out to Maldwyn to go faster. The splashing increased, the rate of progress did not and Aron felt a surge of anger at Maldwyn's efforts.

The boat was gaining solidly on them, close enough now that Aron could count six men in it; four bent over their oars and two holding torches. Maldwyn seemed to be tiring as the boat bore down on him. Aron trod water as the boat cut between him and Maldwyn, turning to block Maldwyn's path. Aron saw it heel over as the men tried to grab Maldwyn. No-one was looking his way and an idea formed in his mind. He ducked under the water and struck out towards the boat, guided by the flare of the torches. He swam under it to surface almost beside the gunwale. He reached up, caught the gunwale and pulled downwards for all he was worth. The boat, already unbalanced by the guardsmen's effort to grab Maldwyn, tipped and capsized, spilling the guardsmen in the water.

Night swallowed the scene as the torches were quenched with a hiss, and for a short while, there was a maelstrom of splashing and yelling. Over a few minutes the splashes faded until there was only the din of the heir of Nandor propelling himself through the water. Aron struck out for the shore as the cold ate the last of his strength.

***

"It was the monster. Sure as anything," said Davo as he passed the spirit flask to Maldwyn who sat with a thick cloak wrapped about him. "I telled yer there's a monster in there."

Aron said nothing but concentrated on tugging on his boots with desperately cold fingers. The boots finally yielded and Aron stood up, water dripping from his clothes.

"We must get away from here. There'll be horsemen upon us in no time and hounds sent from the castle. There's a boat waiting to take us downriver. I hope you've strength enough for a run, my Lord," he said to the shivering Maldwyn. "At least it'll warm you."

CHAPTER 15

The guard sergeant looked nervous as the grey light of early morning struggled to light the chamber. "We lost the trail, my Lord," he said hesitantly. "The dogs found their scent easily enough on the lakeside, but there are just too many other trails when you get into the city,"

As well he might be nervous thought Nicoras. *Lord Hercival is, like his grandfather, not a good man to have to report failure to, particularly at this hour of the morning.*

Lord Hercival growled with dissatisfaction but then composed himself. "Only to be expected, Sergeant. If they'd gone straight for the hills, you would have caught them. At least we know which way they've gone. You've done your best, go and get some breakfast."

He waited until the man had closed the door before crashing both fists onto the wooden table before him and uttering a blistering oath.

"You cannot expect dogs bred to track game across open country to track men through a city, my Lord. It's just not realistic." Nicoras stood with his powerful arms folded in front of him. "To be honest, we should be grateful they found as much as they did."

"Thank you, Nicoras. I assure you I am duly grateful." The heavy sarcasm told Nicoras that gratitude was the last thing Lord Hercival was feeling. "Please tell me something useful now. What is being done to capture these invaders?"

"Message birds have been sent to all highway guardposts with a description of Maldwyn. The posts on the Nandor road are being reinforced. Squads of guards are patrolling the city and near countryside, and I have put word out through our intelligence network offering a reward for information that leads to a capture."

"How much?" Lord Hercival looked up suspiciously.

"Twenty in silver. I hope that meets with your approval, my Lord."

"Not enough. Make it fifty. These men have made fools of us, and I want them in chains before my father finds out, Nicoras." His eyes glittered dangerously. "How did they get in?"

"Over the lakeside wall it would seem, my Lord. We found a grapnel hook and rope lodged in the wall at the spot where a man was seen on the way out."

"What about the sentry at the south tower?"

"He took a crack on the head, remembers nothing. He was found trussed and gagged under a wagon in the rear courtyard."

"What happened to the boat?"

"Found floating upside down in the lake. We've recovered two bodies. No doubt the lake will give up the others in due course." Nicoras hesitated before continuing. "The men are saying it was the lake monster."

Lord Hercival's eyes narrowed and Nicoras anticipated another explosion. "Superstitious idiots," said Lord Hercival, pounding the table again with his fist. "I don't believe that for one minute, do you?"

"No, my Lord. It can only have been the intruders' doing, but I don't understand how."

"No matter how they did it, it makes them dangerous opponents. Ten men we've lost to them and they are going to pay. I swear it, Nicoras. The house of Sarazan will not be mocked."

"We will find them, my Lord. The scum of Sarazan would sell their own mother for ten in silver; fifty will have them fighting to bring these men to us."

"If they're still here. But then there are ways of finding them if they are not. Wake up Master Ezrin and send him to me. Here's something a little more demanding for him than a maid's horoscope. And send up my breakfast."

"May I remind you we still hold the other Nandorans, including Maldwyn's cousin. They are presently breaking rocks in the quarry by the will of the city magistrate."

Lord Hercival sat back with a smile. "Thank you for reminding me of that; I had forgotten them. There may yet be something to salvage from this. Have them brought in to the castle. I'd like to talk to these Nandorans."

***

"Can you find this sheepkisser then? You've heard of the embarrassment he's caused us?" said Lord Hercival, pushing back his plate.

"You can keep no secrets in a castle, my Lord," Ezrin the sorcerer smiled unctuously. Now that Hercival needed something perhaps there was a chance of him gaining a little respect. He was not overly vain, but a man of learning deserved some honour. "It may be possible, depending on what he has left behind for me to work with," he said in measured tones.

"Explain." Lord Hercival's brow furrowed with puzzlement and suspicion.

Hercival had never listened, Ezrin remembered, when he had tried to tutor him and his brother in the arts of wizardry.

"It is quite simple, my Lord. I need something which has been in close contact with the subject, preferably part of him, to assist me in finding him. It is much like a hound needs a man's shirt to give him the scent. Blood would be best, but hair or even nail trimmings would suffice. Did the Nandoran leave a hairbrush or comb behind?"

"I've no idea, but no-one has been in his room today. If you wish to have it searched, Nicoras will provide a squad of guardsmen."

"There's no need of that, my Lord. I've seen the guardsmen's idea of searching. I'll go myself and I'll find more than they would I'll wager."

"Very well. Keep me informed of anything you find."

The tall grey-haired sorcerer turned to leave and permitted himself a small smile of satisfaction. Now Lord Hercival would learn the value of his arts.

***

Ezrin stood on the threshold of the tower room and looked carefully round it to take in its entirety. It measured roughly three paces square; nearly half its area was taken up by the pile of straw that had served as a bed. There was a rough chair, a wooden chest that still contained the clothes Maldwyn had been sent from Nandor after he was captured, and a bucket. The bucket had been emptied recently Ezrin observed, as he surveyed the chamber, all the better for his comfort. Theoretically it should be possible to obtain a reading from ordure, but it was not something he was prepared to countenance. He moved to the chest, lifted the lid, and there on top of the clothes was a hairbrush and comb. He picked them up and turned them over in his hands; there was plenty of hair caught in the teeth of the comb.

"You cannot escape me, Maldwyn of Nandor," he said.

***

"This is him, my Lord."

Nicoras indicated the man flanked by two armed guards standing at the door to Lord Hercival's chamber. Lord Hercival looked at the bedraggled figure before him. Tancred's once rich clothes were torn and stained, his face was scratched and dirty and Lord Hercival caught the rank smell of him from where he sat three paces away. He did not, as Lord Hercival judged, look dangerous, but there was an air of defiance in his stare.

"Dismiss the guard, but you stay," Lord Hercival said to Nicoras. With a nod to the guard, Nicoras pushed Tancred into the centre of the room and took his place with his back to the closed door.

"Tancred of Nandor," Lord Hercival said evenly and was gratified to see Tancred stiffen at his name, the defiance replaced by anxiety. "Yes. I know who you are, and what you came here to do. I would like you to tell me where your cousin Maldwyn is."

"You think I have no honour?" blustered Tancred.

"I don't believe you can afford honour," said Lord Hercival calmly. "We will find him with or without your aid, but you have an opportunity to help yourself. I suggest you take it. I could hang you and no-one would raise an eyebrow."

Tancred seemed to deflate further at these words. "I can be of much more use to you alive, and perhaps we both have an opportunity to help each other," he said uncertainly.

Lord Hercival eyed him suspiciously. "What do you mean?"

"I would think we share a common situation, you and I. I am heir to Earl Baldwin after Maldwyn. If he falls, I inherit. You are the second in line to Sarazan. I would call that uncommonly similar." Lord Hercival looked up at Nicoras. The man's battered face was unreadable.

"And what are the consequences of this similarity?" said Lord Hercival evenly.

"We are in positions where we can assist one another."

"In what way should I need your aid?"

"Second sons are always dependant on their father's good opinion in a way that first-born are not." Tancred paused to examine the effect of his words before continuing. "I could ensure your father's good opinion of you."

"How?" Lord Hercival fixed Tancred with a hard stare.

"If I were Earl of Nandor, Sarazan would find me a loyal and reliable ally."

Lord Hercival snorted derisively. "Why bother? Why not send a tenth of our strength and stamp your pathetic little army flat, then take Nandor for ourselves? Why I myself might be Earl of Nandor then."

"Oh you could certainly do that, but would it be worth your

trouble? For trouble it most certainly would be."

Lord Hercival laughed. "You think you could stand against us?"

"Militarily no, but do you think Nandor completely friendless at court? How many would take side with us simply to oppose you? Consider the example of Caldon, now in outright rebellion against the High King, and all because they moved against Darien. Moreover, have you considered the cost of garrisoning Nandor? It is a poor place, and you would never recover in taxes what it would cost you to hold it. How much better if the Earl of Nandor was a loyal vassal paying a measure of tribute each year for the protecting hand of Sarazan?"

Lord Hercival looked up Nicoras. "What do you think?"

Nicoras paused for a moment before speaking. "He's right about the cost of sustaining a garrison, and there's no reason of strategy for us to hold Nandor. The proposal has some merit."

"And what would be your price for this?"

"That my cousin Maldwyn does not survive his recapture. That should be easy to accomplish. He's stupid enough to fight any number of your troops when he's found," said Tancred, a small smile of triumph on his lips.

"So you will assist us in the recapture of your cousin?" asked Lord Hercival mildly. "Where is he then?"

"Alas, that I do not know," said Tancred.

"You ask me to trust you in great matters of state, yet you refuse me the littlest aid that would advance our cause. What game are you playing?" Lord Hercival half rose from his seat, fists clenched in anger.

"No game, my Lord. I assure you. You misunderstand me," said Tancred hurriedly. "We had no plan for the escape of Maldwyn. We knew nothing of Sarazan before we arrived and we laid no schemes. I truly do not know where he is now, or where he is headed. We had nothing planned, nothing at all. I can only tell you of the two men with him."

"That would be a start," said Lord Hercival.

"One of them is an ordinary guardsman. A native of Sarazan. He is a dirty little sneakthief and pickpocket by the name of Davo. The other is from Darien. He is very young, and goes by the name of Aron, son of Eamon. He is dark of hair and eye, slim and dangerous with a blade. He murdered the swordmaster at Nandor and impressed my uncle enough that he sent him with us. He'll be the only one who knows where they are going. Watch for him, and hang him when you catch him."

"That is all you have?" said Lord Hercival.

"Yes, my Lord. Why should I hide anything from you?" Tancred paused. "My friend."

"Why indeed?" said Lord Hercival coolly. "Why indeed? Well then - friend. I have no doubt you would appreciate a bath, a change of clothes and a decent meal. Nicoras, have our friend escorted to the guest quarters."

Nicoras opened the door and spoke briefly to the guards outside, then conducted Tancred out of the room.

"A moment, if you please, Nicoras," Lord Hercival said, "and shut the door." Nicoras did as he was bidden. "What did you think of our new friend?"

"What he has told us accords with what we already know. The thief and the youth. But it has cost him nothing. He is, I think, an eel, my Lord; that would twist and turn in your hand if you tried to grasp him."

Lord Hercival smiled. "But eels may be caught in a net, eh Nicoras? I think it would be prudent to place a guard at the door to our friend's chamber. I would not wish to lose another Nandoran guest. You may go, and send the scribe to me. I have a letter I wish to send to Earl Baldwin."

CHAPTER 16

The fat-bellied cargo boat ploughed its way down river at a decent speed, its sails filled by a fresh north-westerly breeze. Aron opened one eye as the sunlight played across his face. He paused for a moment to recollect where he was. The water sang under the blunt prow of the boat and he remembered the mad dash through the streets and alleys of Sarazan, the driving fear of pursuit as he, Davo and Maldwyn ran from the lakeside. They had collapsed with exhaustion and relief when the skipper had cast off as soon as they had stepped aboard, then huddled together on deck in their blankets as the current carried them away from the dark city. They were safe, for the moment at least. With Maldwyn and Davo sprawled on the deck sleeping off the night's excitement, Aron savoured the peace of the moment, knowing it could not last. It was tempting to think of the reward awaiting him in Nandor, but the reality was they were getting further away from Nandor with every hour that passed. He had hoped to slip quietly out of Sarazan unnoticed, but men had died. He had not intended this, but their deaths had raised the stakes and made pursuit certain.

The captain appeared at the head of the ladder that led from the two cabins below deck. He was a plain-looking man with thinning dark hair who had looked Aron in the eye as he stated his price and shook his hand firmly when Aron handed over the coins. He had offered him a cabin, but the price had been too high so the three of them were deck passengers. Aron hoped for dry weather; otherwise it would be a miserable trip. The captain glanced across at Aron as he made his way to the steersman at the stern of the craft and nodded.

As Aron woke up more, he became aware of how long it was since he had eaten. He reached into his pack and pulled out the dried meat and oatcakes he had bought the previous night. The captain walked over from the stern.

"The price includes meals. We'll not cheat travellers on my ship."

"Thank you for reminding me," said Aron with relief. Their funds had not stretched to more than a few days' rations.

"It's not a feast, but it's what I'm having," said the captain. Aron followed him to the head of the stairway and waited while he went below. He returned with a small loaf of bread and a lump of strong yellow cheese.

"How long to Oxport?" asked Aron.

"Five days, if the weather holds. We've a full cargo, so I've no plans to stop along the way."

The captain looked directly at Aron as if measuring him for a suit of clothes. *He's wondering what or who we're running from*, thought Aron.

"You cause me no trouble, and you'll be safe on my ship," he said and returned to the helm.

As he ate Aron sat and watched the scenery slip by. The air was mild; sunlight dodged between the clouds, and the green of leaves on the trees showed spring was well advanced. The country on either bank was extensively farmed rolling pasture with every so often a village clustered around a landing jetty where small streams joined the river and swelled it to a broad, even flow. Occasionally they passed ships being towed upstream by teams of horses, and there was an exchange of greetings and news shouted across the water. At the junction of a major tributary they passed a large town with boats of all sizes tied up to the many landing wharves. Aron scanned the wharves anxiously looking out for someone who might be watching for them. He saw no such observer but felt that that meant nothing.

Sometime after midday Maldwyn and Davo awoke; a crewman came with bread and cheese which they consumed with relish. As Maldwyn ate, Aron was aware that the Nandoran was studying him intently, and prepared himself for the inevitable questions. Finally Maldwyn finished his meal, brushed off the crumbs and looked directly at Aron.

"Davo I know well, but who are you and how do you come to be my rescuer?"

Aron smiled. "Easy enough to answer. My name is Aron, and your father sent me." *And your mother persuaded me*, he added silently.

"Surely not you two alone?"

"No. There were six of us. Your cousin Tancred was in charge."

Maldwyn's face registered surprise.

"Not Captain Thalon?" Maldwyn asked. "I would have thought him the man to command such an expedition."

"Too obviously Nandoran in his accent. Your father sent those men who could pass without suspicion in Sarazan."

"And where is my cousin now, and the rest of the party?"

"Don't rightly know, my Lord," Davo chipped in. "Didn't come back the night afore last and then the Sarazan guard attacked the inn."

"After that we took the first chance we had to come for you," said Aron.

"Is it possible they were taken by Sarazan?" asked Maldwyn.

"Probable enough," said Aron gloomily. "And so by now Sarazan knows exactly who they are looking for."

Maldwyn was silent for a moment, his brow puckered in thought, then he burst out. "We must go back and rescue them. Honour demands that as Tancred risked all for me then I, in my turn, must take a similar risk for him."

Aron resisted the temptation to reach out and strangle him. Davo looked similarly dismayed.

"With respect my Lord, this is most unwise," said Aron slowly and tactfully. "Firstly, we don't know where they are. We're only guessing that Sarazan holds them. Secondly, there are three of us, with little money and few weapons. Thirdly, the whole of Sarazan is now roused against us. I don't know how many of their guardsmen died in your escape, but you can be sure that it was enough that they'll pursue us with all their might. We'll be very fortunate if we evade them ourselves. We have to look to our own survival before we can worry about Tancred. My task, as your father laid it upon me, is to return you to Nandor." Aron sat back hoping that Maldwyn had enough sense to acknowledge the realities of their situation.

"Honour can take no account of such things. I know what must be done and I command you do it."

Aron closed his eyes and took a deep breath before he answered. "I am no sworn man of Nandor. You do not command me."

Maldwyn looked taken aback.

"Did not my father command you on the errand?"

"He did. He held that I owed Nandor a debt, and this was the way to pay it."

"What debt?"

"I killed a guardsman."

"Who?" Maldwyn's voice rose in register as he grew more animated.

"I believe his name was Marek. It was in a tavern beside the marketplace."

"Big Marek? The weaponmaster? How? Is this so, Davo?"

Maldwyn seemed stunned by this and turned to the little man who had sat silently beside them.

Davo nodded. "True my Lord, an I seen him take every one of the lads one by one with practice woods. Cleaner an better'n Marek ever was."

Maldwyn looked hard at Aron and said nothing. Aron decided to press his advantage.

"My advice is that we continue to Oxport," he said. "That is what I intend to do."

There was silence for some moments then Maldwyn spoke. "What will we do in Oxport?"

Aron let out the breath he had been holding, the peak of the crisis had passed.

"We should be able to find a ship to take us up the coast. We can trek into Nandor over the western range. Spring should be well on by then and it won't be too hard on the hills."

"It'll take a good long time though," said Maldwyn. "And all the while Tancred is in the hands of Sarazan."

"True, but I see no other way. We may be able to send a faster message to your father from Oxport to let him know that at least you are free. It would strengthen his hand in dealing with the Duke."

"Can we not do that before Oxport?"

"I know a few people in Oxport who will shelter us for a short time. Before then we are on our own. Even when we are beyond Sarazan's borders, the Duke has a long reach," Aron said looking around as if he expected to see the Duke's cavalry on the riverbank.

Maldwyn fell silent for a while and then asked for news of Nandor. This brought Davo out of his shell, he was happy to relate the gossip of the town and castle. Aron hoped the little man would have the wit to keep quiet about Maldwyn's sisters and their attachment to him.

***

"I have found him, my Lord." Ezrin stood in the doorway of Lord Hercival's chamber. Nicoras looked up sharply from a map that he and Lord Hercival were studying, and noted that Ezrin seemed taller and more confident than at their previous meeting. Dust motes danced in the late afternoon sun streaming in through the narrow slit of the window lighting the table and leaving the rest of the chamber in shadow.

"Where?" Lord Hercival's question was as sharp as an order.

"He is on a boat heading downriver," the sorcerer replied. "The other two are with him."

"Yes, yes, but where? How far downriver?" Lord Hercival scrabbled with the map to find the course of the river.

"That is less easy to determine. He doesn't know and there were no landmarks that I recognised."

Ezrin's confidence drained away and Lord Hercival's face tightened into a scowl.

"What do you mean? How can you have found him and not know where he is?"

Lord Hercival stood back and his face was lost in shadow as Ezrin's eyes struggled to make the adjustment from the sunlit table.

"It's more a limitation of Maldwyn than of the magic. The hair he left behind preserves a link to him in the spirit world. I can follow this to him, and then I can see through his eyes, and to some extent know his mind. The trouble is his eyes see nothing that I recognise. He doesn't know where he is so I cannot pluck it from his mind."

"So this magic is useless to us," said Lord Hercival.

"Not entirely, my Lord," Nicoras intervened from the shadows." We now know they are on the river. We will find whose boat they are on soon enough, and where that boat is bound. In the meantime, I suggest the wizard here goes back to watching Maldwyn until he sees something he recognises."

"I don't know the river very well, my Lord," Ezrin turned to Hercival.

"Never mind, we can send someone who does to sit with you. You describe what you see to them until they recognise something. See to it, Nicoras," commanded Hercival. "Thank you, Ezrin, do as we suggest and you will yet earn our gratitude."

The wizard, his mouth a thin line of anger, withdrew.

"I begin to understand why my grandfather had so little time for wizards, Nicoras," said Lord Hercival with a heavy sigh.

"I think you are being overly hard with him, my Lord," said Nicoras. "He has found them for us, and we may very well need him further."

Hercival snorted in reply before speaking. "What resources do we have down that way to catch our fugitives?"

"I would guess they are already past Thrieve. There are two garrisoned towns further downriver, my Lord; but if you'll take my advice we should not take them in either place."

"Why?" Hercival's brow furrowed again.

"Things have a way of going wrong when there are too many people about, in my experience. Also, in the strictest legal sense, we do not have the right to stop a boat on the river. By the treaty your father signed with Oxport, we have no right to close the river to navigation or hinder trade on it."

"Damnation, Nicoras!" Lord Hercival slammed his fist onto the table. "Can I not do what I please in my own land?"

"With respect my Lord, it is your father's land. This is why I suggest we take them in some out of the way corner where there will be no-one to hinder us and no witnesses."

Lord Hercival stood rigid for a moment, but then unclenched his fists and turned back to the map. "Yes, of course. Thank you, Nicoras, practical as ever."

CHAPTER 17

Maldwyn spoke. "Davo said you killed ten Sarazan guardsmen when they attacked your lodgings." He and Aron were leaning on the rail of the boat watching the sun sink behind the low range of hills that formed the edge of the river valley. "I can see why you don't want to return."

"I see no sense in putting my hand into the wasps' nest more times than necessary," Aron said, scanning the bank. The boat had moored for the night some five paces out into the stream; enough trees grew right down to the towpath to provide plenty of cover for anyone trying to approach unseen, though the river seemed deep around them. Aron felt uncomfortable at this, but it was beyond his control; the river had enough snags and mudbanks to make the most foolhardy skipper take pause before attempting to navigate it in the dark.

"Davo exaggerates the tale, it was only four guardsmen," Aron added.

"That is still an amazing feat," said Maldwyn his eyes shining with admiration.

"I had them at a disadvantage. They were coming into ground they didn't know, and they didn't know what they were facing."

"You're too modest. If I'd done that, I'd have some minstrel make a song about it. It would make a fine ballad; you killed the weaponmaster of Nandor, despatched four Sarazan guardsmen and singlehandedly lifted me from a heavily defended castle with less fuss than a herdsman rounding up a flock of sheep, yet you're no older than me." Maldwyn stopped and looked at Aron, his face suddenly serious. "This is the stuff of legend, Aron. How is it that you're here? Who are you? I mean no intrusion and I owe you a great debt, but I'd like to know whose hands I'm in."

Aron recognised the offer of friendship implicit in Maldwyn's question. Davo had been incurious to a fault about Aron and, in all honesty, Aron was dubious about the merits of the little man's friendship. Maldwyn was a completely different case. For a start he was honest and almost painfully transparent. Full of impossible notions of honour but, once his friendship was given, Aron guessed, intensely loyal. Aron would need good friends if they ever managed to return to Nandor.

"It's no intrusion, and you are right. If we are to win through to Nandor we have to trust each other. It has been a while since I have had companions and I've dropped out of the habit of talking about myself."

Aron looked up and saw Maldwyn's blue eyes fixed on him. *No lies for this man,* he thought.

"I was born the son of the guard sergeant at the castle of Darien. My mother was a serving girl in a tavern in Darien; the fever took her when I was very young; I have no memory of her. I spent my childhood years in the castle of Darien mothered by the cooks and housemaids and spoiled by the guardsmen. The Earl took me in to be a companion to his son Cordra who was of an age with me. He thought Cordra would learn better if he had a companion at his lessons. We become fast friends; I was given a room in the castle and had all the lessons Cordra had. So, in due course, I was taught by the weaponmaster of Darien as if I was a nobleman's son. Cordra was an average pupil, but my tutor soon found that I had a talent. After that he devoted all the time he was allowed to teaching me."

Aron paused there and looked east to where the first stars shone out in the deep purple sky; east towards far distant, lost Darien.

"I heard of the fall of Darien," said Maldwyn as if unsure whether he was trespassing on painful ground.

"Aye, and what did you hear?" Aron laughed, his voice hard and bitter. "Did you hear of the three months of siege? Did you hear how the Saxish mercenaries the Earl had hired turned their coats and opened the fortress to Caldon? Did you hear of how the Earl and his men were hanged from the walls of their own castle?" He turned away from Maldwyn then and spat into the water.

"How did you escape their fate?" Maldwyn asked cautiously.

"I was already in the Holy City with Cordra. When the Earl got word of the advance of Caldon's forces he sent us with the ladies of the household to his wife's family."

"Didn't your honour burn at this? How could you bear to be sent away like a maid?" Maldwyn burst out. "I would have insisted on staying."

"Then you would be dead too, and for no purpose. Would two extra blades have made a difference? I think not. The only thing that would have made a difference would have been the discovery of the Saxish treachery. No, Maldwyn, only a fool puts all his eggs in the one basket, and that is as true of Earls as farmers. Had we stayed, the House of Darien would now be extinct. As it is, Cordra is Earl of Darien. One day he will reclaim his inheritance, and I will stand beside him." Aron's fists clenched with determination.

"And Nandor shall stand beside you." Maldwyn reached out and grasped Aron's hand. "I swear it upon the honour of my house."

"Thank you. I shall remember when the time comes." Aron was genuinely moved by Maldwyn's impulsive offer, though he wondered if Maldwyn would still feel that way when the time came.

"How did this bring you to Nandor? It is a long way from the Holy City."

"That is a tale that does not reflect well on me," Aron sighed. "I was shown great kindness in the Holy City. Many people opened their hearts to us of Darien when the news of the Earl's fall broke. Cordra's mother is sister to the Duke of Kyria who stands close to the High King. He took us into his household and arranged for me to be admitted to the Academy."

"The Academy!" gasped Maldwyn, "I should have realised."

"Cordra thought it would be an honour for Darien, and that an Academy trained weaponmaster would be a useful companion for an Earl-in-exile." said Aron remembering the joy the news had brought him. As he recalled he had grinned incessantly for a week.

"Is it as wonderful as I've heard?"

"That depends on what you've heard. If you expect splendid buildings then you would indeed be disappointed. Nor are there great numbers of blademasters; hardly more than half a dozen fulltime. Most of the instruction is by blademasters who are in the Holy City with the nobles who employ them. There are, I suppose, around thirty students at various stages of study from freshmen up to newly graduated masters looking for their first post. Most of the pupils are from households which already have a blademaster or are near the Holy City; otherwise they wouldn't have got a recommendation in the first place. I'm the first student from Darien."

"I dreamed of going, but never got a recommendation. Nandor could not afford an Academy-trained blademaster. That's something I shall put right. I'll speak to father when we get back, with your help of course. But how did that bring you to Nandor? I would never have left such a situation."

"As I said, the tale doesn't reflect well on me. I was happy at the Academy, and I did well enough at the disciplines, but something one of the masters said led me astray."

"How could that be?" said Maldwyn, puzzlement in his voice.

Aron paused, wondering how Maldwyn would react; would he understand the doubt that had crept through Aron's mind at the instructor's words?

"It was one of the blademasters. He spoke to the advanced students seeking, I think, to caution us against overconfidence. He said that it was all very well being the finest bladesman in the exercise yard, but it was completely different when the man before you was a real enemy. He said he'd seen the most excellent swordsmen freeze when the moment came to kill and then be killed themselves because of their hesitation. He was looking straight at me when he said it."

"You felt he insulted your honour? Questioned your bravery?"

"No. He made me doubt whether I would kill when the time came. I needed to know whether I could do it. I would be no use to Darien as the finest swordsman in the exercise yard who couldn't bring himself to kill."

"What did you do? Challenge the instructor?" asked Maldwyn.

"Certainly not. He was one of the finest swordsmen I've ever seen. I wouldn't have lasted a minute against him. You may have heard that in the Holy City tavern fights are a public entertainment and much money changes hands in wagers."

"What kind of fights? Brawls?"

"No, swordfights. Like the arena, but less formal. The oddsmakers pay the magistrates to keep the Watch from interfering." From the shocked expression on Maldwyn's face Aron knew he had not heard of this. "I became attached to a group of Darien exiles who were sworn to hunt down the servants of Caldon. Usually this took the form of goading them into a tavern fight and then I killed them."

In the silence that followed Aron remembered the first fight: the cries of the crowd, the burning lustful eyes of his target as he savoured the easy kill he thought awaited him, and the way those eyes had faded to a blank distant stare as his life flooded out of him through the gash in his throat. Those eyes had haunted his sleep for a long time.

"So what went wrong?" askd Maldwyn

"I suppose I was too successful and became too well known. The Caldons recognised me and wouldn't be drawn into fights, and I wouldn't kill them if they didn't draw a blade. It was getting too close to murder. Then they sent an assassin after me."

"How did you survive the assassin?"

"Luck. Pure blind luck. He shot at me in the street with a crossbow, but the fellow I was with looked quite like me, and he shot the wrong man. It seemed a good idea to leave the city for a while after that."

"How many did you kill?"

Aron paused for a moment. "Nine, I think; ten if you include the assassin." Maldwyn stared wide-eyed at him as he thought about what Aron had told him. Aron guessed that Maldwyn had never killed a man and that the same doubt that Aron had faced nagged at him. Somewhere upstream there was a splash followed by a second. Aron's right hand jumped to the knife in his left sleeve, then he relaxed. "Just a fish," he said.

Maldwyn stared at the knife for a long moment before speaking. "You made no mention of a sweetheart."

"No. I haven't met one yet," said Aron. *Or have I?* "The life I've been leading the last few years has kept me away from the kind of girl that would win my heart." He looked down at the water with a frown as he remembered how Caldon's men had tried to trap him with a pretty tavernmaid and so nearly succeeded.

"So where did you go from the Holy City?" said Maldwyn after an embarassed pause. "And how on earth did you finish up in Nandor?"

"I wandered without plan or direction hiring out as a bodyguard or teaching the blade to the clumsy sons of gentlemen. In Oxport, I taught the blade for a season and I happened across a Saxishman who had been at Darien. I dealt with him, but succeeded in bring another half dozen of them down on me, one a wizard of some power. My friends in Oxport advised me to lose myself for a while and I hired as a caravan guard for a wool merchant trading in Nandor. So that is how I came to be in the tavern by the market where Marek and Davo were drinking. I'd been in the town less than an hour before I killed Marek."

"So it was the blindest chance that made you my rescuer. Surely this shows the gods are on our side. If father had sent out across the realm to find the finest and boldest man, he could have done no better. And he found you in a tavern in Nandor market." Maldwyn's laugh echoed across the river.

"Not so." Aron smiled. "Marek found me, though I daresay he regretted it."

They talked as the sky grew dark and the mist rose from the river the cloak to banks in deep shadow. Maldwyn was as keen as his sisters had been to know about life in the Holy City though his interests were more focused on the Academy of Weaponmasters and the various tournaments at which the nobles jousted. Aron did his best to satisfy Maldwyn's curiosity and tried to make him understand that much greater victories were won by smooth-tongued men in the drawing rooms of palaces than ever were won by feats of arms upon the field. Eventually the talk slowed as full night descended to the point that the two young men could no longer see each other.

CHAPTER 18

The old river captain was sitting beside Ezrin as the sorcerer hunched over his crystal describing what he saw through Maldwyn's eyes. "I know where they are," he said. "I know that hill with the ruined walls and the trees grown up through them. You sure they're beeches?'
"They're beeches," said the sorcerer without looking up. "There's a bend in the river coming up. The fortifications are on a hill that sticks out and the river bends around it."
"That's certain then. I know right where they are. No doubt at all."
Ezrin sat up and covered his crystal with a dark cloth. "Excellent. I think we deserve some lunch, and then we'll go and see Lord Hercival."

***

"Are you quite sure of this?" Lord Hercival leaned across the table towards the two men who stood before him.
"I've been thirty years on the river, my Lord and the Master described the ruins at Castle Bend exactly." The old riverman spoke with calm authority.
"Good. Then we must consider how best to net these fish." Lord Hercival turned to Nicoras. "Twenty men should suffice. Have the garrison at Erkimar send a patrol up to meet them."
"Very good, my Lord. Do you have a plan as to precisely how they'll take them?" Nicoras replied. Lord Hercival paused. *No you haven't, my Lord* thought Nicoras.
"It's no easy matter to seize a ship, my Lord," the old riverman said. "Is it something your lads would've practised?"
"No. These are infantrymen of the garrison. They would be proficient in spear and blade against an enemy or an unruly crowd."
As Nicoras spoke, Lord Hercival scowled silently.
"There's none that'd be watermen and used to boats, my Lord?" said the riverman.
"None," said Nicoras for Lord Hercival. "How would you go about seizing a boat on the river? In thirty years you must have seen it done."

"It'd best be done with two boats and a rope stretched between 'em. You come up on either side of 'em. The rope holds 'em fast an' you go in from both sides at once." The riverman gestured with his hands to show how it should be done.

"Could the Erkimar garrison do such a thing, Nicoras?" asked Lord Hercival.

"I doubt it, my Lord. They've no-one with any notion of boat handling. You could drown half the garrison."

"Then there has to be another way. Why can we not seize them when they're moored-up for the night?" asked Lord Hercival.

"Same problem, my Lord. They'll moor out in the stream so you'd need boatmen to get to them. It'd be too easy for bandits to seize a boat otherwise."

"How then do we achieve this simple, yet seemingly so difficult, task?" asked Lord Hercival. There was silence around the room.

"I believe I may be able to offer a solution, my Lord." They all turned to stare at Ezrin. "Is there perchance some small village with a landing stage or an inn beside the river, good and isolated where they might be seized without hindrance?"

"Plenty of places answer that description, but why should they come ashore before Oxport?" said the old riverman.

"If you select the place, my Lord then, by my arts, I shall force them to land."

Lord Hercival stared hard at Ezrin. "You can ensure they must land?" he said sceptically.

"I have no doubt of it, my Lord," said the sorcerer firmly.

"There is an inn beside a ferry crossing some way down the river," said the riverman. "There would be time for your men to march up from Erkimar before the boat reached it. If the wizard here can make them land then where else would they go? There is nothing there but the inn. But how will you do it? The river is broad and slow-flowing with no obstacles."

"Broad and slow, eh? All the better for what I have in mind." Ezrin smiled mysteriously. "They will land."

"Very well," said Lord Herival dismissing Ezrin and the riverman with a wave of his hand. "Nicoras draft a message to the commander at Erkimar. A troop of infantry to the inn at the ferry. They are to lie hidden and seize the Nandorans when they land. You know what Maldwyn looks like, but get a description of the other two from that weasel Tancred, and don't forget to warn them about the Darien bladesman. Send three birds; I want to be sure this message arrives. Have the commander take charge of this himself. We know what these people are capable of, Nicoras, and I want them alive."

***

Captain Elthorn, commander of the Erkimar garrison, frowned as he read the message the pigeon keeper had brought him. "I don't believe it. Three birds for this," he said irritably to Lieutenant Gerom, his second in command.

"What is it sir? Is it war?" asked Gerom.

"No. Nothing so momentous. Lord Hercival commands me personally to take a troop to the Ferryboat Inn upriver and arrest three fugitives who will be landed there from a riverboat."

"They must be very important for three birds to be sent though sir."

"I hardly think so. Listen to this." He read from the despatch. "Lord Maldwyn of Nandor, who is about twenty years, tall, thin and awkward with long dark hair that sticks out like a stork's nest. A grave threat to the realm no doubt. The other two are an older man and a youth of similar age to Maldwyn. The older man is short, slim and sharp-featured; he is a thief and pickpocket, but cowardly and unlikely to be violent. The youth is from Darien. He is tall, slim, dark and apparently very handy with his blades. His Lordship warns us of him most particularly."

"Be worth taking a few crossbows then," said Gerom. "What's a Darien accent sound like? Can't say I've ever heard one."

"I've no idea, but we're going to find out. Good idea about the crossbowmen, Gerom. His Lordship commands me take these men alive if at all possible, and there is no sense in crossing swords with a bladesman if we don't have to. I'll take twenty men, that should be enough."

"The Ferryboat Inn is on the east bank, isn't it sir?"

"Yes, it is. Therefore we must conduct ourselves discreetly."

***

"Alas. Truly the gods have deserted us."

Earl Baldwin drained the wine jug of its contents and hurled it across the hall of Castle Nandor to shatter against the wall. Lord Hercival's courier had just left and the four Nandoran guardsmen who had journeyed with him from Sarazan stood around embarrassed by the Earl's reaction.

"What on earth is all the noise about?" Lady Alice appeared at the foot of the stairs that led to the upper floors of the castle. "What is happening, Baldwin? Is it Maldwyn?"

Seeing her husband's distress she hurried across the hall to him as fast as her long skirts would allow. Celaine appeared on the stairs and scurried down after her.

"Send for Thalon, muster the men," declared Earl Baldwin. "We march on Sarazan."

"Why? What has happened?" said Lady Alice.

"Our best hope is defeated. Sarazan hold Tancred for ransom of five hundred crowns. Nandor is ruined."

"Slow down, Baldwin. Tell me what happened," said Lady Alice as she reached her husband's side.

He thrust the message scroll at her. "Read it and see for yourself."

"What is it, mama?" asked Celaine.

Lady Alice quickly scanned the message. "Sarazan have Tancred."

Celaine, her face set grim, spat out a short and unflattering description of her cousin. Lady Alice looked somewhat surprised at Celaine's reaction, but said nothing.

"What are we to do, mama?" said Celaine.

"Summon every man and boy and ride on Sarazan," cried Earl Baldwin. He stumbled over to the cabinet where the wine was kept. One of the guardsmen started to move then looked quizzically at Lady Alice.

"Don't be absurd! You will do no such thing," Lady Alice said firmly. "But fetch Captain Thalon all the same if you please, Thomi." The guardsman turned and headed for the door. The Countess stared at the three remaining men as if seeing them for the first time.

"You three were with the expedition; Kriss, isn't it? Tell me what happened."

The guardsman called Kriss looked at the other two shamefacedly before he spoke.

"We was in a tavern in Sarazan."

"Looking out for information and that," interrupted one of his companions.

"We was with Lord Tancred, under his orders and all," said the third.

"Go on," said the Countess her voice tight with emotion.

"We got into a fight and the city watch came and took us. They didn't know who we was, so the magistrates set us to breaking rocks. But they must've found out 'cos the Duke's guardsmen come to the quarry and took us to the castle." Kriss recounted the tale with his two comrades nodding assent. "They took Lord Tancred off and put us in a pit in the dungeon. Then they came and said we were going back to Nandor 'cos they had a message to go to Lord Baldwin, m'lady."

"There were seven of you as I recall. Where are the other two, Davo and the Darien boy?" asked Earl Baldwin.

"I don't know, my Lord. Lord Tancred took against them and left them back at the lodgings when we went out into the town. The Darien boy said he'd found someone who'd sell us information, but Lord Tancred wouldn't give him the money."

"So they're still in Sarazan?" said Lady Alice sharply.

"Suppose so, my Lady. The castle was in a right fuss when we left, but we didn't see them, did we lads?"

The other two murmured negatives in chorus.

"You sent for me, my Lord." Captain Thalon entered the hall with Thomi a step behind him.

"Yes Thalon," Earl Baldwin and Lady Alice spoke in unison and then stopped, waiting for the other to continue. Lady Alice was first to continue.

"Lord Tancred has been captured by Sarazan and they are demanding ransom for him. It seems that we have no other option than to plead our case before the High King and throw ourselves on his mercy. We shall need to leave as soon as possible. Please see to the arrangements."

"And you really think that he will take our side and forget that Nandor stood against him?" said Earl Baldwin.

"Is this not the same king who spoke of healing and reconciliation and justice for all?" replied Lady Alice.

"And then filled his council with his friends?" said Earl Baldwin.

"Do you see another choice? One that does not bring ruin upon us?"

Earl Baldwin snorted in reply.

"Very good, my Lady," said Thalon crisply. "Who will be going?"

"Why, we all shall. It is high time the girls were presented at court." With that Lady Alice turned and swept across the hall towards the stairs followed by Celaine.

CHAPTER 19

Aron stood on the deck watching the countryside slip by as the flat-bottomed boat continued on its way. The river here was broad, and the steersman had to keep a lookout for other craft; mostly the coracles of the fisherfolk whose poor villages they passed every so often, but occasionally another trader passed by with shouts and a waving of signal flags. From this Aron gathered that there were no obstacles ahead of them.

"We should reach Erkan by sunset," the captain said to Aron, his words plucked away by the sharp breeze. "We've a good wind and the weather looks set fair."

He pointed towards the west; there was a distant line of dark cloud, but most of the sky was sprinkled with broken white cloud that the sun was trying to peer through.

Aron moved slowly towards the stern where Maldwyn and Davo sat. Aron was bored; Davo was playing dice with Maldwyn, trying to teach him some trick or other that Aron had no interest in. He reached for his pack and dug out his whetstone and did what he always did when he had time to pass, sharpened his knives.

After a while, Aron became aware that the air had grown colder. He looked up; on the eastern bank there was a long two storey building with a jetty beside it. On the other bank was a similar jetty with a ferryboat moored to it. Looking skyward, he saw dark clouds piled up blotting out the sun.

The captain followed Aron's gaze and walked along the deck toward him.

"I don't like the look of that," he said. "Don't feel right. The wind's telling me one thing and my eyes another. Gonna come right over us that lot." He gestured with a grimy finger. "I think I'll shorten sail."

He called out to the deckhand, who emerged from below deck and began to take down one of the sails.

"Good tavern that," he again gestured with the grimy finger. "Good place to stop a night, the Ferryboat, reckon I'll call in there on the trip back." He looked at the clouds again. "Them ain't natural, don't like it at all."

He turned and made his way back to the steersman. Aron stood staring at the boiling clouds for a minute or two and then stepped over to where Davo and Maldwyn were still focused on their dice.

"Get your gear together. There's bad weather coming."

Maldwyn looked up. "Time for one more game?" he said.

"No. Now," said Aron firmly.

The first squall hit the boat within a minute, heeling it over where it teetered for agonising moments on the point of capsize before righting itself. The captain shouted for his crew to get the sails off the mast as he fought for control of the steering oar. The crewmen ran for the ropes holding the sails and loosed them so that the sails tumbled to the deck. The boat righted itself just before the next squall hit and, with the sails down, was buffeted but didn't come so close to capsize. Aron, Davo and Maldwyn clung desperately to the rail as the wind beat at them and waves broke over the deck. The captain, having won his struggle for control, steered for the safety of the riverbank as more squalls battered at his craft, but the storm hadn't finished with them.

Davo looked up from where he clung towards the west; the wind swept his lank hair from his face and he shrieked in terror. Aron followed his gaze and felt a heart-stopping moment of intense fear. A dark pillar of whirling, raging water rose out of the surface of the river and climbed into the boiling clouds. Furious gusts of wind tore at the boat's rigging as the waterspout raced straight for them.

Aron reached for his pack and took a tight grip of it, wrapping the straps around his wrist, and waited for the impact.

"Get hold of your pack, Davo," he yelled at the top of his voice over the roaring wind. "It'll keep you afloat."

The ravening tower of water circled for a moment then dashed the final distance towards the boat. Aron, Davo and Maldwyn were flung through the air as the craft was plucked from the water and lifted skyward before it was spat out to crash back into the raging waters upside-down.

Aron surfaced surrounded by debris. He spat out a mouthful of bitter river water and struck out for a barrel that bobbed a few armslengths away. He grabbed it and pulled himself up to look around. There was no sign of the waterspout, the clouds no longer churned and the surface of the river was covered with gear from the ruined boat.

Davo, splashing wildly, broke surface ten paces distant. Aron gathered the pack that was still attached to his wrist and swam over to him. He managed to disentangle himself from the little man before Davo drowned them both and got him to clutch a floating spar instead. Maldwyn was further away but was swimming noisily towards them.

Between the two of them, Maldwyn and Aron propelled Davo to shallow enough water so that they could wade to the bank. Aron dragged his pack to dry land and then removed his shirt. He checked that all his blades had survived the soaking and then he began to wring the water out of the shirt. Looking out across the river he saw the Captain and a crewman swimming for the far bank, and offered silent thanks that the decent man had been spared from drowning.

"What on earth was that?" gasped Maldwyn as he sat on the bank to recover from his ordeal.

"Nothing natural, I think," said Aron. "It came straight for us and then disappeared as soon as it had run over us. That sounds like wizardry, powerful wizardry."

"Sarazan?" asked Maldwyn.

"Who else?"

"How'd they find us?" gasped Davo, still breathless.

"You know Sarazan well enough to guess how long our sailing would have remained secret. And who knows what wizards can do?"

"So they'll be able to find us again," said Maldwyn.

"Yes, probably," said Aron. " So let's get moving."

The three of them gathered up their gear and pushed through the undergrowth towards a muddy path that led along the river margins in the direction of the tavern they had seen from the boat.

***

In his tower in Castle Sarazan, Ezrin smiled in satisfaction as he leaned back from his crystal and stretched. He was exhausted from the effort of summoning and controlling the storm and would need to sleep for twelve hours to regain his strength, but he had every reason to be pleased with his work.

"Go to Captain Nicoras," he commanded his servant boy, "and tell him the fugitives have landed."

***

Captain Elthorn watched as the three bedraggled figures approached the tavern.

"Pass the word. Let them get inside then we'll move in and take them," he said to his sergeant who slipped away quietly through the woods.

Elthorn had been curious about how Lord Hercival had known the three would be coming ashore at this point and he'd been utterly shocked by the ferocity of the waterspout's destruction of the riverboat.

"All this trouble about three fleabitten foreigners" he'd said to Gerom when he'd first read Lord Hercival's message, without realising the magnitude of the trouble.

After what he'd just witnessed it was obvious that Lord Hercival wanted these three very much and he didn't want to have to be the one to face his Lordship's wrath if they got away again. He drew his sword as he watched the three figures approach the tavern door.

***

Aron pushed open the heavy wooden door and stepped forward onto the flagstones, conscious for a moment that water still dripped from him to leave little puddles in his footsteps. A few heads turned at their entrance before resuming what they had been doing, but one group in a circle around the fireplace took particular note of the new arrivals. The low hum of conversation in the room stopped as the three men walked to the counter. The group beside the fire put down their mugs and stood up drawing knives or clutching cudgels, two of them moving up to block the doorway. Aron, Davo and Maldwyn stood with their backs to the counter as the men encircled them. Then one stepped forward with a long knife in his hand. He was at least ten years older and a handswidth taller than Aron with a deep chest, thick shoulders and the face of an unshaven pig.

"Good to see you again boys," said Pigface with a gap-toothed smile. "I believe we have some unfinished business."

Aron let his pack fall to the floor and felt the hard wood of the counter at his back as he faced the circle of enemies, a tight knot of fear in his stomach as he reckoned the odds; at least a dozen hard-bitten caravan guards faced them. His right foot found a small wooden stool and without looking down he slipped his foot under it. The fingers of his right hand closed around the handle of the throwing knife he wore sheathed along his left forearm, and all the time he kept his eyes on the men before him, awaiting their move. Suddenly the door crashed open and mail-clad warriors surged in.

As everyone turned, Aron was first to react; he flicked out his right foot sending the stool flying at the same time as drawing the knife from his left arm. The stool caught Pigface in the groin as the knife hit the first warrior just below the chin. At that the room exploded into chaos as the caravan guards turned on the new enemy. The soldiers reeled in dismay and confusion; they had expected three men and little resistance. Now they faced almost equal numbers of tough and seasoned ruffians. Crossbows twanged and wounded men screamed in agony, but the caravan guards drove forward, forcing the first group of soldiers back into their fellows. The crossbowmen struggled to reload in the crush and succeeded only in hindering the swordsmen. The soldiers attempted to fall back but only pressed into more men trying to get through the door. The front rank, their swords too long for such close hand-to-hand fighting, were falling to the long knives of the guards. The men crowded at the door were under attack from a hail of bottles and mugs thrown by Davo and Maldwyn and were unable to respond or escape. The caravan guides, sensing their enemy weakening, pushed forward and drove the soldiers backwards where they tripped and fell over their already-felled comrades leaving them helpless before the rampant ruffians.

Aron saw the caravan guard's advance for the opportunity it was. He grabbed Davo as the little man sought to join the forward rush.

"Come on, let's get out of here. You too," he said turning to Maldwyn. "Before they remember who they were originally going to fight."

He scrambled over the counter dragging his pack after him and pushed through a curtained door into the room behind. Looking around he realised he was in the kitchen.

"Food," Aron called to Davo and Maldwyn. "Grab as much as you can carry."He picked up a basket of loaves and then caught sight of a man cowering beneath a table, presumably the tavern-keeper. Their eyes met for a moment and, overcome with guilt, Aron dug in his pouch and threw some coins on the floor, then was moving again to the door at the far side of the kitchen.

He opened the door and cold air struck his face, chilling his still-damp hair. He led the other two into the yard and, hearing the stamp of restless beasts, ran to the stable opposite. There were about a dozen rough-coated horses in the stalls, enough for the number of caravan guards.

Why not? Aron thought. "Horses, boys," he called. "Let's get out of here quick. Bridles only."

They bridled their chosen horses in double quick time,

mounted and rode out of the yard leading the rest of the horses. Sounds of conflict still came from the far side of the tavern. *The soldiers must have regrouped and fought back*, Aron thought.

When they were clear of the tavern they kicked their mounts into a gallop and loosed the others, but they were well-schooled beasts and did not scatter as Aron had hoped. There was nothing more to be done other than put as much distance as possible between them and the soldiers, so Aron turned his mount's head towards the road that lead away from the river.

CHAPTER 20

The three men rode until the darkness of the night made the track hazardous. Maldwyn, as befitted a nobleman, rode easily, still carried by the adrenaline high from the fight in the tavern. Davo, in contrast, bounced awkwardly and cursed almost continuously. Aron grew tired of his complaints and snapped at him.

"Better a sore arse than a stretched neck."

Davo continued to curse, but under his breath. Aron rode on with more ease than Davo but not in complete comfort. The food he had gulped down as they fled from the tavern sat uneasily on his stomach and a headache had grown from a vague discomfort to the point where every jolt from his horse released sharp needles of pain through his head. The road they had followed from the ferry had deteriorated with the miles into a rough track that threatened to fade out entirely. Several times the way had forked and Aron had been entirely unsure which was the major path. Maldwyn and Davo had offered no guidance and Aron had chosen almost at random, distracted by the fever brewing in him.

"Halt. We go no further today," Aron called out and steered his mount off the track towards a grove of scrubby trees.

The grateful Davo was already out of the saddle, but Maldwyn pivoted his horse on its haunches and prepared to argue the case for continuing.

"There is still light enough for a few miles further. You said we were certain to be pursued."

Aron looked about his head throbbing with pain. In the gloom he could make out tumbled walls under the scrub and the chatter of a stream somewhere near.

"This looks as good a place as any to stop. We must rest the horses. There's decent enough grazing and water here."

After a moment Maldwyn accepted this and dismounted. Davo took the horses to the stream before securing them for the night while Maldwyn set about gathering wood for a fire. Aron sat very still on a crumbled wall trying to will his stomach to calm.

Davo returned from watering the horses and produced a bottle from the depths of his pack, he pulled out the cork and after taking a long drink offered it to his companions. Aron waved it away with a tired shake of his head.

"Are you alright?" Davo asked.

Aron looked up at him. The light was fading fast and he could barely make out Davo in the gloom. He opened his mouth to speak, but his stomach rebelled and he vomited onto the grass between his feet. He tried to stand but his legs gave way and he sprawled across the turf. He made another effort to rise but a further spasm of retching seized him and, as he raised himself on his elbows, he lost control of his bowels.

Davo called out for Maldwyn and he came, dropping firewood as he ran.

"He looks like he's far gone in drink," Davo said. "I bin like that a few times. But he ain't bin drinking." He looked down at the sprawled figure at his feet. "Give him some of the water and I'll turn him so he won't choke if he gets sick again."

Davo caught Aron by the shoulders and dragged his dead weight to the shelter of a tree, then turned him to lie on his side. Aron groaned softly but otherwise did not react. He coughed and spluttered at the water Maldwyn gave him but at least he kept it down. The two men set the fire close enough to warm him, spread his cloak over him and settled down for the night.

"He'll be better for a night's sleep," Davo said and reached for his bottle.

***

Aron did not immediately recognise where he was when he woke. Davo and Maldwyn lay nearby, rolled in their cloaks and asleep, half-buried in the layer of mist that rose from the turf. But where he remembered tumbled mounds of rubble buried in undergrowth there now stood an elegant building; pale walls shining in the moonlight, splendid flowering vines twined around the door pillars climbing to the red-tiled roof. A warm golden light gleamed invitingly from the wide doorway giving the place something of the appearance of a ship of light sailing on a cloud sea. Aron threw off his cloak; his guts were quiet now though he still had a faraway headache. He stood up, confused that his clothes were unsoiled, and walked towards the golden house knee-deep through the mist. *Am I mist-*

walking? he asked himself. It was both like, and unlike the walks in the mist he had taken under the influence of the wise woman's potion.

Cautiously Aron moved nearer until he could look inside. Within was filled with lush plants; shrubs in the full flower of spring and apple trees bearing golden fruit, all bathed in the sunlight of midsummer. Birds sang unseen and a warm breeze scented with honeysuckle caressed his skin. In the midst of the grove stood a pool of clear water. Aron suddenly felt parched as if he'd not drunk for days. He stepped across the threshold and as he did so a figure appeared from the greenery somewhere to his left. He turned at the movement, but saw only a silhouette as if the light shone directly behind the newcomer. He froze. His hands sought his blades, but failed to find them.

"Welcome stranger and fear naught. Drink, if that is your need. There is no trap here."

The voice was a woman's; low and rounded with laughter bubbling at the edge. Aron relaxed, but his right hand still sought the knife hilt.

"Come into my garden and let me see you," she called, her voice soft and inviting.

Aron stepped forward until the light was no longer behind the speaker and he could see that she was a woman of extraordinary beauty; smooth of face and full of bosom, her long flowing hair the colour of ripe corn. She smiled as she walked towards him and Aron felt as if the summer sun shone upon his face.

"It is so long since I had a visitor here. Won't you tarry awhile?"

Aron looked into her eyes, unable to decide what colour they were. She reached out and took his hands in hers. A scent reminiscent of sweet hay filled Aron's nose as he allowed her to lead him into the luxuriant undergrowth.

"My bower is nearby. You may rest there and tell me of what passes in the world," she said, her voice as sweet as a dove's call.

"I cannot stay here, my Lady. My comrades and I are fugitives," said Aron. "Pursuit may overtake us at any time."

"This is my place and no-one harms my guests." There was a firmness and power in the soft voice as she led him to a grassy bank covered in daisies and buttercups.

"What is your name, lady? I cannot rest in your bower without knowing whose guest I am," said Aron.

"Hush now, rest is what you need." She laid Aron down on the grass and then sat beside him. Laying her hand on Aron's brow she looked into his eyes. "I feel the fires burning in your blood; rest here and I will cool you." She produced a white metal cup and a ewer of clear water. "Drink. There is healing in the waters of my well."

Aron took a draught of water and a great coolness flowed through him. The pain in his head seemed to flow out into her hands as she gently caressed his forehead.

"You're a pretty lad for one so dangerous, Aron son of Eamon," she said softly. "I think I might keep you here with me though that would displease some of my followers." Her lips gently brushed his and Aron felt his body respond to her nearness.

***

"I can't wake him," said Davo. He was kneeling beside the still figure of Aron who lay between the cold ashes of the fire and the spreading roots of an oak tree. "Splash some water over his face, that'll do it," said Maldwyn. "That's what my nurse always did to me."

"Already tried that," replied Davo. "Didn't work. What're we gonna do, milord?"

Maldwyn looked around at the woods that surrounded them on all sides. The track that they had followed the previous evening seemed to lead no further, and he had no idea where they were.

"We have no choice in the matter," Maldwyn said after a moment's consideration. "We stay here until he is fit to travel. Make sure he takes plenty of water and wait until the fever breaks."

"What about them lads behind us?"

"We'll conceal ourselves as best we can and hope they miss us. How fast do you think we would be able to travel with him as he is? There's another thing too."

"Wassatt?"

"We oughta wash him."

"But he's shit hisself"

"Exactly why we need to wash him. We can't leave him lying in it."

"Don't see why not."

Maldwyn was silent for a moment as he pondered on Davo's concept of personal hygiene. He reached for a water carrier. "I'll get some water. You get his breeches off."

Davo recoiled. "I'm not touching him, not like that."

Maldwyn thrust the water carrier at him with a sigh. "Very well. You get the water then."

***

Aron awoke in soft arms, his head cradled between the breasts of the Lady whose name he did not yet know. His head was clear and he felt strong and filled with energy, he was also hungry. His stomach growled at the very thought of food. Her hand reached out and caressed his head.

"So you're awake at last, my sweet." Her voice was like a summer breeze in the long grass of a hay meadow. "And hungry now, I shouldn't wonder. But which hunger shall we satisfy first." She chuckled and moved so that a plump nipple slid across Aron's lips. Aron reached out his tongue and licked the sweetmeat offered him.

"Food later then," she said running her hand down Aron's belly towards his groin.

***

"I suppose I have to let you go back."

The Lady's soft voice caressed Aon as he lay back lazily on the grass and let her feed him.

"Now the water fever you took from the river is burned out. But mind; you'll be weak yet when you return. I'll send a guide to you. Now I've found you, I can't have you getting lost in the forest."

"How can I thank you for all your kindness? I am forever in your debt," said Aron as he looked into her eyes. "How will I find you again?"

"Keep me always in your heart and I will find you. Now you must go." She bent her head to kiss him and Aron felt himself falling asleep as her cool lips held his.

***

"He's awake." Davo called out to Maldwyn in the still morning air. Maldwyn came running from where he had been tending the horses.

"Thank the Gods. How is he?"

Aron tried to raise himself up on one elbow, his head spun and he was obliged to lie back down. He tried again more slowly and succeeded in sitting up.

"Hungry," he smiled weakly and then wrinkled his nose in disgust, "and in need of a wash. How long have I been asleep?"

"Four nights and three days," replied Davo. "We've bin real worried about you and there's almost no grub left."

Aron looked around their camp site and seeing the overgrown stones of the tumbled walls rubbed his eyes in disbelief. Where was the lady's house?

"Four nights, all that time? I don't understand." Then, as he remembered what had brought them here. "What of the soldiers? Are we not pursued?"

"There has been no sign of them," said Maldwyn, looking around as if to confirm his statement. "The track we followed ends here and we've seen no-one at all."

"I doubt we've seen the last of them. Now what did you say there was to eat? Is there any ham left?" Davo shook his head. "Well, have you managed to catch anything? There must be game in these woods," said Aron.

Davo looked helplessly at Maldwyn who looked equally blank.

"We tried," said Maldwyn. "But we didn't catch anything, and our snares disappeared from where we'd set them."

"There's oatmeal. You can have porridge," said Davo. Aron groaned inwardly; just what he needed to restore his strength. Still it was better than nothing.

"It'll do until the guide gets here."

Davo and Maldwyn looked suspiciously at him.

"What did you say? What guide?" asked Maldwyn.

Aron paused a moment then shook his head. "Never mind. Is there any clean water?"

Maldwyn looked at him curiously and then went to fetch a water pouch. Aron sat staring at the ruined walls trying to reconcile the sight with his memory of the building in the dream. Who was she? She had avoided telling him, but he was sure it was important that he know. She had said she would send him a guide; if one appeared that would be the proof of the dream. He didn't want to believe that it had all been illusion, but he would await the proof.

Eventually Davo interrupted Aron's ponderings with a pan of warm oatmeal porridge. Aron ate it without relish, the lumpy consistency and bland flavour too much of a contrast with his memory of the Lady's gifts.

"You know's where we is, don't yer?" Davo spoke softly so that Maldwyn, who was tending the horses twenty paces away, wouldn't hear. "Cos I don't reckon he's got much idea. He's brave enough and alright with the horses mind, but I wouldn't want him in charge when there's thinkin' required."

"He's going to be Earl of Nandor," said Aron quietly.

"Then the gods help 'im."

"His mother'll keep him heading the right way," said Aron.

"Clever woman, Lady Alice, dangerous too," said Davo with a meaningful glance at Aron.

"Hush now, what was that?" Davo's head swivelled in response to Aron's sharp enquiry.

"What was what? I didn't hear nothing." One of the horses snorted as Maldwyn's brush caught a tangle in its mane. "It's just the horses."

"No, it's not. See over there." Aron pointed between the trees where a greenclad figure moved lithely through the undergrowth. Davo whistled softly to get Maldwyn's attention, and the three of them watched in silent interest as the figure walked right up to them.

"Are you the guide?" asked Aron.

Maldwyn and Davo looked at him, mystified.

"Yes, I suppose so. The Lady told me to come and see to you, if that's what you mean. I'm Araiminta."

The voice identified the stranger as a woman even before she threw back the hood of her green cloak to reveal her greying hair. Though her face was lined, her dark eyes sparkled with vigour.

"I'm Aron of Darien, this is Lord Maldwyn of Nandor and Davo." Aron indicated the others, who continued to stare at him as if he were mad.

"Are you ready to leave?" Araiminta asked.

Aron tried to stand up, but everything blurred alarmingly and he sat down again. Araiminta offered her hand. Aron grasped it and was surprised by the calluses and the firmness of her grip.

"Up you come, young man. I don't think you're in any state to be walking yet. The Lady said one of you had been ill." Araiminta turned to Davo and Maldwyn, who stood watching her with their mouths hanging open. "Why don't you two bring a horse over for your friend and get packed up? Then we can be on our way. Come along, we haven't got all day."

Davo and Maldwyn turned and walked towards the horses in bewildered silence.

"You'll need feeding up for a few days before you're going anywhere, my lad. My cottage is just a step away and I've a good stew in the pot. I've been keeping an eye on you since you arrived, but the Lady only told me last night you needed help. Till then I thought you were bandits or suchlike."

"We didn't see you, at least, they didn't," Aron indicated Davo and Maldwyn who were packing up their gear.

"They weren't meant to, but I saw them trying to trap my animals.

You might well have been bandits, it wouldn't be the first time."

"You took the snares."

"Thought it might persuade you to move along."

"Who is the Lady that you speak of?"

Araiminta turned to look at him as if he was simple. "The Goddess Iduna. She that we call the Lady. This is her place; the mother of all her sacred places. Though few now remember. Once, long ago, she was widely worshipped, but now there are only a few who follow her. The warrior's god and merchants' gods of luck and profit have driven her out of the towns and villages. I am keeper of the temple. How is it that you enjoy her favour yet know her not?"

"We came here as fugitives; I fell ill of a fever and we camped here because there was clean water. I dreamed of the Lady in my fevered sleep. She was kind to me; she fed me and cooled my fever with water from her well."

"Did she indeed? You are most fortunate. Is that all she did?" She eyed him suspiciously. "Did she feed you a golden apple?"

"Not that I recall. I saw some growing in the grove by the pool, but I don't remember eating one."

"She has retained some propriety then." Araiminta wrinkled her nose as she said this, sounding to Aron like an aunt discussing a favourite but wayward niece. "Can't say as I blame her though. You're a handsome lad, and there's been none but old women coming to her for years."

Aron felt his face begin to colour. "Our pursuers may appear at any time," he said. "I would not have you put yourself in harm's way on our account."

"Oh. I'll be fine, they won't find me. This is the Lady's place and she'll see no-one under her protection comes to harm."

"Your horse is ready, Aron," called Maldwyn.

Davo brought the horse over and helped him mount up. Then the three men set off following Aramainta as she strode through the trees.

CHAPTER 21

Captain Elthorn looked over at the surviving caravan guards where they sat in a sorry huddle guarded by four crossbowmen. He spat to one side and wiped his mouth on his sleeve. "What's the final tally of the damage they've done us, Gerom?"

"Five dead, ten wounded, but four of them can ride," said Lieutenant Gerom who himself had a bandage round his head covering a deep cut in his scalp. "Not including myself, sir."

No doubt he had a raging headache, but declined to mention it. *Sound lad,* thought Elthorn. *He should do well if he survives this*.

"Hang the lot of them. Take them across on the ferry and string them up," said Elthorn. "They've cost us dear this day and this is the least payment we can take."

"Are we going after the three that got away, sir?"

"That is entirely up to you now, Gerom. I am handing over command of this sorry mess to you." He saw the surprise register on Gerom's face. "I shall draft a message to Lord Hercival reporting the full details of what happened here and tendering my resignation. I shall accept full responsibility for everything. What you do from this point on is entirely your decision, but I would caution you of four things. Firstly, the fugitives are reported to have fled away from the river into the forest. That is outside Sarazan's lands and you have no legal right to pursue them there. Secondly, you have wounded men in your care. Thirdly, you have no-one who can track through woodland, and finally you have only a handful of men who can fight, and one of the fugitives is known to be skilled bladesman."

"Very good, sir," said Gerom stiffly. "But why are you standing down?"

"I suppose you could call it cowardice, Gerom, though I call it self-preservation," Elthorn said bleakly. "As I'm afraid you will find shortly, Lord Hercival is much like his grandfather, the Old Duke, and not a reasonable man when it comes to dealing with failure. And you don't have to call me sir anymore."

"No sir. I mean, no. I don't think you're a coward." Gerom

stumbled over the words. "What are you going to do now?"

"Right now, Gerom. I'm going back into that inn and I'm going to get drunk. What are you going to do?"

Gerom paused for a minute in thought. "I'm going to hang those caravan guards, then I'm going get the wounded back to Erkimar."

"Good lad. You'll be fine," Elthorn said and turned away towards the door of the inn.

***

"Incompetent idiots," shouted Lord Hercival. He hurled his drinking glass across the room where it shattered against the wood panelling.

"My Lord?" Nicoras hurried into the room. He had seen the messenger heading for Hercival's chamber and some intuition had told him that the news was not good. *That's my wages for a month he's just broken*, he thought.

"They got away." Hercival raged. "Our men got themselves embroiled in a fight with a bunch of locals and let them get away."

"Have they gone after them?" asked Nicoras even though he feared the answer.

"They have not. It seems they are retreating to Erkimar to lick their wounds. The commander says that he has resigned his post and placed some green lieutenant in command. I want him in chains, Nicoras. I want him flogged. He has disgraced the house of Sarazan."

"What is his name, my Lord?"

"Elthorn." Hercival spat out the name.

"Very good, my Lord." Nicoras remembered Elthorn as a quiet man, tough and competent. He wondered what had gone wrong at the Ferryboat Inn and what he would have done if he'd been in charge. "Is there anything else, my Lord?"

"Yes there damn well is. Dig that wizard out from wherever he's hiding. Thanks to that cretin Elthorn we have to find Maldwyn again."

***

"I don't think you appreciate the gravity of the situation?" Lord Hercival said to the tousled Ezrin, his voice tight with frustration. "The prisoners have eluded our forces. I need you to find them again while our men are still close enough to catch them."

"I understand completely, my Lord," muttered Ezrin sagging wearily before Lord Hercival's anger, his eyes dull and red. "But I cannot do it. It is a simple matter of the nature of magic. The manipulation of the storm was an enormous effort, it drained my psychic powers and I can work no magics until I am recovered."

"I don't want to hear arguments. I need you to find Maldwyn of Nandor. Now!"

"But, my Lord. You do not understand. You would not race your finest horse after a long day at the chase. Of course not, your riding master taught you this years ago. It is the same with magic. I must recover my strength before I can work the simplest spell."

"You are not a horse and this is not a day's hunting. I require you to find Maldwyn of Nandor."

Ezrin was about to dispute the point when Nicoras intervened to save the old sorcerer.

"Let us go and see what the cooks can offer you. I'm sure your powers will be much repaired by a good meal. By your leave, my Lord."

Nicoras put his arm around Ezrin's shoulders and guided him to the door before turning back to face Hercival.

"I did not ask for your opinion, Nicoras," said Hercival, his mouth a thin slash of anger.

"He is an old man, my Lord and we need him too much," said Nicoras levelly. "And His Grace, your father, thinks highly of him."

Hercival's eyes glittered dangerously and Nicoras thought for a moment that he was going to have to defend himself, but the moment passed.

"Thank you, Nicoras, for reminding me," said Hercival icily. "Very well. Take and feed him and get him back to work as soon as possible."

CHAPTER 22

Lady Edith of Nandor kicked her feet in frustration against the side of the bed she shared with her sister.

"Oh be quiet, Edith, and go to sleep," said Celaine.

"But I can't. It's too early and I'm too awake. Can't you hear the music downstairs? I want to go down and listen for a while."

"Well you can't. Papa said no, so go to sleep." Celaine rolled over turning her back on her sister.

It's so unfair, thought Edith. They had been travelling for nine days now on the way to the Holy City and the Court of the High King, and she hadn't been allowed to do anything. For the first three nights they had stopped at manor houses within Nandor, but once they had passed out of her father's lands they had had to stay at inns just like any other travellers; though of course they only stayed at the better ones. And every night Edith and Celaine had been packed off to bed straight after supper. It wasn't as if they had been riding hard enough to tire the girls; on the contrary the Nandor caravan moved at a very sedate pace and Edith, who rode very well, was bursting with energy and curiosity. Celaine, by contrast, was quiet and listless; to Edith it seemed as if Celaine couldn't wait to get to bed each night, as if she had some tryst in the world of dreams.

It was so unfair; Edith could still hear the music in the common room downstairs, she even recognised some of the songs the singer had massacred. She just wanted to see a little of life beyond the castle and town of Nandor. The Holy City wouldn't be any fun at all if she was going to be kept in and sent to bed all the time. Resolution hardened in her mind. She sat up in the bed and slipped out from beneath the covers.

"You're going to get into so much trouble," murmured Celaine sleepily, but Edith was undaunted. She stepped into her gown and, after a moment's scrabbling in the gloom, found her shoes.

The tavern was substantial and catered to large travelling parties such as merchants' caravans. Its upper floors contained several suites of rooms for the use of rich travellers who wished for peace and distance from the poorer customers. The Nandor party occupied one such suite; their small entourage of servants and soldiers had a dormitory across the yard.

Edith crept silently down from the second floor drawn by the swirl of the music that rose up the stairs. The ground floor common room was spacious, with a stage at one end for performers, and was packed with people, but Edith barely noticed; her eyes were on the stage. A slim man in a bright yellow shirt with shoulder-length dark curls was singing a rousing hunting song accompanied by pipe and drum. The crowd were stamping along to the drum beat and shouting out the choruses. Edith blushed when she heard the words which made it clear that the huntsman's quarry was a maid rather than the usual game, but she still pushed her way through the throng towards the stage. The song finished, the singer drained his tankard and then asked what they wanted to hear next. A dozen different voices called out suggestions, some of which Edith recognised, some sounded utterly obscene, still more insulted the singer and his apparently unmarried parents.

The singer began another song, one which Glynis had taught Edith so she sang along as she gazed, wide-eyed, at the singer. Behind her though, the catcalls had not died down and she noticed that the singer was slightly offkey. He looked around the room with a nervous air between the verses until their eyes met. Then with a broad grin he stepped down from the stage in front of Edith and caught her by the hand.

"Here's a maid who loves a song," he called to the crowd as he pulled Edith onto the stage. Edith thought of pulling away, but the crowd cheered the singer's words and the noise lifted her.

"What do you know, little lady?" asked the singer; Edith's mind whirled for a moment as she feared she had forgotten all the songs she'd ever sung.

"How about Bringing in the May?" said the piper with a sympathetic smile.

Edith relaxed instantly. She'd learned that song in the nursery and sung it a hundred times. "Yes. I know that one," she said.

"After four then," said the piper nodding to the drummer.

The music began; the singer took Edith's hand and quietly counted her in to the start of the vocal part. Edith felt the rhythm of the song pick up and the words flowed into her mind, she forgot about where she was as the melody lifted her and carried her away.

"That's lovely, but sing up, girl. They'll not hear you at the back," the singer whispered in the space after the chorus.

Edith began the next verse with greater volume as her confidence grew, and by the end of the song the crowd were joining in the choruses with gusto. The applause washed over her along with a few ribald suggestions which Edith chose to ignore.

"I think they like you. Would you like to sing one more?" whispered the singer. A voice from the crowd called out for a song Edith knew, and she nodded quickly to the piper who struck up the melody straight away. The familiar tune flowed through her and she rode it with her voice until it delivered her to the end breathless and exhilarated. She would happily have sung all night and certainly the crowd wanted to hear and see more, but the singer took her hand and, with exaggerated ceremony, kissed it then led her off the stage.

Hands reached out to her and voices called asking her to come and have a drink with them, but she ignored them all as she walked on air through the hall. One great hairy fellow stood swaying in her path, demanding a kiss and she received another great cheer when she pushed him away and he fell sprawling over a stool. She paused and gave a theatrical curtsey before pushing open the door and walking out into the cool night.

Outside the sky was clear, Edith lifted her face to the breeze and looked at the stars which seemed brighter than she ever seen. Softly she sang the chorus of Bringing in the May to herself; she felt more alive then she ever remembered, and wished Aron had been there to see her sing. She heard the noise of movement behind her and turned to see a tall figure step through the door.

"Ah, the little songbird," he said, silhouetted by the lantern that hung over the door. Edith looked around hurriedly, there was no-one else in sight.

"And pretty too."

He moved toward her. Edith stood her ground unsure of what to do. The musicians had just started another song in the hall, another hunting song. The crowd was stamping and singing along; more than enough noise to cover any cries for assistance. Edith reminded herself she was an earl's daughter and stood up straight, looking the man squarely in the eye. He took two long strides towards her and seized her in his powerful arms. Edith squealed in surprise as his lips pressed down on hers. His unshaven cheek scratched her face, she could taste the ale on his tongue and the sweat on his body. She lashed out and felt her knee connect with something solid. Her assailant grunted in pain and loosened his grip. Edith twisted from his arms and ran across the cobbled yard, but her soft shoes were not made for running and within a few paces he had caught her again. Strong arms swept her off her feet and pinned her arms. She shrieked in fear and defiance, but another chorus of the song drowned her cries. She could see he was making for the stable block and was two paces from the door when Edith heard boots on the cobbles behind her. A voice rang out in challenge.

"Release her."

The abductor turned to face his challenger and Edith saw Captain Thalon advancing across the yard, his sword in his hand.

"This is none of your business, old man."

"Oh, but it is," said Thalon levelly. "Now take your hands off her."

The stranger released Edith, pushing her to the ground, and drew his own blade. Edith crawled out of the way of the two men as they circled each other and then watched in terror-stricken fascination as the fight began. The stranger swept into the attack and Thalon was forced back in desperate defence as blow after blow rained in on him giving him no opportunity to carry the fight to his attacker. Thalon was a competent swordsman, but his reflexes were slower than his opponent and each attack was barely parried as he gave ground before the younger man.

Inside the hall the song finished in a storm of applause. In the quiet before the music started up again, Edith screamed for all she was worth; no-one seemed to notice.

With every breath the end of the fight seemed imminent; Thalon was tiring and the stranger seemed as fresh as ever. Edith looked about for some weapon she could use to help Thalon, but the courtyard was bare. She resolved to throw herself at the stranger's legs to trip him the next time he came within reach, but before she had the chance the fight was over. The stranger thrust then changed direction. Thalon tried to respond but stumbled, and his blade was knocked from his hand. In the blink of an eye the stranger's point was at the old man's throat as he scrabbled desperately at the cobbles.

"Still think it's your business, old man?" The stranger sneered.

"Hold!" The voice of command rolled across the yard. "That is enough."

Two crossbowmen scuttled into the yard and took up position with their weapons trained on the stranger. Behind them, the speaker rode into the light cast by the hall windows. He halted before the combatants and calmly took off his riding gloves. The stranger kept his point at Thalon's throat as he waited for the newcomer to speak.

In the hall the song finished, and the horseman waited for the applause to die away before speaking.

"You, girl." He pointed at Edith. "Come forward into the light."

Edith stood up and walked slowly forward, her head held high.

"You are no tavern wench. What happens here?"

"What business is this of yours?" The swordsman sneered, his point never wavering from Thalon.

"I do not like your tone of voice, soldier. You will have more respect in the presence of your betters."

The horseman slid fluidly off his mount and stepped forward. He was half a hand's width shorter than the man he faced, but it seemed to Edith that he was somehow taller and more commanding. The swordsman stood uncertain of his next move. He withdrew his blade from Thalon and slowly turned it towards the newcomer.

"Do not raise your blade to me, sir," the newcomer said, his voice chill and even. "It will be the last thing you do."

The swordsman stood still staring at him, his eyes narrow and glittering with hatred. The horseman stood calmly before him and it seemed to Edith that everyone held their breath. The swordsman's blade lifted slightly as his muscles regrouped. In that instant the horseman clicked his fingers and the two crossbows sang as one. The swordsman began to move forward and was then jerked backwards as the two bolts struck him in the chest tumbling him like a skittle. Edith screamed as his body sprawled bloodily on the cobbles in front of her. The horseman leapt forward nimbly and took her hand.

"Fear, not my Lady, he is past being any danger to anyone." He turned his attention to Thalon who was sitting with his head between his knees, and still breathing heavily.

"Are you hurt, good sir? It was a fine fight you put up."

"I was overmatched," said Thalon gruffly. "But I couldn't let him harm the girl."

"There speaks a true knight. Allow me to assist you, sir."

The horseman reached out his hand to Thalon who took it and, with some effort, rose to his feet.

"Your arrival was most timely, good sir," said Thalon. "May I know to whom I owe my life?"

"But of course." He smiled, flashing brilliant white teeth framed by a close-cropped beard. "I am Petter, Lord Tirellan, at your service."

"I thank you from the bottom of my heart. my Lord. I am Thalon, captain of Nandor and this is my Lady Edith of Nandor, daughter of Earl Baldwin."

Edith curtsied as Thalon introduced her. Lord Tirellan reached out, took her hand in his, and with an elegant bow, gently kissed it.

"'Delighted to make your acquaintance, my Lady," he said, his blue eyes shining in the lantern light.

CHAPTER 23

Araiminta's cottage lay tucked in a fold of the hills that hid it from prying eyes. A clear stream flowed through the neat garden which was planted with orderly rows of vegetables. The cottage itself was a sturdy construction of roughcut logs and mud-covered wattle with a reed-thatched roof. Araiminta led them around to the back of the cottage, where a dozen chickens scratched in the dirt around the woodpile.

"Leave the horses here," she said, indicating an open-sided barn whose roof looked in need of repair. "Choose whichever of the sheds takes your fancy. There isn't room in the house for all of you, and he needs the bed." Araiminta gestured at Aron who looked up sharply.

"I feel fine," said Aron.

"Don't argue, young man. You've just woken up from a fever sleep and I know how weak that leaves a body," said Araiminta, her tone indicating that she expected no argument. "You need a few days of rest and good food. Fetch your gear in and I'll stoke up the fire."

Aron had to admit that it sounded an enticing prospect as he climbed off his horse; even the short ride had tired him.

"What should we do?" asked Davo.

"Put your gear down then make yourselves useful," said Araiminta briskly. "There's plenty to be done in the garden, and the chicken house needs mucking out." Davo looked at Maldwyn in dismay.

"You can't have him working in the garden, he's an Earl's son," said Davo.

"Is he really? No doubt he eats the same as other men," said Araiminta. "Then if he wishes to eat, he has to work the same as other men."

There was no argument after that. Araiminta hustled Aron into the interior of her cottage, dusty and aromatic with drying herbs. He was wrapped in a patchwork blanket and laid on a pallet with soft pillows beside the fire where Araiminta's stewpot simmered on an iron trivet. Davo and Maldwyn were banished to the vegetable garden after a few minutes instruction on what were weeds and what were not. Araiminta busied herself with preparing vegetables, humming a little tune as she peeled and chopped.

***

Ezrin the sorcerer bent over his crystal and tried to clear his mind. He had slept less than he needed, but Lord Hercival's demands rang in his ears. He grasped a single hair culled from Maldwyn's comb, rolling it between his fingers. He began the deep breathing pattern that initiated the focusing and gazed deep into the crystal. The familiar surge of vertigo heralded the beginning of the trance, but the crystal did not clear to give him the view through Maldwyn's eyes. Instead thick clouds of fog swirled all around him and he knew that he was not with Maldwyn.

A little knot of frustration tightened on Ezrin's brow; he had never experienced such a complication to this unsophisticated piece of magic. He drew a deep breath and pushed more of his reserves of mental strength into the crystal imagining a beam of sunlight piercing the fog. The beam reached forward perhaps two or three paces and illuminated nothing but cloud which seemed to grow thicker. Ezrin relaxed and then threw his mind into imagining a wind sweeping the clouds aside; a gale, a veritable tempest. The fog swirled but did not break, and Ezrin felt as if he was trying to sweep aside sand rather than moist air. He strained for a moment longer and then, defeated, dissolved the focus.

Sweat slicked Ezrin's face and body as he drew air back into his lungs like an athlete after a hard race. His palms were bloodied where his nails had dug into the flesh, he reached for a flask of spirits and gulped down a large mouthful. His head still buzzed from the effort that he had made in trying to push the clouds aside.

How could I have failed? It seemed as if he'd been shielded from Maldwyn. *But how?* He knew how shielding worked, indeed he had done it himself, but his countermeasures should have been enough. *Certainly there are mages in the world more powerful than me, but not so much stronger that my strength would not move them, force them to reveal some portion of their identity. No mage on earth could so completely nullify my probes like that..* The shielding had been so complete that he had not the slightest clue to the identity of the shielder. *Inhumanly strong,* the thought crossed Ezrin's mind, but he dismissed it. *In my learning and practice of magic I've come across very little evidence of the great powers. I'll try to locate Maldwyn again tomorrow; meanwhile I need something to say to Lord Hercival.* For the hundredth time he wished he was dealing with the Duke. *A far more reasonable man.*

***

Aron dozed on the couch, lulled into sleep by the burble of the gently boiling cauldron. It did not seem to him that he slept for long, but the room was dark when he opened his eyes and he was aware of a layer of mist that rose from the floor. The faint scent of sweet hay came to him as the mist rose, there was a burst of light as if a door had opened and then Iduna stood beside him glad in a flowing gown, green as spring leaves.

"Araiminta has you well looked after then," Iduna said, her voice soft like the cooing of a dove.

"I did not realise who you are, my Lady," said Aron, suddenly in awe of the Goddess.

"You cannot be afraid of me. Not after what has passed between us." Then she bowed her head and lightly kissed him. As their lips met Aron felt a warm wave of contentment flow through him.

"Soon you'll be strong enough to leave. Once you leave my garden you will be beyond my protection. I will not be able to hide you from those who seek you and your friends."

"How many were there? Are they near?" asked Aron in sudden alarm, thinking of the soldiers they had fought back at the inn.

"Just one," said Iduna. "A mortal, but quite powerful. You would think him a wizard, I suppose."

"That comes as no surprise. I thought the storm that capsized our boat was nothing natural."

"'Tis a dangerous world out there." Iduna smiled sweetly. "You have only to say the word and you may stay here with me."

"I cannot leave my companions to face the dangers, I must go back. I owe you so much, Lady. How can I repay you?"

"Keep me always in your heart. That is payment enough." She bent to kiss him again and in the corner of his eye Aron saw the mists begin to rise.

***

Aron awoke with Araiminta's rough hand on his forehead; a small lantern hung from a hook on a rafter above him among bunches of drying herbs, its soft glow lighting the room. He realised that he had slept past sundown.

"The fever's gone. Sleep well, did you?" said Araiminta softly.

"Or were you with my Lady?"

"I dreamed of her again," said Aron. "But I don't understand at all."

"'Tis not for you to understand the ways of the Gods. She chose you; just be thankful and be worthy of her. Did she tell you to keep her always in your heart?"

"Yes. How did you know?"

"Do you think you're the first handsome lad to catch her eye? You be sure you keep your promise. She is fickle and jealous if crossed, and you would not wish to carry her anger."

Aron sat up and looked Araiminta straight in the eye. "No-one may say that I do not keep my promises."

"Good, then you will know only her love." She turned to the cauldron simmering over the fire. "Are you ready for something to eat?"

***

Aron spent two further days under Araiminta's care before she declared that he was fit to travel. Davo and Maldwyn got through a lot of work around the garden and outbuildings. The vegetable patch looked in thoroughly good shape, but Maldwyn's hands were blistered from the spadework, while Davo's back ached ceaselessly from bending to pull weeds. Both men were eager to leave as if they had entirely forgotten the pursuers that had driven them here.

As they mounted up Aron noticed the horses looked fitter and sleeker from their few days of rest and good grazing. He wished he could have stayed until he felt as good as they looked; it had been a long time since he had felt as truly at peace as he had here.

Araiminta strode beside them as they rode through the woods to guide them back to the road they had left in their haste to flee the pursuit. Sunlight dappled the forest floor and the air was warm with the promise of summer. Aron rode along lost in thought paying little attention to the path they took. It was one thing to vaguely believe in the existence of gods, it was quite another to have their existence so dramatically confirmed. He recalled the tales he had heard of the rivalry of the gods, their feuds and petty jealousies. *Am I now a pawn in such a game?* He struggled to remember if Iduna had featured in any of stories he had heard. Araiminta had described her as fickle and jealous if crossed; how was he to know what would displease her? In all the stories there was a price every mortal paid for the gods' help; this uncertainty would be part of his. As for the rest, no doubt he would learn the full price as the story unfolded. *Not a comforting thought. But, without Iduna's intervention I would be dead of river fever.*

Aron was so wrapped up in his thoughts that he didn't notice the figure who stepped out in front of them as they rounded a bend in the path. His horse stopped abruptly, jerking him back to reality. The man was dressed in a green hooded tunic with brown breeches and carried a drawn sword. Aron's right hand instantly sought the blade at the nape of his neck before he remembered that he had left it buried in the throat of a Sarazan guardsman back in the Ferryboat Inn. Two more men, similarly garbed and armed, stepped into the path behind the first.

"Ho now, travellers! There is a toll you must pay to pass through our forest," called the first man, his face hidden by the hood.

Aron tensed as he prepared to urge his horse forward to ride the man down; then he spotted the archer. He was some thirty paces away standing on a grassy hillock, an arrow nocked, his bow half-bent, a circle of arrows pushed into the turf before him. Aron relaxed and then grabbed Maldwyn's sleeve to restrain him.

"Only a suicide rides at an arrow," said Aron, pointing out the threat. "If he has any skill at all, you'd be spitted thrice over before you reach them."

"Oh!" said Maldwyn with a curse. "I didn't see him." He relaxed a little, glaring at the man before him.

"Off the horses, if you please," the first man said evenly, gesturing with his swordpoint.

Aron slipped easily off his horse, keeping his eyes on the archer, wondering if there was some way of seizing the swordsman before the arrow arrived.

"Move away from the horses and keep your hands up where I can see 'em," the robber directed.

His two fellows moved forward to the horses as the four travellers walked backwards away from their mounts up the road towards the archer. The first robber, his sword held high, kept at least five paces away from Aron and the others.

"That's far enough," he rasped.

Aron risked a look over his shoulder at the bowman; his bow was still half bent, the arrow ready to fly in a split second, but as Aron watched the man began to twitch. Aron heard an angry buzz as the bowman flicked his hood at the air around him. The point of the arrow wavered as the man tossed his head around and then with a scream, dropped the arrow to beat at the air around him with the bow and his free hand.

Aron turned and drew his sword in one smooth motion and charged the robber. The swordsman, distracted by his comrade's screams, was barely in time to meet Aron's attack. He just parried the thrust at his throat, but it left him off balance to meet the next. Aron's blade slashed through hood and cheek, laying bare his teeth. The man screamed in pain, but turned his blade to meet the next attack. Aron stepped back a pace.

"Get that archer," Aron yelled to Maldwyn and Davo who were staring open-mouthed at the spectacle before them.

Maldwyn turned and ran towards the archer, who was still flailing wildly at the air. Davo dived into the undergrowth. Aron stepped forward to resume his attack with a thrust that changed direction at the last moment and laid open the robber's thigh. The man shrieked in pain, dropped his sword and fell to his knees clutching at his wounded leg.

"Mercy, master, mercy," he sobbed. "I'm just a poor man. I never meant you no harm."

Aron paused for a single breath, and then slashed the grovelling man through the throat. Blood sprayed across the grass as Aron turned to face the other robbers who hesitated for less than a heartbeat before running for the undergrowth.

Aron watched them flee and then bent to clean his blade on the dead man's tunic. Araiminta watched him but said nothing. Maldwyn walked up carrying the bow the archer had discarded in his flight.

"He surrendered," Maldwyn whispered hoarsely. "You killed him after he surrendered."

Aron stared at him for a moment. "Don't they execute robbers in Nandor?" he said, his voice cold and even.

"Quite right, young man," said Araiminta firmly. "I know these men. They would have taken everything we had and very probably killed us all."

Aron walked to where his horse stood and began to collect his scattered gear. Maldwyn stood looking at the body, his face pale. Davo emerged from the undergrowth.

"He's real good, int he?" said Davo. "Best I ever seen."

"I've never seen a man killed like that before, not close to," said Maldwyn softly. "I didn't realise there'd be so much blood."

Then he turned and ran for the undergrowth, a hand over his

mouth. Davo sniggered then knelt beside the body and began to rummage through the dead man's pockets.

Aron began repacking the gear, joined after a minute by Davo, and when Maldwyn reappeared they mounted up and rode off along the path without a word.

The sun was well on to the west when they reached the junction with a larger path.

"This is the road to the Holy City," said Araiminta. "Now I must leave you if I am to reach my cottage before dark."

"How can I thank you for your kindness?" said Aron, wondering if he should dip into their small fund of coin to give her something.

"I did but hear my Lady's voice and do her bidding. Her favour is reward enough. I pray she will continue to watch over you as she has done so far."

"The bees, you mean?" said Aron. "I thought that was you."

"Nay," Araiminta shook her head. "I do not have that sort of power. That was most likely my Lady's work, though she did not speak to me."

"It was a most fortunate coincidence if not," said Aron. "How long is her reach? Will she still be able to watch over us when we get to the Holy City?"

"I really don't know," replied Araiminta after a moment's thought. "There was a shrine in the Holy City. I know where it stood, but I don't know if it still exists. She may still have some presence there. Keep her in your heart and she may find you."

So saying she turned and strode off down the path. Aron watched the sturdy figure until she vanished round a bend in the path and then turned his horse's head towards the Holy City.

***

"My Lord, I have news" said Nicoras from the doorway of the chamber. Lord Hercival looked up from the hound he was petting.

"What is it?" he said sharply.

Nicoras stepped into the room, closing the door behind him.

"Earl Baldwin of Nandor and his household are on the road to the Holy City."

"That is most interesting," said Hercival steepling his fingers. "What possible business could they have there? Baldwin of Nandor hasn't been to court for years without number, so why go now?"

"Seeking husbands for his daughters perhaps?"

Hercival looked at Nicoras and raised his eyebrows in sceptism. "I suppose that is just possible, but a much more likely explanation is that they are to meet up with Maldwyn and the others."

"But Tancred said there was nothing planned beyond getting here."

"Do you believe that?" Hercival stood up to express his point more forcefully. "Tancred of Nandor is a born liar. Not even Baldwin is stupid enough to send out a rescue force with no plan for getting back."

He was interrupted by a knock at the door.

"Enter."

The door opened and Ezrin stepped into the room looking pleased with himself.

"I have located Maldwyn of Nandor and his companions, my Lord," the sorcerer said. "They are on the old road from Erkimar to...."

"The Holy City." Hercival interrupted.

Ezrin stared at him in astonishment. "How could you know that? I have only this minute found them."

Hercival smiled at him. "Thank you Ezrin, that will be all."

Ezrin turned slowly and left the room with a baffled look on his face.

"It seems we need to travel to the Holy City, Nicoras," said Hercival. "We'll need Ezrin, of course, to locate them precisely, and a small squad of men to take them."

"My Lord? Do you intend to go yourself?"

"It seems I need to. The attempts to capture them have so far failed due to the incompetence of those in charge. Who can I trust to carry this out?" Lord Hercival's voice was hard and unforgiving. "It's what Grandfather would have done."

"May I humbly point out that your father quite specifically placed Sarazan in your hands until his return. By leaving you would be disobeying his express command," said Nicoras cautiously.

Hercival scowled at him but said nothing.

"I also see no alternative to informing the Duke of the situation as soon as we arrive in the Holy City," Nicoras continued. "It would look most odd if we do not, and he is in any event, certain to find out about it. You know very well it is impossible to keep anything hidden from his spies."

Hercival's scowl deepened.

"Furthermore I have grave doubts about the legality of seizing

Maldwyn and the others in the Holy City. We could end up in the High King's dungeons."

"Enough!" Hercival pounded his fist on the table startling the hound so that it barked at him. He kicked out at the dog, his boot catching it in the ribs. The hound yelped in pain and sought refuge under the table. "Your point is made. I will stay here and entrust this to you. You will seek out my father and tell of all that has passed, but by the time you do that I want Maldwyn of Nandor in your hands. You can use that lizard Tancred to entrap him. And I want Aron of Darien dead."

CHAPTER 24

Lord Tirellan stretched himself theatrically out on a couch. "May the Gods deliver me from men like Baldwin of Nandor." Petter. It's such a relief to be back amongst cultured people, Cristoff."

"Who is he, and where is Nandor?" asked his steward.

"No-one of any significance from the far back of beyond. Gods, I need a drink."

Cristoff stepped to the door and opened it enough to call an order to the page who stood in the corridor. "He served your purposes nicely enough, Petter. A respectable country Earl to travel with, it could hardly have been better. No-one would dare ambush such a party."

"I know, but I found him such hard work. He knows nothing of art or music. All he wanted to talk about were his hounds or that land dispute with Sarazan." Lord Tirellan mimed an expansive yawn. "I lost count of the number of times I vowed to strangle him with his own bootlaces just to get away from the sound of his voice."

Cristoff plumped a couple of cushions and slipped them under his lordship's thighs. "Such are the travails the chivalrous knight must endure. I know how you love playing the hero, my Lord, but is it really worth it?"

" Not if it means spending my life with men like Baldwin, I'd rather take poison." Lord Tirellan pulled a sour face. "Fortunately I will have some time here in the company of civilised men, Cristoff. My Lord Caldon's next move is likely to be northward."

"Northward? What's there up there that's worth the effort?"

"Silver. The barbarians have mines in the mountains, and my Lord needs to replenish his coffers. Those Saxish clansmen were exceedingly expensive. Besides the move threatens no-one and fits very nicely with his stance of penitent; so he bids me to seduce the great men around the throne. Sing them songs of peace and reassurance, he said."

"I can think of no-one better as a seducer. I'm less certain of the singing."

"Thank you so kindly, Cristoff. You know, I think Lady Celaine of Nandor might prove useful here. There's certain to be a lot of functions to attend, and I'll need a lady on my arm. One has certain expectations to fulfill and she is so touchingly naïve."

"Quite. I imagine we'll have to dress her of course."

"Oh of course. Can you imagine what she'd turn up in otherwise? It would certainly be woollen."

Cristoff turned away in mock disgust. "I doubt that she has ever worn a scrap of silk. I don't suppose she can dance a step either, poor child."

"I'll have to invite her to dine here first then. I wonder what her table manners are like? And I suppose I'll have to endure her dreadful father once more," said Lord Tirellan pulling a face.

There was a discreet knock at the door.

"Enter," called Lord Tirellan.

A dark-haired pageboy came in carrying a jug and a tray with two goblets. Both men watched him with close interest as the boy glided across the room.

"There is a messenger outside who would speak with you, my Lord," the boy said in a near whisper.

"Pour the wine then send him in, boy," said Lord Tirellan

The page poured the wine with trembling hands before leaving the room, and a moment later a man clad in the livery of Lord Tirellan's personal staff entered. Lord Tirellan looked up expectantly.

"Did you deliver the letters, Joris?"

"Yes, my Lord."

"And were they all accepted?"

"Yes, my Lord. Every single one." *As well they should be*, thought Lord Tirellan. *The seal of Caldon should ensure that they received the most urgent attention of the nobles they were addressed to.* "Thank you, Joris. You have done well. You may go now."

The messenger marched smartly from the room. When the door had closed Lord Tirellan picked up the goblets and passed one to Cristoff.

"Now we wait for the replies," he said with a smile. "I think the next few weeks are going to be most stimulating. Do we know what those Darien scum have been up to recently?"

"It seems they've been very quiet since that most unfortunate fire, my Lord."

"Do we know where they've moved to?"
"Not yet," Cristoff took a sip of wine. "But we will."

***

"Oh, I'm so excited." Lady Celaine of Nandor stood by the window looking out onto the street. "Look at all the wonderful clothes."

The street was filled with people taking an early evening stroll rather than working people going about their business, and everyone seemed to be wearing their finest. Pairs of young women arm-in-arm, strutting young bloods with a girl on each arm, and married couples all dressed in vivid colours walked slowly by, stopping to greet each other or watch the juggler who stood at the street corner.

"You know, Mama, I'm going to need some new clothes if Lord Tirellan invites me to a reception as he promised."

Lady Alice looked up from her embroidery. "He only said that he would try to arrange such an invitation."

"But didn't you think he was most attentive to me? He isn't married, is he? I'm sure he's interested."

"He did not say that he is married and, yes, he was attentive, but no more than is polite in elevated circles I'm sure," said Lady Alice. "Calm yourself, Celaine, and don't raise your hopes too high."

Lady Edith kept her head down over her embroidery and sniffed angrily as her sister chattered away. She had been made to ride with the servants at the back of the party, and Lord Tirellan had not spoken to her, though he had enquired after her health on the first morning after the incident in the tavern. Edith thought this most unfair since her actions had been the cause of them joining up with Lord Tirellan's group. The inn they were now staying at had been recommended by Lord Tirellan and was perfectly comfortable, although Edith did not like most of the food they served. The meat was always covered with strange-tasting sauces, and she had heard the maids on the stairs laughing at her when she asked to have her meals served plain. The city was huge and so busy; she had never seen even half as many people, and no-one seemed to smile as they rushed about in such a hurry. She wasn't really interested in clothes in the way Celaine was, so she hadn't taken much notice of what the city ladies were wearing. Probably the real ladies of quality went about in closed carriages. Indeed in her opinion, the best dressed women she had seen had been standing in the street outside a house, and when she had lingered near them Captain Thalon had hastily hustled her away.

Edith wondered where Aron was. She knew he hadn't been captured along with Tancred but that was the last they had heard, though she thought of him often. She had had one dream about him, so strikingly vivid that she was sure it was a true-dream, but nothing had come since. She wished he was here; he knew the Holy City and would surely show her the sights and real wonders. Even the Kingsday fairs had been a disappointment without someone to enjoy them with, and her mother had made sure Edith was kept away from all the most interesting entertainments.

Edith's reverie was broken as her father clattered into the room, his boots thumping on the wooden floor.

"Oh Papa," trilled Celaine. "Is there any news? Anything from Lord Tirellan?"

With a smile Earl Baldwin drew out from his tunic a small sealed scroll.

"I believe this bears his seal," he said, and passed it to his wife.

Lady Alice broke the seal and unrolled the message.

"Lord Tirellan requests the company of the Earl and Countess of Nandor for dinner at his residence two days hence," she read. "And Lady Celaine of Nandor is also invited."

"Oh Mama, how wonderful." Celaine turned to her father. "Papa, I shall need a new dress."

Earl Baldwin frowned. "I'm sure what you've brought with you will be good enough."

"Baldwin," said Lady Alice sharply. "Lord Tirellan is a very sophisticated man, and he'll expect to see Celaine at her best." She turned to Celaine. "You will certainly have a new dress. I'll go with you to choose one tomorrow, and perhaps get one myself."

"What about me?" said Edith.

Lady Alice looked again at the scroll. "It doesn't say anything about you, dear."

"That means you're not invited," said Celaine.

"That's not fair," cried Edith. She threw her embroidery across the room and stamped out, slamming the door behind her.

***

Nicoras and the squad of Sarazan guardsmen, accompanied by Ezrin and Tancred, rode into the Holy City in the late afternoon and headed directly for the Duke's residence, located in the most select area of the city, adjacent to the Palace. They dismounted when they arrived at the gatehouse which was the only way through the high wall that protected the Duke from the rest of the city. The guardsman on the gate recognised Nicoras and saluted smartly before opening the heavy wooden gate. Nicoras left the party in the courtyard and made his way to the office of Theobald, the commander of the Duke's guard.

Theobald was sitting beneath a large map of the city, a ledger open on the desk before him. When Nicoras entered the room he closed the ledger with a thump and sprang to his feet, a broad smile on his face.

"Nicoras, the last man I expected to see." He clapped Nicoras on the back in greeting. "What brings you here? Will you have a drink?"

He tugged a cord that hung on the wall to summon his orderly and waved Nicoras to a chair. Nicoras sat down glad that he had caught Theobald when the commander had time to relax. He counted Theobald a friend, but he was well aware that if duty and friendship collided, Theobald would unhesitatingly choose duty. The soft-footed orderly entered the room, Theobald ordered a jug of cooled wine and then turned his attention to Nicoras.

"I bear a letter from Lord Hercival to His Grace which will explain all."

Nicoras opened his belt pouch and produced a roll of paper that was sealed with a fat blob of red wax bearing the Sarazan crest.

The orderly returned with a jug and two glasses that he filled with straw-coloured wine before silently withdrawing. Theobald picked up the glasses and passed one to Nicoras.

"His Grace is not here. At present he is hunting with his Majesty, and it is uncertain when he will return. Lord Reginal accompanies him," said Theobald.

Nicoras nodded slowly at this information, took a sip of wine and then replaced the letter in his pouch.

"We lost a prisoner," Nicoras said gruffly. "We're here to get him back at Lord Hercival's command."

"Lost a prisoner? How did that happen then? He must be someone of importance for his Lordship to be bothered with him."

"Maldwyn of Nandor," replied Nicoras wearily. "Got out over the back wall in the middle of the night and swam the lake. We lost six men."

"Six men? How could you lose six men?" Theobald's grey eyes fixed intently on Nicoras.

"The boat capsized. We only found two bodies."

"How did he get over the back wall? Where was the sentry? Asleep, I suppose," snorted Theobald. "I hope you had him flogged."

" No. He was found unconscious under a wagon with a lump the size of an egg on the side of his head."

"Hmm," grunted Theobald and took a mouthful of wine. "Why on earth were we holding Maldwyn of Nandor?"

"We captured him along with a couple of soldiers up in the Tymion valley that Nandor claims belongs to them. He attacked a hunting party, wounded one man quite badly."

"Martis's balls! We've lost six men over that worthless bit of scrub. I thought the Duke had forbidden anyone from going up there, so what were they doing? There's not even any decent game up there."

"It was Lord Hercival and a group of his friends."

"Ah. That kind of hunting party. So six men died because Lord Hercival chose to disobey his father and show off to his friends?"

"It's worse than that. We lost another four in trying to seize a party of Nandorans in a tavern in Sarazan city."

"Did you get them?"

"Not the ones we were after, but we caught another lot." Nicoras took another sip of wine. "We caught Maldwyn's cousin Tancred. I've got him here with us."

"We've lost ten men and we hold Tancred of Nandor." Theobald looked at Nicoras over the rim of his glass, his expression sympathetic. "I can just imagine what his Grace will say about this."

"Fifteen men. We lost another five in a fight in a tavern on the river trying to pick up Maldwyn and his two companions."

"Fifteen men. Is that the final total? What on earth is happening? Is Maldwyn of Nandor some kind of god?"

"Far from it, from what I know of him. He seems as great a fool as his father, but one of his companions, some Darien exile, is reputed to be from the Academy."

"He must be one of the real ones then. But still, we shouldn't have lost fifteen men. How many more will it take? You know I don't hold with putting men at risk unnecessarily."

"Lord Hercival was most insistent upon the point. My task is to recapture Maldwyn and dispose of Aron of Darien. I have Ezrin with me to assist in finding them."

Theobald took a mouthful of wine and looked at the floor thoughtfully.

"I can see why his Lordship is so insistent, but I think his father will see things differently. You have explicit orders from Lord Hercival and you have to follow them, but I'm bound to say that the Duke will countermand them the instant he returns. That is only my opinion though and, of course, you must follow your orders until told otherwise." Theobald studied his glass, which was nearly empty, and then continued. "There's plenty of room for your men here, and if you need any further resource then I'll do what I can. I'll have that letter sent up to his Grace by courier; you have a few days before his reply in my estimation. Pass your glass over and have another drop of wine. I think it's rather good, don't you?"

Nicoras offered his glass and Theobald poured the wine.

"Are you certain that Maldwyn is here?" asked Theobald.

"Ezrin is able to locate him and has tracked him ever since they left Sarazan. If he isn't yet here then he is coming here. Lord Hercival had word that Earl Baldwin and his family were on the road to the Holy City too. It seemed unlikely to be a coincidence."

"Our people can find out about Baldwin for you. The city is alive with spies and watchers of all kinds. You'll know within an hour of his arrival."

CHAPTER 25

Aron and his companions approached the Holy City along one of the smaller roads that led to the capital. On either side the fields of farms and market gardens flourished on the rich soil, supplying the needs of the population. Despite the traffic of farm carts of every size the surface of the road was in good condition; even minor streams were bridged rather than forded, and the ditches had evidently been dug out since the turn of the year. As they reached the crest of a small hill the prospect of the Holy City unrolled before them. The sun reflected from the white walls of the citadel of the High King as it rose above the haze of ten thousand hearthfires. Hidden in the haze, Aron knew, were the richest houses in the kingdom and the blackest hearts.

The Holy City was similar to Sarazan in that it had long ago outgrown its defensive wall; beyond that it had all the characteristics of other cities, but on a much grander scale. The ambitious and the poor, the desperate and the dissolute of the kingdom had come to build their lives drawn by the legend of its prosperity. The result was an unplanned sprawl of shanty towns and fine villas, crowded tenements and airy mansions all jostling for position around the court of the High King.

"Beware in crowds. If you are jostled, even by children, especially children, look straightaway to your purse," Aron said to Davo and Maldwyn. "And be careful how you return a stare; there are professional duellists on the streets who will provoke a fight to create a spectacle."

"I remember you told me," said Maldwyn. "But I'm still amazed the High King allows it."

"Duelling is a great public entertainment; it would be a lot of trouble to suppress it. And then there's the money. The oddsmakers make a fat living from the gambling on the fight. They pay their taxes and pay a swordsman or two to keep business brisk."

"You done it?" asked Davo.

"It suited my purpose at the time to fight a couple of duels of this sort, yes," said Aron. "I fought the minions of Caldon in public, and profited handsomely."

"We could make a bit of money then," said Davo brightly.

"Unlikely," said Aron with a hard stare at Davo. "Most of the oddsmakers would remember me." But Davo's comment had brought forward a worry. Araiminta's supplies had lasted them well, but were nearly spent; they were running short of coin and would have barely enough to purchase lodgings. At last resort the horses could be sold, but Aron was most reluctant to lose the flexibility they provided. He needed to make contact with the Darien exiles quickly.

***

The streets of the Holy City were thronged with people of all description and the three travellers were forced to dismount and lead their horses through the crush.

"Is it always this crowded? I've never seen so many people before," asked Maldwyn looking around nervously. "I feel uncomfortable."

Just then a porter carrying a wooden chest barged him aside and was lost in the crowd before Maldwyn could regain his feet.

"No, it isn't normally this bad," said Aron. "But you must keep your wits about you."

"Where we goin' anyway?" said Davo. "I'm hungry."

"I'm going to an inn that the Darien exiles used to frequent. It's as good a place to start as any, even though it has been some time since I was last here."

***

The inn was called the Silver Moon; a long low building roofed with wooden shingles, it stood in a district of workshops, forges and small, ramshackle houses. Despite its rundown appearance, it was as crowded as everywhere else. The three travellers lodged their horses with the stable boy and went into the dingy taproom which was too full for them to get a table. Aron asked a serving man why it was so busy.

"Where have you been living that you don't know tomorrow to be King's Day?" answered the serving man.

His derisive laugh was taken up by those around him that had heard Aron's question. Cheeks burning, Aron tried to retreat to a corner, but his way was blocked by a large shaven-headed man in a black leather jerkin with a crest embroidered in silver upon the breast. He held a tankard in his left hand; he reached out until it struck Aron's shoulder and spilled its contents down his arm.

"You'll pay for that, you clumsy peasant," snarled the man, his right hand resting on the ornate sword hilt at his hip. The taproom fell silent. Aron looked the man in the face for a long moment. He judged him to be in his mid twenties; the long thin scar across his unshaven cheek proclaimed him a swordsman. The ghost of a smile played across Aron's lips as he too, found his sword hilt.

"You are making a mistake, my friend; perhaps you would allow me to get you another drink," he said quietly.

"Not enough," sneered the man through a half smile. "Not nearly enough, bumpkin. Let's take this outside."

There was a scurry of activity as most of the people in the taproom tried to get out into the tavern yard. Aron caught hold of Davo in the crush.

"Find the oddsmaker that's running this and get the wager on."

He passed over the pouch that contained the last of their coin.

"'Ow much?" asked Davo, grabbing the pouch with both hands.

"All of it."

Davo slipped away into the crowd. Aron and Maldwyn stepped into the yard to find that a wide oval of onlookers had formed with Aron's opponent at the far end. Several voices were shouting odds over the noise of the excited mob. Aron handed his pack to Maldwyn, drew his sword then unbuckled his sword belt, and handed that to Maldwyn as well.

"Are you sure you know what you're doing?" whispered Maldwyn.

"Sure," replied Aron with a strange distant smile, and then stepped forward raising his blade.

"Stick it to him, Kovac," a harsh voice yelled.

Kovac raised his blade and stepped out to meet Aron. A hush fell on the crowd.

Kovac moved forward on the balls of his feet as if he was walking on hot sand, his blade moving in a tight circle as he focused on Aron. Aron took two steps forward and awaited Kovac's first move. There was a moment's silence as the two men looked at each other and, it seemed, everyone held their breath. Then Kovac attacked. The crowd roared with approval and excitement. Aron tried to blot out the noise of the crowd. *Be the centre of the storm; focus only on your opponent's hand and blade, move only in response to him.*

Kovac attacked fast and with precision, his thrusts powerful yet controlled, his blade a blur in the twilight. *He is used to winning quickly,* thought Aron as he blocked a slash to his neck followed by a thrust to the groin. *The odds are probably weighted to this, and he'll become frustrated when he can't break through. Just watch and wait.*

The crowd howled for blood as Aron fought a defensive fight, anticipating well, blocking the frenzied attacks. Already cries of derision could be heard; they were used to the quick kill. Aron circled warily, content to parry and forestall Kovac's attacks which were becoming noticeably slower. Sweat was breaking out on Kovac's brow; soon he would make an error. Aron waited, holding him at bay, waiting for the mistake. The mob screamed in frustrated anticipation. Aron continued to circle, keeping clear of the front rank of the crowd, wary of the tripping foot. Kovac was breathing heavily now; Aron could see doubt in his face as he continued to thrust forward, more warily than before.

As the minutes passed and the fight continued with no blood spilt, the crowd grew quieter, sensing that their favourite was struggling and their wagers were in danger of costing them dear. Somewhere at the back of the assembly someone called out "Ten crowns on the stranger." Other voices joined him as the oddsmakers struck new bargains.

Kovac must have heard the shouts because at that moment the balance of the fight changed. Aron moved smoothly onto the offensive with sharp thrusts, too fast for his opponent to do anything other than block and retreat. The noise of the crowd increased as they anticipated the bloody conclusion. Kovac was tiring badly now. Once and then twice, Aron's blade nicked him; washing his hairy arms with scarlet without doing any serious harm. His blocks grew more and more desperate as Aron drove him backwards around the yard, the crowd parting before them.

Suddenly it was over. Aron thrust high and turned his wrist in mid thrust, directing his point downwards. Kovac's tired arms could not react fast enough and Aron's blade slashed into his groin cutting through the big artery. He squealed in agony as blood gushed down his leg and collapsed forward onto Aron's blade which sank deep into his chest.

A great roar of cheering burst from the crowd as they surged forward. The foremost seized Aron and lifted him onto their shoulders so that he could receive the acclaim.

"Best fight I've seen for months."
"Splendid, absolutely splendid."
The voices all around were yelling and cheering. Somewhere in

the middle of it all, as he was carried through the crowd, Aron managed to grab Maldwyn for a moment.

"Pass your hat round for the victor," he instructed before Maldwyn was shoved aside by the crush

After a few minutes Aron was carried to the taproom door and allowed to regain his feet. A mug of ale was thrust into his hand which he drained to great cheers and then went inside. The taproom was empty save for the serving boys, Aron headed for a table in a dark corner and ordered another mug of ale. The crowd flowed in after him and the room became noisy with shouts for ale and spirited re-enactments of the fight.

Aron sat quietly at his table, breathing slowly and deeply as he had been taught, seeking to calm the surges of emotion that rushed through his mind. *Be thankful you have survived again and take what lessons you can.*

With a scuffle of feet Davo arrived at the table; he called to a potboy for more ale and pushed a leather purse across to Aron. It was heavy. Aron unfastened the drawstring and poured a few coins onto the table. The gold glinted dully in the lantern light.

"I got in before the fight started, got real good odds," Davo said, his smile displaying his yellowed teeth. "We got stacks of money."

And how much have you squirelled away for yourself? Aron wondered briefly then dismissed the thought. *There's more than enough here to keep us in decent lodgings for a few weeks.*

A moment later, Maldwyn pushed his way through the crowd and also laid money onto the table. There was no gold, but a good selection of silver and copper coins.

"They were glad to give something; lots of them said it was the best fight they've seen." said Maldwyn, his eyes shining with excitement. "It was the best I've seen. I mean, I know you must be good, but I never realised." He tailed off when he caught Aron's eye.

"Have a drink, Maldwyn, then we'll go," said Aron quietly.

"You don't want to stay here?"

"No," said Aron. "We can afford better now. And besides, I just killed a man. He would have had friends." He looked around the room. "We're safe enough for a while, but I don't want to be here when the crowds thin out. And I don't hear any Darien accents."

Calling to the potboy, he ordered a round of ales and some food.

Some time later, feeling better than he had for days, Aron roused his companions to leave. The other customers of the tavern stood back to give them a clear path to the door and applauded them all the way out. The landlord met them at the door and ceremoniously tore up their bill.

"I'd be pleased to see you back here any time," he said with a smile. "That was the best fight we've ever had here."

***

"But I don't understand why he picked on you," said Maldwyn as they walked away from the tavern. The streets were far less crowded now and the three men were able to stroll freely.

"He heard me say I didn't know what day it is," replied Aron. "And assumed I was some strawhead as ignorant of bladework as I was of the city. That is an attitude that many city dwellers possess; that all there is worth knowing is to be found in the city and that everyone who lives in the country is an idiot."

"But he could have picked on me," said Maldwyn. "I didn't know it was King's Day."

"Welcome to the Holy City," said Aron.

He flicked a glance over his shoulder and then stopped in the doorway of a shop, peering to look into the interior for a few moments. He glanced up the street then moved on. As he walked he fiddled with the strap of his pack and then cursed as it slipped off his back onto the cobbles. He knelt to pick it up and again looked back up the street to confirm his suspicions as the other two waited for him.

"Someone is following us," Aron said as he stood up.

Maldwyn began to turn to look behind them.

"Don't look around, just keep walking," said Aron. "Keep straight on up this street. Walk slowly and I'll catch you up."

With that he slipped into a narrow alley that led off from the street into the dark. He hurried down the alley and emerged into a narrow lane, then turned to parallel the main street going back towards the tavern. Thirty paces along he came to the mouth of a second alley leading back towards the main street. He ran down this to the junction and waited in the deep shadow. A thin, shabbily dressed man walked past. Aron reached out, grabbed his coat sleeve and pulled him into the alley. Holding a knife along side the man's nose he said softly.

"Why are you following us?"

CHAPTER 26

The thin man went limp in Aron's grasp. "Aron. It is Aron isn't it?" He gasped. "Don't you remember me? I'm Tamon."
Aron looked hard at the man. The dim light of the street lanterns did not show him enough of Tamon's face. Davo and Maldwyn ran back down the street to stand either side of Aron. The few people on the street ignored them and hurried about their business. *If this is an ambush, it's a very poor one,* thought Aron.

"Walk out into the light so I can see you," Aron commanded.

Tamon did as he was told and walked towards the nearest lantern with Aron close behind. There had been a man named Tamon amongst the Darien exiles. He had arrived in the Holy City a few weeks before Aron had been forced to leave. Was this the same man? Tamon turned to look at Aron from under the lantern.

"Now you remember, don't you?" Tamon said.

The accent was certainly Darien and the thin features looked somewhat familiar. Aron paused a moment and then put the knife away.

"It's been a long time, Tamon. I didn't recognise you."

"I thought it was you when I saw how you handled him back at the tavern. I didn't know you were back."

"We only arrived today," said Aron. "We went to the Silver Moon in the hope of finding a few Darien folk."

"There's too many people know the Moon for Darien folk, so we don't go there much anymore," said Tamon reflectively. "Only for I was passing and saw the crowd."

"Can you take me to Esson?" asked Aron.

"He's dead," said Tamon. "Killed when Caldon fired the house in Cooper's Lane."

"Who else was killed?"

"Too many. Lamat, Hami, Snellin and Ralf that you would know, and a dozen more besides. Thorold and Manni were knifed in the street. We've had a rough time since you left. Caldon's men came down hard on us after Tirellan arrived."

"Tirellan is here!" exclaimed Aron. "But he is under the same sentence from the High King as Caldon."

"I don't know what's going on, or if he's still here" said Tamon. "But he's been here right enough."

"Is Cordra alright?" asked Aron, gripped by sudden concern for his friend.

"Well enough. There's talk of him getting married."

"Good thing if he does. He needs to ensure the succession. Who's the bride?"

"They say it'll be Nerissa, daughter of the Duke of Letra."

"Letra would be a fine ally." Aron remembered the girl as being rather short and plump with a squint, but her father was a rich and powerful man with a fine reputation as a soldier. "Who's leader of the exiles now?"

"Lionel," said Tamon.

"Good. Can you take us to him?"

Tamon looked suspiciously at Maldwyn and Davo for a moment before he spoke. "Follow me."

Tamon set off up the street; Aron motioned to the other two to follow.

"He'll take us to my friends," Aron said and turned to follow the fast disappearing Tamon.

Tamon led them through gloomy streets and dark stinking alleys until they arrived at a door in a high white-washed wall. Tamon rapped on the door, somewhere up above a window squeaked open. Aron looked up but could make out nothing in the darkness. A small peephole opened in the door, Tamon muttered a password and after a scraping of bolts, it was opened. One by one they crossed the threshold to be scrutinised in turn by a heavily built man who held a hooded lamp. Aron could not see his face beyond the lamp.

Tamon set off up the narrow stairs that rose before them; somewhere above a candle lantern provided enough light to see by. Aron, Davo and Maldwyn passed the doorkeeper and climbed the stairs. Behind them they heard the bolts grind back into place. At the head of the stairs they entered a wide unfurnished room.

"Wait here," said Tamon. "I'll see who is around."

He walked across the room and opened a door in the far corner.

"Your friends seem very suspicious," said Maldwyn.

"With good reason if Tirellan's here," said Aron.

"Who is this Tirellan? I heard your reaction to his name. Is he an enemy?"

"He is Caldon's right hand, his executioner." Aron's voice was cold and hard. "He butchered the garrison at Darien, including my father."

"And he is here, in the Holy City?"

"He's been here, though I thought he was under sentence for treason. His agents have killed half a dozen of my friends since I left."

"This ain't good news then," said Davo.

"It is and it isn't," replied Aron. "He is a calculating and ruthless killer and it's not good news that he's hunting the friends we have here. However, I have sworn his death and anything that brings him within my reach is good news." He smiled grimly.

The door at the far end of the room crashed open and a large bearded man, a thick riding cloak thrown over his night clothes, strode in.

"Aron," he roared, his arms outstretched. "It's so good to see you."

Aron stepped forward to meet his embrace. "Lionel, it's good to be here."

The two men hugged for a long moment before Lionel released Aron.

"I had no idea you were coming. How long have you been back? And who are your friends?"

"I arrived today," replied Aron. "Lionel, this is Lord Maldwyn, heir to the Earldom of Nandor."

Lionel bowed from the waist and offered his hand. Maldwyn bowed elegantly in return and grasped Lionel's hand as he introduced himself.

At least his mother taught him manners, Aron thought.

"And this is Davo, a soldier in the service of Nandor." Davo imitated Maldwyn's bow. Lionel did not shake his hand.

"I need a favour, Lionel," said Aron.

"Of course," said Lionel expansively. "Anything."

"My friends are fugitives. I killed a man tonight and there are soldiers after us guided by a wizard. We need somewhere to hide up for a few days until I can arrange to get them out of the city."

"Stay here. There's plenty of space and we're well guarded. But tell me, who's hunting you?"

"Sarazan."

"Ummm," said Lionel thoughtfully. "Not good."

"Only for a few days. Until I can get them on their way back to Nandor."

"Keep them out of the way then," said Lionel. "But here I am forgetting my manners. Have you eaten tonight?"

"Yes. We ate in the Silver Moon," said Aron. "All I really want at this moment is a bed."

The tiredness had crept up on him since they had arrived at the house of the exiles and he had been able to relax his alertness. Now he felt his eyelids trying to close of their own accord.

"Of course. I'll catch up with you in the morning and you can tell me the full story of what brings you here."

***

Aron was woken by the noise of the pigeons that roosted on the window sill of the dusty attic room he had shared with Maldwyn and Davo. They slept on as the morning sun crept across the floor. Aron lay in bed thinking about the chances that had brought him back to the Holy City and what now had to be done. It certainly seemed that fate had guided his steps, for he'd had no plan of returning, yet here he was and with Tirellan in reach. Fate, or something more? *Is this your doing, Lady?* he thought, remembering Iduna and her bower.

Maldwyn grunted as he turned in his sleep. *What am I to do about them?* Aron wondered. Just because there had been no sign of Sarazan's pursuers recently did not mean they had given up. Iduna had warned him that someone searched for them; most likely a wizard that had a lock of Maldwyn's hair or something similar, and could scry him whenever he chose. *You missed that didn't you? Should have brought his hairbrush with him.* And there was the unnatural storm that had wrecked their boat, the wizard again? *How far is Sarazan prepared to go? It was a fair guess they might be in the Holy City, but would they trail them further?* Aron looked over at the slumbering figure of the Nandoran. Could he leave Maldwyn to make his way back to Nandor unaided? Would he be likely to reach home? *Unlikely*, Aron thought. Even without pursuit it was a better than even chance that Maldwyn would find trouble.

So he had to go with them to Nandor, but that could not happen until he had dealt with Tirellan. The prospect of returning to Nandor with Maldwyn, leaving behind Tirellan's dead body, was most attractive. Earl Baldwin would have to stand by his promise of reward and Aron was much taken with the idea of seeing Maldwyn's sisters again. His memory supplied Davo's mocking voice *"So which one do you want?"*

He closed his mind to the remembered question. The outcome would probably have very little to do with what he wanted so it was best not to speculate on it. He had to get to Nandor first, and before that he had to find a way to Tirellan. He tried to think about how he could get close enough to kill him. It had to be personal; something like a poisoned arrow was out of the question. Tirellan must know who his nemesis was. He wanted to stand beside Tirellan as the light faded from his eyes and tell him that he died to avenge Darien - then he would consider the question.

***

The sun was high when Aron awoke again, roused by a servant calling to him that breakfast was past ready and likely to spoil if he didn't come soon. Davo and Maldwyn's beds were empty. Aron leapt out of bed and pulled on his clothes in a fury of worry lest the other two had already finished their meal and gone out to explore the city. He hurried down the stairs after the servant and followed him through the house to a plain dining room. At the table sat Davo and Maldwyn taking their ease as they grazed in a leisurely fashion on the food set out before them.

"So you've finally woken up," said Davo with a laugh. "I 'ad to hold Maldwyn back, totherwise there'd a bin nothing left."

Maldwyn looked aghast at this allegation, but Aron had been awake long enough to recognise the look in Davo's eye.

"And you've taken nothing but water yourself because it's a fast day," he said lightly looking straight at Davo.

"There's plenty left," said Maldwyn earnestly.

"There's some really manky fish," said Davo. "Dunno what they've done to it, but it's all brown."

"Smokies? They've got smokies," said Aron, lifting the lid of a metal serving dish. "I haven't had smokies for years. I used to love them."

He dumped several large spoonfuls onto his plate along with a hunk of bread.

"Don't know how you can eat that," said Davo pulling a face.

"Food of the gods," said Aron through a mouthful.

"We was thinking we'd 'ave a look around the city today," said Davo. "Being as how it's our first time 'ere."

Aron almost choked on his bread. "You'll do no such thing," he coughed, trying to get the words out past the crumbs.

He tried to say, "You're still a fugitive, Maldwyn,", but the words came out as a splutter without form as he tried to communicate his displeasure at Davo's proposal. The splutter turned into a coughing fit and then hiccups. Maldwyn came and thumped him on the back but to no avail. He was still hiccupping when Lionel came bustling into the room.

"Good morning, good morning. Did you sleep well?" he said to Aron who hiccuped in reply. "I've news you'll want to hear. Tirellan's back."

"Where?"

"Here, in the city," replied Lionel. Aron hiccuped again.

"Let me get you something for that." Lionel turned and left the room.

"Tirellan. He's your enemy isn't he?" said Maldwyn. "Let me aid you in this. Let me pay back some of the debt I owe by hunting him down for you."

"No, Maldwyn," said Aron. "I will take my revenge on Tirellan first hand. This is a matter of blood."

The dramatic effect of this statement was somewhat diluted when Aron hiccuped violently at the end. Maldwyn looked disappointed and ready to argue the point, but Lionel returned with a cup of liquid which he passed to Aron.

"What is it?" asked Aron between hiccups.

"It's just a little honey in warm water; my grandmother swore by it. Just drink it slowly and in a few minutes you'll be fine."

Aron looked dubiously at the cup and then took a sip. "Excuse me Maldwyn, but I must speak with Lionel. When we're done, I'll find some practice blades and we can resume your tuition if you wish," he said.

Maldwyn and Davo took the hint and left.

"Tell me about Tirellan," Aron said and then took another sip.

"He came back a few days ago; we believe he was in Caldon."

"How is it that he is allowed to be here? Isn't he still under the sentence of exile?"

"In the public face of things, yes," said Lionel. "But in private, he is Caldon's envoy and is allowed to freely come and go."

"But Caldon is still in rebellion against the High King and his servants are supposed to be seized and imprisoned wherever they are found."

"Again that is the public face of it, but in private the High King is negotiating with Caldon. According to Kyria, His Majesty has no greater wish than to see the kingdom healed."

"Leaving Darien in Caldon's grip," said Aron, his fists clenched. "I thought the King prided himself on being a just man."

"He does," replied Lionel. "But he sees this as a price he is willing to pay to bring peace, and that peace he desires more than anything. More than that, there's a new king in Peresia, who seems to want to reopen their claim to the southlands. His Majesty needs all his nobles behind him."

Aron sat in silent thought a moment before he spoke. "How long has the King been talking to Caldon?"

"Tirellan first arrived nearly a year ago. He has been back to Caldon several times. We believe they are close to agreement."

"Fool! It will cost him his throne. He should confront Caldon while he still can. Otherwise Caldon will pick off his allies one by one just as he did with us until he's too strong. There are reasons aplenty to kill Tirellan; this is but one more. But it must be soon."

"We've been trying since he first appeared in the city and got nowhere. He's always surrounded by half an army of guards and has the devil's own slyness. Our hand cannot be detected in it, otherwise we would forfeit any sympathy the King holds for us, and he has made continuous war on us. Did Tamon tell you of what happened to the house in Cooper's Lane?"

"Aye." Aron nodded grimly. "There must be some way to get to him."

"He rarely steps outside his mansion, and when he does he's surrounded by at least a dozen guards. He's protected against sorcery too. Kyria's wizard probed him for us and he's shielded. Caldon's wizard may have set him up with a talisman-based shield, but seems more likely that he's been dabbling himself."

"Really. What's the evidence?"

"Coopers Lane for one thing. Why would the place go up like an oil store? There was a big pulse of magical energy around the time the fire started. Every wizard felt it, but no-one recognised it. It could have been him."

"That just makes it all the more important that we get to get to him as soon as possible. Have you any ideas?"

"There's one possibility." Lionel paused.

Aron eyed him suspiciously. "What is it?"

"Lord Tirellan has enjoyed the pleasures the city offers," Lionel said, picking his words carefully. "And we have discovered he has certain tastes that he has indulged whilst he's been here." Aron looked at him even more suspiciously.

"Go on."

"He has a taste for young men. He likes to beat them and then take his pleasure with them. It's rumoured that he's killed more than one. He dismisses his servants and guards on the nights when he does this."

"That sounds like an invitation to visit him."

"We thought so. A group of us went over the back wall the last time."

"What happened?"

"We didn't get past the dogs."

"Poisoned meat takes care of them."

"Not these dogs." Lionel shivered at the memory. "Man high with glowing eyes and jaws dripping fire."

"Hellhounds?"

"We didn't stop to find out. But there's no way past them without using powerful magic and that just exposes whoever helps us." Lionel paused. "There is another way though."

"Which is?" said Aron, his suspicions dark as a thundercloud.

"There is a procurer in the city who supplies the boys. He pays in gold. There are people poor enough to take the risk," said Lionel, turning his head so that he did not meet Aron's eye. "The procurer has been persuaded to assist us."

"Are you suggesting that I offer myself as a prostitute for this man to supply to Tirellan?"

The disgust thickened Aron's voice so that he almost spat the words out.

"It's the only way I can see to get close to him. He likes them dark and slender like you," Lionel said and turned back to face him. "How much do you want to kill him?"

Aron sat in silence for a while turning the proposal over in his mind. At last he reached his decision. "I'll do it."

CHAPTER 27

Theobald smiled as Nicoras and Ezrin entered the guard commander's room.

"Have you news for us, Theobald?" Nicoras asked.

Theobald smiled and indicated they should sit down.

"Certainly there is some news, and some that will be to your liking, I believe. Do sit down." Theobald's attention moved to the tray on his desk; he lifted the lid of one of the cloth-wrapped jugs and inhaled the aroma. "Would you like a cup? I have peppermint or raspberry."

"No thank you," said Nicoras. "Now what news have you?"

"Patience, Nicoras," chided Theobald. "Would you like a cup, Master Ezrin?"

"Ah yes, thank you," said the wizard as if surprised that he had been asked.

Theobald poured for himself and Ezrin as Nicoras fidgeted irritably. Finally he spoke.

"News then. The king is expected back the day after tomorrow, but our lord will not be returning with him, so you have a little more time, gentlemen. His Grace is at present visiting the Duke of Westport, and it is not yet known when he will return. I doubt he has received your message yet as the courier bringing this news crossed with the one bearing yours."

"How long do you think we may have?" asked Nicoras.

"Another two days before His Grace receives the message and then it depends on his business in Westport. At least a week, I should think."

"Hmm," Nicoras frowned. "Tell Theobald what you've found, Ezrin."

"Maldwyn of Nandor is in the city. He is staying in a house with a group of people he thinks of as the exiles. Their leader is called Lionel, and they are friends of Aron of Darien. He doesn't know where the house is because he arrived there in the dark and he hasn't left it."

Nicoras looked at Theobald inquisitively. "What do you make of it?"

"Almost certainly they are the exiles of Darien and they are trouble. There has been a nice little war on the streets of the city between them and the Duke of Caldon." Theobald poured himself another cup. "They're a wild crowd. You certainly pick them, Nicoras."

"Do you know where this house might be?"

"No, I don't. You weren't thinking of charging in there, were you?" Theobald looked sternly at Nicoras. "I would advise most strongly against it... it will certainly be heavily defended."

Nicoras frowned and stared into his cup for a moment. "Do you have any news of Earl Baldwin?"

"Ah yes," Theobald said. "Earl Baldwin and his family have taken rooms at an inn called The Seven Stars, and what is more, have been seen in the company of Lord Tirellan. I thought that might interest you."

"We'll set a watch on The Seven Stars immediately, but what's especially interesting about Lord Tirellan?" said Nicoras.

"You've not heard of him? That does surprise me. I thought his reputation had spread far and wide. Not a man to get on the wrong side of, and he just happens to be the Duke of Caldon's pet wolf."

"What's Caldon got to do with this?"

"Nothing, I hope. His Grace would be deeply displeased if this affair tangled him in Caldon's nets."

"So why is Baldwin associating with Tirellan?"

"Who can say? It is just possible that Baldwin doesn't realise who and what Tirellan is." Theobald smiled in amusement. "I wonder what the Darien exiles are going to make of this news?"

***

"The fish are rising nicely, Cristoff," said Lord Tirellan as he read the last of the four message scrolls that had arrived that morning. "The Earl of Dunmore invites me to dine and play cards. The Peresian ambassador invites me to luncheon; now I wonder what he wants to talk about? Lord Calshot invites me to hunt his estate with him and the Duke of Norrish bids me to a ball. Do you suppose the Lady Celaine can play cards, Cristoff?"

"I would suppose she can play beggar-my-neighbour and other such nursery games," replied Cristoff with a snigger. "Though I wouldn't play against Lady Alice for more than pennies."

"A beautiful and clever woman," said Tirellan. "And dangerous. Fortunately she is harnessed to that buffoon, which limits her power."

"You know, Petter. I thought you were exaggerating how awful Earl Baldwin is. I can see now you were merely being polite. I mean, the man was roaring drunk. I had to endure his interminable ravings about his land dispute for the whole night."

"Come now Cristoff, you exaggerate. I distinctly recall he fell asleep before midnight."

"Well perhaps, but it seemed like the whole evening. How do you wish for me to answer these?" He indicated the message scrolls.

"Accept Dunmore, Norrish and the Peresian ambassador, stall Lord Calshot. I don't wish to leave the city just now, there will be other replies coming and Calshot's estate is too far away for anything less than eight days absence."

"Will you be escorting Lady Celaine to the Ball?"

"I suppose I will need a suitable lady on my arm. Can you think of some way of ensuring that her father cannot attend, short of poisoning him?"

"No, my Lord," said Cristoff. "It is the sworn duty of a knight to bear fortitude with a good grace."

"You have such a wonderfully sympathetic character, Cristoff. Have you considered becoming a priest?"

"Frequently. But then I would have to spend the rest of my days praying for the redemption of your soul, my Lord."

"A more worthy use of your time I could not conceive of," Tirellan said with a broad grin. "Has there been any news of those Darien scum?"

"None at all. They seem to have gone to earth completely. I'm confident they'll turn up soon though. You know how the city is; you can't keep anything secret for long. There was a very good wager fight at the Silver Moon a few nights ago."

"Oh really. A shame we missed that, who was it?"

"You remember Kovac; big, shavenheaded right-handed swordsman. He did his usual trick of picking out some innocent punter and got stuck with someone who could really fight."

"Really? What happened?"

"It was a classic by all accounts. The punter drew him on, toyed with him for a while then skewered him. Just your style, Petter."

"And who was this punter?"

"No-one knows for sure, but someone thought he looked like

that Darien assassin we had so much trouble with about eighteen months ago."

"Really?" Tirellan reacted sharply. "If there is any chance at all that it's him, then I want him found."

"I've already put the word out, my Lord."

"Hmm. Shame about Kovac, he used to put on a good show. Good swordsman, but always likely to underestimate an opponent. Have you heard anything from Bazarkis the procurer?"

"Yes. He says he may have something that will interest you, though the price will need to be higher."

"It costs what it costs, Cristoff," sighed Tirellan. "I need something to look forward to."

***

"I don't trust him and I don't like him," said Lady Alice with some force. "I know he's well-connected and that just makes me more suspicious. And there's something wrong with the way he looks at me and the girls."

"He seems a perfectly decent kind of a fellow to me. Even if he does prefer dancing to hunting," replied Earl Baldwin. "How's the fellow supposed to look at you then?"

Lady Alice paused for a moment, searching for the words Baldwin would understand. "With respectful interest."

"What's that then?"

"The way you would look at a horse you were thinking of buying, or a good hound that belongs to a friend."

"Hmm," Earl Baldwin snorted. "Is it not enough for you that he's a nobleman with lands and substance, and he's interested in our daughter?"

"But why is he interested in Celaine?" Lady Alice fixed her husband with a hard stare. "She's young and beautiful, but that's all. You know we offer no great wealth or alliance, and that hasn't been enough for a dozen men far less eligible than Tirellan. She's been disappointed too many times already, and I don't want to see it happen again."

"Why does it matter? Tirellan's a rich and powerful man with wide influence. He'll be an excellent ally for Nandor. He can arrange an audience for me with the High King. What more do you want?" Earl Baldwin drained his glass and then lifted the jug to see if any wine remained. "Dammit, this jug's empty, call the maid to fetch me another."

Lady Alice rose to tug the bellrope that would summon the maid. She wanted to say no; that Baldwin had already drunk two jugs and it was only mid-afternoon, but she knew it would do no good to start an argument now. She wanted to say that Celaine deserved to be more than a dynastic pawn, deserved a husband who would love her and treat her well. She tugged the bellrope and sat down in silence. It was an old argument and there was no point in restarting it.

"Lord Tirellan sent around the name of a dressmaker with his invitation. Celaine will need a dress for the ball," Lady Alice said mildly.

"More blasted expense," grumbled Baldwin. "Do I look as if I'm made of money?"

"For a man like Lord Tirellan, it is essential that his escort reflects well on him. You said yourself that he is a man of wide influence, who moves in the finest circles. Celaine simply cannot be shown up. It would reflect badly on his Lordship, and it would reflect badly on us. Come to that, I shall need a dress myself."

"Why?" Baldwin looked disconsolately into the bottom of his glass.

"You don't imagine that Celaine is going alone to the ball with Lord Tirellan! That would be most unseemly, and don't tell me you'll be keeping an eye on her because I know what you'll be doing." Lady Alice regarded her husband sternly. "You'll be talking to anyone that will listen about the iniquities of Sarazan, and boring them to death most likely."

"I er, well. Try not to spend too much then." Earl Baldwin knew when he was beaten. "Where's that blasted maid got to?"

***

"I'm bored," declared Maldwyn.

"So'm I," replied Davo. They were sitting in the afternoon sun with their backs to a wall, on a balcony overlooking the inner courtyard of the Exiles' house where a few of the exiles were aimlessly kicking a ball of rags about.

"It's all right for Aron. They're all his friends and I'm sure they've got lots to catch up on, but I don't know anyone and there's nothing to do."

"I agree," Davo said mournfully. "No one wants to play dice with me no more, an' I caught up on the sleep I lost getting here. I wanna go an' 'ave a look around the city."

He idly flipped a lump of moss down onto the head of one of the footballers.

"Exactly," said Maldwyn. "The greatest city in the kingdom right outside the door and we're shut in like naughty children. All my life I've listened to stories about the wonders of the Holy City. I want to see them. I was hoping Aron would show me, but he hardly has time for us now."

"Reckon we slip out an' have a look around. We'll keep our eyes peeled for Sarazan's men, but they won't try nothing. There's too many people around for that an' besides, we're armed."

"How will we get back in?" Maldwyn scratched at the back of his neck.

"Don't worry about that, my Lord." Davo grinned slyly. "Most of the guards are good lads an' owe me a bit o'money."

***

"He's on the move at last, Captain," Ezrin said as Nicoras entered his room. "He's going to look around the city with the little thief. Aron of Darien is not with them."

"Where are they?" Nicoras asked sharply.

"He doesn't know," replied Ezrin, gazing into his viewing crystal once more. "He's walking past a timber yard; there are good houses on the other side of the street. The exiles' base seems to be close to a lot of woodworking workshops."

"Where is that?"

"I don't know. I'm sorry, Captain, I don't recognise anything. I know the city about as well as Maldwyn."

"Then we need Theobald's map and someone who does know the city," said Nicoras. "I'll get them. You keep watching."

***

"Isn't the King's Keep magnificent?" said Maldwyn. "I'd heard of the size of the walls, but I was still surprised to actually see them. They make Castle Nandor look like a child's play house. There will be some building work when I return. I will talk to father and persuade him of the need."

The two of them were leaning against a wall eating hot slices of pork wrapped in a flat bread and watching the bustle of the market around them. Their eyes followed the younger women, dressed as they were in light summer skirts that were semi-transparent in the strong sunlight.

"Some new kit for the lads wouldn't go amiss, my Lord. If you don't mind me saying so," said Davo as Maldwyn paused to wipe the hot pork fat from his chin.

"Yes. Of course. The old lot looks rather rough when you look at the guards at the Keep."

There was silence for a moment as Maldwyn considered rebuilding Castle Nandor.

"Is there anything else you specially want to see, my Lord?" Davo asked. Maldwyn did not reply immediately, but looked down at his boots as he chewed the last of his snack.

"Is there? Could we go to a," his voice trailed off and he blushed. Davo looked at him curiously. "I mean. I've heard of such places, but."

"My Lord?" Davo struggled to conceal his grin as he waited for Maldwyn to get to the point.

"Could we go to one of those places that have......girls?"

"What girls would those be my Lord?" Maldwyn avoided meeting Davo's gaze which prevented him seeing Davo's struggle to keep a straight face.

"Girls who will go with you if you pay them."

"Why would you want to go to one of them, my Lord?"

"Dammit." Maldwyn looked at Davo then, as if daring him to laugh. "Because I've never been with a girl."

Davo thought for a moment. Certainly in Nandor there were taverns where it was known that some of the wenches would be compliant for the right money. But not if you were the Earl's son; there was nowhere that Maldwyn could have gone, and there had been no gossip about him flirting with the castle maids.

"I'm sure there are such places in the City, my Lord, but I'll need to ask the lads back at the Exiles' place. Can't take you to just any place."

"Why not?"

"Wouldn't do for you to catch a dose of the pox, my Lord."

"I hadn't thought of that."

"You should, my Lord. 'Tis a dreadful thing, the pox," said Davo. "But if we go to one of the better places you should be alright. What kind of girl d'yer want?"

"What do you mean?"

"What do you want her to look like? Fat, skinny, blonde, dark? They'll 'ave all kinds, yer know."

"Blonde, I think." Maldwyn smiled. "Blonde and slim and not very tall, but with nice brown eyes."

"Right you are, my Lord," said Davo. "I'm sure we can find one like that for you."

***

"How much do you know about Earl Baldwin?" said Lionel.

"Why? What's happened?" replied Aron, caught off-guard by his tone.

"Earl Baldwin has found a friend in the city," Lionel frowned so deeply his eyebrows met in the centre of his forehead. "He has been keeping company with Lord Tirellan. How do you explain this?"

Aron sat very still, stunned by Lionel's revelation, trying to assimilate the news. At length he spoke.

"Baldwin is here? Why? What's going on?"

"I thought you might answer that. How is it that he associates with Tirellan?"

"Earl Baldwin is straightforward and none too bright. I doubt he knows who Tirellan is, or who he is associated with. He has taken him on his word as a gentleman, but I don't understand why he's here."

Lionel looked straight at Aron, his eyes cold. "Are you confident enough of your opinion to risk our safety on it?"

"Baldwin doesn't know Maldwyn is with us. Maldwyn doesn't know his father is in the city," said Aron earnestly. "And I didn't know until you told me."

"Do you intend to reunite Maldwyn with his father?"

"That has been my quest ever since I got him out of Castle Sarazan."

"He must not be able to pass on our location here. There is too much at stake."

"He hasn't left the house since we arrived," said Aron. "Keep him here until I can take him to his family. He's never been to the city before. I can make sure he'll never find the house again."

"Be sure," said Lionel grimly. "You know how Tirellan would use the information."

Lionel was silent for a long time, his brows knitted together, as he thought.

"If it were anyone else than you," he said at last. "I would have his throat cut to preserve our secret. See him safely away from here and he will live."

"I will go and see Earl Baldwin and make the arrangements. Where is he lodging?"

"We don't know where they are staying. But we will."

"They? Who is with him?"

"His wife and a daughter. Tirellan escorted them to Duke of Norrish's ball."

"What! Which daughter? What on earth is going on?"

Aron's stomach tightened at the thought of Tirellan with Edith or Celaine.

"The older daughter, I believe. It looked like the usual sort of thing by all accounts. He danced with her several times. Pretty girl, I'm told," said Lionel with a half smile.

"But we know Tirellan isn't interested in women."

"Then they're cover for something else. The question is does Baldwin know what's going on?"

"I very much doubt it. He probably thinks Tirellan is going to marry his daughter."

He thought of Celaine and her long list of disappointments, about to get longer it seemed.

"They're in for a disappointment then," said Lionel.

"Poor girl, she doesn't deserve any more heartache," said Aron.

"Oh. You know her then?" said Lionel catching the tone of Aron's voice.

"Yes. There are two daughters. They're both very pretty and very nice, and don't belong in the same world as the likes of Tirellan."

Lionel raised one eyebrow inquisitively and smiled at Aron.

"Just another reason to kill him," said Aron flatly. "Any news on that?"

"Bazarkis the procurer reports that Tirellan's been asking for his usual entertainment. Bazarkis passed on your details. Are you ready?"

"I've been practising unarmed with Kyria's weaponmaster. But I hope I can get a hidden blade in with me."

"Don't count on it. You know how clever Tirellan is. You keep practising and in the meantime, we'll keep Maldwyn of Nandor confined. Once you've disposed of Tirellan he can go to his father."

CHAPTER 28

It was around midday and the two girls were sitting in the bedchamber they shared in the Seven Stars. Celaine was still in her nightgown. "It was so wonderful, I don't know where to begin," said Celaine.

"What time did you get in?" said Edith as she brushed Celaine's hair. "It seemed very late."

"I heard the watchman call four of the morning when Lord Tirellan's coach brought us back. It's such a beautiful coach, with black horses and four coachman all dressed up in scarlet livery."

Edith said nothing and continued brushing.

"The Duke's mansion is just so splendid. It had so many lamps it was as bright as a summer's day. The ballroom was huge, bigger than the whole of Castle Nandor and you've never seen so many servants."

"Did Lord Tirellan dance with you?" Edith asked evenly, aware that she was going to be told whether she wished it or not.

"Yes. Three times. And I danced with Lord Merrish, Count Anador and lots of others that I can't remember. Lord Merrish said my accent was charming."

"Are you sure he wasn't laughing at you?"

"Oh no. He was far too nice for that."

"Is he handsome?"

"Well yes, I suppose so. Not as handsome as Petter."

"Who?"

"Petter, Lord Tirellan."

"He said to call him Petter?"

"Yes. He was wonderful for the whole evening." Celaine seemed entirely unaware of Edith's increasing irritation with the subject. "And he wore such a lovely coat of silk with lace cuffs. He was quite the finest dressed man there."

"Did Papa enjoy the evening?" Edith decided to change the subject at this point.

"Oh yes," said Celaine. "He met someone who promised to get him an audience with the King."

"Really! When?"

"Oh, today I think. He's probably already gone. What's the matter? You shouldn't curse like that."

Celaine bent to retrieve the hairbrush Edith had dropped.

"I thought we would all go. I wanted to see the palace, and the King and everything. It's just not fair. Papa will get it all sorted out and then we'll go back to Nandor and I won't have seen or done anything."

"Oh, I'm sorry, Edith. But think; you'll be able to come and visit me here all the time after I'm married."

***

Earl Baldwin strode into the sitting room of the Seven Stars and threw his wet cloak at a chair; it missed and fell on the floor.

"How did it go?" asked Lady Alice, laying aside her embroidery to pick up the cloak. "Did you see the King?"

"I saw him, and spoke with him at length. Do you know what he wanted at the end of it? Some piece of paper to prove Nandor's claim to the land, as if my word was not enough!"

"But I can see his point," said Lady Alice calmly. "No doubt the Duke will swear equally as strongly that the land belongs to him. How is the King to choose?"

"In favour of his friends no doubt."

"Well, if you believe that then there was never any point in coming here. What said His Majesty of Maldwyn's ransom?"

"Better news on that. His Majesty said he would speak most strongly to the Duke, and that he disapproved of the taking of hostages in time of peace."

"The land doesn't matter provided we get Maldwyn back."

Baldwin opened his mouth to reply but then thought better of it.

"Surely there's a record of the grant of the Earldom?" continued Lady Alice. "There's a chest full of documents at the back of your hanging cupboard at home. You have looked in there, haven't you?" Lady Alice stared hard at her husband.

"Father never mentioned the existence of any such warrant," said Baldwin defensively.

"You should have Tumas go through the contents of that chest and catalogue them properly. There could be any manner of thing in there."

"Yes dear," said Baldwin. "Is there anything to drink up here?"

"It's barely midday," said Alice with a frown. "How did His Majesty leave things?"

"He gave me his word that he would enquire into it and speak to me again."

"The King gave you his word. What more could you reasonably want?"

***

"Alright, my Lord. I think I've found just the place for yer." Davo grinned, exposing the gaps in his teeth. "The prettiest young ladies can be yours for a mere twenty silver pieces."

"Twenty silvers?" exclaimed Maldwyn, he sat up from the bed where he had been lounging. "Do you know how many sheep you could buy for twenty silvers in Nandor?"

"Well they are the prettiest girls in the city, but if yer'd prefer sheep, my Lord." Davo displayed more gaps.

"Oh no. I mean." Maldwyn turned red, to Davo's great amusement. "Twenty silvers it is then. Where is it?"

"Half Moon Street in the Tailors' district."

"We could go today."

"They don't open until after sundown and we need to get a change of clothes."

"Why?"

"It's a classy place and yer dun't look like a nobleman. Yer looked in a mirror? That's the same shirt yer've had on since yer left Sarazan."

"So? I'm the heir to the Earldom of Nandor." Maldwyn straightened his shoulder and stuck his chest out.

"So bollocks. They ain't gonna let yer in. How's yer going to prove yerra nobleman? Yer don't sound like a nobleman and nobody's even 'eard of Nandor and we're supposed to be keeping quiet about who yer is anyway. Or 'ave you forgotten Sarazan's still after yer?"

"Alright so, I'll get a new shirt. When can we go?"

"When you look like sommun they'll let in. We'll go tonight if yer get some decent clothes."

"Why are you so fussy all of a sudden?"

"They throw yer out an' most like I'll get a kicking too. The doorkeepers is famous there."

"So where am I to get clothes?"

"Same as everone else, buy 'em. We've got the money. Get Aron to take us out or send in a tailor. He can't 'ardly refuse, he needs 'em as much as yer. Or ask Lionel, yerra a nobleman ain't yer? Yer can't be going round looking like a scarecrow."

***

"I think this is what we've been waiting for," Ezrin said, smiling broadly as he faced Nicoras. "Lord Maldwyn is planning a visit to a cathouse in Half Moon Street in the Tailors' district. He's been thinking of little else all day."

"Where's Half Moon Street?" Nicoras turned to the map that was pinned to the wall.

"The Tailors' district is here, Captain." Theobald's servant pointed on the map. "I know Half Moon Street, and I have heard of the brothel there. It has the reputation of being expensive."

"It's a good way from here then," said Nicoras. He thought in silence for a moment. "Is there an inn nearby where we can take a room?"

"Several, Captain," replied the servant.

"That's what we'll do then. We'll install you in an inn nearby, Master Ezrin. You can tell us when Lord Maldwyn's coming, and Tancred can lead him straight into our arms." Nicoras cracked his knuckles with a little smile of satisfaction. "I'll take a dozen men and some crossbows to discourage any resistance. No livery though; we can't show Sarazan colours on the street or we'll have the King's guard down on us. And we'll need to make sure none of the men guarded Maldwyn when he was in Sarazan otherwise he might recognise them. Right, let's get moving. These places don't open until after sundown so there's time enough to get set up tonight if we move smartly."

***

Maldwyn stood in the bare room displaying his new shirt and breeches; he had even managed to get a shine on his boots.

"What a treat for a lucky girl. You could be the crown prince hisself. Let's be gone then, we mustn't keep the ladies waiting," said Davo. "Shame Aron ain't coming, but then he wouldn't really enjoy hisself. He's far too serious for a young fella."

"He's got a lot on his mind," said Maldwyn.

"Do him good to have a night out on the town," chuckled Davo. "Now do yer want to go for a drink or two and maybe a bite o' summat before we head up to Half Moon Street, my Lord?"

"No, I think we'll go straight there. We might seek a tavern afterwards, perhaps. I'll-um - see how I feel."

They made their way downstairs to the exit door. The doorman nodded to Davo and drew back the bolts. They stepped out into the street and heard the bolts rattle back into place behind them. They strolled in a leisurely fashion down to one of the main thoroughfares. At this point of the day, just after sunset, but with the sky still light, there were many people abroad. None were bustling about business wearing their workaday clothes. This was the time when the city people took the air dressed in their finest, maybe stopping for a gossip with friends or to take a drink at a tavern. Strolling musicians played for the crowds and sweetmeat sellers cried their wares.

"Celaine and Edith would just love this," said Maldwyn. "All these colourful clothes and the people just parading around. When I'm Earl, I shall bring them here and take a house for a month every year."

Davo smiled as he thought about the time when Maldwyn would be Earl. A good friend of the Earl might prosper; someone who had shared danger with him and who knew his secrets might do very well. Maldwyn was like his father in that he would stick to his friends through thick and thin, and always make sure they were well looked after.

By the time Maldwyn and Davo reached Half Moon Street the residents of the Tailors' district were hanging out the night lanterns.

"That's the place," said Davo, pointing to a discreet, but stout door in an otherwise blank wall. "Knock and ask for Mistress Lively. I'll wait for you in that tavern." Davo pointed to a hostelry a few yards further on. "Enjoy yourself, my Lord."

Maldwyn clutched the pouch of coins and marched up to the door with his shoulders held square. He rapped firmly on it and took a pace back to stand under the lantern so that the doorkeeper could get a good look at him through the peephole. After a moment the door swung open and Maldwyn stepped inside.

***

"They're moving, Captain," said Ezrin. "They're heading for Half Moon Street."

Nicoras took a look up and down the street. "Still busy, too many witnesses if Maldwyn makes a fight of it. We'll lift him when he comes out. You can tell us when that is."

"The very minute, Captain."

"Excellent," said Nicoras. "We'll sit outside the door and then grab him."

Nicoras ordered a runner to go round alerting his squad.

The runner returned after a while. "All in position, Captain."

"Good, now we just wait."

Time passsed and the sky darkened from blue to star-speckled purple, but the streets remains busy.

"This will make it easier, Captain," said Ezrin, looking up from his crystal. "Maldwyn is going to meet the other one in the tavern up the lane afterwards."

"Fine. We'll take him there. Send the runner around again."

***

The tavern was light and airy with comfortable chairs, and the serving wenches were pretty. It was not to Davo's liking. There were no dark corners and no dice games and the wenches' bright smiles had a 'hands off' quality about them. Davo sat down in an inglenook with a bad grace and prepared to wait for Maldwyn.

The ale was good enough that Davo was drinking four tankards to the hour as he imagined what the young lord was up to and watched the tavern fill up. He had barely noticed the new arrivals until he was on his sixth tankard and Tancred walked in. Davo choked on his ale and nearly dropped the tankard. Tancred did not appear to notice Davo immediately, so the little man withdrew as far as he could into the inglenook and kept the tankard in front of his face. Tancred sat with a group of men, all with the haircut and demeanour that said 'soldier' to Davo; another group sat at the next table. All of them drank very little and watched the door out of the corners of their eyes.

What's going on? thought Davo, his stomach filled with ice. *What's that bastard Tancred doing here and who are these soldiers?* Whatever the answer, he was certain it added up to trouble.

He sat in his corner trying to work out what he should do. The only exit was on the far side of the tavern. To reach it he would have to walk out in front of Tancred and the soldiers. As he considered he became aware of the pressure on his bladder, the natural consequence of the ale he had consumed. In a very short time the pressure became intense; Davo briefly considered refilling the tankard he had just drained but doubted that it would prove sufficient. He slipped from his corner to the door that led to the back yard and the privies. No heads turned to follow his progress.

The yard was contained by the high walls of the adjoining buildings, leaving no exit. Davo relieved himself into the barrel and hurried back into the taproom just in time to see Maldwyn enter, a dreamy smile on his face. Maldwyn took four steps into the room before Tancred stood up.

"Well met, cousin," said Tancred, an oily grin on his face.

"Tancred," said Maldwyn, his mouth falling open in surprise. "Wha...what are you doing here?

"I could ask you the same question, except that I know what you've been doing. Not something that your father would approve of, I think, cousin." The oily grin broadened.

Maldwyn turned red and spluttered incoherently as he tried to answer.

"I think we should go now, don't you?" Tancred took Maldwyn gently by the arm.

"Where are we going?" said Maldwyn resisting Tancred's efforts to push him towards the door.

"Away from the wickedness and temptation."

"But I have to meet people here." Maldwyn twisted away from Tancred's grasp and picked up a stool, holding it by one leg.

"If they are frequenting such places as this then they are not friends worth having," said Tancred smugly. "What would your mother say?"

"Who are these people?" said Maldwyn as the soldiers stood up. He looked desperately around the room, then dropped the stool as they moved to surround him

"Just some friends of mine," said Tancred. "You've fallen in with some very low company and I've needed their help to find you."

Davo watched in dismay as the soldiers hustled Maldwyn out of the taproom followed by Tancred. No-one looked in his direction as the room emptied. He thought for a moment or two and then followed them through the door. *Aron is going to kill me for this*, he thought.

A few paces down the street, the soldiers stood in a protective circle around Maldwyn and Tancred. As Davo watched, another man walked up to them and the soldiers saluted him.

"Well done, Tancred," said the man. "Good to have you back with us, Lord Maldwyn."

Maldwyn froze for a moment as he recognised Nicoras, and then turned on Tancred.

"You treacherous dog," he cried, seizing his cousin by the throat. "You'll die for this."

He wrestled Tancred to the ground before the strong arms of the soldiers broke his grip and pulled him away. Tancred sat in the middle of the street gasping for breath. Looking up, his eyes met Davo's.

"Him too! Get him too," shouted Tancred pointing up the street.

Davo turned to run, but before he had taken five paces two crossbows twanged and the impact of the bolts pitched him face down before the tavern door.

CHAPTER 29

The sun was barely up before the Duke of Sarazan, who had arrived very late the previous evening, summoned Theobald and Nicoras to attend him. "Can someone please explain why His Majesty so urgently wishes to see me to discuss the matter of Nandor?"

The Duke of Sarazan spoke in a moderate and reasonable tone that all those present recognised as concealing extreme annoyance. He had arrived very late the previous evening, and now the sun was barely up before he had summoned Theobald and Nicoras to attend him. His eldest son, Lord Reginal, stood silently behind his father's chair.

"Earl Baldwin of Nandor had audience of His Majesty yesterday, my Lord," said Theobald.

"Did you not receive the despatch that I sent, my Lord?" said Nicoras. "It was sent the moment we reached here."

Nicoras had a headache and was unprepared to meet his master at this early hour. He had permitted his men to have a small celebration to mark Maldwyn's recapture last night.

"I did not receive any despatches," said the Duke sharply.

"The courier was sent to the royal hunting lodge, but by the time he reached it you were probably on the way to Westport," said Theobald. "He's probably on the road between here and Westport."

"And what were the contents of this despatch?"

"I haven't actually read it, of course, my Lord," said Nicoras.

"Of course not," said the Duke, giving Nicoras a hard stare. " But I'm sure you can tell me what I need to know."

"It began in that strip of disputed land," said Nicoras. "Lord Hercival took a group of his friends riding up there." The Duke's jaw tightened, but he said nothing. "They were attacked without warning by a band of Nandoran soldiers led by Lord Maldwyn, the Earl's son. They repelled the attack and captured some of the Nandorans, including Lord Maldwyn, though they did suffer some injury."

"Serious injuries?" asked the Duke with concern.

"Serious enough. One fellow may never ride again and will always walk with a limp. Anyway, they captured Lord Maldwyn and took him back to Sarazan and Lord Hercival sent to Nandor demanding ransom."

"I understand now why his Majesty wishes to see me," said the Duke, his face stern. "This is the very thing he is striving to end in the Kingdom. Have I not just returned from Westport where I urged the Duke to end his feud with his neighbour Lord Egil? How does this look to his eyes? Years I have spent in cultivating his trust, and this act of stupidity will undo it all. Theobald, dispatch the message birds at once and summon Lord Hercival here. Reginal, it seems you must return to Sarazan to take charge, since I cannot rely on your brother."

"Yes, father," said Lord Reginal, his face serious. "This is most regrettable."

The Duke fixed Nicoras with a cold eye. "That does not explain why you are here."

"Maldwyn of Nandor escaped from Castle Sarazan, my Lord, and we pursued him," replied Nicoras. "We recaptured him last night. He's confined in a room here, my Lord."

"Escaped? How?"

"He got out over the back wall and swam the lake."

"Is that all?" asked the Duke bleakly.

"We lost some men in the pursuit, my Lord."

"How many?"

"Six in the boat and another five in taking the Nandoran rescue party."

"Rescue party?"

"Earl Baldwin sent a group of soldiers under his nephew Tancred to rescue Maldwyn. We've got Tancred too."

"Baldwin sent soldiers into Sarazan?" The duke's mouth was a narrow slit of anger beneath his beak of a nose.

"Yes my Lord. We captured all save two. Those two got away downriver with Maldwyn and we tracked them to the Holy City with Master Ezrin's aid. We lost another five men trying to take them in a tavern on the river."

The Duke sat in silence for a moment before he spoke, his eyes seeming fixed on some point far beyond the room.

"So, not only have I incurred His Majesty's extreme displeasure and lost half a platoon of trained soldiers, but all the nobles of the kingdom will be laughing up their sleeves at me for losing a prisoner and letting Earl Baldwin, of all people, get the better of me. Do you see any redeeming features in this black farce?" He turned to Theobald and Reginal.

"No father," said Lord Reginal. "Only Nandor is not blameless in all this. It was their attack that precipitated it, and they also sent soldiers into Sarazan city itself."

"Hmm. True, but I fear it will avail me little to go crying the wronged man before His Majesty."

"Do you have some other approach in mind?" asked Lord Reginal.

"No."

"What should we do with Maldwyn of Nandor?" asked Nicoras.

"Hang on to him this time," replied the Duke grimly. "That will be all for now."

Nicoras and Theobald bowed and left the room.

"I would not wish to be in Lord Hercival's shoes when he faces his father," said Theobald quietly.

"Nor I," replied Nicoras.

***

Aron careered down the stairs from his attic, a cold knot of fear in his stomach and crashed into Lionel's room. "Have you seen Davo and Maldwyn?" he said breathlessly. "Their beds haven't been slept in. They haven't been at breakfast and I can't find them anywhere in the house."

"I've not seen them," said Lionel with a worried frown. "They're usually the first to the table. I gave orders that they were not to leave the house unaccompanied. What do the doorkeepers say?"

"Those I've spoken to say they haven't seen them."

"Then someone is lying." Lionel stood up, his fists clenched. "They can't have got out without someone's help. I'll ask them again. Have you any idea where they could have gone?"

"No. I haven't really spent that much time with them recently. I've been too busy preparing to face Tirellan."

"Could Maldwyn have found out where his family are lodging?"

"I don't see how, since we don't know. I don't think he knows they're in the city. I certainly haven't told him." Aron struggled to keep his annoyance under control. "This is all I need. I'll have to go out and look for them."

"No. Let me speak to the doorkeepers first. Fools!" Lionel thumped his fist on the table. "You know as well as I do how soldiers can relax if the danger isn't right in front of them. I'll double the guard." He stalked around the room a deep frown on his face. "Maldwyn was asking for new clothes yesterday, and I had a tailor brought in to see to him. I thought you wouldn't want him sent back to his father in rags. I wonder if there's a connection? Dammit, they've probably been taken up by the watch for brawling in some tavern. I hope Maldwyn's had the sense to keep quiet about who he is. I don't want to think about what could happen if Tirellan's got him."

"This is my responsibility," said Aron grimly. "I brought them here. I should find them."

"No. You need to be close by for when Tirellan sends to Bazarkis for you. That could happen anytime. You can't do everything; focus on what's important."

***

"Tell me something interesting, Cristoff," Lord Tirellan drawled. "What does the future hold for me?" He lay back on the cushions of his chaise longue and lifted a cup of herbal tea to his lips.

"Well, let us see what the new day brings." Cristoff opened the pouch containing the morning's despatches. "The Duke of Westport bids you to attend a performance of a new musical entertainment he has commissioned."

"Westport, by the Gods! That is unexpected. When is it?"

"Tonight, my Lord."

"So I'm an afterthought." Lord Tirellan smiled. "But it shows that I'm creating a stir if he invites me so late. Accept immediately."

"Very good, my Lord. Will I send to Earl Baldwin asking him also?"

"Oh, I suppose so. I need an ornament on my arm. The child may even enjoy it, though the Gods only know what Baldwin will make of it. He'll probably nod off and snore like a pig, but I can't bring the one without the other. Still, I don't have to endure him for much longer."

"My Lord?"

"My job is nearly done here and I have succeeded brilliantly. I have prepared the ground so that enough of the nobles of the court will not stand against Caldon when he re-enters. Nor will he have to abase himself overmuch, and after a well-judged period of repentance he will not lack for friends. Then we can take our proper place in society."

"And what of Lady Celaine?"

"No doubt she will be returning to Nandor shortly when her father's business here is concluded. I can't imagine Earl Baldwin developing a taste for life at court, really, can you?" Lord Tirellan smiled sweetly. "And when she is gone I shall miss her slightly, but I'm sure I'll get over it in a few days. And she can look back fondly on this episode and think of the favour I have done her in introducing her to a level of society she would have otherwise never reached. Have we any news of how Baldwin's dispute progresses?"

"The Duke of Sarazan was summoned to appear before His Majesty this very morning. He arrived at the palace in a fine temper, I'm told. He is unlikely to be pleased at your involvement, my Lord."

"I can live with his displeasure. He was never likely to support us anyway. Now that His Majesty has taken the matter in hand resolution will not be far away. I wonder how Baldwin will like the royal judgement?"

"Even he is not stupid enough to dissent, surely?"

"I think it would be dangerous to attempt to set limits on Baldwin's stupidity," said Lord Tirellan. "But let us not dwell upon him. In a few short days he will be gone. What other news?"

"The Earl of Dunmore invites you to another evening of cards the day after tomorrow."

"No doubt he hopes to win back the money I took off him last time, and it would be churlish to refuse." Lord Tirellan smiled. "Another profitable evening in prospect, Cristoff."

"Do you wish for an escort for the evening, my Lord?"

"No. I think not. Lady Celaine is charming enough, but I am growing weary of her. Is there anything else?"

"No, my Lord."

"Then fetch me my writing case. I must write to Caldon to tell him of my triumphs, and, I think, send to Bazarkis. We will entertain his latest offering in two days time."

"Very good, my Lord."

"And stand down the guard for that night."

"Is that wise, my Lord?"

"It depends how many witnesses you want there to be. I prefer none."

"I was just thinking of last time, my Lord, and the rumours of that Darien assassin."

"I shall cast my usual warding; it proved most satisfactory didn't it? There's no suggestion that he has magical abilities, is there?"

"No, my Lord."

"Then have a little faith, Cristoff. As long as I live, nothing can get past my pets without my permission. Cease your worrying, and tell me how to establish my temple. How can I draw the faithful to the altar of Galgulla?"

"Answering a few prayers would put you ahead of most gods, my Lord."

"Heal the sick, raise up the unfortunate?"

"For a price. Not too many though, you would not wish to attract too much attention."

"Certainly not, at least at the beginning. Besides most of the unfortunate richly deserve their fate. I prefer a secret cult for the chosen few."

"Including His Grace?"

"I think not. My Lord of Caldon believes in nothing beyond his own destiny. His son, however, is a quite a different matter."

"And he may be High King one day."

"Indeed, and a glorious day that will be." He took a sip of herbal tea. "We will need premises, Cristoff. Discreet, of course, but well-appointed."

"This will not be cheap, my Lord."

"No, but then immortality seldom is."

"Immortality?"

"Yes, Cristoff. Such is the gratitude of gods to those who serve them well."

***

"Is there any news of Maldwyn and Davo?" asked Aron.

"I've found who let him them out and they're already regretting it," said Lionel, his voice edged with anger. "But no, there's been no news of them yet, nor is there any hint that Tirellan has them." His voice softened slightly. "However, we've found where Earl Baldwin is lodging. They're at an inn called The Seven Stars. I've sent a couple of men to have a look and find out whether Maldwyn is with them, but I've much bigger news..... I've heard from Bazarkis. It's to be the day after tomorrow. Forget about Maldwyn, Tirellan's the target. Are you ready?"

Aron stood silent for a moment and then nodded. "I have to be," he said quietly.

"Did you practice again today?"

"Five hours. I don't believe there's anything more I can do. Not in the short time we've had."

"Have you got everything that you need?"

Aron smiled and reached into his belt pouch and drew out a slim object which he tossed to Lionel. "This is what I'm going to kill Tirellan with."

Lionel caught it and turned it over in his hands. It was a short black-handled knife, its blade the length of his index finger. He drew it from the soft leather sheath and tested its edge. "Sharp enough, but how are you going to get it in? Tirellan's guards are good and you're certain to be searched."

"I know. That's why it's the size and shape it is. I'm going to stick it up my arse."

Lionel's expression froze in surprise, then a moment's disgust flashed across his face. "Will you be able to draw it quickly enough?"

"I think so," said Aron. "I've been practising." The look of disgust passed across Lionel's face again. "Don't look at me like that. Where else can I put it? If you have a better idea, I'd like to hear it."

Lionel looked at the floor; there was a long pause before he spoke. "No. I've no better idea. Can you move with it?"

"Yes. It isn't comfortable, but I can walk. I haven't tried doing more. I hope that all I have to do is wait until I'm alone with him and then I can kill him."

"Don't let him die too quickly."

"He won't if things run my way." Aron smiled grimly. "So what is to be done about Maldwyn and Davo?"

"Will you stop worrying about them and concentrate on Tirellan? I've doubled the guard and made sure everyone knows we're on alert. If Caldon comes we're ready."

"They're my friends and I'm responsible for them. Maldwyn's never been in a big city before, and I was supposed to look after him. What can I tell his father?"

"Maldwyn was told to stay in the house and disobeyed. You're hardly responsible for that. He's old enough to face the consequences of his actions," Lionel said firmly. "You know what this city is like; someone will have seen them and the information will be for sale. I'll make sure the right people know that we'll buy. If Tirellan's got them we'll know soon enough. Anyway, Tirellan isn't going to be a problem for much longer."

CHAPTER 30

Their shadows stretched long before them as Aron and Lionel walked through the city to the house of Bazarkis. All about them the streets were filled with people making their way home at the end of the working day. Lionel did not speak, and Aron was glad of the silence; he had too many thoughts in his mind for him to want the distraction of idle chatter. The whereabouts of Maldwyn and Davo, the involvement of Baldwin with Tirellan, Tirellan with Celaine; all these tumbled in his head and underlying everything was a tension that sharpened his every sense. Tirellan, face to face, at last.

Bazarkis' house stood in a street of fine tall stone-built houses, the residences of prosperous merchants. There was nothing to mark it out; it was totally anonymous. Lionel approached the door and tugged on the bellpull. After a few moments the door opened and a huge doorward silently conducted them inside. The interior corridor was floored with glazed tiles and the air carried the hint of exotic musky perfumes. The doorward led them up a fine wooden staircase to a small drawingroom, and gestured for them to sit on a cushioned bench, then left closing the door behind him.

"How much does this man Bazarkis know?" asked Aron quietly.

"Very little," replied Lionel. "As much for his safety as for yours. He knows we want to get you close to Tirellan, that's all."

Aron looked around at the rich wall hangings, rugs and carved furniture. "There's a lot of money gone into this house," he said.

"Bazarkis has grown fat on supplying the specialised needs of his customers."

"So why is he helping us?"

"We have given him no choice. Until a few years ago, Bazarkis was just a brothel keeper and procurer, one amongst many, unremarkable but ambitious. He discovered that there is a great deal of money to be made out of catering to the perverted tastes of some rich men. Men who want more than a pleasant companion for an evening, far more. Men like Tirellan. That there are such people might not surprise you; but what would surprise you, is how many there are." Lionel paused and looked suspiciously around the room. "Bazarkis recruits his victims from the poor and unfortunate. He offers them gold, but for some the price is their life. He has used some of our people. The families came to me to help find them. I know what became of their children......they do not. If Bazarkis does not do all I demand, the families will find out. You know our people well enough to imagine what they would do. They might even ask you to kill him."

"I will gladly when I'm done with Tirellan."

"No. We must hold our silence. That is part of the price."

Aron was about to dispute this when the door opened and a well-dressed, dark-haired man of about forty walked in.

"Ah, Commander Lionel. So good to see you again. This must be your young man."

His eyes remained cold as he greeted them, none the less Lionel shook him firmly by the hand.

"Now then, young fellow. Let me have a look at you."

Bazarkis walked slowly around Aron, examining him as if Aron were a horse he was considering buying. Aron shifted uneasily, uncomfortable under Bazarkis' gaze. "Hmm, not bad. Not bad at all. Should clean up very nicely."

Aron was unsure whether he was flattered or not. "What's your name, lad?"

"Aron."

"Well Aron, you're a fine-looking fellow. I'd consider taking you even without the circumstances."

Aron said nothing and tried to avoid catching Bazarkis' eye.

"I hope he knows what he's letting himself in for." Bazarkis turned to Lionel. "I don't want Lord Tirellan angry with me. He's been a good customer, but I know enough of him to know he'd be a very bad enemy."

"Oh. He knows alright, don't you Aron?" said Lionel with a tight smile. "I'm sure there will be no complaints about Aron from Lord Tirellan tomorrow."

"Well, I hope not. My customers trust me; if it gets out that I did this for you I could be ruined."

"I have given you my word," replied Lionel. "No-one will find out from us."

Bazarkis stared at Lionel for a long moment with a far off gaze then he shrugged. "To business then. We must prepare Aron for his evening's work."

"Prepare me?" said Aron guardedly. "In what way?"

"You can hardly go dressed like that." Bazarkis plucked at Aron's plain and threadbare tunic. "And when was the last time you bathed? Lord Tirellan is a man of taste and refinement. You can't go to him looking and smelling like a vagabond. We have clothes here that will fit you and be far more to his lordship's taste. Come."

Aron passed Lionel his pouch containing the black-handled knife, and followed Bazarkis from the drawingroom, across the landing and into another small room. Several wardrobes with full length mirrors in their doors lined the far wall, and the room was filled with flowery scented warm moist air from the steaming bathtub that stood in the middle of the fine mosaic floor. Two women stood beside the tub.

"These ladies will wash, dress and prepare you," said Bazarkis. "I'll come back in a while to see what they've made of you." With that he left, closing the door behind him.

Aron looked at the two women; they were both in their late thirties, he judged, simply dressed in plain blue dresses in the manner of servants. There was amusement in their eyes as they looked at him.

"Come on then, love. Get your clothes off." said the taller dark-haired woman. Aron hesitated.

"I think he's shy, Terris," said the shorter plumper one with a laugh. "What are you hiding?"

Aron felt the blush rising to his cheeks.

"You won't get far in this business if you can't take your clothes off in front of strangers," laughed Terris. "Do you think we have to undress him too then, Shara?" Aron stood frozen to the floor as the two women advanced on him.

"Don't worry, my dear, we won't hurt you," said Terris reaching for his waist. Aron jumped involuntarily as her fingers touched him.

"Oh a little bit ticklish are we, love?" Aron jumped again as Shara's fingers touched his neck. "Is this your first time? We'll be gentle."

Both women giggled as Aron turned scarlet. Working swiftly and deftly the women stripped Aron's clothes off as he squirmed, gasping and giggling from their touch.

"So what was it you were hiding my darling?" said Terris as Aron stood naked before her.

"I can wash myself, thank you ladies," Aron whispered huskily.

"Oh no. Master said we have to scrub you proper," said Shara. "In the tub with you. We put some lavender and rose petals in it so's you'll smell nice."

Aron stood a moment under the women's gaze and then reluctantly stepped into the tub. The warm water swirled up around his legs as he slid into its embrace, then Terris and Shara attacked him with their washclothes. As they washed him his body began to respond to their touch.

"Oh careful, Terris," laughed Shara. "We've got a live one here."

"Tis a shame to waste it, but you're going to need it later."

Terris smiled at Aron, her dark eyes sparkling with mischief. Aron's cheeks flamed.

"Enough! I am clean." Aron surged out of the tub to stand naked and dripping on the floor. "Now what else is to be done?"

Shara put down her washcloth and stood back with her arms folded under her substantial bosom to look at Aron.

"I like 'em with a bit of spirit. Reckon you'll need another bath after your night's work," she said with a broad grin. "I'll look forward to that."

"Just get on with it, will you," said Aron, resisting the strong temptation to put his hands over his groin. "Give me a towel."

"Yes, master," giggled Terris as she fetched a towel.

"What should he wear then, Terris?" said Shara. "I think the dark blue would suit his colouring."

"Yes, that would work. Maybe white or cream leggings to show off those dancer's legs."

Shara opened one of the cupboards and sorted through the contents coming up with a long dark blue tunic.

"Try that," she said as she continued to pick through the contents of the cupboard.

Aron took the tunic from her and slipped it on. The material felt soft on his skin, softer than anything he had ever worn.

"Suits him very well," said Terris. "Though it will cover his pert little bottom."

Aron reddened again.

"What do you think of these?" Shara held up a pair of creamy white leggings. "Try these on him."

She tossed them to Terris who caught them deftly.

"I can put them on perfectly well by myself," protested Aron.

"But it's more fun this way."

Terris winked at him and ran her hand up his thigh. Aron turned even redder.

"Stop embarrassing the poor lad and get him dressed," said Shara. "There's still lots to do."

"I'm clean and I'm dressed," said Aron as he pulled up the leggings. "What else is there?"

"Your hair to start with," said Terris.

"What's wrong with it?" asked Aron as he scrubbed it energetically with a towel.

"Don't do that, you'll make it all frizzy," said Terris snatching the towel. "It needs properly setting."

"What?"

"Making it curl. Shara'll do it. She's a dab hand with the tongs."

"I don't want my hair curled."

"It's not what you want that matters. Your customer prefers curled hair, so curled hair you will have." Terris smiled knowingly at Aron. "You've got nice hair, but I do love a man with curls in his hair."

"Come and sit here and I'll do your hair," said Shara. "And sit still."

Aron did as he was told as Shara fiddled with the tongs, which she heated over a candle flame for what seemed to him an extraordinarily long time before applying to his hair.

"Now are we done?" he asked when Shara finally finished.

"There's just your face to do," said Shara standing back to examine her handiwork.

"No!" said Aron in dismay.

"Have to do the job properly. Your customer will expect it," said Terris bringing out a small leather pouch. "This is your first time with a gentleman of quality, isn't it? Well they're different, let me tell you. There's nothing too good for them, the money they're paying. So you have you hair curled and your face made up and you says 'yes my Lord, no my Lord, anything you please my Lord' and make sure you says it respectful, or the master here will have the hide off your back. But you do it right, and there's good returns if they like you. Shara there, she was a most favoured friend of a duke, weren't you dear?" Shara sighed and smiled. "'Til she wore him out and the old fellow snuffed it. Now hold still, 'cos if you move and smudge it I'll have to start all over again."

Aron did as he was told and held still as Terris worked with her set of brushes and sponges. She seemed to take an eternity, and the longer she worked the more the brushes tickled and the more his nose itched. He longed to scratch, but that could smudge the artwork and prolong his embarrassment. Finally she stepped back.

"There now, I'm done. And don't you look lovely. Let him have a mirror, Shara, and see how pretty he is."

Shara brought a large gilded handmirror and held it up for Aron to look into.

Aron stared at the image in disbelief. What he saw was the face he had shaved that morning, but changed in a most unsettling way. It was as if he had a twin sister and now beheld her: dark-rimmed eyes, moist red lips and peach tinted cheeks framed by a fall of dark curls. A girl stared back at him. A pretty girl too, a girl that he would take a second look at in the street.

"Wouldn't you just want to eat him, Shara?" said Terris.

Aron looked away and shook his head, but the image would not fade. He looked again, turning his head to catch the profile view. The brow of his reflection furrowed as he turned it over in his mind. He looked attractive, pretty, beautiful even. A cold shiver ran down his back and he turned from the mirror feeling as if he had just looked over a vast cliff.

"Come along then," said Terris. "Stop mooning around like a lovestruck girl. Master'll be waiting."

The two women led Aron back to the small drawingroom where Bazarkis and Lionel sat, two glasses and a half-full decanter of red wine showed how they had passed the time. Lionel looked up as Aron and the two women entered the room, but his gaze slid past Aron without recognition.

"A very good job ladies," said Bazarkis as he handed Terris and Shara a silver coin each. "He looks absolutely delicious."

Terris and Shara left the room in a torrent of giggles. Aron's cheeks flamed under the layer of powder. Lionel looked again at Aron and his mouth dropped open.

"God's blood is that you, Aron?" he asked in a whisper.

"It's me," replied Aron quietly.

"I'd have passed you in the street and never known you," said Lionel struggling for words. "It's your hair."

"Surprising what curling irons, a little rouge and powder can do," said Aron with a wry grin.

"My carriage will be ready shortly, then you must go. Your customer particularly disapproves of tardiness," said Bazarkis. "Would you like a glass of wine before you go?"

"No, thank you," said Aron. "I wouldn't want to spoil my lip paint."

Bazarkis chuckled. Lionel stared and shook his head in disbelief. At that moment a servant came in and spoke softly to Bazarkis.

"Very good," said Bazarkis. "The coach is ready. Please follow my man and he'll take you to it. I wish you a," he paused for a moment, "profitable evening." Then he left the room.

"How much did he pay you?" asked Aron quietly, one eye on Bazarkis' servant.

"Twenty, in gold," replied Lionel.

"I wonder how much he charged Tirellan."

"Seventy."

"That is a man who richly deserves to die slowly and painfully."

"Yes, but not tonight. Are you ready?"

Aron nodded silently.

Lionel handed him the pouch contained the sheathed knife, reached out and took Aron's hand and gripped it firmly. "The gods be with you, Aron," he said hoarsely.

Aron wondered what Iduna would think; would she be with him under the circumstances?

"I'll see you tomorrow," said Aron. "Leave word with the doorwards that I'll be back late."

"Ah, I will. But wash that stuff of your face before they see you, or they won't let you in."

Aron smiled and then turned to Bazarkis' servant who stood quietly by the door. "Time to go," he said and walked to the door.

***

Aron sat alone in the coach as it clattered through the streets towards Lord Tirellan's mansion, his stomach taut with tension as he tried to focus on the task before him. For a moment, he felt like leaping out and running in the opposite direction, but then he thought of all the effort that had gone into getting him here and the moment passed. He remembered all who had died by Tirellan's hand or order, and a cold flame kindled in his heart melting away the nerves. Tirellan would pay the price tonight. While it was tempting to made it lingering and painful, Aron doubted that he would be afforded the opportunity. So Tirellan would die quickly then; a cleaner better death than so many he had killed, but dead none the less.

Aron pulled aside the window blind and looked out to see where they were. He recognised the street - they were close to

Tirellan's mansion. He drew out the slim black-handled knife from his pouch and then eased down his leggings.

***

The coach slowed as it passed through the open and unguarded gates of Lord Tirellan's mansion.

"We're here, master," called the coachman, as the coach pulled up before the portico. Aron stepped down from the coach and, as the doorward's seat was empty, tugged on the bellpull beside the door.

The door was opened by a tall slender man with blond hair and beard wearing white leggings and flowing shirt of blue silk. Aron recognised him as fitting the description of Cristoff, Tirellan's steward and partner in depravity. Cristoff looked Aron up and down and smiled approvingly; then he took some coins out of his pouch and paid off the coachman.

"Come this way," Cristoff said, his voice a light tenor.

Aron stepped across the threshold into a fine airy hallway lit by lamps burning scented oil. The floor was tiled with a fine mosiac centrepiece and a large mural of fauns dancing with shepherdesses covered the wall that faced the door. Aron paused to admire the mural as Cristoff closed the door.

"Magnificent, isn't it?" said Cristoff. "It took the artist a year and a half. His Lordship is a connoisseur of beautiful things."

Aron shivered as he tried to reconcile the magnificent painting before him with the countless brutal acts that Tirellan had committed.

"This way," said Cristoff holding open a door at the side of the mural.

The door led into a wood-panelled corridor, and Aron followed Cristoff past paintings and cabinets filled with fine silverware. At the end of the corridor another door stood ajar; Cristoff pushed it open and led Aron into the room.

"Petter, he's here."

Petter, Lord Tirellan turned from what he was doing and Aron got his first sight of his prey. He was slightly shorter than Aron, but heavier in the shoulder; his dark hair was short and a neat beard and moustache framed his mouth. He was dressed in a simple tunic and leggings and moved with an easy fluidity that spoke of a trained physique.

Tirellan scrutinised Aron much as Cristoff had, but his blue eyes lingered longer on Aron's body. Then he smiled showing even white teeth.

"Splendid," he said. "Bazarkis excels himself."

Aron had to consciously avert his eyes from meeting Tirellan's gaze in challenge. Looking down he took in the dagger at Tirellan's belt that was larger than those commonly worn for decoration

"Well worth the price," said Cristoff.

Aron noticed that he, too, wore a large dagger. Have to wait until they're undressed, he thought.

"Wine for all," said Tirellan.

He turned to a sidetable that bore a decanter and tray of goblets. Aron watched intently as he poured and then passed Cristoff a goblet. Cristoff took a sip.

"This is a good one," said Cristoff appreciatively. "Where did you get this?"

Tirellan passed Aron a goblet. Aron eyed it suspiciously. Tirellan took an appreciative mouthful from his own goblet. "Yes, it is rather fine. I picked up a cask in Peresia last year. Surprising for such a young wine, I should have bought more."

Aron watched as Tirellan and Cristoff both drained their goblets and refilled them from the decanter. *Can't be poisoned then if they're drinking it so freely,* he thought and took a cautious sip. There was nothing unusual about the taste of the wine. Aron looked around curiously, wondering what they wanted him to do.

"Just stand there so we can look at you for a while," commanded Tirellan. Aron did as he was told and watched as they gossiped and occasionally looked his way. *I wish they'd get on with it,* he thought; the tension in his stomach making him very conscious of the concealed knife. He took another mouthful of wine. *I could take them right now.* He looked out of the corner of his eye at Tirellan. *Remember Tirellan is Academy trained. He's probably as good as you are; better to wait until you can be certain of the kill.*

Still Tirellan and Cristoff did nothing . Aron stood looking at the finely decorated walls and carved furniture, better even than the household of the Duke of Kyria. The air was thick with the scent of perfumed oil from the lamps and Aron felt a trickle of sweat run down his body. His head swimming slightly, he looked down at his goblet and saw it was empty. Surely he couldn't had drunk it all, he didn't remember. He looked up sharply and the room kept moving. He shook his head to clear it, but that made it worse.

Tirellan looked at Aron and smiled. He picked up a small

hourglass from a side table.

"I believe you win, Cristoff," he said.

There was nothing wrong with the wine, thought Aron desperately. *The drug was in the goblet before he put the wine in.* He tried to move, to attack while he still could, but his body felt as if he was moving through some thick fluid. Tirellan and Cristoff stepped forward and caught his arms. He tried to resist, but his strength seemed to leak out of him and they half carried, half dragged him towards a door in the far wall.

Cristoff pushed the door open with his foot and Aron saw into the room beyond. It was only small, built originally perhaps as dressing room. Secured to one wall was a whipping frame, with leather straps to bind the victim to the bloodstained wood. Beside it stood a rack of whips, wicked metal spikes, slim pincers and other implements of torture. Opposite stood a pair of velvet upholstered couches piled high with pillows.

Aron struggled, but Cristoff and Tirellan easily overcame him and strapped him face first to the rack. Cold horror spread through Aron and he would have collapsed to the ground if he wasn't secured. He felt the cold touch of steel on his back as his tunic and tights were cut from him to leave him naked. The room spun and the darkness at the edge of his vision threatened to claim him. All was silent for a moment; then the first lash of the whip tore a line of fire across his back. Aron shrieked in agony; a second lash fell and the vomit rose in his throat cutting off his scream. He clenched his arse tight to hold the concealed knife. A third stroke slashed into his buttocks and he emptied a mouthful of bitter fluid onto the tiles. *Too late*, he thought fleetingly, *the drug's done its work.* His vision blurred; he looked down into a mist that seemed to be rising from the floor. Another blow fell and the mist thickened as Aron tottered on the edge of an abyss of darkness. He seemed to hear his own voice screaming in the distance and the last thing he saw before the world turned black was a pair of blue eyes smiling at him.

CHAPTER 31

Earl Baldwin stamped into the room heading directly for the bottles on the table beside the fireplace. "Damnation take the man,"

"I take it that His Majesty has not taken our part in his judgement," said Lady Alice, her face a mask of calm.

"Stupid little pup who shouldn't even be given charge of a flock of chickens,"

snarled Baldwin, his face mottled red and his hands shaking as he struggled with the cork.

"What did he say, papa?" asked Edith.

Baldwin's reply was a wordless roar of rage as the corkscrew slipped out of his hand. He picked up the bottle and broke the neck off against the stone of the fireplace then filled the largest goblet to the brim.

"Sit down Baldwin, before you burst something," said Lady Alice. "And don't curse in front of the girls."

Baldwin snorted in reply and took a deep draught of wine which provoked a violent coughing fit resulting in him spilling a good portion of the wine. Tears ran down his scarlet cheeks as he strove to control the cough. After watching his struggles for a minute, Lady Alice put aside her embroidery.

"Go and help your father, girls."

Edith and Celaine shared a glance and then went to Baldwin. Celaine took the wine bottle and goblet from him and Edith slapped him firmly between the shoulderblades before mopping his tunic with her handkerchief.

"Now sit down and tell us exactly what His Majesty said without cursing," Lady Alice said.

Baldwin collapsed onto the chair and sat gasping, trying to regain his breath. Celaine and Edith returned to their seats to await the news.

"Blasted little jackanapes," spluttered Baldwin.

"Baldwin, will you get to the point," Lady Alice said, her eyes narrowed with annoyance. "Did you see the King?"

"Yes," snapped Baldwin, pouring himself more wine.

"Is he going to make them release Maldwyn?"

"No," said Baldwin from behind his goblet.

"Do we have to pay the ransoms and cede the land?"

"No."

"What then?" said Lady Alice.

Edith and Celaine held their breath awaiting the news.

"Damn fool said that he had no means of deciding between us, as if I were lying to him. He's not fit to be king if he can't tell an honest man when he sees one."

"But what's going to happen, Papa?" cried Edith.

"Because this idiot can't see the truth when it's under his nose, it's to be settled in the arena by trial of champions."

Baldwin took another mouthful of wine. There was silence for a moment while the ladies considered the news.

"When?" said Lady Alice her usually smooth brow furrowed.

"The next tournament," muttered Baldwin in reply. "Day after the next full moon."

"And who is to be our champion?" Lady Alice fixed her husband with a hard stare. "It will not be you, Baldwin."

"Why not, dammit?" Baldwin raised his head defiantly. "The honour of Nandor is at stake."

"You are too old and too slow," said Lady Alice. "I absolutely forbid it. We will forfeit rather than you risk your life in such a manner." Baldwin glared back at her, his fists clenched showing the knuckles white. "There's no good looking at me like that. You know very well Sarazan has three or four Academy trained masters at his beck and call, any one of whom would cut you to pieces in a few moments. When do we have to name our champion?"

"By sundown the day after tomorrow," said Baldwin gruffly.

"Then we haven't much time," said Lady Alice. "We need to find someone to take this fight for us. It will be expensive, but that can't be helped now." She shot a look at Baldwin who was reaching for the wine bottle. "Would you leave please, girls. Your father and I have a lot to discuss."

Edith and Celaine stood up, and with a curtsey to their parents, left the room closing the door behind them.

"I wish Aron was here," said Edith as they stood on the landing. "He'd be our champion."

"But he's not here, is he?" replied Celaine. "Anyway, we don't need him. Petter will do it. He's Academy trained too, you know."

"What makes you so sure he'll do it?" said Edith a little more sharply than she intended.

"For the honour of Nandor, for my honour. He wouldn't want a wife from a dishonoured house. Petter is a very honourable man." Edith said nothing but rolled her eyes. "I shall ask him myself, he wouldn't refuse me."

"You sound just like Papa with all that talk about honour," said Edith.

Celaine had the grace to look embarrassed.

"Well, have you got any ideas then? We have to do something."

"When are you next seeing Petter?" asked Edith.

"I shall go to him today," said Celaine. "He doesn't dine until late, there's time enough."

"We should go right now then." Edith nodded at the door behind her. "Before they arrange something else."

"I'll just ask Mama if we can go."

Celaine moved towards the door, but Edith blocked her.

"Let's just go. They'll be busy for hours. We can be back before they're finished."

"But what'll Mama say?"

"If you ask her now, she'll say no. Just change our shoes and go."

Edith steered Celaine towards their room where they exchanged their slippers for street shoes. Celaine paused in front of the mirror, a hairbrush in her hand.

"There's no time for that," Edith said as she shooed Celaine away from the mirror. "You look fine as you are."

Together they tiptoed past the door to their parents sittingroom and then down the stairs. Through the open door of the taproom, they saw Captain Thalon and two other Nandorans at a table, engrossed in a dice game. Holding their breaths, the girls flitted silently past out into the street. Dusk was falling and already some of the buildings had their night lanterns lit. As was usual for this hour there were many people about; watching a juggler, buying sweetmeats from a pedlar or just strolling in the warm evening air.

Edith felt a little thrill of excitement as she looked around at the scene. "Which way is it?" she asked.

Celaine paused and looked around. "It's this way, I think," she said, setting off towards the thickest part of the crowd; Edith had to scamper to keep up with her.

A few hundred paces on Celaine headed off down a well-lit

side street where the press of people was thinner. They made faster progress, until Celaine halted in front of a shop.

"Isn't that lovely? Don't you think it would suit me?" Celaine said.

Edith looked into the shop. A wedding gown was displayed on a mannequin. Edith turned to her sister who was staring longingly at the gown.

"Is this on the way, or did you come here to just look at that?"

"No, no. It's on the way, but isn't it beautiful? I just had to stop for a minute."

"Now you've seen it, let's go." Edith plucked at Celaine's sleeve without response.

"Don't you want to look at one for yourself? It won't take a minute."

"I'll do it when we've got more time," said Edith, biting her lip. "Now I really think we should go. How much further is it?"

"It can't be very far. It doesn't take long in Petter's coach. There should be a lovely square with a fountain at the end of this street."

To Edith's relief, Celaine turned away from the shop and headed down the street.

There was indeed a square at the end and a small garden where a number of young women were strolling or gossiping in small groups. They were as finely dressed as the women Edith had seen when she first arrived in the city, and a number of them carried small dogs in baskets at their elbow.

"Oh look at those sweet little dogs," said Celaine moving towards the nearest dog-bearing woman with Edith following.

"Isn't he lovely. What's his name?" Celaine reached out to stroke the dog which bared its teeth and growled at her. The woman looked at her suspiciously. Up close, Edith could see that she wore a lot of facepaint and the roots of her blonde hair were dark.

"What do you want?" said the woman showing yellowed teeth.

"I just wanted to see the little dog," said Celaine.

"Piss off, you stupid little bitch," said the woman pulling the basket out of reach. "This is my patch."

Celaine stepped back in surprise as the woman spat at her, and tears started to well up in her blue eyes. Edith grabbed her sister and pulled her away as the woman bent, scooped up a handful of dirt and hurled it at them. The other women in the square turned from what they had been doing to stare at the commotion; a few bent to find missiles to throw. The sisters hitched up their skirts and fled down the street, stumbling on the cobbles, pursued by a volley of rubbish and invective.

The pursuit did not last beyond the first corner though Celaine and Edith kept on running well beyond. Eventually they halted in a quiet side street and stood hands on thighs gasping with the exertion.

"Why was she so horrible?" sobbed Celaine once she had breath enough to speak. "I don't understand; people are so strange here."

Edith hugged her close and fought to control the anger surging through her; she wanted to go back and slap the woman until her teeth rattled. She pulled out a handkerchief and dried Celaine's eyes.

"How can I go to see my Lord looking like this?" said Celaine plucking at her disheveled hair. "And I'm sure my eyes will be all red too."

"I think I can hear water," said Edith. She walked a little way down the street to an archway. "Come here Celaine, there's a fountain. At least we can rinse off the worst of it."

"Have you got any soap?" asked Celaine as she walked shakily towards Edith.

"No, of course not," said Edith. "We'll just have to do what we can."

She walked to the fountain in the centre of the little square and sat on the low stone surround. Celaine came and sat down beside her. Edith drew out a handkerchief from a sleeve, dipped it into the pool and started scrubbing at the worst stains on Celaine's dress. Celaine fished in her reticule and found a hairbrush which she wetted and started to brush her hair.

"How far is it to Lord Tirellan's house?" asked Edith.

"It can't be far," said Celaine, concentrating on her hair. "I'm sure we're heading in the right direction."

Edith was about to answer when she noticed the man watching them from an archway on the far side of the square. She plucked at Celaine's sleeve as the man, aware that he was being observed, walked towards them. Edith glanced around; the shutters were closed on all the buildings overlooking the square and there was no-one else in sight.

"Good evening ladies," he said as he reached them. "Are you together?"

Edith looked at him suspiciously. His accent was that of an educated man and he was quite well-dressed, though his clothes seemed rather worn. He was only slightly taller than her as she stood up to face him.

"Yes," she said hesitantly, glancing at Celaine.

"Are you sisters?" he asked with an oily smile.

"Yes," said Celaine.

"And how much for the pleasure of your company?" He reached into his coat and pulled out a leather pouch. "I have money. Come along, girls, it's not a hard decision. An evening of your time for half a crown."

He held out a grimy hand with silver in it.

Edith turned to look at Celaine, confusion in her eyes. Celaine sat holding the hairbrush, her mouth open, saying nothing. As Edith turned back the man stepped forward and grabbed her. Edith gasped in alarm and astonishment as she felt his arms around her. His hold tightened as she squirmed and she felt his tongue slip into her mouth. Celaine stepped up behind him and hit him over the ear with the hairbrush. He loosened his grip on Edith, half turned towards Celaine, and then Edith brought her knee up sharply between his legs. The blow was somewhat cushioned by her skirt, but she felt her knee make contact with soft flesh. The man stared at them for a moment, eyes bulging and then doubled over in pain.

"Run," cried Edith.

They both gathered up their skirts and pelted up the nearest street, Celaine still clutching the hairbrush. They didn't halt until they emerged from a side street into a square that was thronged with people. As they careered to a halt and stood gasping, heads turned to stare. Edith didn't care who was watching and collapsed down on a low wall. Sweat dribbled into her eyes as she panted for all she was worth. Celaine came and propped herself beside her sister and was quietly sick.

"I hate this city," whispered Celaine wiping her mouth with Edith's handkerchief. "Everyone is so horrible. I want to go home."

"We can't," said Edith, her eyes closed and her breathing almost returned to normal. "We have to get to Lord Tirellan. Someone has to fight for us; otherwise we'll be ruined."

Celaine's reply was somewhere between a whimper and a gurgle.

"Which way is Tirellan's house from here?" asked Edith.

Celaine looked around. "I've no idea," she said hopelessly.

"Then we'll have to ask someone," said Edith. She looked around the square and spied a respectable looking middle-aged couple strolling arm in arm nearby. "They'll do. Come along Celaine," she said offering her sister an arm up.

"Excuse me, good sir."

Edith started, but before she could continue the wife gave her a cold stare, turned her head away and hauled her husband off across the square without a word.

"Well, whatever is wrong with them?" exclaimed Edith.

"Everyone in the city is mad," replied Celaine.

"Let's try them." Edith pointed to a knot of young men who were watching them with interest from the doorway of a tavern.

"I don't like the way they're looking at us," said Celaine, but Edith was already walking purposefully towards them.

"Could any of you fine gentlemen tell us the way to Lord Tirellan's residence?" Edith said firmly.

"Why certainly, miss," said the foremost of the lads, a tall well-built fellow with a cowlick of dark hair falling across his eyes. "But first we must fix a price." He smiled mischievously at Edith.

"What had you in mind?" said Edith looking him straight in the eye.

"Show us your legs," came a voice from the rear of the group. The tall lad grinned. "Show me and my friends your legs, and I'll take you there myself."

Edith stood speechless for three breaths studying the lad's face. She saw amusement and mischief, but she thought, no evil. Someone thrust a stool towards her. Then her mind was made up. She skipped up onto the stool then took hold of the muddied hem of her skirt with both hands and with a mischievous smile slowly raised it to the middle of her thighs. She stood for a few moments ignoring the chorus of whistles and shouts of more and higher, and then hopped down in front of the tall lad, a tingle of excitement running through her.

"Now take us to Lord Tirellan's," she said looking him straight in the eye again. The lad took a deep breath and glanced around at his cronies.

"The price was agreed and paid," said Edith firmly.

"She did what was agreed," said one of the fellows. "You owe the maid. See you later, Will."

Will said nothing for a moment and then smiled. "If you'll come this way, girls."

He directed them towards a sidestreet. Celaine, her face white and thin-lipped, gave Edith a furious glance as she walked past the Will's group of friends and then hurried out of earshot of their laughter.

Will strolled easily through the dark streets, chatting away happily, completely undeterred by the girls' silence. In the time it took to reach their destination, they learned that he was apprenticed to his uncle who was a bootmaker, that he lived with his widowed mother and three sisters, and had never been further than a day's walk from the city. Finally they turned a corner and stood before a fine white-painted house surrounded by a wall decorated with an armorial crest every three paces.

"Lord Tirellan's house as promised," said Will turning to face the girls with a smile. "And may I know who I have had the pleasure of escorting?"

Edith smiled at the young man. "Lady Edith, of Nandor and this is my sister Lady Celaine." Will's cheery expression froze and he bent in a deep bow.

"My apologies, ladies," he said in a strangled whisper. "I had no idea who you were. Please forgive my friends and me for our behaviour."

Edith smiled at him. "Thank you for being our guide, Will. You were a friend when we needed one."

"With your permission, I'll leave you now, ladies." Will stood up and with a tight smile turned and hurried away. As soon as he was out of earshot Edith burst out laughing.

"How could you do that?" said Celaine. "Displaying yourself in front of that crowd. What would mother say?"

"I did what I had to do to get us a guide," said Edith. "I don't care what mother would say and anyway, she isn't going to find out. And it worked, didn't it?"

"But it was such a risk. He could have been any kind of criminal."

"But he wasn't," Edith smiled mischievously. "He was quite nice, wasn't he?"

"In a common sort of way, I suppose," said Celaine. "But I still think you were mad to do it."

"We're here now. Let's do what we came for."

"We can't go in looking like this. Let me brush my hair first. You need to do yours too."

A few minutes later the sisters, their appearance slightly less unkempt, approached the house.

"What are you going to say to the gateman?" asked Edith. "He might not let us in if we're not expected."

"He will at least send for Petter. You know how servants gossip, everyone will know who I am."

They walked up to the gate and saw the gateman's post empty with the gate wide to the night. Edith looked around for a moment and then walked in.

"Where are you going?" hissed Celaine.

"Inside. There's light in some of the rooms, so we'll find someone who can tell us where your precious Petter is. Now come on," replied Edith. "Or don't you think he'll be pleased to see you?"

Edith started up the gravelled driveway to the entrance, and Celaine followed a moment later.

"I don't understand," said Celaine when they reached the entrance. "There's usually someone either here or at the gate."

Edith tried the door which swung open at her touch. "Never mind, let's see if Petter's at home." They stepped into the lamplit hallway.

"What's the smell?" asked Edith wrinkling her nose.

"Scented oil," said Celaine. "Petter burns it in the lamps. Isn't it lovely?"

"Choking more like," said Edith holding her nose. "Isn't that an incredible picture."

She pointed to the mural of the fauns and shepherdesses.

"Petter's got lots of beautiful things," said Celaine airily. "He's probably through here." She moved towards the door beside the mural. "Don't touch anything."

Together they walked down the wood-panelled corridor, Edith wide-eyed at the richness of the decorations.

"This is a treasure house," she whispered. "It's like a fairy story."

Ahead of them the door was ajar and as Celaine approached it, she set her shoulders back and her head up. She pushed open the door and walked in followed closely by Edith.

The girls looked around the empty room. On a table stood three wine goblets, two of them still with red wine in them. Other than that, there was no sign of anyone. Celaine noticed the door in the far wall stood ajar and that the lamps were lit in the room beyond.

"He might be through here," she said." I've never been in there, so I don't know where it goes."

"Then let's see," said Edith.

CHAPTER 32

Aron opened his eyes to a world of white. He shook his head and dark shadows swam in a pale background. He pushed himself up from where he lay and lifted his head above the layer of mist that clung to the ground. Around him trees and bushes grew out of a white sea. He stood up and regarded his surroundings. Above, the sky was cloudless blue with barely a breath of wind. In front, a small valley with the shadows of the trees stretched long across the grass, the ridge on the far side perhaps five hundred paces distant. Behind him was a scrubby wood in the full leaf of summer though strangely silent with no birdsong or buzzing insects.

Morning or evening? thought Aron. Already the mist was thinner around his feet, the air chill on his naked body. *Morning then, but where? The spirit world?* He tentatively ran his hands over his back exploring the sites of remembered pain and found no injury. *Am I dead then? This doesn't look like any afterlife I've ever heard of.*

The sight of two horsemen cresting the ridge interrupted his musings. They halted and one pointed in his direction. Aron heard the distant blare of a horn, and then a pack of hounds appeared on the ridge. The horsemen kicked their mounts into a gallop and headed down the slope directly towards him, the pack at their heels.

After a moment's hesitation, Aron turned and ran for what looked to be the thickest part of the wood. He paced himself as he ran, as if this was one of the hare and hounds chases at the Academy, except that this time the hounds were real. He could hear them howling as they picked up his trail at the edge of the wood. He looked for a tree to climb; but every one was either too large, tall pines with no handholds within reach, or too small to take his weight. He ran on picking his way, trying to keep to dense enough parts of the wood to hinder at least the horsemen. Thin branches lashed across his naked body as he crashed through the foliage, dodging to avoid the thicker boughs, looking continuously for some refuge. The ground sloped away ahead of him. *Please let there be a river at the bottom of the hill,* he thought as he heard a hunting horn blare somewhere behind him. The horn was answered by the baying of the hounds, closer now than before. Aron pushed himself to run faster. *I'm done for if I twist an ankle now*, he thought, ignoring the pain from feet bruised by the rough ground.

Aron heard the splash of water ahead of him and, breaking through a screen of bushes, he came upon a stream. *Too small to offer a real chance of losing them*, he thought as he jumped in; the water blissfully cool on his injured feet. He waded downstream for some thirty paces before hauling himself out onto an overhanging branch and back to dry land again. Then he set off continuing downhill, tracking the path of the stream. Behind him the cries of the hounds echoed through the wood.

The slope flattened out and the scrubby bushes gave way to lusher greener plants. As he ran, Aron was aware that the ground was softer underfoot. The trees were smaller too, willow rather than pine. He ran on, each breath burning in his chest. The cries of the hounds faded; *they've lost the trail* he thought. Then a minute later, a horn blasted and they gave tongue again. Aron looked around desperately for some refuge where he could rest up, catch his breath and think. Ahead of him was a high bank of reeds; he plunged into it and sank shin deep in water. He splashed through the screen of reeds and found himself looking out over open water.

To his left and right the water stretched a good distance, five hundred paces perhaps; the shore ahead of him was much closer, maybe fifty paces. Aron splashed forward as the cries of the hounds grew closer.

By the time the dogs came in sight, Aron was hip deep and nearly halfway across the lake. The leading dogs bounded through the shallows and then swam towards him. Aron turned to face them and saw the two horsemen push through the reeds and halt their mounts in the shallows. He was close enough to recognise his pursuers as Tirellan and Cristoff.

How is it that they have horses and hounds in the spirit world? Aron thought as he stared at them. *I thought you brought only your essence here.*

He had no more time for questioning as the first dog was almost upon him, teeth bared, growling deep in its throat. Aron reached out his left hand; the dog snapped at it. Aron pulled his arm away and threw his weight onto the dog's back pushing it under the water. He threw a leg over the struggling beast as if trying to ride it, as the second dog seized his right arm in its jaws. Hot needles of pain leapt up his arm. Aron clamped his legs around the first dog, bearing down on it and then caught the second dog's muzzle with his left hand and hauled it below the water. The second dog tore at Aron's body and legs with its claws. Aron held on struggling for balance, gritting his teeth against the pain as a third dog sank its teeth into his shoulder.

After an eternity the second dog released its grip on his arm allowing Aron to get a new, firmer hold on it. The first dog ceased struggling. Aron stood up and then rolled to bring the third dog under the water. A fourth dog snapped at his face.

"Damnation Cristoff, this fellow's game." Lord Tirellan's voice carried over the water. "Never had one fight like this. Let's get him moving again before he slaughters the whole pack."

He raised his horn to his lips and blew a blast. The dogs turned immediately and began to swim for the shore.

Aron looked up at the sound of the horn, but retained his grip on the now limp second dog.

"Encourage him to get moving, Cristoff," called Tirellan.

Aron tensed at the words.

"Certainly, Petter."

Cristoff slid a light hunting bow from its hanging on his saddle and nocked a arrow. He took brief aim, smoothly bent the bow and let fly.

Aron saw the bow bend and lifted the body of the dog up before him. He fell backwards off his feet. He felt the arrow strike the dog, the point punching right through the body to just scratch his chest. He dropped to the lake floor and struck out for the far shore, holding his breath for as long as he could before surfacing to breathe.

Tirellan turned his horse down the long axis of the lake and pointed to the far end. Cristoff wheeled his horse the opposite way and kicked it into a hand gallop. Tirellan blew his horn, and the dogs, after a moment's confusion, divided into two roughly equal packs and chased baying after the riders.

By the time Aron reached the shore both Tirellan and Cristoff were out of sight, hidden by the trees, though he could still hear the hounds. He sat down for a moment's rest on a stretch of coarse grass and inspected his wounds. His right forearm was bleeding freely from the dog bite as was his left shoulder. His stomach and thighs were scratched from the dog's claws and though they burned fiercely they weren't deep.

I have to keep moving, he thought. *If I rest for too long I'll stiffen* and be unable to run. He pulled himself up and lurched into a trot away from the lakeshore. *But where am I going?* He thought of what he knew of the spirit world. *Not much really, just the walking in the mist and Iduna's bower.* He remembered her face and what she had said when he asked how he would ever find her again.

Keep me always in your heart and I will find you.

He pushed through a stand of bushes, flinching as the branches swept across his lacerated body, seeking some hiding place; but this side of the lake was the much like the other, mostly scrub and willow. Ahead of him the wood seemed thicker with bigger trees. He struggled to move faster, but his legs seemed unable to respond. *I can't go much further,* he thought desperately. He stumbled over a root and nearly fell. Dark specks danced for a moment in his field of vision as he pulled himself up. Horn blasts sounded from left and right. *Round the end of the lake now.* He ran on, gasping for breath. A stand of pines reared up in front of him, one of the trees growing up at an angle. *A shallow enough slope to climb?* It looked possible. Aron halted at the foot of the tree. *I'd be safe from the dogs up there, but Cristoff has a bow. I'd be an easy target and there'd be nothing I could do.*

Beyond the pines grew a thick bank of tangled gorse and thorn. Aron looked around at the fallen wood and selected a likely looking branch. He hefted it in his hands; a tool to clear a way through the undergrowth, but also a club to use against the dogs. *But what then? I can't run much further and I can't kill all the dogs.* He looked at the undergrowth and a desperate plan formed in his mind. *If the undergrowth is thick enough, I can draw the dogs in, but Tirellan and Cristoff won't bring their horses in. Then I can circle round and come out behind them, despatch one of them, take the horse and escape.*

He moved forward into the undergrowth, the baying of the hounds now loud on either side of him. It was impossible to move quickly and Aron collected many more scratches from the thicket. He could feel his arm and shoulder stiffening as he eased his way carefully through using the branch to push the larger bushes. *If I clear a way, it'll only lead them straight to me.* The sound of dogs now merged behind him. *They've reached the point where I came ashore. The dogs will be into the bushes soon.* He struggled forward bearing to his right through the dense dark heart of the thicket. *I hope this undergrowth is deep enough.*

A horn blew somewhere away to his right. *Soon.* He drove onwards a few more paces before the tumult of the dogs became mixed with the sound of cracking branches as they pushed into the thicket. Distancing his mind from the pain it brought, Aron forced his way through the tangled foliage expecting at any moment to break into clear ground. *I should be out of this by now,* he thought. *I'm lost.*

Aron could hear the nearest dogs individually pushing their way through the undergrowth. He readied the club and turned to face the oncoming threat. The first dog came in sight behind a screen of branches. It leapt forward snarling, but snagged itself on a snare of thorn, and Aron brought the club down on its head with all his strength. He had no time to see the effect as a second dog appeared through the same gap. Aron thrashed at it, but the branches took most of the blow and the dog fled howling. Aron turned and continued his push through the thicket. Ahead of him the foliage seemed to grow thinner.

A horn blew close at hand and he heard the noise as something large crashed its way through the undergrowth. Either Tirellan or Cristoff had driven their horse into the thicket. Cursing, Aron pushed the foliage out of his path, and broke through into clear ground. He stumbled and almost fell to his knees, exhaustion running through his veins. He looked quickly around, but this place seemed to bear no relation to the wood he had been in before. The thin scrubby grass had given way to rich succulent sward, the twisted thorns to strong, clean-limbed fruit trees, even the air seemed warmer. Behind him the noise of the hunt's passage through the tanglewood told that they were on his heels.

Aron forced himself to run, but his strength was spent and he could do no more than stumble a few paces to a sturdy apple tree. He turned to face his pursuers as they burst through the undergrowth, the dogs baying in delight at the sight of their prey. Lord Tirellan blew a triumphant blast on his horn to halt the pack. He urged his mount forward to stop a few paces from Aron. Aron stood his back against the tree, holding his club defiantly, facing the circle of his enemies.

Lord Tirellan looked down at Aron, his face lathered with sweat from the ride. "I must congratulate you on an excellent chase, young man," he said smiling broadly, his blue eyes shining with pleasure. "Quite the best we've had. Such a shame it has to end."

He dismounted and drew his sword from where it hung at the saddle. He shook himself to free his muscles, rolling his head around in a circle, before raising the blade and turning towards Aron.

"Before we finish it, I should like to know what you expected to do with the nasty little knife you were hiding. It must have been most uncomfortable. Did you think we wouldn't find it?"

Aron raised his head to spit at Tirellan but didn't have the strength.

"How dare you come to my home and behave in this manner?" The voice was that of a woman, a very angry woman. Aron and Tirellan both turned to look at the speaker. Iduna stood before them dressed in pure white, her eyes blazing with anger.

The smile on Tirellan's face froze. "Iduna," he gasped.

The dogs turned to her; the pack leader bared its teeth and snarled. Iduna glared at it for a single icy moment.

"This is my place and I will not have your dark magic defile it."

She snapped her fingers and the dog fled howling, its tail between its legs. The rest of the pack followed, and in a few heart beats they were out of sight, their mournful howls the only reminder of their existence.

"You, I don't know, though I know your sort," said Iduna looking at Cristoff. "But you should know better than to come here again," she said turning to Tirellan who seemed paralysed by shock.

"Who is this damned witch, Petter?" asked Cristoff reaching for his bow. "Tell her to go away before we get upset with her."

Iduna turned to face Cristoff. "Do not use that word in my presence."

"I'll do as I please," said Cristoff. "I think you've outstayed your welcome." He nocked an arrow and, taking aim at Iduna, bent the bow.

"No. Cristoff!" cried Tirellan.

"Goodbye witch," said Cristoff and released the arrow.

Iduna stood quite still, but Aron saw her eyes blaze for a moment. The arrow veered away, missing her by an armslength and carrying on, flying a complete circle, ending where it had started with Cristoff.

Cristoff stared in disbelief as the arrow curved back at him, until it struck him in the chest. He opened his mouth to scream, but blood filled his throat. He gurgled and slid sideways off his horse to the ground, his blood spilling out and staining the rich turf. Tirellan ran to where he lay and cradled his friend's head in his lap burying his face in Cristoff's hair. When he looked up tears streamed down his face.

"He's dead," he raged. "You didn't have to do that, Iduna. He was no threat to you."

"He died because he was a fool," said Iduna, no hint of sympathy in her voice. "But how much greater a fool are you to bring your evil to this place? You have broken your promise to me, Petter.

There is no-one in your heart save yourself."

"You could have spared him, Iduna."

"As you would have spared this one," said Iduna glancing at Aron. "I think not."

"Have mercy, Iduna," Tirellan said softly. "You loved me once."

"How can you speak of it when you have brought dark magic to my home? You have become an abomination, Petter."

There was sadness mixed in with the anger, Aron thought, as he listened to her words. *Iduna had loved Tirellan!*

"Would you have me beg, my Lady?" said Tirellan.

"It is beyond anything you could say."

Aron heard finality in her voice and, by the look on his face, Tirellan did too. He laid Cristoff's head gently on the grass and stood up; his legs red with blood. He raised his head to meet Iduna's gaze. A single tear trickled down his cheek. Then it seemed to Aron as if the air itself twisted like a sudden eddy in a pool of water. When his vision cleared a statue of flawless white marble stood before them the exact likeness of Tirellan, the tear forever frozen on his cheek.

Iduna stood a moment facing the statue and then turned to Aron, her face wet with tears.

"Beloved," she said, her voice choked and husky.

Aron stepped away from the support of the tree to go to her, but his legs folded under him and he pitched forward onto the grass. Instantly she was beside him, pillowing his head on her breast, probing his wounds with soft fingers.

"How did you find me?" whispered Aron.

"You called me, my love; and you kept your promise," she said softly. "Hush now; it is healing you need and for that you must rest. Sleep now and when you wake you shall tell me all about it."

Aron felt a languorous warmth spreading through him and was vaguely aware that she had picked him up in her arms as easily as a mother picks up her infant. Before she had taken a dozen steps he was asleep, his head cradled against her shoulder as she carried him through the orchard to her bower.

CHAPTER 33

Edith laid her hand on the door handle. "Hello is there anyone there. Hello.....?"

The final syllable trailed off into a squeak as she beheld the room before her. Lord Tirellan and Cristoff were sprawled naked and unmoving on a pair of couches, their bodies speckled with dark red splashes. Their fine clothes lay in a heap on the floor beside a discarded pair of silver handled whips. Spread-eagled on a frame attached to the wall in front of them was a naked figure; back, buttocks and legs red raw and bloodied, a pool of blood and filth congealed on the tiles beneath them. The room stank of blood, sweat and vomit mixed with the scented oil of the lamps.

Edith stood with her eyes and mouth wide open, staring at the room, forgetting to breathe until she gasped for air. Then Celaine pushed past her and ran to Lord Tirellan.

"Petter, Petter. Wake up." She patted his cheek lightly. "Petter. You have to wake up."

Edith slipped past her and knelt to examine Cristoff.

"He's dead," she said after a moment, her voice shaking. "Whatever are we going to do?"

"He can't be dead," wailed Celaine, she shook Tirellan's head. "Wake up, wake up." There was no response.

Edith took her sister's hands and stopped her shaking the body. "He's dead too, Celaine," she said gently.

"No! He's going to marry me," wailed Celaine shaking Tirellan more forcefully.

When he did not respond she flung herself over Tirellan's body sobbing deep wracking sobs. Edith held her shoulders for a moment, but then decided to let her cry and moved to investigate the body on the frame. She shivered in disgust and sympathetic pain as she looked at the cruel wounds. She forced herself to undo the leather straps binding his legs and then, standing on a stool, she reached up and untied his wrists. She all but dropped him as his dead weight slumped in her arms.

"Celaine, Celaine. Help me with him," she said, her voice breaking in panic. Celaine looked up blankly, her face streaked with tears. "Help me, Celaine. I can't hold him."

Edith tried to shift the man's weight to support him more easily, but the stool tipped and slid on the bloody floor. With a shriek the two of them collapsed in a pile. Edith's head hit the floor with a thump and she cried out in pain.

"Edith. Edith, are you alright?"

Celaine's shaky whisper seemed to come from a long way away. She felt a hand patting her cheek.

"Edith, wake up, please."

Edith groaned and opened her eyes to see Celaine kneeling beside her, her eyes wide with fear. Edith rubbed at her eyes to clear away the blood that was smeared across her face. She tried to sit up, but pain flashed alarmingly in her head. She groaned and lay back again.

Celaine went over to the couch where Lord Tirellan lay. She took a cushion, placed it gently under Lord Tirellan's head and then brought the rest of them over to where Edith lay, pinned under the bloody body. She lifted Edith's head and slid the cushions under her one by one, then sat and silently wept until Edith felt able to move without her head splitting. With Celaine's help, Edith eased herself carefully out from under the body, and cradling his head in her lap, she looked into his face. Recognition dawned.

"Aron?" she whispered, staring in shock at his curled hair, rouged cheeks and painted lips.

"But what's he doing here?" said Celaine. "And why is his face painted like a girl?"

"I don't know. I don't care," cried Edith. She buried her face in Aron's chest and sobbed her heart out for the end of her world. She didn't understand how he could be here, why he looked as he did. All she knew was that something was terribly, monstrously wrong.

Somewhere in the midst of her tears she became aware of Celaine plucking at her shoulder.

"Edith, we can't stay here, I'm frightened."

Edith turned and looked up at her sister's wild, tear-stained face.

"They're all dead," whispered Celaine breathlessly.

"Let me say goodbye," said Edith.

She bent to brush a stray curl from Aron's face and softly kiss his rouged lips. Suddenly she sat up.

"Celaine, he's alive. He's breathing."

"Are you sure?"

"I felt it when I kissed him," said Edith. "I'm sure."

"Let me see." Celaine bent over and gently lowered her lips to Aron's. "Oh, thanks be," she whispered. She looked up, her eyes very wide. "We must get him away from here."

"We must cover him with something," said Edith. Celaine nodded blankly, but did not move. Biting her lip, Edith looked around the room. Gently lowering Aron's head onto a cushion, she stood up and walked decisively to the door returning a moment later with a heavy velvet curtain. Celaine was sitting cradling Aron's head in her lap.

"Here, help me wrap him in this," she commanded.

Celaine reluctantly released her hold on Aron, and they gently rolled him onto the curtain; tears starting anew in Edith's eyes as his wounded back was exposed again.

Edith told hold of Aron's ankles. "Now take his shoulders. No, get right under his arms and lift."

Celaine did as she was told and together they lifted Aron and awkwardly carried him out of the little room into the sitting room before depositing him gently on a fine silk rug.

"Oh, he's so heavy," said Celaine. "We'll never carry him all the way back."

Edith looked down at the polished wooden floor and then smiled grimly. She reached down and pulled at the rug. It slid a little way across the floor. She pulled harder.

"Come on," she said. "We can get him as far as the door like this."

Taking turns they slid the rug with its unconscious cargo across the room and down the wood-panelled corridor to the entrance hall.

"Now what?" said Celaine. "We can't slide him outside."

Edith was silent for a moment.

"We need a barrow or a ponycart," she said. "You stay here with him. I'll go and see what I can find."

Celaine sat down on the rug, lifted Aron's head into her lap and gently rocked him stroking his curled hair, her face vacant. Edith watched her for a moment and then slipped out of the front door hoping there was still no-one around. She scampered around the side of the house following a gravel path praying it would lead to the stables. Her prayers were answered when she found a handcart standing in the middle of the path piled with garden tools. She tipped them off and hurried back to the door with her prize.

Celaine started at the sound of Edith opening the door
"I've got a handcart," said Edith. "It was the best thing I could find." Celaine stared at her wide-eyed, still cradling Aron.

"Well, come on, Celaine. Let's get him onto the cart."

Celaine did not move. Edith came and shook firmly by the shoulders. "Get up, Celaine."

Celaine stared back, her eyes unfocused.

"Celaine. We have to get him onto the cart and take him out of here."

Celaine rose mechanically.

"Lift him then," said Edith, bending to grasp Aron's feet.

Celaine held Aron by the shoulders and together they half carried and half dragged him outside to the handcart. Gasping with the exertion, they dumped him onto the cart. Celaine looked at her sister.

"You're all covered in blood," she said distantly.

Edith looked down at her dress; it was indeed soaked with Aron's blood from where she had held him. *I can't walk across the city in this state.*

Edith turned to go back into the house. "Come on then," she said "Help me find something to wear."

Celaine, her arms still around Aron, shook her head.

"I'll stay here with him. Bring a pillow to put under his head too."

Edith gave her sister an old-fashioned look and then went back into the house. She thought briefly about exploring other rooms but remembered the clothes Lord Tirellan and Cristoff had discarded.

Celaine was standing stroking Aron's hair when Edith returned wearing Cristoff's shirt.

"That's a dead man's shirt," said Celaine. She retreated from Edith. "You shouldn't wear it, that's unlucky."

"Yes, it's Cristoff's shirt. But he doesn't need it now, and I do. I can't walk around the city covered in blood."

Celaine shook her head.

Edith looked down at Aron and, as if on cue, he stirred and moaned.

"I've got to wear it," she said urgently. "We'll get taken up by the Watch and then we'll never get him back. I brought a pillow too."

Edith held out the pillow. Celaine stared at her wild-eyed, then snatched the pillow and placed it beneath Aron's head.

"Right. Let's go," said Edith briskly. "Don't be standing there like a mooncalf, Celaine." She shoved the cart forward. "Help me push, it's heavy."

"Careful," cried Celaine. "Don't be so rough with it, you'll jolt him."

She scurried to catch up with the cart and adjust the pillow beneath Aron's head.

"Then help me push."

Together the girls pushed the cart up the drive and out into the city. There were fewer people around now, and most of the shops they passed were dark and shuttered as they rattled through the cobbled streets. The taverns were in full swing, and more than once they had to steer around over enthusiastic revellers spilling out into the street. It was on one such occasion that they encountered the City Watch rounding up a crowd of drunken brawlers.

"What have you there, ladies?"

A tall young man wearing an officer's insignia asked politetely, but insistently as the girls tried to steer around the melee. He stepped forward and raised his lantern to examine the cart.

"It's our cousin," said Edith. "He's drunk again and Mama sent us to find him."

"And you are?" he asked, turning back to face them.

"Lady Edith of Nandor. This is my sister Celaine, and this...." She paused to indicate her cargo. "Is Tancred."

"You are out late, ladies, where are you headed?"

"We are lodging at the Seven Stars."

"These streets are not safe at night for the likes of you." He looked to where his men were making ready to march some of the brawlers off to the Watch House. "I can't spare more than two men, but please allow me to give you an escort."

Edith smiled in assent, pleased that he had offered what she did not dare ask for.

"Kal, Barri," he called to two Watchmen. "Escort these ladies to The Seven Stars."

The two Watchmen saluted sharply and marched over to where the girls stood. They both took a brief look at Aron, then one of them took the handles of the cart and set out at a brisk pace for the inn.

To the girls, it seemed a very short time before the Watchmen halted in the yard of The Seven Stars. They saluted politely and hurried away leaving the girls with Aron.

"You stay here, I'll go up and fetch Mother," said Edith.

She pushed open the door and ran two steps at a time up the stairs to the suite that the Nandor party had rented. Lady Alice was sitting beside the fire, working on a piece of embroidery. She heard the door open, looked up and abruptly put the embroidery down.

"Edith! Where on earth have you been?" she said sharply, rising from the chair. "Look at the state of you. What have you been doing? Where's Celaine?"

"She's downstairs, Mama. Come quickly," Edith said breathlessly. "We've got Aron and he's hurt."

Lady Alice caught the urgency in her daughter's voice and jumped to her feet. "Where? Show me."

"In the yard."

Edith turned and hurried down the stairs with her mother close behind.

"Where did you find him?"

"Er ....I'll explain later," replied Edith.

She reached the door to the yard glad to postpone further questions. They clattered out into the yard where Celaine was bent over the still figure of Aron.

Celaine lifted his head as her mother approached. "He's still alive, Mama," she said, her voice shaking.

Lady Alice lifted Aron's eyelids and probed his neck lightly searching for a pulse.

"Yes, just." She looked at Celaine's pale tear-streaked face in the lantern light. "You go upstairs, Celaine." she said firmly. "We'll take care of him."

"But Mama -."

"Now, Celaine! And send the porter out here on your way up."

Celaine stood for a moment under her mother's gaze then turned for the door.

"How long has he been like this?" asked Lady Alice.

"I don't know," said Edith. "He was unconscious when we found him."

"Milady." The porter appeared in the doorway, almost filling it. Lady Alice turned to him.

"Ah good. This young man needs to be taken up to our rooms and we shall need another bed made up for him."

"Very good, my Lady."

He stepped forward, picked up Aron in his arms and carried him inside. Edith and Lady Alice followed him up the stairs to the Nandor suite where the porter laid Aron gently on the rug before the fire in the sitting room. Lady Alice bent to examine Aron more closely, and attempted to unroll the curtain that wrapped him. Her hand came away sticky with blood.

"I'll send a maid up directly, my Lady," said the porter." Will there be anything else?"

"I think we'll need a bathtub and plenty of warm water," said Lady Alice.

"Very good, my Lady," said the porter. He left the room, closing the door behind him.

"What are we going to do?" asked Edith.

"This cloth has to come off him and he needs cleaning, but you are going to bed, young lady."

"But Mama, I can help."

"You've done quite enough for one night and, if I'm any judge, Celaine needs you more than I do. Make up a sleeping draught for both of you, and then go to bed. The maid can help me."

Edith stood defiant for a moment, but a knock at the door forestalled what she had to say.

"Enter," called Lady Alice.

The door opened and a sleepy-eyed maid came in carrying bedding. There was another knock at the door, and a moment later the porter was placing a copper bathtub beside Aron. A second maid arrived carrying a large steaming jug of hot water followed by another with cold water. They mixed the bath to a comfortable temperature and then gently lowered Aron, still wrapped in the bloody curtain, into the water. Edith stepped forward to assist but her mother stopped her.

"Make up the sleeping draught and go to bed, Edith."

"Yes, Mama."

Edith took a last look at Aron and felt the tears begin again. She turned to her mother's medicine chest and began to mix the sleeping draught.

***

It was still early morning when Celaine and Edith hurried down to the sitting room as if seeking reassurance that they hadn't dreamed the night's events. Despite the draught Edith had barely slept, her head ached and every time she had tried to relax the same questions tumbled over in her mind again. *How badly was Aron hurt? What had he been doing there? Why was his face painted?* Beside her Celaine had slept peacefully.

Lady Alice sat dozing in a chair beside the bed where Aron lay face down, his back bare. Her head jerked up as she awoke to the sound of her daughters.

"How is he?" asked Celaine.

"Still unconscious," said Lady Alice, rubbing her red-rimmed eyes.

"Did you stay up all night?" asked Edith.

Lady Alice nodded. "I had to soak that curtain off him then clean his wounds." She glanced at Aron and shivered. "It's just as well he's unconscious. He'd be in agony otherwise. Who did this to him?"

Edith looked uncomfortably at Celaine. There was a moment's silence before Celaine spoke.

"It was Petter," she said, her voice tight with emotion. "Petter and Cristoff."

"Perhaps you'd better start at the beginning," said Lady Alice gently. "Where did you go last night?"

"We went to ask Petter to be our champion," said Celaine. "I thought...."

She stopped and choked on her tears. Lady Alice reached out and took Celaine in her arms letting her cry herself out. Edith stood awkwardly, not wanting to watch, her eyes pricking at Celaine's distress and the sight of Aron's wounds.

"You went to see Lord Tirellan," said Lady Alice gently. "And you found Aron there?"

"There wasn't anyone around when we got there first," said Edith. "No servants or guards or anyone."

"Go on," said Lady Alice. Celaine sat on the floor beside her, wiping her eyes and nodded in agreement.

"So we went into the house and found this little room and they had him there, tied up and naked and they'd been whipping him, but they were dead when we got there, weren't they, Celaine?" Celaine nodded again.

"Dead! Lord Tirellan is dead," said Lady Alice. "Are you sure?"

"Yes, and Cristoff too," said Celaine with a sniff and a gulp.

"How?" said Lady Alice. "Did they have any wounds?"

"No," said Edith. "There wasn't a mark on them."

"And where was Aron?" said Lady Alice.

"He was tied to a frame on the wall," said Edith. "And he'd been whipped all down his back."

"So you untied Aron and brought him back here. Did anyone see you?"

"We met a group of Watchmen and two of them brought us back," said Celaine.

"But we were a long way from Lord Tirellan's when we met them," said Edith. "No-one saw us near the house."

Lady Alice nodded, but said nothing. After a long moment's silence Edith said. "What do we do now?"

"We wait," said Lady Alice. "I've sent the maid to find a wise woman for Aron. And we have to decide what to tell your father." Edith looked over her shoulder. "Where is he?"

"Still in bed," said Lady Alice, her face expressionless. "There's something else I need to talk to you about before the wise woman arrives."

Edith and Celaine heard the edge of uncertainty in her voice and looked at each other, but said nothing.

"She's more than a healer. She is a priestess of Iduna, the goddess I have followed in my heart all my life. We will pray to Iduna, for her help in healing Aron. Your father does not know about this and would not, I think, understand or approve. I have waited for a time that seemed right to tell you of this, but fate has chosen for me. I would be very glad if you would join us in the prayers."

Edith and Celaine looked at each other again with smiles on their faces. "Mama, we've known about this for ages," said Celaine. "And of course we'll pray with you."

Lady Alice's eyes opened wide in surprise. "How did you find out?"

"Lots of little things," said Edith with a grin.

"Those prayers you used to say over us when you thought we were asleep," said Celaine. "And things you and Glynis said when you thought we couldn't hear."

"Does Maldwyn know about this?" said Lady Alice suddenly concerned.

"I don't think so," said Celaine. "He doesn't really notice things like that."

Lady Alice relaxed. "Well, I'm glad you know about it. The priestess should be here soon."

"Will she be able to help him?" asked Edith.

"Who can say? We can only hope."

"But he will live, won't he, Mama?" said Celaine, her smile suddenly gone.

"I don't know. I've seen men die of what seemed the slightest thing, yet others have survived what I thought would certainly kill them. He's strong; he survived being poisoned with brown bonnets."

"But there must be something we can do," said Edith.

"Yes, dear," said Lady Alice. "We can pray."

The silence that followed was broken by a discreet knock at the door.

"Enter," called Lady Alice.

The door opened and a maid stepped in. "Begging your

pardon, my Lady, but the wise woman is here," she said.

"Very good, show her in," said Lady Alice rising from her chair.

A stout, red-cheeked, plainly dressed woman walked in, laid down her satchel and bowed fractionally to Lady Alice.

"You were asking for me, my Lady," she said, a hint of questioning in her voice

"May the light of summer shine on you always," said Lady Alice.

The wise woman smiled at her words. "And the Goddess keep you in her heart. I am Lorai."

Lady Alice turned to where Aron lay still unconscious on the bed.

"He has taken a grievous hurt and will not wake."

Lorai knelt by the bedside and examined Aron.

"The wounds are clean and there's no fever. That is good, but he should be awake." She lifted up an eyelid, frowned and then touched his lips lightly with her tongue. "Drugged, and with a powerful one too. Someone didn't want him to wake."

"What can you do?" asked Lady Alice.

"I'll dress his wounds with comfrey and honey then we'll pray to the Goddess. He's wandering in the spirit world with this drug, we may be able to guide him to her. This would be better done at the temple."

"I agree," said Lady Alice. "We cannot keep him here."

Lorai went to her satchel and brought out a pouch and a brown jar sealed with waxed cloth. From the pouch she scattered chopped comfrey leaves onto Aron's back and then poured the contents of the jar over the leaves. With a spatula she spread the honey evenly across his wounds covering every bit of raw flesh. Then she produced two candles from the satchel and, taking a light from the hearth, placed them on either side of Aron's bed.

"Now we pray," she said.

CHAPTER 34

Aron awoke to birdsong and the scent of summer flowers; the surface beneath him was soft and the sun was warm on his back. Eyes still closed, he cautiously tested his wounded body; his arm and shoulder the dogs had mauled, his torn and bruised feet. There was no pain; everything worked as it should.

Soft as a butterfly's wing, something brushed his forehead. He opened his eyes. Iduna sat over him, her hand poised above his face.

"Awake at last," she said, her voice as soft as a dove's call. "Come and drink; you must be thirsty."

She held out a white metal cup. Aron sat up and drank, as he drank he felt the tiredness wash out of his body. He stretched out his arm and looked at where Tirellan's hound had torn his flesh. There was no scar, no sign that anything amiss had happened.

"All is healed," Iduna said and bent to kiss him, her lips as sweet as a ripe pear.

They lingered long over the kiss before they parted.

"I am in your debt again, my Lady," said Aron. "How will I repay you this time?"

"Just the same way as you did before." Iduna smiled. "By keeping your promise to me."

Aron gazed up into her eyes which were as green as summer leaves.

"What happened to Tirellan?" he asked and her eyes seemed to turn to grey before she answered.

"He will stay here with me."

"You knew him before?" Aron asked cautiously. "He said you loved him once."

There was a long pause before she answered and the warmth of the sunlight seemed to fade.

"I misread his heart. The world has changed and I am diminished. This would not have happened before."

"Before?"

"When I had many followers. When your world was younger."

There was an edge of sadness in her voice and her eyes seemed very dark and glistened with unshed tears. "He learned something of the ways of this world, but the knowledge festered in his heart and he sought only dominance. There are others here. He found one and they aided him."

"So that's how he possessed the horses and hounds."

"Certainly," said Iduna bleakly. "There will have been a price for them."

"A price?"

"In blood. They prize youth and innocence; no doubt he found it for them. They crave a foothold in your world, and for that they would grant anything. Now that the foothold is established they will not relinquish it. They will wait; there is always another fool seeking power and dominion to open the way for them."

Aron shivered at the memory of Tirellan's hounds, and wondered what innocent had purchased them with their lifeblood.

"You must purge your heart of the hunger for vengeance," said Iduna, suddenly grave. "It would consume you as he was consumed."

She slid an arm around his shoulders.

"But let us talk no more of such things," she whispered as her lips sought his.

***

They laid Aron in a small room that looked out into the garden of the temple face down on the bed they had brought from the inn. The temple itself was small and hemmed in by larger buildings, accessible only down an alleyway.

"I somehow expected it to be larger," said Lady Alice to Lorai. "As this is the largest city in the kingdom so it should have the largest temple"

"Our lady is a goddess of woods and fields," Lorai laughed. "Look around you, my Lady. Do you see many trees?"

Lady Alice looked around; true, there was a grove of trees in the temple precinct, but beyond all was brick and stone.

"Then where is the mother temple?" she asked.

"There isn't one," said Lorai. "Not any longer at least. But some of the old scrolls we have suggest that there was one, deep in the country, halfway to Sarazan."

"What became of it?"

"Destroyed in one or other of the wars, no-one remembers. There never was any central control or great hierarchy of priests. We've just gone our own way. I think our lady prefers that."

Two other women carrying candles and bundles of herbs freshly cut from the temple's garden joined them. Lorai took two candles and placed them either side of Aron's head and then scattered the herbs all around him.

"What are those for?" asked Edith.

"We must ensure that his wounds don't fester," said Lorai, wiping her hands on her apron.

Celaine picked up a handful and sniffed at it.

"Tansy and Elder. They'll keep the flies and evil vapours away. But there's something else too."

"Well taught I see, my Lady," said Lorai with an approving smile. "We have added rue to the mixture, which perhaps is what you do not recognise."

Then they prayed, although to the girls it seemed that they simply sang. They recognised some of the songs as ones that Glynis had sung to them, though some of the words were different. Edith also noticed that her mother stumbled over some of the words as if the songs were unfamiliar.

The song finished and Lorai took a taper and lit the candles beside Aron. Then she lifted up her arms and spoke in a clear voice.

"Iduna, Lady of our Hearts, hear us as we call to you. Reach out to our lost brother and draw him to you. Heal him, nurture him and send him back to those who love him and wait for him." She lowered her arms and turned to Lady Alice. "It is done. We can only wait and see if she answers. He'll be thirsty when he wakes; be sure he drinks plenty."

"What do we do now, Mama?" asked Celaine as Lorai and the other women left the room.

"As she said, we wait," said Lady Alice. "There must always be two of us here. The first thing he sees when he wakes must be one of us."

"Of course, Mama," said Edith. "But why?"

"He is our only realistic chance," said Lady Alice. "He must be our champion, so we must bind him to us."

"I don't understand," said Celaine. "Why wouldn't he fight for us anyway?"

"Perhaps he will, we can't be sure," said Lady Alice. "We have no idea where he's been. The last we knew of him was in Sarazan. Where's he been since?" She looked down at the prone figure, her lips pursed. "How did he come to be in Lord Tirellan's house with his face painted and his hair curled?"

She looked at her daughters inviting them to answer.

"Don't you trust him?" said Celaine, her lower lip trembled and her eyes glistened. "But I thought...."

"I'm just saying that we have to be careful," said Lady Alice more softly. "If he wakes to find us tending to him then it is far more likely that he will repay our care. Then perhaps we may find some answers."

"But what will Papa say?" said Edith.

"You leave your father to me," said Lady Alice with a smile. "He'll agree when I remind him of the cost of the alternatives." Somewhere nearby a bell struck the hour. "I had best do that immediately." She turned to the archway. "You stay here with our patient and I'll return later. Send for me immediately if he wakes."

She walked out into the sunlit morning.

"We'll need chairs," said Edith looking around the bare little room.

"And water for when he wakes," said Celaine. "The priestess said he must drink."

"And something to eat. Do you have any money?"

"No. Do you?"

Edith shook her head.

"Oh well, I'm not hungry anyway," said Celaine. "I couldn't eat. Not with him lying there like that."

"I'll get us something to sit on. I won't be long." Edith walked out into the sunlight.

When Edith returned carrying two stools, the sun had slipped behind a large cloud and the little room was quite dark. Inside Celaine was curled up weeping beside Aron. Edith put down the stools and went to her. Saying nothing she put her arms around her sister and hugged her.

"I just can't forget that room, and the smell," sobbed Celaine. "It was so horrible." She looked at Aron. "And his poor back." She turned to Edith with wide frightened eyes. "What are we going to do if he dies?"

"He's not going to die," said Edith fiercely.

***

Aron awoke in Iduna's arms, his head pillowed on her chest, his fingers tangled in his hair, the sweet hay scent of her in his nose. He sighed contentedly.

"I hear prayers for you," she whispered. "My priestesses cry your name to me, women weep by your bedside, and one of them carries your child."

Aron sat up with a start, eyes and mouth wide open. "What did you say?"

Iduna smiled, eyes sparkling mischievously. "One of them carries your child."

Aron felt as if all the breath had been sucked out of him. "Lady Alice," he gasped.

"The very same."

"Does she know?"

Iduna's smile broadened. "She knows. How could she not?"

"And she prays for me?"

"She prays for you as do her daughters."

Aron's mind filled with their faces and his heart burned with a longing to see them. Iduna looked at him, the brightness of her eyes fading, her smile becoming wistful.

"The road is grievous and filled with pain." Tears glistened at the corners of her eyes. "You are welcome to stay."

She glanced meaningfully at a dish of golden apples that sat on the grass nearby.

"I never yet turned aside from a road because it was hard." Aron looked at her, but found it difficult to meet her eyes. "Would you wish me to stay?"

"I would."

Aron's heart turned over at the sadness and longing in her voice.

"Why did you tell me they're praying for me?"

"How could I deny the mother of your child?" She looked at him defiantly and a tear ran down her cheek. "I will not lie to keep you with me."

His heart breaking, Aron reached for her.

"The road need not be walked just yet."

***

Aron awoke to pain and thirst. His last memory was of Iduna's face close to his and her whisper.

"Keep me always in your heart, and you will always find me."

Now his back burned with a constant pain as if he lay too close to a great fire. He tried to roll on his side and sit up, but a lash of pure agony surged through his back and he flopped back face down onto the bed. He gasped with the pain and a shadowed figure moved beside him.

"Mama, he's awake." A girl's voice. *Edith or Celaine?* He struggled to focus on her face in the candlelight, but she remained a blur as she threw her arms around him and planted a tearful kiss on his face.

"Come away, girl, and let me see to him." The room grew brighter as Lady Alice came in carrying a lantern and knelt by Aron's bedside. "Thank the Goddess, our prayers are answered. Run and fetch Lorai, Celaine."

Celaine scurried out of the room. Lady Alice put down the lantern, poured a cup of water and lifted it to Aron's lips.

"Drink. You must be parched. Just raise your head a little."

Aron lifted his head, wincing with the pain the movement brought and drank thirstily.

"Where am I?" he croaked when the cup was empty

"The temple of Iduna," she said stroking his hair and raising the cup to his lips again.

"How long?"

"It is a night and a day since the girls found you at Tirellan's and brought you here."

"How?"

"We'll talk later, when you're stronger." She paused to wipe a tear from her cheek. "You just concentrate on getting better."

She kissed him and then straightened up hurriedly as she heard Lorai and Celaine approaching. Lorai went straight to Aron's bedside.

"How are you feeling, young man?" she asked laying a hand on his forehead. "You've no fever, thank the Lady."

"Everything hurts," groaned Aron.

"No doubt," said Lorai. "But we can't leave you lying there too long. You need to be up and about, or you'll lose flexibility as you heal."

Aron groaned again in reply.

"But he's in pain," cried Celaine. "Can't you do something?"

"I have the milk of the poppy, but that has its own dangers. It would be better if he could bear it....can you do that, lad?"

"Tomorrow," rasped Aron. "Give me the poppy tonight."

Lorai pursed her lips in disapproval, but reached into her bag and drew out a small bottle.

"For tonight only."

She poured a measure of the milky liquid into the drinking cup and passed it to Aron; gasping with pain, he propped himself up on one elbow to drink.

"You must drink plenty, my lad," said Lorai. "You've lost blood and you must make more." She watched as he drank the cupful. "Sleep tonight and we'll have you out of bed tomorrow." She turned for the door, speaking to Lady Alice as she left. "Make sure he drinks as much as he can take. I'll be back early tomorrow."

Aron held out the cup, Lady Alice refilled it and he drained it to wash the bitter taste from his mouth. Behind him Celaine rearranged the pillows so that he could at least partially sit up without lying on his wounds then sat on a stool beside the bed as close as she could get to him.

Aron felt the drug begin to have its effect; the bright fierce pain of his wounds faded to a distant, almost pleasant glow. He moved experimentally and while there was pain, it seemed that it belonged to someone else. He lifted himself and turned to sit up, resting on the pillows. He half expected to see the mist creeping across the floor as when he slipped into the spirit world, but it did not happen this time, which was just as well; Iduna had permitted him to return, but would she do so again? That he owed his life to her was undeniable, but he was not yet ready to surrender his independence. She loved him now, but the storytellers told many tales of the fickleness of the gods and he'd seen what happened to those who displeased her. He didn't fancy a future as a garden ornament.

"What happened to Tirellan?" he asked.

There was a moment's silence; Lady Alice looked meaningfully at Celaine.

"He's dead," said Celaine quietly, an edge of sadness in her voice. "He was dead when we got there, Cristoff too."

"He killed my father," said Aron, his own voice sounding to him as if someone else at the end of a long corridor spoke the words. "And the rest of the Darien garrison."

"Oh," said Celaine, her voice full of dismay. "He seemed so nice and clever to me."

She sounded very young to Aron at that moment.

"We had no idea," said Lady Alice. "We met him on the road. He did us a great service and, as we were strangers in the city, we were grateful for his aid."

"But why are you here at all?" asked Aron.

"We came to see his Majesty," said Lady Alice. "It seemed our only hope when Sarazan demanded ransom for Tancred too."

"Petter arranged for father to see the King," said Celaine. "I was going to ask him to be our champion against Sarazan to free Maldwyn and Tancred."

"Maldwyn?" Something nibbled at the edge of Aron's memory. "But Maldwyn was with me."

"With you?" Celaine's mouth dropped open in astonishment.

"But why didn't you bring him to us?" said Lady Alice.

"Haven't you seen him?" Aron looked at them feeling as if they were on the shore and he in a boat drifting away. "I took Maldwyn out of Castle Sarazan and brought him here, to the city with Davo. But we didn't know you were here."

"Where is he now, then?" asked Lady Alice. "Sarazan would scarcely agree to a trial of champions if they didn't hold him."

"He went missing a few days ago," said Aron slipping further away downriver. "I hoped he might have come to you."

"We haven't seen him," said Lady Alice. "We wouldn't need a champion if we had."

"Will you be our champion?" said Celaine, clutching his hand, her eyes very wide.

"Of course I will." Aron heard someone say with his voice.

CHAPTER 35

Lord Hercival paused outside his father's study to run a comb through his hair before knocking on the door. *I will not let him humiliate me. I'm his son too,* he thought, but his stomach still tightened with anxiety when he knocked and the voice called 'enter'.

"Hercival. You took your time."

The Duke was seated behind a large wooden desk, his hook-nosed face reflected in the highly polished surface.

"No good to see you, did you have a pleasant trip, father?"

Hercival looked around for somewhere to sit down; there was nowhere save the rug.

"Don't take that tone with me," said the Duke sharply. "Did you see your brother?"

"No, father. He must have dallied on the way."

The Duke frowned and glared at his son.

"He will take over the running of Sarazan which you cannot be trusted with. Now I want you to explain to me this affair with Nandor. To save you the trouble of lying, I will tell you what I already know."

Hercival felt his stomach tighten further.

"You and your worthless ragtag of friends went to the manor at Two Fords at the mouth of the Tymion, against my specific instructions. There you drank, caroused and abused all you found. When two of the kitchen girls fled your attentions, you and your friends pursued them up the valley into woods where you met Maldwyn of Nandor. Have I missed anything?"

"May I not visit my own property? Grandfather left the manor to me."

"Not when I've expressly forbidden it."

Hercival looked at the floor.

"They attacked us without warning," he said.

"No, they did not," replied the Duke coldly. "You had time enough to withdraw."

"I was defending the honour of Sarazan." *Surely he can't*

disapprove of that? thought Hercival defiantly. "It's what Grandfather would have done."

The Duke glared at his son and took his time before replying.

"Let me tell you what I have been doing for the last six months for the honour of Sarazan. At His Majesty's instruction, I have been visiting Lords around this kingdom trying to heal feuds. So how does it make me look to have a neighbour's son held for ransom in my house? I'll tell you. It makes me look a knave and a hypocrite, or else a fool who can't control his children. So where does that leave the honour of Sarazan?"

Hercival kept his eyes lowered to avoid his father's stare.

"His Majesty," continued the Duke in a calm, even voice, "was not impressed; which is most regrettable as we had been discussing the possibility of Princess Lucienna marrying your brother. I think you can appreciate the honour this would bring to Sarazan. Look at me, damn you!"

Hercival raised his eyes to meet his father's furious gaze, feeling as if he was a child again.

"Your reckless disobedience has threatened all this and now Mikael has to risk his life to mend it."

"What? Why?"

"His Majesty has decreed that the dispute will be settled in the arena by trial of champions, and I have no alternative than to comply if I wish to retain a shred of dignity. Mikael, being the truly honourable man he is, has demanded the right to be our champion. It seems the only way out of this tangle of folly that you have landed us in."

"So what's the problem? Mikael can take care of anyone that Nandor has."

"Do you think so?" The Duke glared. "They have named Aron of Darien as their champion."

"But he's just...."

Hercival groped for the words, but the Duke cut him off.

"Just a very dangerous swordsman. Academy trained, and a real threat to Mikael. I should have thought he had done us enough damage and that you would have some respect for him."

"I had no idea," said Hercival lamely, wishing that the conversation was over.

"Quite," said the Duke coldly. "Yet you chose to ignore Master Ezrin's warning. This whole tragic mess flows from you and decisions you made. I am gravely disappointed with you, Hercival. At your age I had command of an army, yet I find I am unable to trust you with the running of a pie stall. You will remain under my direct supervision until such time as you show signs of maturity. Now get out of my sight."

"Yes, father," said Hercival.

He turned for the door, his cheeks burning. He more than half expected his father to call him back to say something more but the Duke did not speak.

Hercival stalked back to his rooms anger seething in his heart as he reviewed the meeting. Everything he had done was for the honour of Sarazan, the way that noblemen of honour had acted for hundreds of years, and if it was at the expense of a neighbour then that was what had made Sarazan powerful. His grandfather would have understood. He wished the old man was still around. He would have thought his son had water in his veins instead of Sarazan blood. Perhaps his father was right about Ezrin though, even if his warning had been vague. Hercival mentally kicked himself; had he heeded the wizard, Aron of Darien would have been hanging from the gatehouse before he could do any damage. At least that was one thing he could do something about. Everything was for sale in the Holy City, even someone's death. He wondered how much an assassin would cost, more than the small amount of coin he had probably. He strode into his room straight to a chest of drawers, and took out a jewelled dagger; a present from his grandfather. *Appropriate*, he thought, *the old man would approve of this*. He should be able to pawn it for enough to buy Aron's death. He slipped it into his belt pouch and turned for the door. It was still early in the day, but he knew of a tavern where he should be able to buy the kind of men he needed.

***

The Duke of Sarazan was sitting with his head in his hands when he heard the knock at the door. He pulled himself upright with a grimace and then called out, "Enter."

His expression relaxed as he saw his vistor was a short but athletically built man of around forty.

"Ah, Mikael, come and sit down," the Duke said. "Will you take a drink?"

"Thank you no, my Lord. Not now that I'm in training," said Mikael.

"When have you ever been out of training?" said the Duke. "You don't mind if I do?" He turned to a shelf behind him and selected a bottle from the several that stood there. "I know it's early, but under the circumstances."

"You've spoken to Hercival then."

The Duke sighed wearily. "I have, and he is quite unrepentant." He poured a generous measure of red wine into a goblet. "So what have you discovered about this Aron of Darien? Was he truly at the Academy?"

"Oh yes. And highly thought of too. A serious young man, not impetuous as so many of them can be at that age."

"Dangerous?"

The Duke took another sip of wine.

"Certainly."

"You don't have to do this. One of the other blademasters could take your place. Young Morin could do with the experience."

"It's what you pay me for," said Mikael evenly. "And besides, how would it look if I passed on it and Morin got himself killed?"

"You're far more valuable to me than Morin. Who else can I rely on for sound advice? And where would I get another chess partner?"

"One who lets you win, you mean."

"Seriously, Mikael. I've lost too many friends in these last few years. You're irreplaceable and I would be happy if one of the others took your place. The Tymion valley is not worth a drop of your blood spilled."

"Is that an order, my Lord?"

"No, Mikael. It's a request."

"One I must regretfully decline. I have to do this. I am the senior blademaster of Sarazan. The land may be worthless, but the honour of Sarazan is not. This Aron hasn't fought in the arena before, I have many times. He may not handle the occasion. He's a young man and may make a young man's mistake and I will be waiting."

"I thought you said he wasn't impetuous?"

"He may not be, but he will still feel all the pressure."

"You make it sound so simple."

"It is, my Lord."

"If only other things were too," sighed the Duke. "Tell me what I should do with Hercival."

**

"Were you looking for something in particular, my Lord?" asked the serving man as he placed a tankard of ale on the table, slopping much onto the floor.

"Why do you call me my Lord?" asked Lord Hercival, squinting at the man in the halflight of the taproom.

"The way you speak, the clothes you wear, the way you look at people."

There was no respect in the man's attitude. Hercival felt a chill shiver of fear run through him.

"Now what are you looking for?"

"Some men to perform a small task," said Hercival. "I'll pay well."

"Local or upcountry?"

A knife scar writhed across the man's unshaven cheek as he spoke. Hercival thought for a moment about leaving the tavern right then but instead said, "Local."

"You might want to talk to them lads then." The man gestured at a corner table. "If you don't mind they're Saxish."

Hercival looked over at the corner. Three large men sat there in shadow. He could just make out the long dark hair caught in ponytails and the leather waistcoats that were characteristic of the Saxish clansmen.

"Thank you," he said, expecting the serving man to move away then but he didn't, and Hercival realised that he was expecting to be paid for the information. He dropped a small coin onto the table; the man swept it up and scowled at him.

"Thank you, my Lord," he muttered before turning away.

Hercival drank his ale and took a moment to consider what he was going to say; then, heart pounding, he walked over to the clansmen. Three pairs of dark eyes turned to look at him.

"Whaddya want?" asked one, his harsh accent so distorting the words that Hercival could barely understand him.

"I'm looking for someone to do a little job for me." Lord Hercival glanced around to check that there was no-one in earshot. "It's local, here in the city."

"Yeah." The dark eyes glinted. "Kind of a job?"

"There's someone I want taken care of."

"Permanent?"

"Permanent."

There was a wolfish flash of teeth. "It cost."

Lord Hercival smiled. "How much?"

"One hundred." The clansman grinned at his companions. "Fifty now and fifty when it's done."

"Sixty now. We can't cut fifty three ways equal."

Hercival paused a moment, unsure if they were making fun of him.

"Done," he said and reached for his purse. He counted out sixty silver coins and laid them on the table. The clansman took one at random, raised it to his mouth and bit it.

"Good. Now we drink," he said waving to the potboy. "Who's the mark and where we find him?"

"His name is Aron of Darien and he is attached to the household of the Earl of Nandor."

At his words the clansmen began an animated conversation in their own guttural tongue. Hercival sat bemused until the first clansman turned back to him.

"You say Darien?"

"Yes. Aron of Darien. Is that a problem?"

Hercival had a moment of panic wondering how he would get his money back if it was a problem.

"No problem." The clansman grinned his wolfish grin again. "Where we find him?"

"The Earl of Nandor and his family are staying at the Seven Stars Inn. Aron is my height, slim, with dark hair he wears to his shoulders." Hercival silently thanked the loose tongues of Tancred and the Sarazan soldiers. "If you watch the Earl's daughters then Aron will not be far away." He paused a moment. "He's good with the blade."

The clansman nodded and smiled evilly at Hercival. "That's alright. We not fighting a duel."

"Is there anything else you need?" said Hercival, hoping that the deal making was over. His bladder suddenly felt very full.

"And who are you, me Lord?" said the clansman with the same smile.

"Lord Hercival of Sarazan, and I can be found at...."

"Don't worry, me Lord." The clansman cut him off. "We find you when it's paying time." Hercival felt a thrill of fear run through him at the words.

The potboy arrived with four tankards. The clansmen took one each. "Now we drink."

Hercival reached reluctantly for the final tankard wondering how long he was expected to stay; he crossed his legs and hoped it wouldn't be long.

***

Aron shifted the cushion on the stool beneath him. It hurt to sit, but then it hurt to stand, or even to breathe too deeply. The last few days had been the hardest of his life as Lorai and the other priestesses had urged him to first stand, and then walk despite the pain. He watched Celaine as she knelt by a bed in the sunlit herb garden talking with one of the priestesses. He'd barely had a waking moment to himself; Lady Alice and her daughters had been in constant attendance, but their watching had somehow made the pain worse. Their presence a reminder of his failure to bring Maldwyn home. Celaine turned and saw him watching her; she smiled and for a moment his pain was lessened.

Celaine stood up and turned towards him, brushing earth off her skirt, the sun picking out the chestnut shades in her hair, which she wore loose and flowing as was the fashion for unmarried girls in the city. Aron thought at that moment that she was probably the prettiest girl he'd ever seen.

"They've taught me so much in the time I've been here," said Celaine. "And they're going to give me seeds for my garden."

She knelt beside him and, to Aron, it seemed that there was a sadness about her this morning, and as she turned from his gaze he thought her eyes looked moist.

"Will you be sad to leave the city?" he asked.

"Well, yes and no," she said not looking at him. "It's so rich and exciting, but it's cruel too." She was silent for a moment and then turned back to him." I dreamed about you last night. About the fight." Her eyes glistened with tears. "I dreamed he killed you."

Aron reached out and took her hands in his.

"Not all dreams come true," he said.

***

Aron walked slowly down the streets, dark and gloomy even in full daylight, that led to the exiles' house. It wasn't a great distance, but today was the first day that he had felt strong enough to attempt it.

He paused to wipe the sweat from his face; it was full summer in the King's City now and the air throbbed with heat. The doorway was within sight, but Aron was tired and thirsty, his wounds itched under the dressings, he had a headache and wanted to sit down somewhere in the shade. He gritted his teeth as he pushed himself to walk the last few yards. His head swam a little as he rapped on the door. After a short delay the peephole in the door opened.

"Whadya want?" a harsh voice asked.

"Let me in," said Aron.

"Password."

"No idea." Aron closed his eyes against the sun's glare reflecting off the white wall and struggled to remember. "It was turnip stew six days ago."

"If you don't know the password, you can piss off."

"Don't you know who I am?"

"No. Now piss off."

The peephole banged shut. Aron sat on the doorstep hands over his eyes as the pain in his head flared. This was the only way in he knew of, and Lionel and Tamon the only people he knew inside. The other exiles he'd met only briefly, but they ought to know his name. He waited for the pain to ease, then stood up and banged on the door again.

The peephole opened. "You again. I told you to piss off."

"Tell Lionel, Aron is here."

"So you're Aron, are you?"

He sounded unconvinced. Aron struggled to contain the anger that was growing inside him.

"Tell Lionel I had to cut my hair to get rid of the curls."

"You what?"

"Just tell him."

The peephole banged shut again. Aron stood defiantly before the door, sweat running down his face, waiting for something to happen. Eventually he heard hurried footsteps on the other side of the door, it swung open and Lionel stood before him.

"It is you, thank the Gods." Lionel stepped forward and flung his arms round Aron who winced at the contact with his partially-healed wounds. "I thought we'd lost you when you didn't return. We heard about Tirellan, but where've you been?" He released Aron from the bearhug, held him at arms length and looked at him, his cheeks streaked with tears. "You look terrible. What happened?"

"It's a long story," said Aron.

"Come on in and tell me about it."

Aron followed Lionel inside and walked past the hulking shaggy-haired figure of the doorward who gave him a long hard stare as he passed. *What's got into him?* thought Aron. *Just because I'm who I said I am.* Something in the man's gaze made him shiver despite the warmth of the day.

Lionel led him to a cool airy sitting room two floors up where Aron made himself comfortable on a low couch while Lionel fetched drinks.

"So where have you been since you left Bazarkis' house?" said Lionel handing Aron a mug of ale.

"Last few days I've been at the temple of Iduna. Don't look so surprised. I've been with the healers, I needed them."

"Where did things go wrong? You got to Tirellan's house?"

"The coach took me straight there," said Aron. "The place was unguarded, and wide-open, no-one around except Tirellan and Cristoff. Tirellan tricked me. I saw him pour wine for himself and Cristoff, and I made sure they drank before I touched mine. The wine was clean, the drug was in the goblet. I should have known."

"They drugged you?"

"Yes." said Aron, the words bitter in his mouth. "Drugged me, tied me and whipped me."

"So how did you get away?"

"Edith and Celaine. They came looking for Tirellan, found me and took me to the temple. Without them I'd be a dead man for sure." Aron paused and took a drink. "And now I have to pay my debt to them with an arena fight against the champion of Sarazan."

"Sarazan eh? Is this connected to that fellow Maldwyn you brought with you?"

"Yes. It's his ransom that's at stake."

"I thought so because we learned that he was seized by a group of Sarazan's soldiers in a tavern in Half Moon Street."

Aron's heart sank. He'd been hoping Maldwyn would turn up somewhere and that Sarazan's claim to hold him was a bluff.

"What was he doing down there?"

"The other fellow that was with you, Davo. He'd been asking the lads about brothels and there's a high class one down there."

Aron cursed. The story seemed all too plausible.

"Damn fool. Why couldn't he do what he was told for a few days? What happened to Davo?"

He could tell from Lionel's face that he was not going to hear good news.

"He's dead," said Lionel quietly. "Shot down in the street by Sarazan crossbows. I'm sorry."

Aron took a deep breath and bowed his head.

"That's hard. But there are worse deaths. He was never going to make old bones, probably saved him from the gallows anyway." He took a deep draught of ale and stared at the floor. "I'll miss the little bastard though."

"Who's the opponent in the arena fight?" asked Lionel.

"The champion of Sarazan, a fellow named Mikael. All I know about him is that he's old. He's been the Duke's principal blademaster for twenty years and is said to be his closest friend."

"He must be good to have lasted this long," said Lionel thoughtfully.

"Exactly my thoughts."

"When?"

"Day after the next full moon."

"That's soon; are you going to be fit?"

"I'll have to be."

Lionel took a mouthful of ale and thought for a while before speaking.

"Tough fight," he said grimly.

"Very tough," said Aron. "I really need to practice. Can you get hold of Kyria's blademaster and arrange something? I'll need my kit from here, too."

"I'll send someone to fetch your things immediately and there'll be no problem with Kyria." He stepped to the door and spoke briefly to someone outside. "Where are you going to be staying?" he asked.

"At The Seven Stars with Earl Baldwin and his party. I've been at the temple long enough."

"The old women not to your taste?" Lionel grinned at Aron.

"More comfortable than your attic," Aron said laughing.

Lionel smiled and took another mouthful of ale. "How much should I stake on you to win?"

Aron looked back at him. "Not a penny."

Lionel caught his mood and the smile vanished. "That bad?"

"That bad."

"And high stakes."

"If I lose, Nandor is ruined. They lose the land and paying the ransom will leave the daughters without dowries."

"Not a nobleman in the land would marry them then. And if you win?"

"Sarazan gives up all claim on the land, and releases Maldwyn and his cousin Tancred, though as far as I'm concerned they can keep Tancred."

"What do you get?"

"Not money. Probably the offer of a position in the household and maybe marriage to one of the daughters."

"Tempting. I hear they're beauties." Lionel smiled knowingly at Aron.

So which one do you want, Aron remembered Davo's mocking words. "Nandor's a long way from anywhere and it rains a lot," said Aron not wanting to confront the question.

There was a knock at the door; Lionel got up to answer it. He exchanged a few words with the unseen messenger and returned with a half-filled sack. He passed it over to Aron.

"This is all they could find in your room."

Aron took the sack and sorted through the contents. His sword, knives and the pouch of coins they'd won at the Silver Moon were all there.

"I should be going. I'll see you before the fight, won't I?" Aron said gathering up the sack. "Come up to Kyria's mansion when I'm practising."

"Of course; I'll be there every day," said Lionel. "They'd all come to watch if I let them."

Together they made their way to the street door. Lionel examined the street through the peephole before opening it.

"One thing," he said. "You said you were drugged and tied up by Tirellan."

"Yes."

"So who killed him?"

Aron looked at Lionel, wondering whether he was ready for the truth.

"Iduna," he said and stepped into the street.

CHAPTER 36

Aron entered the Nandor party's sitting room still sweating from his exercises.

"Well, it is nice to see you," said Celaine as Aron came into the sitting room. "We thought you'd quite forgotten about us."

"I'm sorry to have disappointed you, my Lady. But I've been training and that's best done before the day gets too hot."

Indeed by this hour yesterday, Aron had run across the city to the Duke of Kyria's mansion and put in two hours intensive practice. He looked at the remains of the breakfast still on the table and reflected that with half the day gone by the ladies were barely risen and there was no sign of Earl Baldwin.

"Aren't you training today?" asked Edith.

"I've already been for a run, but my instructor has other duties today, so I'm working with another blademaster later on."

"So you're free to show us the city for a while then," said Celaine with a happy smile.

"That would be lovely," said Edith.

Aron looked for a moment into the dangerous blue gazes and suddenly it seemed a very attractive idea.

"For a while then before I go training."

"Can we, Mama?"

Edith turned to her mother who was taking her time over a dish of honeyed eggs.

"I don't see why not." Lady Alice smiled and turned to Aron. "You will take good care of them, won't you?"

"They'll be safe with me," said Aron.

"I must go and get ready," said Celaine and turned for the door that led to the bedroom.

Aron reached for a plate.

"I've time for a little breakfast then," he said, and Lady Alice smiled at him again.

***

It was busy out on the streets, and hot enough for Aron not to wear his mailshirt, though he kept his knives and sword; he had after all promised to look after the girls and the city wasn't that safe. At the moment though, he was in danger of being bored to death, as the girls had insisted on stopping to examine almost every shop they had passed. He was idly watching the passing crowd, when he caught a glimpse of what looked like a Saxish clansman. The fellow saw Aron looking at him and ducked away into an alley. Just then the girls detached themselves from the merchant's wares and turned back to Aron, each taking an arm. Aron twisted to see if the clansman reappeared and flinched as his back muscles protested.

"What's the matter?" asked Celaine as they steered him down the crowded street.

"I thought I saw someone I knew," said Aron.

"Not a girl, I hope," said Edith.

"No, no it wasn't," said Aron, still thinking about the clansman.

"You seem very distant today," said Celaine. "Are you thinking about the duel?"

"Yes," said Aron.

"I didn't think heroes ever worried," said Edith squeezing his arm. "That's what the bards say anyway."

"Proves I'm no hero then," said Aron.

"What is there to worry about?" said Celaine. "You'll be fit in time won't you?"

"I hope so. But that's just part of my worries. I've never fought in the arena before. I would expect this Mikael has. He's twenty years older than me and that's a lot of experience. He must still be good otherwise he wouldn't be Sarazan's senior blademaster."

Edith turned and looked at him, her blue gaze turned up to maximum.

"You'll still be my hero if you lose," she said gravely.

"I could easily be dead if I lose."

"Then we'll put flowers on your grave every day," said Celaine and both girls broke into giggles.

Aron grinned despite himself.

"You're being far too serious," said Edith. "I think you need to see a fair. The maid said there's a fair beside the watergate. Why don't you take us there?"

Aron groaned inwardly; shysters and pickpockets would be as thick as fleas on a street dog at the fair, but he knew the girls would love the tawdry glamour.

"This way then," he said directing them towards a quiet lane between high buildings that led away from the main street.

They had gone maybe ten paces along the narrow lane when two tall figures appeared from an alleyway further on and began walking towards them. The leather waistcoats and long dark hair tied back with leather thongs marked them unmistakably as Saxish clansmen. Aron looked over his shoulder; another clansman had entered the lane behind them and all three carried longswords on their backs.

"Just keep walking," Aron whispered to the girls as he freed his arms from theirs.

They moved looking confused as he fiddled with his belt and his sword dropped noisily to the cobbles. As he bent to retrieve it he could hear the boots of the clansman behind approaching at a brisk walk. He glanced up to see how far away the other two were and, crouched in the middle of the lane, fumbled with the sword's fixings. Shielded from the clansman's view his right hand found the dagger in his boot top.

The clansman halted a pace from him. Aron looked up to see him reach over his shoulder to draw his sword. Somewhere up the lane a girl screamed. Bracing his hands on the ground, Aron struck out with his left foot and caught the clansman solidly on the side of his right knee. He staggered sideways and his half-drawn sword jammed in the scabbard. Aron danced upwards and brought the dagger round striking just below the point of the jaw beneath the left ear. The clansman grunted and collapsed like a sack of turnips. Aron picked up his sword, looked back up the lane and then sprinted for the near end.

The two clansmen hesitated for a moment, then drew their swords and pelted down the lane after Aron, shoving Celaine and Edith roughly out of their way. Edith stuck out a foot and caught the ankle of one, who tumbled cursing to the cobbles. He picked himself up and glared back at Edith.

"I'll be back for you, bitch," he grated, then sprinted off up the lane.

Aron rounded the corner and stopped abruptly, sword in hand. He could hear the clansman approaching. *High or low* thought Aron as he held his breath waiting. The clansman reached the corner. *Low.* Aron's sword slashed across the clansman's thigh as he barrelled round the corner, sword held in front of his body. He screamed and collapsed in a sprawl. Aron stepped forward and silenced him forever with a cut across the throat.

The third assassin charged out of the lane straight at Aron without hesitation. Aron side-stepped and a wide slash missed him by an armslength. Aron rebalanced to face him as the clansman whirled to strike again. He danced back as the longsword carved the air in front of him then darted forward to cut his opponent's shoulder. The clansman snarled in pain but did not retreat. Aron looked into his eyes and saw only the madness of blood rage as he launched another attack. Aron blocked the swing of the longsword with his own blade, pivoted on his left leg and kicked the clansman hard just below the right knee. He grunted and stumbled sideways, but stayed on his feet. Aron attacked, instantly pressing his advantage; stepping inside the arc of the longsword, he shifted his sword to his left hand and drew the throwing knife from its sheath at the nape of his neck and brought it up beneath the clansman's chin.

"Drop the sword," Aron said as the clansman's foul breath washed over him. There was a moment's defiance in the man's dark eyes then the longsword clattered on the cobbles.

"Who?" demanded Aron just pricking the stubbled skin with his knifepoint. There was no reply and the defiance re-entered the clansman's eyes. Aron shifted the knifepoint to the cheek just below the left eye.

"There are worse things than dying," he said softly, pressing the point just enough to draw blood.

"Hercival," the clansman said hoarsely. "Hercival of Sarazan."

"Very wise," said Aron. He withdrew the knife a few inches and then struck suddenly below the clansman's ear, stabbing deep into the neck. The clansman gasped, his eyes opened wide in surprise, he spasmed briefly and slumped to the ground. Aron stepped back and looked up to see where the girls were. He sheathed his knife and walked up the lane to the doorway in which they huddled.

"Are you alright?" asked Edith, her voice shaking, her face pale and eyes too wide.

"I'm fine," said Aron.

"We were so scared," Celaine said, and started to cry.

Aron reached out to comfort her but found both girls in his arms. He held them tight as they sobbed and out of the corner of his eye he saw a crowd begin to gather.

"We need to go," he whispered.

"Is it safe?" asked Celaine.

"It's safe, they're all dead," said Aron reassuringly. "Let's go back to the inn."

An arm around each girl, Aron headed up the lane, leaving the three dead clansman to the crowd. They walked in silence as fast as Aron could manage with both girls held close. He glanced back to see if anyone followed them but the lane was empty.

They walked without noticing the passage of time through lanes so narrow that the upper stories of the houses almost touched above them until they came in sight of the Seven Stars. As the adrenaline of the fight left him Aron's back began to glow with a distant ache from the strain he'd put on his wounds. *Could be worse*, he thought. *Three assassins and all I've got is a sore back.*

"Stop here and we'll clean you up," said Edith. "You've got blood on your face; we can't take you back to Mama in that state."

She made Aron sit down beside the horsetrough and with a moistened handkerchief washed the blood from Aron's face and arms. Celaine sat beside him silently holding his hand.

"You were unbelievable, you know," said Edith. "I thought you were dead for sure when that swordsman came up behind you. I've never seen anything like it. Marek never had a chance, did he?"

Aron looked up at her.

"Not really," he said, getting the full benefit of the blue eyes. "He was dead as soon as he drew his sword."

"He's no loss, I never liked him," said Edith. "But you were like something out of the bard's tales."

"You shouldn't listen too closely to the bard's tales," said Aron suddenly serious. "Life's not like that."

"But it is," said Edith. "You appear in Nandor just when we need you most and you rescue Maldwyn from Sarazan. Now you're going fight for us before the High King and win a great victory."

She smiled, blue eyes filled with enthusiasm and hope.

Aron turned away, unwilling to prick the bubble.

"Let's go inside then," he said.

He stood up and immediately Celaine slipped her arm around him.

***

"You're back early," said Lady Alice as Aron followed the girls into the sitting room. She looked at her daughters' faces. "What's happened?"

"We were attacked," said Aron. "Three Saxish clansmen."

"What?" Lady Alice dropped her embroidery in shock. "Are you hurt?"

"No Mama, we're fine. Aron killed them all," said Edith. "All three. It was incredible."

"What's going on?" Earl Baldwin emerged from his bedroom wearing a crumpled and stained robe, his thin hair in disarray. "Who've you killed?"

"Three Saxish clansmen," said Aron.

"Excellent. Well done, my lad. Have a drink." Earl Baldwin smiled broadly and moved towards the wine bottles on the table. He poured two generous glasses of red wine and held one out to Aron.

"Tell me all about it," said Baldwin. "What were they armed with? How did they come at you?"

Aron took a mouthful of wine and had to restrain himself from spitting the bitter brew onto the floor. *How on earth can he drink this?* he thought.

"There were two in front and one behind, all with longswords," said Edith enthusiastically, as Aron struggled to swallow his wine.

"Your ladies can tell you all about it, they had a much better view than me, my Lord," said Aron putting the glass to one side. "If you'll excuse me, I still have a blademaster waiting for me."

"That's all right, lad," said Earl Baldwin. "We mustn't keep you from your training."

Lady Alice caught Aron's eye as he turned for the door and her expression clearly said that the discussion was not over.

***

It was late evening with the full moon riding in a clear sky above the city when Aron returned to the Seven Stars. He had worked long and hard with the blademaster and then accepted his invitation to supper. They passed the evening swapping stories over a bottle of wine with Aron listening intently to every snippet of information about Mikael, the blademaster of Sarazan.

Aron was tired as he climbed the stairs that led to his room beneath the eves and his back ached. He saw the glow of light beneath the door of the Nandor suite and, remembering Lady Alice's expression, thought about passing by. Instead he knocked softly.

"Enter," Lady Alice called.

He pushed the door open and walked in. Lady Alice was sitting with her embroidery on her knee, a stern frown on her face. Aron had seen this expression many times before, but never directed at him.

"I want you to explain what happened today," she said tightly. "You promised me the girls would be safe with you. Celaine was very upset. I've had to give her a sleeping draught to calm her."

"It was nothing I could avoid," said Aron. "The men I killed were assassins hired by Lord Hercival of Sarazan. One of them told me before I killed him."

"Iduna save us."

Lady Alice clasped her hands to her face, dropping her embroidery on the floor.

"The only reason I survived is they were Saxish," Aron said, kneeling to recover the embroidery. "I've been suspicious of Saxishmen since they betrayed Darien at the siege, and when I saw one tailing us I was ready."

"They could have killed you all."

"Yes." Aron passed the embroidery back to her and she caught his hand.

"I'm so sorry I doubted you,"she paused. "Can you forgive me?"

She looked at him her eyes dark in the candlelight.

"There is nothing to forgive," Aron said softly.

"You know that's not true. It was ungracious of me after you have done so much for us already,"she faltered and then continued in a whisper. "I have no excuse except that I stand on the edge of the ruination of my entire life."

Aron was conscious then of how tightly she gripped his hand and looked around guiltily for Baldwin.

"Thank you," Lady Alice said. "Thank you for being here. I've had to be strong for everyone for so long, but there's no-one to be strong for me."

"Baldwin?"

She shook her head slowly.

"Don't judge him too harshly. Maldwyn's capture hit him hard. He's lived all his life in his father's shadow, and the old man never once reached out to him as a father should."

Aron, feeling utterly helpless, said nothing and waited for her to continue.

"I was younger than Edith when I married him. My father was a merchant; he thought it would bring honour to the family, but he didn't live to see his first grandchild." She loosened her hold on Aron to push back a stray lock of dark hair. "At first it was like a dream to be Countess of Nandor, but you have to wake from dreams."

"Where is Baldwin now?"

"Gone. He dragged poor Thalon off to some cockfight. He'll come back drunk again. I don't remember the last time he came to bed sober. I'm so alone in this, and all he does is drink. We could lose everything and I'm pregnant again. I sent Glynis to get the herbs after I laid with you, but they were mouldy and they didn't work." She swallowed hard. "My mother was younger than this when she died in childbed and I'm frightened."

She shivered despite the warmth of the room. Aron looked into her lovely blue eyes and saw a depth of sadness that made his heart turn over. He wanted to tell her that everything would be alright, but he couldn't speak the lie. She took his hands again, leaned forward and very deliberately kissed him, softly at first, but then with rising passion and hunger.

CHAPTER 37

It was still dark when Aron woke. He went to the window of his little room on the top floor of The Seven Stars and looked out eastward over the city. He stood and watched the silver on the horizon pass through pink to yellow as dawn rolled across the land. *Might as well enjoy it,* he thought. *This could be my last one.* The sky was clear and the day promised to be hot. *Must drink plenty of water before the fight.* He watched as the city started to come to life. Then, with the early morning sun on his face, he shaved carefully using one of his throwing knives.

He turned from the window and pulled out his pack to prepare his gear for the day. At the bottom he found the handkerchief Edith had given him back in Nandor. He sat on the bed holding the stained and crumpled scrap, remembering her smile and her laughter and, above all, her blue eyes looking at him, reminding him of all that was at stake today. *You can't think about that; you must clear your mind of everything except your opponent.* He put the handkerchief back in his pack beside his money pouch, spare shirt and leggings. *But I'll take it with me into the arena.*

Aron thought about breakfast. He didn't feel hungry in the least, but he'd need a good solid breakfast and then nothing after; the fight was in the afternoon, the exact time dependent on the bouts scheduled before his. He wondered how the rest of the Nandor party had slept - poorly he suspected. Last night's supper had been a quiet and strained affair as if everyone had suddenly realised the enormity of the next day's events. It was probably the first night Earl Baldwin had gone to bed sober that year.

Aron drew out his sword and whetstone and began to work on the blade. It didn't really need doing, but it was a task to absorb himself in. Once that was done, he worked on each of his knives even though he would not be taking them into the arena.

The knives packed away, he decided it was time for breakfast even though he still wasn't hungry. He made his way down to the Nandor suite to find them all at breakfast, even Earl Baldwin. Edith and Celaine greeted him with nervous smiles. Aron's heart gave a little skip at the sight of them.

"Good morning, Aron," said Lady Alice. "I hope you slept well. Will you have some breakfast?"

"Yes, thank you," said Aron, though he still had no appetite.

"A good jug of red wine should set you up nicely," said Earl Baldwin. "I always like to start the day with a quart or so when I'm hunting."

Aron smiled politetely. "I fear I would be asleep by the time of the fight, my Lord."

"Leave the lad alone, Baldwin," said Lady Alice firmly. "He's the Academy trained one, not you."

Aron served himself with bread, cold ham and a large mug of milk and sat down at the table conscious of Edith and Celaine's silent gaze. He wanted to say something reassuring, but couldn't think of anything.

"When are you going to the arena?" asked Lady Alice.

"Sometime after midday," said Aron. "I need to have plenty of time to prepare and I want to go to the temple this morning. I must thank the priestesses."

"They certainly did a fine job," said Lady Alice. "Who would have thought you'd be fit to fight so soon after such injuries?"

"We should all go," said Celaine which provoked a fierce frown from Baldwin.

"You needn't go if you don't want to," said Lady Alice to Baldwin. "Though you've plenty to be thankful for. Without them there would be no champion for Nandor."

Baldwin grunted in reply.

"I thought not. Suit yourself then. Are you presentable girls? Edith, go and brush your hair. We'll go as soon as Aron is ready."

***

Lord Hercival stalked into the garden, his fists tight knots of anger. Twelve days had passed since he had paid the Saxishmen for Aron's death and he had heard nothing. Clearly they had cheated him and there seemed to be nothing he could do. He certainly couldn't go back to the tavern in search of them on his own, and there was no possibility of taking a squad of Sarazan soldiers with him, his father had seen to that. He ground his teeth with rage.

"Good afternoon, my Lord. I am most glad to see you."

Hercival looked up at the sound of the voice and saw Tancred walking swiftly towards him.

"Perhaps you can tell me what is going on," said Tancred. "Your men haven't allowed me to leave the grounds since Maldwyn was recaptured and now they tell me that everything will be resolved today."

"Ah, Tancred," said Hercival smiling coldly. "In truth today all will be resolved and Aron of Darien will finally meet the end he so richly deserves."

"Why? What is happening?"

"Aron stands as champion of Nandor in the arena this afternoon. Mikael, the senior blademaster of Sarazan, is going to kill him and then your fleabitten uncle will have to pay the ransom for Maldwyn."

"Why is Maldwyn still alive?" said Tancred angrily.

"It's out of my hands now. My father has taken charge of everything."

"And why am I not allowed to leave the grounds?"

"Did no-one mention that we're holding you to ransom along with your cousin?" said Hercival mockingly. "I do apologise for the oversight."

Tancred stared in astonishment at Hercival. "We had an agreement," he said, his eyes blazing with anger.

"Had we? Did I swear an oath? Have you witnesses?"

"You treacherous bastard."

"You're a fine one to accuse me of treachery. Who was it who was only too happy to sell his cousin?" Hercival laughed. "You're a fool to try to play this game of house. You have not the wit for it. Go back to your sheep."

Tancred's reply was to hurl himself at Hercival tumbling both of them to to the gravelled path. They rolled into a flowerbed and Tancred came up on top, his hands around Hercival's neck. Hercival bellowed at the top of his voice for the guards and battered ineffectively at Tancred's head and shoulders as Tancred struggled to apply his full weight onto Hercival's throat.

The blood pounded in Hercival's head and his vision was growing dark when the pressure was suddenly released. He lay back on the soft earth gulping in great draughts of air.

"My Lord. My Lord. Are you alright? Will I call the healer, my Lord?"

Hercival sat up still gasping. Beside him, a sergeant guardsman stared anxiously at him; another two guardsmen were sitting on Tancred, pinning him to the gravel path. Hercival struggled to his feet and then kicked out at Tancred, catching him in the stomach.

"My Lord, stop!" cried the sergeant. "He is a ransom prisoner."

He interposed himself between Hercival and the helpless Tancred. "Your Lord Father ordered that they be correctly treated at all times."

"Damn my Lord Father," shouted Hercival. "Take him then and get him out of my sight."

He turned and strode out of the garden massaging his throat as he went.

***

It was just short of midday when Aron, Lady Alice and her daughters left the Temple of Iduna. Earl Baldwin was pacing up and down in the sittingroom of The Seven Stars when they returned.

"Where did you get to?" he asked. "It's time we were on our way to the arena."

"Sit down, Baldwin," said Lady Alice. "Before you wear a hole in the floor. We've plenty of time. They can hardly start without us." She looked critically at her husband. "Is that the cleanest shirt you could find?"

Earl Baldwin looked at her quizzically. "What's wrong with it?"

"There's a stain on the collar. It looks like soup or gravy. Really, Baldwin. His Majesty might be there, and you can't meet him in a soup-stained shirt."

Earl Baldwin recognised the battle was lost. "If you say so, my dear." He turned and headed for their bedroom.

"Do you think the King will really come?" asked Celaine brightly.

"I doubt it," said Aron. "Though it's possible, as Sarazan is one of his principal supporters. He's more likely to send the Chancellor or one of his deputies."

"Don't let Baldwin hear that, or he'll never change his shirt," said Lady Alice. Celaine giggled nervously.

"I'll fetch my gear," said Aron. "Then we can go when his Lordship is ready."

He walked out of the sittingroom and climbed the narrow stairs up to his room. He picked his pack up from the bed, rolled up his travel cloak and fastened it to the bottom of the pack, flipped the pack over his shoulder. He tested his back one last time and finding it supple and painfree, hurried back down the stairs.

Baldwin had found himself a clean shirt and was waiting with the ladies.

"There's no need for you to all come now," said Aron. "I want time to prepare, but the fight will not be for some hours yet."

"No! Absolutely not," said Earl Baldwin. "You are the champion of Nandor and it is only fitting that you arrive there with all the honour Nandor can muster. Besides we can't risk any more assassins. Thalon and the guard are waiting out in the courtyard and we'll escort you there."

"As you wish, my Lord," said Aron though in his heart he wished it was otherwise; their nervousness was getting to him and he wanted as few reminders of the stakes as possible.

***

They walked through the city, the guardsmen clearing a path through the bustling streets. Few people took note of their passing as Aron scanned the crowds for hints of danger. *Foolishness,* he thought. *If there is danger it comes from above. An archer or crossbowman on a rooftop.* He hoisted his pack higher on his shoulder to shield himself against the imagined dart and felt the sweat beading at his temple and trickling down his back underneath his mailshirt. Edith seemed to catch his mood and reached out her hand to his; ahead of them Celaine and Lady Alice also walked hand-in-hand.

Ahead of them the great bowl of the arena loomed over the buildings of the city, the pale stone of its arches seeming to shine in the midday sun as they joined the flow of people making their way to the tournament. The street led out into a wide field before the arena, its margins crowded with taverns, eating houses and food stalls, the smell from the cooking meat setting Aron's mouth watering. Troubadours, jugglers and acrobats vied for their attention, but the Nandor party ignored them all and marched straight to the main entrance where the arena adjoined the temple of Martis, the warrior's god. Baldwin identified himself to the gatekeeper and they were conducted inside as far as a great iron gate.

"Beyond this gate lies the temple of Martis, and within, the chambers of those that fight in the arena," said Aron. "I must leave you now to prepare."

Edith reluctantly released his hand and looked at him with those dangerous blue eyes. Aron felt she was about to say something, but Baldwin stepped forward.

"Our honour is in your hands," he said and embraced him. "This will be a glorious day for Nandor."

He stepped back and Lady Alice stepped forward and caught his hands.

"Iduna bring you safe back to us," she said with a catch in her voice. She leaned forward and chastely kissed his cheek. Celaine followed and her kiss was on Aron's lips and she held it just a little longer than her mother. She stepped back and held his eyes with hers for a long moment, but said nothing. Finally Captain Thalon took Aron's hand.

"We couldn't have a better champion for Nandor," he said gruffly. "Go and make us proud, lad."

Aron gripped Thalon's hand firmly. "I'll see you all later," he said and then turned to the gatekeeper who opened the great iron gate and muttered a few words of directions.

Aron walked into the temple complex not daring to look back in case his resolve cracked.

The interior of the temple was a pleasant relief from the heat outside. Aron followed the gatekeeper's directions along a long corridor whose plastered walls were decorated with paintings of battle scenes. The corridor led into a chamber where several priests of Martis sat around a dice game. They looked up as Aron entered.

"Yes. What do you want?" said one.

"Aron of Darien. Champion of Nandor. I'm fighting the champion of Sarazan today."

The priest looked up and consulted a blackboard on the wall on which were written the details of the day's bouts.

"Ah, yes. You're early." He picked up a towel from a pile and tossed it to Aron. "Find yourself a cell down there. We'll call you when it's time." He pointed to a doorway. "The bath is at the end of the corridor if you want that, and the altar-room is that way."

He pointed to another doorway. Aron took his towel and headed for the cells and the priest returned to the dice game.

The cells were small, three paces by two, lit by a small window high in the wall with a bench seat wide enough to be a bed. In one corner was a shelf with a large jug of water and below it a bucket. Aron chose a cell at random, closed the door, put his pack down on the floor and lay down on the bench to try to focus his mind on the contest.

***

Maldwyn was lying on his bed when Nicoras came to fetch him. *It's quite a comfortable room for a prison*, thought Maldwyn. The bed was soft, the linen changed frequently, and the food was better than he ate in Nandor. But it was still a prison; he had only an hour's walk a day in the grounds and the rest of the time he was ferociously bored. He spent most of the time thinking of what he was going to do to Tancred when he finally got his hands on him.

The bolts on his door were pulled back and Nicoras walked in with two guardsmen.

"On your feet, my lad," said Nicoras. "Today's the day."

"Who's fighting? Not my father?" asked Maldwyn as he sat up.

"No. Aron of Darien is your champion."

"Thank the gods for that."

"Indeed. Now we can be rid of him. He won't cause us any more trouble once Mikael's finished with him," said Nicoras with a grim smile.

"I wouldn't be too sure," said Maldwyn. "I've seen Aron fight. He's very good."

"Mikael's the best I've ever seen," said Nicoras. "And believe me, I've seen a lot. Now get your boots on; we need to go."

Maldwyn tugged on his boots and then followed Nicoras out of the room and into the courtyard. There a squad of immaculately turned-out Sarazan guardsmen waited for them with Tancred standing in their midst. Maldwyn stared hard at Tancred and noticed that he had a black eye and the side of his face was swollen. *Good, he thought. I hope he's lost a few teeth.*

At that moment the Duke of Sarazan, accompanied by Lord Hercival, rode into the courtyard. Nicoras hustled Maldwyn into the formation well away from Tancred. The guard sergeant called the squad to attention and they marched off behind the Duke out into the city streets.

The Sarazan compound was only a short distance from the arena, but Maldwyn was sweating freely by the time they reached the great stone bowl. The crowd drew aside for them and the gatekeeper bowed deeply to the Duke before hurrying to open the gates. Maldwyn and Tancred, still kept well separated by the guardsmen, were led up flights of stairs and down dim corridors to emerge in a seated enclosure only a few paces above the wide sand floor of the arena. Maldwyn caught his breath at the sheer scale of it, the tiers of seating rising higher than the keep of Castle Nandor. The cushions on the seats showed Maldwyn that these were, save for the royal stand, the finest in the arena. The Duke took his seat at the front, Lord Hercival beside him. Maldwyn was seated on the rearmost row of the enclosure with two guardsmen behind his chair, well away from Tancred. He looked around the arena and saw his family seated in a similar enclosure on the far side of the royal stand. With a surge of joy he leapt up to wave to them, but the heavy hands of guardsmen pushed him down again very quickly, and he couldn't tell whether anyone had seen him. *We must get some finer livery*, he thought. *We look terrible beside the Sarazan household.* He looked around the rest of the arena; it was only about half full, with most people sitting over on the same side as the Sarazan and Nandor parties where the great canvas sails that soared above the arena walls offered some measure of protection from the sun.

Three heralds appeared on the platform beside the royal stand and blew a fanfare. The marshal clad in black and carrying his silver baton of office stepped forward into the centre of the arena. In a great clear voice he introduced the first event, an exhibtion bout between two teams of young swordsmen. The young men ran forward from the shadow of the arena entrance and began a series of fencing exercises. Maldwyn watched with interest, to the amusement of his guards. All around on the public benches people gossiped, ate and drank or just stretched out in slumber waiting for something more exciting.

The exhibition finished, the young men marched out of the arena and the marshal announced the next event as a trial fight to first blood. A buzz of anticipation ran through the crowd, the slumberers sat up and the gossip ceased. Maldwyn learned from the guards that the fighters represented two merchants who were in dispute over a spoiled cargo. Both men wore long mail shirts over stout leather jerkins and had a tough hard-bitten look to them.

"Caravan guards," said one of the guards contemptuously.

The fight was very short. In the first move one of the men thrust at his opponent who slapped the blade to one side and flicked his own blade in to run the point up his opponent's arm. They both stepped back, the marshal cried 'cease'and stepped between them. The crowd booed and whistled as the two fighters withdrew to be replaced by a troupe of acrobats. As the acrobats went through their display the crowd subsided into their previous state.

A cold knot of fear tightened in Maldwyn's stomach despite the pretty female acrobats. *That fight was over quickly. Ours could be over just like that. One slip and Aron's dead and we're ruined.* He thought. *No. Aron's too good for that.* But the knot did not loosen.

***

Aron heard the two fighters go out and return shortly after. *Short fight*, he thought. *Probably to first blood. I'll be on soon.* He sat up and reached for his pack, running through in his mind all that Kyria's blademaster had said about Mikael of Sarazan. "*A very patient conservative fighter, his whole strategy is based around sound defence. He'll let you come at him and when you give him an opening he'll take you.*"

"Then I mustn't give him an opening. I must be as patient as he is," Aron had replied. The blademaster had nodded. "Think you can do that?" he'd said and Aron had replied with confidence. "Of course."

Now was the time to do it. He took another mouthful of water from the jug; he'd drunk nearly half the jugful. *Would that be enough?* he thought. *Depends on how successful I am about not giving Mikael an opening.* He removed his mailshirt from his pack and slipped it on.

There was a tap on the door. "Aron of Nandor," a voice called. "It's time."

Aron adjusted his mailshirt, picked up his sword and opened the door. A priest stood waiting. Aron walked down the corridor the priest by his side. In the chamber where the priests had played dice, two men waited. One was another priest, the other a short man with a neat spade-shaped beard and grey-flecked dark hair. He wore a mailshirt under a shortcoat of seasoned leather and carried a sheathed sword.

Mikael of Sarazan, thought Aron. Mikael watched as Aron approached, but made no acknowledgement.

The priests led the two of them down another corridor to the arena entrance where the marshal stood waiting and then out onto the sandy floor. The bright sunlight made Aron squint after the dim chambers and corridors of the temple.

The marshal addressed the crowd.

"By the will of His Majesty the King the matter of dispute between Norbert, Duke of Sarazan and Baldwin, Earl of Nandor is to be resolved upon the bodies of their champions, Mikael of Sarazan."

Mikael stepped forward and raised his sword in salute to the royal stand.

"Aron of Nandor."

Aron stepped forward and made his salute, noting that the royal stand appeared unoccupied.

"There being no judgement of this matter upon earth it is His Majesty's will that the Gods decide by battle to its conclusion," cried the marshal. "Is it your will that battle be done?"

He turned to face the Sarazan enclosure. The Duke raised his hand in response. The marshal then turned to the Nandor enclosure, Baldwin raised his hand too.

The marshal raised his baton.

"Before the Gods then let it be battle until one can battle no more or does yield."

Mikael drew his sword and passed the sheath to one of the priests then drew away a few paces and turned to face Aron. Aron unsheathed his own sword and gave the sheath to the other priest, then the two priests hurried back to the entrance. Aron turned to face Mikael.

The marshal stepped back from between the two swordsmen and dropped his baton.

"Let battle be done," he cried.

Aron forgot then about the marshal, the priests and the crowd. Nothing existed in his world except Mikael and the sword in his hand. Mikael raised his sword and took up a perfectly posed defence stance. Aron stepped forward, his weight on his toes and adopted an identical stance. He probed towards Mikael and was met with a classically executed block. *Every bit as good as they said*, thought Aron as he stepped back to avoid Mikael's counter. He danced right and thrust forward, quicker this time. Again Mikael blocked and pushed Aron's blade aside with a turn of his wrist then flicked out his own blade in riposte. Aron skipped back and Mikael's blade found only air.

***

Edith sat watching the deadly dance chewing on the knuckle of her right hand, beside her Celaine, deathly pale, twisted a handerchief in her hands so tightly that it began to tear. Despite the warmth of the day Edith felt icy inside and on the edge of being sick. The crowd behind her were stamping their feet on the wooden benches and calling out for blood. She felt like screaming at them to stop. She wanted to run away and hide until it was all over, but dare not take her eyes from Aron. The merchants' champions had shown her how quickly the fight could end, and she had to see the stroke that changed her life utterly even though she knew it would live in her mind forever. A dozen times it seemed to her that Mikael's blade must catch Aron, but each time he miraculously flowed away from it producing more jeers and catcalls from the crowd. *He really is good*, she thought. *Even I can see that, but so is Mikael, how can Aron win?*

***

How can I beat this man? thought Aron as he stepped away from another counter. *Nothing I'm doing seemed to make the least impression on him.* He looked for a moment into Mikael's eyes but they remained as expressionless as ever despite the sweat trickling down his face. *Nothing there but total focus. Just don't give him an opening.*

Aron darted in again with a thrust to Mikael's left side and changed direction at the last moment to stab at his thigh, but the move was blocked as solidly as every other one had been. Aron danced right and backwards to avoid the inevitable riposte and Mikael's blade skimmed past his face a handswidth away. He flicked the sweat away from his eyes, the air he was breathing felt as if it came straight from the mouth of a furnace. *He's twenty years older than me at least. This must be affecting him too.* There seemed no sign of Mikael tiring though as he thrust forward and Aron again danced backward, but this time Mikael put in an extra half step. His point caught Aron and sliced up his forearm. Aron yelled more in surprise than pain as the blood flowed down his arm and the crowd roared in approval. Still no emotion registered on Mikael's face.

***

Lord Hercival sat at his father's elbow watching the fight. Everyone in the Sarazan enclosure was tense and silent. The light scarf he wore around his neck to hide the bruising from Tancred's assault was damp with sweat and chafing in the heat. The mounting frustration of the crowd mirrored his own and he longed to scream out for Aron's blood.

"What's Mikael playing at?" he said to his father. "Why hasn't he killed him yet?"

"Be quiet," said the Duke without taking his eyes of the fighters.

Then Mikael drew first blood. Lord Hercival leapt to his feet and roared with the crowd.

"That's more like it. Now finish him," he cried.

Beside him, his father said nothing, but kept watching grim-faced.

In the arena, Mikael made no move to press his attack and the catcalls resumed from the crowd. Lord Hercival sat down again.

"Gods! What is he waiting for?" he exclaimed.

"Be silent!" commanded his father still not turning his head from the battle. "You know nothing. This Aron is every bit as good as we were told. Mikael is fighting for his life."

There was another roar from the crowd as Aron feinted a

thrust and then flicked his blade over Mikael's block and scored a gash up his swordarm. Lord Hercival sat stunned, his father spat out a curse and clutched the arm of his seat with white knuckles. Mikael took a step back and then resumed as if nothing had happened.

***

To Aron, it seemed that Mikael had slowed a little, which was just as well, for Aron was labouring; his sword grip was slippery with blood from the cut on his arm and his back ached from the wounds of Tirellan's beating. The heat of the arena seemed to snatch the breath from his lungs and sweat ran continuously down his face. *Damn, he's good,* he thought as Mikael blocked another thrust and, with perfect balance, riposted. *And in very good shape too.*

Aron tried what had worked before; the feinted thrust and then the flick over Mikael's blade. This time Mikael read the feint, blocked the flick and then riposted with a slash that nearly took Aron's thumb off as it clattered on his sword hilt. Aron jumped backwards and noted that Mikael was a little slower in pressing forward. *Just keep probing at him, he's feeling it.*

Mikael thrust forward, stabbing towards Aron's groin, careful not to commit too much momentum forward. Aron danced backwards and parried trying to push Mikael's blade aside to give him space to thrust, but Mikael's wrist was stronger. Aron skipped back then forward again, feinting high, thrusting low. Mikael blocked and thrust forward. Aron read the extra half-step, dodged low and left, flicked Mikael's blade aside and stabbed his point into Mikael's calf. For a moment the pain registered on Mikael's face then focus returned. The roar of the crowd rolled over them like a wave breaking on a beach.

That should slow him a bit more, thought Aron. And so it did, but Aron felt very little advantage. Mikael stopped thrusting forward, and simply stood and blocked every move Aron made.

He's making me do all the work, tiring me and waiting for me to make a mistake. Aron's arms felt like lead and he needed an extra time to breathe between attacks. *How much longer can I go on?* he thought, lungs burning and legs threatening cramp.

***

Maldwyn sat very still at the back of the Sarazan enclosure barely daring to hope. He could see Mikael was hurt and had lost the initiative, he was just standing and defending as Aron attacked. Everyone in the Sarazan party could see it. The crowd had stopped jeering and fallen silent anticipating the imminent bloody climax. The duke was sitting rigid in his chair, clutching the arms. Surely Aron would finish it at any moment. Suddenly the Duke stood up.

"We yield," he cried in a loud voice. "Sarazan yields."

Lord Hercival leapt to his feet and caught his father's arm. "What are you doing?" he yelled. "You can't yield now."

The Duke turned furiously to Lord Hercival.

"Take your hands off me and sit down this instant or I shall have the guards remove you. I have had enough of this stupidity. Give them the land and let the boy go free. None of this is worth Mikael's life."

***

At the Duke's words, the marshal stepped forward between Mikael and Aron. The arena rang with the boos of the crowd. Aron let his sword fall to his side and stood panting, unable to believe what had happened, half expecting the marshal to step back and tell them to resume. Mikael's face contorted with anger for a moment before the discipline reasserted itself. He made the briefest of salutes to Aron then lowered his sword and limped slowly towards the entrance, back rigidly straight, looking neither left nor right. Aron turned to the royal stand and wearily raised his sword in salute to some sporadic applause from the crowd.

The guards opened the barriers across the stairways and Maldwyn was first into the arena, his long legs speeding him down the stairs and across the sand. He caught Aron in a great bearhug and lifted him off his feet, yelling in exultation and only releasing him when they were joined by the rest of the Nandor party. Lady Alice threw her arms around Maldwyn and kissed him, tears streaming down her face. Earl Baldwin took Aron's hand, ignoring the blood that still dripped from the wound Mikael had given him.

"The finest day for Nandor," he said, his voice thick with emotion. "You have brought us a wonderful victory and great honour. Now you must have your reward as was promised. The hand of one of my daughters and the rank of blademaster to the House of Nandor."

"You do me great honour, my Lord," said Aron, looking at Edith and Celaine. Both girls were looking horror-struck at their father's words, their tears of joy replaced by tears of shock and disappointment.

"We will long celebrate this day in Nandor," said Baldwin. "And tonight will be the first of the celebrations." He seemed to notice Aron's wound for the first time. "But first you must get that arm attended to."

"The priests of Martis here have a good name for their care of such wounds," said Aron. "They get plenty of practice."

"Then let us get you to them," said Baldwin.

Maldwyn offered his arm to Aron to assist him, but Aron declined and they all walked slowly towards the arena entrance where the acrobats were waiting to start their next display.

"Where's Tancred?" asked Lady Alice looking around.

"He was in the Sarazan enclosure," said Maldwyn craning his neck to look over the heads of the group. "They must have let him go at the same time as me. I wasn't watching, but just you wait 'til I get my hands on him; he betrayed me to Sarazan."

"What?" exclaimed Baldwin. "When? What are you talking about?"

At that moment two priests came forward to Aron; one took his arm to examine the wound.

"I'll be a while, I'll see you later at the Seven Stars," Aron said and then turned to follow the priests into the temple.

***

Tancred ran until his lungs burned, ignoring the yells of outrage as he forced his way through the crowd away from the arena. He halted and leaned gasping against a wall, looking around he realised that he had not the faintest idea of where he was. He mopped the sweat from his eyes and walked slowly to the street corner. If he could see the towers of the King's Keep then he had only to head towards it to get to somewhere he knew. From there he could find his way to his cousins's house. He wondered briefly about what story he would tell them. It didn't really matter, so long as they gave him a change of clothes and enough money to see him on his way. He needed to get back to Nandor before the news of today's events. That should not be too difficult. Earl Baldwin was likely to be too drunk to travel for at least three days by which time he could be halfway to Sarazan.

He reached the corner of the street and looked up to see the towers of the Keep looming ahead of him. What would he do when he got back to Nandor? He didn't know, but he would have plenty of time on the way to think of something.

CHAPTER 38

Aron lay back in the bath, the water up to his chest, being careful to keep his bandaged right arm dry. Despite the warm water, the soft candlelight and his bone-weariness, he still could not relax. The ordeal he had passed through filled his mind.

He was better than me. If Saraazan hadn't conceded I would have died out there. The thought focused his mind. He wasn't ready to go to his grave with the enemies of Darien unpunished. Tirellan was dead, but there were others; Tentra, the treacherous Saxish chieftain, the most culpable of all. He could not accept Baldwin's offer while they still lived.

Nandor was a trap for him; very comfortable but a trap nonetheless. Turning Baldwin's guard into an efficient fighting force would not be enough for him and he would quickly lose his edge without good swordsmen to practise with.

The girls would be heartbroken; He had seen all too clearly the shock on their faces at their father's words. Each had expected to be his bride and been very happy at the prospect. A part of his soul howled in anguish at the prospect of never seeing them again, but it would be better for Nandor if they were to seal alliances by taking husbands from great houses.

They will expect my decision tonight, he thought despairingly. *And Baldwin will be mortally offended if I refuse.* Under any other circumstances it was a handsome reward for a lowly-born sell-sword. *I can't see any other way. I have fought and bled for this reward, and now I cannot claim it. Is this part of your price, my Lady Iduna?* He felt sure she would not approve of his choice. He climbed out of the bath, dried himself with a towel, and then walked slowly back to his cell, his heart heavy within him.

***

Dusk was falling when Aron left the temple. The events in the arena were long finished, but the taverns and eating houses nearby were doing a roaring trade. No-one took any notice of him as he walked wearily away, pack slung over his left shoulder to spare his wounded arm.

The Seven Stars was filled with light and laughter. The smell of roasting meat drifted tantalisingly on the evening air. Music was playing and a girl was singing 'Bringing in the May'. His eyes pricking with tears, Aron re-adjusted his pack on his shoulder and kept walking.

***

This time there was no problem getting past the door at the house of the Exiles. The doorman had been at the arena, and was full of praise for Aron as the oddsmakers had decided that the Duke's conceding meant that bets on Aron had to be paid. Clearly the Exiles had disregarded Aron's advice about betting on him and had won a lot of money.

Lionel was surprised to see him. "I'd have thought you'd be celebrating."

"I need a favour," said Aron. "I need a horse, tonight."

"You're leaving, but why?" Lionel said with furrowed brow. "I heard Earl Baldwin's offered to make you blademaster of Nandor and marry one of his daughters."

"That's why."

"I thought you liked the girls."

"The girls are as sweet as any man could wish for and it's beyond me to choose between them. But I cannot accept the offer while the Saxish traitor still lives. I swore to my father's shade and the oath is unfulfilled."

"Earl Baldwin will be mightily affronted." Lionel paused. "I've recent reports of clansmen in Laranda. I'd be lying if I said I'm sorry about this. Nandor is a long way from the fight against Caldon."

"Yes, it is, too far. And it rains a lot."

Lionel smiled. "We've horses to spare. You've got to go tonight?"

"If I leave it any longer I might change my mind. I'll send word when I've found somewhere in Laranda."

"I suppose you know best. I'll get someone to saddle up a horse for you if I can find anyone sober. Is there anything else you need?"

"Something to write with. Can you get someone to deliver a note to The Seven Stars?"

"Certainly." Lionel moved to a cupboard and brought out ink, quill and a roll of coarse parchment. "I'll go and get your horse ready."

He opened the door and left Aron to compose his note.

A dozen times Aron picked up the pen, poised to write and then laid it down again. *Nothing I can say will make them feel better* he thought. *So just tell the truth as simply as possible.* He took up the pen again and wrote "I cannot choose between Edith and Celaine; therefore I regret that I must decline the great honour you have offered me." He signed his name and then folded and sealed the parchment before he changed his mind.

Footsteps announced Lionel's return.

"Written it?" he asked. "Good. I've got someone to take it round and your horse is ready. That's if you're still sure you're going."

* * *

It was a warm night; the gentle westerly breeze ruffled Aron's hair, and the just past full moon gave enough light to see his way. The road was deserted, the villages he passed through dark and shuttered. *They should have got my note by now.* He pictured in his mind Lady Alice reading his words and saw again the dismay on Celaine and Edith's faces. *Iduna help me. Tell me I've done the right thing.* He had never felt so alone and miserable before. Even the stars reminded him of the happy sparkle of blue eyes. *I'll never look into those eyes again.* Away across the fields a pair of farmyard dogs barked furiously at his passing. He wiped his eyes and dug his heels into to his horse's flanks to hurry him on his way.

THE END

Lightning Source UK Ltd.
Milton Keynes UK
UKOW02n1202050516

273614UK00003B/8/P